LETTERS TO DOGWOOD

BOOK ONE OF A TEXAS BLOOM SERIES

TANYA FISCHER

DOGWOOD GROVE PRESS

Cover Art by Ed+Designs

Print ISBN: 979-8-9864085-0-7
Formatted via Atticus
Publisher: Dogwood Grove Press LLC

To my grandmother, who introduced me to the wonder of books. To my husband, who believed in me from the beginning.

PART I

1

— . —

CHAPTER ONE

ATLANTA, GEORGIA

March 31, 1881

Fleeing the house of Mrs. Aurora Pattinson-Ricci without her knowledge was achieved that morning without any great effort whatsoever.

Lucy Ricci slipped away from the grand Queen Anne Victorian in smart traveling clothes, a matching hat, and hard-soled leather boots which clacked across the paved drive onto the tree-studded sidewalk. Beautiful homes dotted the grand street with dark, sleepy windows and silent owners. The street slept, taking no notice of the events taking place.

Deep brown eyes raised as a cool spring breeze rustled the newly budding leaves of the oak she stood beneath. Her face was dark and slate gray as the coming dawn blurred her features. A smear for a mouth. A dollop of a nose. Two smudges beneath dark winged brows.

This was the first decision in Lucy's seventeen years that she had made of any import. It was also of considerable risk. If she failed in her goals, she could be lost, ravished, or killed.

Risks were nothing compared to the outcome if she succeeded and escaped her mother's wrath, men's scrutiny, and nature's susceptibility to turning foul. But even death was more freeing than remaining here.

The morning sky lightened from heavy gray to lavender as the sun chased away the night. The stars disappeared, and Lucy tapped her boot.

What was taking him so long? Had he forgotten?

A cold sweat dotted her lip.

What if he didn't come?

Then, sounds.

A horse's hooves beat upon the cobblestones, and a murky shape turned the corner.

Relaxing her clenched fists, Lucy burst into motion, flitting from tree to tree until a rented horse-drawn phaeton clattered closer. Its wheels slowed as she dashed into the street, and the man with red sideburns and a low cap tightened the reins just enough for the young woman to alight with the grace of a doe.

"Marvelously done, m'dear," the man drolled, flicking the lead reins with limp, delicately angled wrists. He wheeled the phaeton around with competent execution.

Eying the coarse, freckled hands holding the leather strips, Lucy murmured, "Did you remember my bag?"

Jimmy reached beneath the bench and tugged at a hidden strap. "I didnae forget a thing, Miss Lucy. We've only planned this for nigh on two months." His nasal gentlemen's affectation disappeared beneath the harsh Scottish burr of his homeland.

She smiled at him, though it was strained. Only three people were privy to her whereabouts this morning and the next several days. Meggie, Jimmy, and herself.

She was going back to Texas. Back to Papa and Minnie and the hotel. Back to happiness. Three years before, her mother had seized her from her father, and she'd said goodbye to smiling faces and wildflower-lined roads, and hello to paved streets and upturned noses. Her last memory of Papa was of him standing stiffly on the boards of the sidewalk in front of his hotel. His hat had been old, his face filled with lines of pain as a fourteen-year-old Lucy had screamed for him from the stagecoach window.

Three years of belittlement from Mother and her older sister Beth had commenced. Now, she would finally be free.

Reminded of freedom, she reached over and grasped Jimmy's forearm. "I could not have done this without you, Jimmy," she said with feeling. "Are you sure Mother will not suspect you?"

"Doon't be frettin' none." He patted the slim, gloved hand on his rough sleeve. "We live beyond the outskirts of the city now, and I get on fine with the boss at the mill. He's a Scot, ye ken?" He tapped his nose conspiratorially. "And Mary has the run of her own home, no more sharin' a flat with ten others."

Lucy listened to Jimmy talk fondly of his wife and their many children, and how country life suited their family much more than in the city. The month before, he'd left her mother's employment, but not without a promise to Lucy that he'd be back to help her execute her escape. His sister Meggie, also tired of the daily tyranny of working beneath Aurora, was to meet him on the corner once he'd dropped Lucy off at the train station. It had taken Meggie a bit longer to obtain another reputable position in secret outside the city.

"And ye're sure your da will be there to meet you?" Jimmy was asking.

She cleared her throat. "Yes. He bought a ticket for me just yesterday."

He nodded, satisfied, and they rode the remainder of the way to the train station without speaking, each lost in their reveries.

The Atlanta Union Station was an enormous red structure built in Second Empire style, sporting many glass windows and black shingles upon the turreted roofs. Trains wound their way along mazes of tracks that had no rhyme or reason to Lucy's inexpert eye. A forest-green steam engine was currently parked beneath the huge iron and glass pavilion, steam releasing in white puffs from the smokestack. The ticket booth was easy to spot with its single window and a canvas awning. Buggies and horses were parked hither and tither, blocking the roadways between Pryor Street and Central Avenue. Lucy tried to keep her eyes from growing huge with fear at the immensity of the building and bustle of activity.

Once a muttering Jimmy had found a place to park, Lucy halted him from setting the brake or standing from his seat.

"I need to do this alone. The less we are seen together, the better it will be for you. It's best that Mother believes Papa and I acted alone."

He scoffed. "Miss Lucy, you know I'm not skairt—"

"Jimmy," she pleaded, and her eyes began to swim, halting his words succinctly. "We both know how she is. If she discovers you had anything to do with it, it would be nothing to hire a Pinkerton agent to find you. If anything happened to you, what would become of your wife and children? No. I go alone from here."

Jimmy gazed at her serious face for a moment before turning away, squinting near the ticket booth. "I'd like to see your da come and fetch you before I left you here, at the verra least."

Tugging her green and pink-flowered carpetbag from beneath the bench to hide the color blossoming in her cheeks, Lucy lied, "Oh, he's to wait for me in the pavilion. I'll go ask the ticket clerk if he's bought our tickets, and wave at you when I see him, will that suffice?"

Sighing hard out of his nose, Jimmy muttered a reluctant agreement.

Smiling wide at him to conceal how sick she felt, Lucy hugged him, quick and fierce, then hopped from the phaeton before he could change his mind and see what an utter fraud she was.

No Papa waited for her.

Her father had no knowledge of her plans at all. She was very afraid if she didn't leave now, she would be unable to leave at all. It wasn't just her authoritarian mother that had forced her hand, oh no. It was also the despicable scandal that Lucy had tangled and knotted herself into in the past three months.

She asked the ticket clerk what the time was, hat low, and pretended to walk around the booth as though looking for someone. Pasting a fake smile on her face, she turned and waved at the small figure of Jimmy.

Lucy couldn't risk Jimmy convincing her to stay.

She was afraid if she stayed in Atlanta even one day longer, she'd become someone she hated, someone even worse than her mother.

"HERE'S YOUR TICKET, sir."

Benjamin Stone took the third-class ticket and cattle car stub from the skinny little clerk at the window, tipped his hat to him, and strolled across the depot toward the pavilion with the high, cathedral-like ceiling.

Should've got that damned sleeper car, he thought when the weak morning light outside hit his sensitive, tired eyes. But what was another hard place to sleep when it saved dollars? In the five years that he'd worked steers and led drives, his body should be able to conform to the thin padding of a train bench as easily as it did a bedroll on rocks and dirt. His foul mood followed him to the horse tethered at the end of the station's long boardwalk.

He halted when he saw a slender, fine-dressed woman crooning to his gelding, scratching that fuzzy spot under Reb's chin that made the horse's lips quiver. Ben scoffed audibly at the pathetic animal, but when he made to head the lady off, the woman turned. She grabbed the most godawful ugliest green bag he'd ever seen from her feet and walked away. He got a glimpse of a young, crisp profile beneath a stylish hat before she rounded a building.

Reb's ears perked when he saw Ben.

"Oh, no you don't. I saw you flirtin' with that female. Doesn't matter to you whether she has two legs or four, you still act like you got a pair of stones to do something about it." Ben tugged at the bay's black forelock in passing and whirled with a palm out in warning when the horse bent low to nip at his jacket. "Eh, eh, don't even think about it."

In answer, the equine lifted his tail and added his contribution to the many road apples that littered the area.

"Dadgum filthy animal. You act no better than a mule." Ben shook his head and untethered the horse.

Reb's manners may have been atrocious, but when the train hooted in the distance, Ben mourned that he had to lose the animal's company and put him in a cattle car. The black and red steam engine appeared around the corner first, then the remainder of it trailing behind, lithesome as a snake. It hissed, spit, and clattered something awful, bringing with the thousands of tons of black metal the hot smell of oil that blasted everyone within twenty feet.

"Alright old boy, let's load up." After the cattle cars were emptied, he showed Reb's ticket stub to a conductor and led the placid horse up the narrow ramp. They were old pros at this, that was certain, but Ben felt the weariness of six months' constant travel like a load of bricks. It was high time to settle down.

Once Reb was put away, Ben grabbed the edge of the car and jumped to the boardwalk, nodding once or twice at other passerby and their livestock, unsmiling. The strain of being in a big city had worn him down like an old tooth ground too near the nerves. Every social interaction was a jolt; a talkative old timer could make him sweat, and a young child begging for a sweet closed up his throat. He was a man made for solitude, for long Texas nights where the sky stretched broad and black with millions of stars. Animals in their paddocks and pastures would lay down, nocturnal bugs would rustle and chitter, and the hoot owls would talk to each other. In the big country, it was impossible to feel lonely.

Here, no one was still. People squirmed with the purpose of ants on a disturbed mound, swarming everywhere until every corner you turned, you bumped into a body. He'd drifted here from Texas to Tennessee and Kentucky, looking for the best prices to sell the horseflesh he'd accumulated and trained south of the Mason Dixon. His last stop in Atlanta had proved fruitful; none of those fancy thoroughbreds had the stamina of a good quarter horse, but he'd raked in the coins from training the hotblooded stallions those fancy dudes were so keen on riding, lining his pockets with cold, hard cash. Yesterday, he'd visited the bank and had it wired to his old bank in Texas.

And now, he was tired. He wanted a home.

He felt in his soul it was time to go back.

If he wanted any kind of relationship with his little brother, it was time to stop running.

Once in the third-class passenger car, he chose the area in the back that was the least congested with people. He nabbed the empty seat to the left, sprawled his legs until his rear found comfort on the shallow padding, and lowered his hat onto his face for a bit of shut-eye. The dirty leather pressed over his eyes, more inviting than a silken eye mask. If it kept anyone from making idle conversation, all the better.

LUCY PASSED THE conductor with a weak smile as she made her tentative way down the aisle of the third-class train car. Someone was smoking a pipe near the front, and the pungent bite of tobacco was a fragrant layer unable to conceal the more malodorous aroma of mildewed leather seats and body odor.

Her heart hammered at a frantic rate through her legs, arms, and throat, and a clammy sweat of the guilty beaded her forehead and lip.

The car was full of a motley crew of people; families, married couples, and bachelors. No women alone that she could see. She pasted on a mask of unconcern, her nose lifted with confidence, her eyes darting left, right, left, right, trying to find a seat that would be the most bearable to occupy for hours at a time. She threaded past weathered old men, svelte businessmen in suits with gold watches glinting, two husbands with their wives and children.

A baby drew her eye, peeking sleepily from the arms of a young mother who whispered to her husband and their young female relative. The small family had snagged a bench in the very back, perhaps hoping that would disturb fewer people if their baby decided to cry. Across the aisle from them was a seat with a lone man, fast asleep in his worn travel clothes, a faded brown bandana at his collar, and a dusty black cowboy hat perched on an upturned face. As she shuffled closer, she saw a sliver of his neck, tanned a deep brown and almost completely hidden by a stretch of glossy black beard. His sweat-stained shirt had a button missing. Considering he took up half the bench, she reasoned he would be too broad of shoulder to fit anyone next to him larger than a lone lady like herself, and made her decision.

She took a careful seat between the sleeping man and the curious baby at the back of the car and told herself she'd be perfectly content there for the next long, nervous hours. The babe had followed her progress, his small, dimpled fingers splayed on his mother's breast. The mother discreetly moved the hand to the side.

For numerous, tense minutes Lucy remained rigid, eyes shifting from the window to the door of the train car, waiting for her mother or law enforcement to burst in and take her back home. Her foot jiggled and her bag was heavy in her lap. The conductor shouted something, but her ears weren't listening, and she held her breath.

What did he say?

The train began to chuff, and its wheels screeched as multiple cars groaned forward. Progress was slow at first, but they eventually gained speed, and she felt her shoulders slump from their set, unyielding posture.

The baby, old enough to crawl and wanting to do so right away, began to fuss.

Loudly.

A glance at her seat cohabitant confirmed that he still slumbered, but the mother and father of the screaming child began to argue with one another. Lucy tapped her fingers, not looking at the troubled couple but also unable to ignore when the little tyke attempted to do backflips from its mother's arms.

She rummaged in her bag and produced a shiny, bright candy. Lucy flourished a peppermint stick that was thick and wouldn't easily break off in front of the squalling boy's red, contorted face. Within seconds, the screaming broke off into cooing. Wet, blue eyes were round, and plump fingers reached.

"I hope this wasn't too forward," Lucy murmured apologetically to the relieved mother as the baby commenced a slobbering attack on the peppermint stick.

The woman shook her head in reassurance. "Oh, don't worry none. I'd rather a mess than a caterwauling. I was scared they'd kick us right off the train."

They conversed for a good, long while, and made introductions. They were the Stuarts, and their baby's name was William. Lucy introduced herself as Anne, and it was strangely uncomfortable, like wearing stolen shoes. The fear that she would be found out was a steady trickle adding to a river of paranoia. Little Will had soon fallen asleep not even halfway through the candy, so they let a comfortable stall halt their conversation in the hopes that he'd remain so.

Scenery flew past the window in a colorful blur, mostly trees, and it gave the glass pane the appearance of a smudged green painting. Occasionally, a town or homestead would fly past, and Lucy would lean closer before they disappeared into the trees.

She'd done it.

She'd snuck away in the early morning hours and had crept like a thief to the train depot.

After Jimmy had reluctantly pulled the phaeton away, Lucy had returned to the ticket booth. Buying the ticket under a different name was easy, and she'd made up a story about herself in case anyone asked. Her name was Anne, and she was traveling back home to her husband after a long visit with family.

No one had asked.

A kink in her plan appeared right out of the gate, however, when she was informed that the train en route from Atlanta to Houston was being serviced, and the next one wouldn't be ready until after noon.

At noon, her mother would be combing the streets for her.

Pretending she wasn't panicking, Lucy made the swift decision to ride to Jackson, Mississippi.

"You sure?" The wiry clerk had asked. "It'll take longer. You'll have to switch trains. Could get expensive."

"How expensive?"

"Depends on if you grab a Pullman or not."

In the end, she'd decided on the cheaper, albeit slower route.

Take the train to Jackson, Mississippi, opt for a stagecoach between Jackson and New Orleans, board a sleeper car to Houston, then one last stagecoach ride home. Once settled, the clerk had written down the false name, took her money, and handed her a ticket with instructions, rules, and her arrival time in Mississippi. Her success had been so easy that she'd stood like a mute until he'd frowned at her and called, 'Next!'.

Now, she was one step closer to Texas. To Papa. To be sure, he'd be furious with her, but she'd make him understand.

Sighing, she reached into her bag and grabbed an apple. Now that her stomach was no longer in knots, she was famished. She polished the shiny, blushing apple with her cuff and wondered if Papa and Minnie had changed much in her three-year absence. Certainly, their little girl that had been forced away those years ago had changed from a laughing adolescent to a somber woman. Would they be ashamed of her actions?

Lucy bit crisply into the apple, the knot of worry returning. She pictured herself standing before her father. He would tower over her in justifiable anger, shaking with rage, finger pointing in accusation at her rash and ludicrous decision. Excuses bubbled up, arguments of defense her only weapons.

Papa, Mother sent me to a horrible school, so far away...

Papa, she had the preacher make a sermon about me...

The woman is completely unhinged, a raving lunatic...

My sister's beau proposed marriage to me, and his mother tried to pay me to stay away...

At that, she closed her eyes and covered her face with a shaking hand. Had she become such a vile person? It seemed unbearable to tell him such a shameful truth. He may very well disown her and send her back to Atlanta to mete the consequences of her actions. She'd thought she'd been so sly, manipulating a man into sending a secret letter that would cure her unhappiness.

It proved her right, she thought savagely. She was knocked clear off her high horse and now she could revel in her place on the hard dirt, covered in the dust of her poor choices.

Even though she chastised herself, that secret part of her crowed that she was on her way home. She'd just have to be smarter, more cautious, or the next time she was knocked off her saddle, she may very well land in a pile of horse manure.

Well, if she was to work smarter, she'd better start thinking. Straightening into a more confident pose, she took another bite of the apple, analyzing every step of her journey, the expenditures, and the amount of money she had remaining. If her calculations were correct, she'd make it home with five dollars to spare.

The man beside her twitched in his sleep, and she paused in her chewing, distracted.

She glanced at the slumbering male that shared her bench.

Men had become infinitely more interesting to her, being such large and hairy creatures full of awesome physical strength so much greater than her own. And he was quite large, this man. What his face looked like beneath his hat, she could but wonder. Probably tanned and weathered like his hands, which were clasped lightly. Thick, rough fingers interlocked just below his waistband. They could probably crush a windpipe without hesitation. The breadth of him was astounding.

Compared to Peter, this man was a Clydesdale to a carriage horse. Compared to her, she was fragile as a yearling. His legs were long and thick, thighs large and muscular under his dark trousers. His shirtsleeves were up, exposing thick, sturdy wrists dusted with hair, and even in repose, his forearms were roped with muscles and blue veins.

Swallowing the half-masticated apple in her slack mouth, she squirmed with guilt and shot furtive looks around like the peeping Tom that she was. No one had noticed her ogling, and she determined to behave like a lady and looked elsewhere. Her next bite was resolute. Even through the constant clattering of the train on the tracks, it was loud. She almost choked on it when the sleeping man next to her stirred, legs tautening, muscles bunching in his limbs and torso as he eased upright from his relaxed slouch. His hands came apart to pluck his hat from his face, twirling the worn leather once before it was jammed on a thick crown of mussed black curls.

The cowboy's face was haggard with exhaustion, tan from sun exposure with the softest beard Lucy had ever seen. He was as different from Peter as a leather settee to the gleaming buffalo rug at its tapered feet. His beard did put Lucy in mind of a buffalo, all soft brownish-black curls, dense and wild.

Beth would find this man—obviously working class—repulsive, with his worn clothing and body hair. Lucy found him completely arresting.

And then, she found him alarming, because she had woken him up.

Heart beating fast in remorse and fear, she watched her bench mate rub his eyes and blink them open. The delicate skin beneath them was unlined but tinged in the blue bruising of the unrested. He was neither young nor old, but weary, and his eyes were the shade of a dusky blue night sky when the stars were still shy, and the sun went to sleep behind the horizon. She stared at him, nervous, as eyes vivid against his tan registered their surroundings.

Blue reflected the shimmering light from the window.

Then, they skimmed over the people in the rows of seats in front of them.

Lashes, dark and thick as a line of kohl, rimmed eyes that paused for a long moment on her green valise, flickered with something, thick brows twitching together.

Finally, the disturbing scrutiny completed its slow journey to land, in accusation, on her.

IT FELT AS though a two-ton steer was pressing down on his head, making it heavy, eyelids burning and tired.

He'd drifted in and out of restless sleep as people filled the seats in front of and around him after he'd boarded the train. Someone had taken a seat next to him with a breath of soap and talcum powder. A woman. A baby screamed forever, and he'd wanted to weep, but he'd ignored it until the crying stopped, and soft feminine voices and the pleasant odor of laundered clothes and soap helped him drift into black dreamland.

In his dream, he smelled apples. He was in an orchard, walking between rows of trees alone. It was early winter but no red fruit loaded the branches, though he could smell them. Someone bit noisily into an apple, and he whirled around. Behind him, his mother snacked on a blushing yellow and pink fruit, cheerful and smiling, brown eyes happy. Ben felt something tug at his consciousness, the niggling sense that he was being watched.

He woke with reluctance, slow, digging his heels in. Sound came back to him in a rush. Clattering train wheels, low voices in conversation, the crunching of what sounded like strong horse jaws making short work of an apple. Reb?

Awareness kicked in and he sighed.

Might as well wake up, he groused.

He was just so damned tired.

Sitting up was an effort, and he jammed his hat back on his head and rubbed his aching eyes. Blearily, he opened his grimy lids and blinked, owlish, at the people in the rows of seats in front of him. Hats with feathers, bonnets, black bowlers, ten-gallon; all were attached to the heads of muttering folk determined to keep him awake.

Now, who in the Sam hell was chewing so loudly it woke him from a sound sleep only a screaming babe could disturb?

A flash of sickly green caught his peripheral vision, and he glanced at the familiar ugly carpetbag from the depot. No. Surely God hadn't become so cruel that He'd planted that little first-class miss that had charmed Reb into the same seat as his own. And yet, there she was, a modern replica of Eve herself with a half-eaten apple in the palm of her hand. He glared at it for a moment before putting himself out of his misery and finally looked at the face of the oppressor of his nap.

He met wide, dark eyes.

Light olive skin, pillowy parted lips the color of red wine, dark arched brows, delicate ears.

Ah, hell, he despaired. It was Eve, indeed.

To his shock, he watched a blush climb out of her high neckline, up her neck, to bloom across her cheekbones. She gave him a sheepish, apologetic smile, and to Ben's dismay, his heart began to pound in reaction.

He countered her smile with a curt nod and turned away. Spoiling for a fight at an uncharacteristic burst of adrenaline, he struggled not to shift in his uncomfortable seat. He figured his rear was molded permanently into the shape of a saddle, and anything flatter than curving leather would always be a trial to sit on.

Eyes drilled holes into his profile. Did he have a five-dollar piece on his face? Jewelry? The key back to Eden?

Eve cleared her throat. "Good morning," she offered. "I hope I did not wake you."

Maybe he could pretend not to speak English. *No hablo Ingles, senorita.* His Spanish was rusty enough for his mother to turn in her grave, but if it spared him from a forced conversation, he'd make up words if he had to.

Crunch.

His eyes jumped back to her.

In the growing silence, she'd taken a huge bite of her apple, and was now pretending to look out the window. It was awkward as hell. A delicate feminine jaw chewed the apple, and its aroma permeated the air between them, better than any perfume those rich ladies liked to wear. She even looked a bit well-to-do with her erect posture, fancy hat, and expensive wool suit. But he couldn't remember a lady ever munching on an apple as ferociously as this one did.

"I needed to wake up," was his non-answer. He picked up his hat far enough to run rough fingers through hair in desperate need of a cut before replacing it. Unable to help it, he watched her surreptitiously. She'd stopped chewing and was considering his hands with the kind of intensity that made a body interested.

Stop lookin' at me like that, lady.

It wouldn't surprise him if he was still dreaming. Where were her menfolk? They'd set her pert little behind straight. "Don't look at strange men" was one of the top unspoken rules of traveling women; looking incited mischief. Especially if the looker looked like her.

The lady was speaking again. Unbelievable.

"I'm Lucy Ricci." She frowned and bit that maroon lip. Although her voice was low and clear, and she enunciated her words as perfectly as any city miss, there was a hint of a southern drawl. The way she spoke suggested intelligence, the surety of her words, the expressions on her face.

"Ben Stone," he murmured, tipping his hat, which felt ridiculous to do when one was seated. He hoped she didn't want to shake hands. A man didn't shake hands while sitting, just like he didn't put his hat on his bed or the dinner table.

She didn't.

Instead, she reached into her bag.

"Would you like one?"

He closed his eyes for patience while she joyfully pawed through her God-awful bag until she found what she was searching for. A perfect apple, large as her fist, with a stem and leaf still attached to it.

Yessiree, she came from money.

She wasn't acting like it. She looked so hopeful, that he couldn't help his next words.

"You know, I read about this once in the Good Book."

He watched her eyes register his meaning, and instead of getting offended and ignoring him from then on in a huff, she smiled. Big. It turned her whole face heart-shaped. Its brilliance blinded him, and he felt the corners of his lips curl up despite himself. She looked even younger.

"Ah, found me out, have you?" She laughed and nudged her offering at him.

Forced to accept her munificence or look like a horse's ass, he held it loosely between his fingers.

"It's not poisoned, you have my word," she goaded after a pause, lips twitching. "And we're far from Eden."

"Maybe I'm just waitin' for you to fall asleep before I eat it." Said in such a serious tone, he was again afraid that she'd get her feelings pricked. And again, he was allowed the pleasure of another smile, this one accompanied by rosy cheeks.

"Oh, I did wake you, didn't I? Alright, I'll fall asleep right away so you can exact your revenge."

He snorted and shook his head. He really was a horse's ass, probably turning more and more into Reb by the day. At the thought, he offered, "I saw you at the depot. Before. You were petting my horse."

Miss Ricci leaned closer. It was only an inch, but he noticed.

"That blood bay beauty?" she breathed. "I walked by him and could not resist petting him. He's built like a quarter horse, but his coloring is comparable to any Thoroughbred show horse.

"I couldn't resist," she teased, "complimenting him."

If she'd told him she was a whore in disguise and wanted to rent them a room in Jackson, he couldn't have been more pleased. His shoulders relaxed a bit, and he twisted the stem of his apple. "Yeah, he's getting on in age, but he's decent for an old man. Too bad he was already cut when I bought him." He stopped. There he went again, talking like a rough cowhand in front of a pure lady—

Nodding, Lucy glanced at his fingers and added, "I thought so, too. He would have thrown some fine foals." Not such a ladylike thing to say, but a sensible one, and he found himself liking her more by the minute.

They continued their conversation safely on the subject of horses for an hour until his posture was fully relaxed, and his apple was a mangled core. He noticed her own had been neatly consumed and was symmetrical all around. When she glanced askance for a wastebasket, he didn't think twice and opened their soot-grimed window, grabbed what was left of her apple, and tossed both of their cores across blurred shrubbery. If she was shocked that he'd touched the fruit that she'd gnawed on for the better part of their conversation, she hid it well.

"So where are you headed, Mr. Stone?"

He wished he had a toothpick. His tongue ran a brief pass over his teeth. "Back home to Texas."

Lucy's dark eyes skittered from his mouth and she played with a thread on her bag. "I thought that's where you were from. Your accent makes me homesick," she added with an incredulous shake of her head. "I don't know if it's coincidence or fate, but that's where I'm about as well. Back to Dogwood, Texas. What city do you hail from?"

Dogwood. It sounded familiar, then it clicked into place like the cock of a revolver. Suspicious, he frowned at the blue sky outside, wondering why God would place a beautiful woman practically in his lap who just so happened to live a two-hour ride away from the land he intended to buy outright from his father.

"Our ranch is about a day's ride from Huntsville," he answered, forceful in the vagueness of his answer.

"Oh, then you're not so very far from my town," she smiled, and her nostrils gave a brief flare. "Well, if you ever find your way into Dogwood, be sure to stop by the Dogwood Hotel. Papa just acquired new gas lighting, and I know for a fact that the bedsheets are fresh for every stay. Minnie and I used to do it together." Her eyes glinted with emotion. "The steak is superb and so is the pie." She broke off at the last, and he watched her swallow with the wariness of a miner seated near a lit fuse of dynamite.

His legs shifted, a large, square knee jiggled, then lay still. "Steak and pie are soundin' real good right about now."

She pretended to look in her bag, a nervous habit, and her blinks were vigorous. "Then you must stop by one day, just for the food, even if you have no business that way. It will be on the house."

Feeling a bit desperate, his leg waggled again. "Can't be too good for business, a free meal to a stranger."

"Perhaps we could be friends by the end of our journey. I could dearly use one."

Forthright and candid. He didn't know how to handle women like those. Not anymore. It felt like a trick. His attraction to her cautioned, because the more she talked, the more interested he felt. It was Trouble with long lashes and a pretty smile. He didn't need woman trouble right now.

It shook him up.

The last time he'd felt so out of his element, he'd tenaciously brought his mother up to his father. The force of John Stone's backhand had near about stove his teeth in. Then, his Pa had chased him off the Stone ranch for good measure.

He felt that familiar provoking urge for space now.

So, he did what he always did when he felt cornered. He attacked.

"I'm surprised you're travelin' alone, Miss Ricci." He let disapproval leak into his tone.

"I—"

"Your pa, brother, or husband ain't worried you're out and about without a chaperone?"

"Women do not always require chaperones, Mr. Stone. And I have no brothers, nor am I married." She skirted his question, then looked quietly furious with herself.

"So, your pa is fine with you being all on your own?" he persisted.

"Of course, he is." Her spine couldn't have been stiffer if she'd sat upon a railroad pike. "I'm staying with a friend in Jackson. I shan't be completely alone, I assure you."

It didn't escape his notice that her voice had lost all trace of a comfortable accent and was brittle as a city mayor's during election season.

"That's good," he said with feeling, and having erected her walls enough to please himself, he hunched lower into the mildewed leather scent of his seat, legs sprawled, and pulled his hat back over his face. In the dark of the hollow crown, he repeated, "That's real good."

2

— · —

CHAPTER TWO

T heir train screeched to a halt in Jackson, Mississippi just before dusk.

Lucy waited for a conductor to alert the passengers of the runaway status of a girl with her description. She watched with wary eyes when he appeared, but instead of marching down the aisle to detain her, he merely smiled at the people in front and helped them disembark the car in an orderly fashion.

Wishing there weren't so many steps in this confounded journey home, Lucy peeped at Ben Stone. Choosing to forget the more unpleasant portion of their conversation, she mustered a smile.

"Mr. Stone, it was a pleasure to meet you, and I wish you safe travels."

When he stood, he towered over her, blocking out the window behind him. He offered an ungloved hand and she took it without hesitation. A hot pulse surged through her, and she was grateful for the glove she wore that hid her clammy palm. His fingers were strong, and his forearm barely flexed at her weight when he helped her stand. Lucy imagined what it would feel like if they were skin-to-skin. Once at her feet, she was neck-level with him. She hid her surprise that he was of average height. The breadth of his shoulders and intense presence were nonetheless substantial, and she felt very small next to him.

"Pleasure was mine, Miss Ricci. If I ever go through Dogwood, I reckon I'll take you up on that steak and pie." She loved that his voice was so deep, and she hated that they hadn't met under normal circumstances.

Before their handholding became awkward, she turned it into a handshake. His hand shook hers in a warm, firm clasping of delicately gloved knuckles against a calloused thumb, then, he released her, and they made their way down the aisle after the Stuarts. After they stepped onto the boardwalk, he went right, and she straight. The loss was keen enough to hollow her stomach, but Lucy ignored it and assured herself it was hunger.

Theirs was the last stop of the day, and she reached the ticket clerk just as he was locking the depot building's door, cashbox under his arm.

"Where would I acquire a ticket to the morning stagecoach to New Orleans, sir?"

The clerk didn't glance up and hooked a thumb to his right and gave her an address. "They'll be closing soon, ma'am. Best hurry."

"Yes, sir."

The stage office was halfway down Main Street, and her back grew damp and sticky from the stressful possibility she'd make it too late. The train station had been notified by a wire from her mother by now, she was sure of it. If she was turned away and given to the local law enforcement, she would die. She'd shrivel into a husk and float into the breeze down Main Street.

For now, however, she steeled her spine and rounded the corner onto Main.

Stars were losing their shyness and peeked through the darkening veil of the sky. A man on stilts lit streetlamps in slow, measured steps. If he fell, at worst he'd break his neck or an arm at best. In the orange glow of his wake, the alleys and smaller roadways grew darker, their depths indeterminate gateways to hellish dimensions where invisible beings with red eyes lurked.

Thankfully, it wasn't hard to find the stage line. A coach pulled away from a boardwalk on the left and entered a livery a few buildings down to the right. She watched as more and more people carrying luggage left the rather small building. Foremost, she would pay for the ticket under a false name, a different one than the alias she'd used in Atlanta.

And this time she would stick to it!

She blamed giving her real name and background to Mr. Stone as a temporary leave of her senses. It had to have been his pretty eyes. No one should have eyes that distracting, particularly not bearded cowboys.

Ahead of her, a movement caught her eye. A large shadow led a larger, four-legged shadow into the street. The broad shape of the man's silhouette was instantly familiar.

Speak of the devil.

She took a precious minute to watch the way he walked, like the piston of a well-greased machine in a factory, smooth and rolling. Lucy found herself scurrying in his direction, her bag held before her like armor, and she knew the second he heard her. Ben's dark silhouette glanced back, then halted. His horse turned his head, delicate ears perking.

"Miss Ricci?" came his dark, low voice. She shivered.

"One and the same," she admitted, hot and sheepish in the obscuring gloom. The sun had set, and she glanced worriedly at the stage office. "They'll probably be closing soon," she speculated, chewing a nail for a weak moment before remembering ladies didn't do such things. "I should be a bit hastier and pay for my ticket before they're sold out."

"You're takin' a stage? Train would be faster." He hadn't moved from his spot, and in the shadows, the dim outline of his beard moved with his frown.

"Yes," she agreed, "and far more expensive. I'll take the through train from New Orleans to Houston and take another stage from there."

"Outlaws still rob 'em." The censure in his voice pricked at her pride. Didn't he think she'd thought of that? Of course, there were dangers!

"I've taken measures for safety," was all she said. "All I want is to get my ticket and find a room to sleep in."

"Your friend not here to pick you up?" He'd begun walking again, and she followed, as obedient as his horse.

Lucy felt extreme guilt that he'd caught her in a lie and bit her dry lips. "There is no friend. I didn't want anyone to know that I was alone." He'd stopped walking, and she felt some dark emotion rolling off him in waves. She wished she could see his eyes. "I am sorry, truly. It was not my intention to lie—"

"If you're wanting a room alone, you're probably too late by now," he interrupted and continued walking. She had to skip ahead to keep up with his long strides. "You'll have to bundle with someone or find a cot in a hotel kitchen."

She hated how he spoke to her. Gone was the easy camaraderie from the train bench they had shared, the sense that they were equals. The impatience in his words, as though he were explaining something to a fool, rubbed at the raw place she thought she'd left behind her in Atlanta. Well, he wasn't her father or even her brother. And if his eyes were beautiful, she thought inanely, then all the better that they went separate ways. She'd had enough of men to last her a lifetime.

"I am not afraid to sleep on a cot, or even a dusty corner somewhere, Mr. Stone." She gave a haughty twitch of her chin. "All that matters is getting home, so what is a little discomfort? Where are *you* sleeping, hm?"

A man's voice from a black alley to her left startled her, and she moved in animal instinct to the closest source of protection.

She could feel him shrug, so close had she scooted to him. "Probably the livery, if no one's got a room."

The livery? She imagined dusty hay, manure smell, and flea-infested blankets draped over a shivering Ben. Contrition wilted her prickliness.

"Oh. Well, you should probably find a room in all haste. Could you—" she paused, then swallowed her pride. "Would you—mind doing me a favor, Mr. Stone? Would you wait while I purchase a ticket to New Orleans, and perhaps walk me to the hotel over there? It's awfully dark, and I'm alone—" she drifted off, miserable that he'd think her an incompetent traveler, yet needing him to believe it.

"'Course, ma'am." The formality and forced lightness made her cringe. He tipped his hat at her to precede him, so she acquiesced and struggled not to bound up the wooden stairs cattycorner to the stage office. Her muscles stretched deliciously after being seated on a train seat for so many hours. She reached for the door latch and paused. A quick peek proved that Ben had indeed followed her and was waiting with long-suffering patience in the light from the office window.

Perfect.

She yanked at the door, half afraid it was locked and was gratified when it swung out. There were two men at the counter, and tobacco smoke hung like fog around the room. One man counted a sheaf of money, and the other puffed on a pipe. They both looked up in question when she shut the door behind her. The younger man counting silver coins and greenbacks was a slender fellow with prominent ears. His eyes shot to his partner, and she couldn't miss the swift alertness between the two.

"Hello," she chirped as though her mind wasn't racing, and her bag wasn't slipping out of her perspiring palms. "Do you have a spot available for the stage going to New Orleans?"

The older, overweight man with the pipe blinked rapidly and joined his friend behind the counter. He shuffled through papers, and out of the corner of his mouth past the pipe, he murmured something. The younger man with shrewd eyes looked up from a slip of paper, giving her person several lingering passes before going back to his note.

"Name, Miss?" he asked all business.

The name popped into her head and shone as bright as the light at the end of a long and arduous tunnel. "Stone. Eve

Stone." After a pause, she added with a touch of sternness, "And it's 'Mrs'. That's my husband." She pointed out the tiny window to Ben, who dug through the saddlebags of his pretty blood bay gelding.

"No ticket for Mr. Stone?" the young man asked dubiously, laying his note down. Uncertainty clouded his earlier vigilance.

"He prefers to ride alongside, but I could not possibly be on horseback for that length of time." She shuddered delicately.

"Hm," grunted the older man, and his mustache followed his frown around his pipe stem. "We have one that leaves in the morning at seven-thirty sharp, ma'am. How much luggage you have?"

Lucy suddenly didn't want either man to get a good look at her telling green bag, so she hid it behind her back and thrust her chest forward, smiling with confidence even though her fingers trembled. "A large valise, approximately thirty pounds. My husband will have the rest in our saddlebags."

He nodded and wrote a few things down. She licked her lips when she couldn't see what he wrote. Probably WE FOUND HER in bold letters. Her upper lip had just begun to sweat when he wrote a ticket out for her, and she dug a few hidden bills out of the bag she laid at her feet in elation.

"Thank you, Mr...."

"Pettiford, ma'am."

"Thank you, Mr. Pettiford." She was beyond relieved and wanted to jump and shout with joy as she laid her money on the counter and hightailed it out of there before they could call her back.

Only, when she exited the building, her breath of relief froze in her throat and choked her when Mr. Pettiford called out from the wide-open doorway, "Mrs. Stone! Eve Stone? You forgot your ticket!"

THE EXPRESSION ON Miss Ricci's face reminded Ben of the time his pal Sol fell from his horse, dead drunk, and got the breath clobbered out of him from the hard-packed ground.

Wide-eyed disbelief and chagrin.

He almost expected those pretty pink lips to emit wheezing. It was nearly enough to make Ben smile if he wasn't so damned furious. What he ought to do was give her rear the hiding that it deserved.

Instead, he stood calm and composed while the little fool struggled to transform her face from shock to a placid smile. She turned and plucked her ticket from the outstretched hand with a grateful murmur, then descended the steps to pause beside him in breathless hesitance. She held her breath, and her eyes couldn't seem to decide whether to meet his or stay trained on her hard-won ticket.

The man that had chased her watched them, hawk-like, from the lit doorway. Unsmiling, he jerked his head to Ben. "You two been married long?" His arms were crossed in suspicion, the light from the office behind him filtering red through ears that stuck out from his face like bat wings.

Lucy was small and still beside him. Her bag had never appeared larger or as ugly as it did now, dangling from her bloodless fingers. Those clutching hands and the smug skepticism of the suddenly unfriendly office clerk decided him.

Ben leaned down and snagged the wooden handles of her bag, ignoring her fluttering hands as he took it away. "Here, I'll take that, *dear*." Then, he stood straight and gave the stage clerk a hard, direct stare. "We've been married near to a year now. Reason why you're askin'?"

Bat Ears uncrossed his arms pretty quick after that and held his hands up with a placating laugh. "Oh, no harm in asking, sir! We've had an emergency wire to look out for a runaway from Atlanta. There's a reward for her detainment to the nearest authorities." His voice carried in the night air around them.

Lucy came alive then, and turned around, hands clutching at her breast. "Oh, that poor family. We understand the need to authenticate who I am. Here, hand me that bag, darling. I believe I have a copy of our marriage papers in here somewhere. What was her name and age, sir?" She pretended to dig in the bag that Ben held for their imaginary marriage certificate, dropping items on the ground and chatting.

The clerk shifted his feet and brought out his pocket watch. Ben watched him sigh beneath lowered lids.

"No, no, that's quite alright, madam. The girl is about sixteen in age, plain and plump of figure. Brown of hair and eyes. Her name is, ah, Lucille Richards, or something similar. I'd have to double-check." By the snap of his watch face, the hound was off the scent and he was as ready to find a bed as they were.

Sixteen? Ben thought, sick at heart from his earlier errant thoughts from the train. But then he wondered, *plain and plump?*

"Oh, dear, if you're certain," Lucy frowned. Her hands were poised over the mess she'd made in her search.

The man grunted and backed into the doorway. "Quite sure. If you notice anyone of that description, just make note of where she was, what time, and drop the information off either here or at the sheriff's office."

Ben tipped his hat to him while the girl next to him deposited dropped items back into her carpetbag and managed to remain impassive though his mind was reeling. He grabbed Reb's reins in a loose grasp, then eased a decidedly heavy arm over Miss Ricci's stiff little shoulders, turning them towards the dim haze of the clapboard buildings to their right. She followed along without a peep.

Anger built in him as it always did when lying women tried to manage him.

He'd been managed since he was ten, thanks to a bored, well-meaning stepmother. Where had that got him, he wondered. Shamed and shunned by the respectable people of the town. He'd found that he did quite well by himself without any housewife's say-so, and for five years of living alone, had vowed that no one would run roughshod over his wants and needs. Not his Pa. Not the old man's wife.

And not beautiful little liars like this one.

There was something else in the furious stream of his thoughts as he led her closer to the livery. Some emotion that he refused to admit to himself or give voice to attempt to smother his anger. It had no place in their present circumstances.

It felt suspiciously like worry.

When he imagined runaways, he pictured desperate children forced into thinking like an adult through either poverty or fear. She was neither poor of material things nor bruised of spirit. He tried to remember if she'd acted like a spoiled brat, or if she'd pouted or bragged about her ease in life. There was nothing. She'd been proud of her father's hotel in Texas and had told him how she'd helped with the wash. Rich women didn't touch laundry. In the time since he'd met her that morning, she'd been friendly, humorous, and not at all what he would imagine was a girl fleeing her home and worried family.

Even so. The deceit ate at him, withered up his liking for her. It was hard enough to trust people. She'd offered him kindness on the train, and then used it against him for her own deeds, whatever they were. He hardened his heart against the fondness he'd possessed for her. It was time someone gave her a talking-to.

Ben halted their funeral march just outside the livery's open doors.

"You're that missing girl. That why you're lying, telling people I'm your husband?" He took his arm from her shoulders, and cool evening air seeped through the thin material of his worn shirt.

"Yes." Her voice shook, and she sounded so wretched that he wanted to feel sorry for her. "I did not want strangers knowing my real name. In Atlanta I used 'Anne', and here I'm 'Eve'. I'm so sorry I used—"

"You mean strangers like me? You told me your real name on the train, first thing." His quiet, wrathful sarcasm slipped out. "Or is Lucy Ricci even your real name?"

"Yes, it's Lucy Ricci." Lucy shot him a challenging look so quickly he would've missed it if he hadn't been so focused on her face. Her efforts to hang her head after that dark look lost their authenticity, and he felt a cruel, knowing smirk twist his face. Little Liar. "I was not purposefully trying to be deceitful, Mr. Stone. I just...I didn't want...There's—" She took a deep, bracing breath. It was fully dark now, and she gestured to the warm light of the livery doorway. "May I explain myself while we get your horse bedded down?"

We? Just who in the hell did she think she was? They weren't a '*we*'.

"No." His mouth pressed into a thin line, uncompromising and stern. "I don't think you realize what kind of fool thing you did back there."

That idiotic show of meekness disappeared, and she gawked up at him, offended.

Ben took a looming step toward her, practically breathing down her high neckline. "You can't be goin' around, claiming strange men as your husband, little miss. Any other man, and you could be buzzard food in a gully somewhere by morning."

Her mouth opened and closed, her eyebrows knit, and the elusive spark was back. *Better than lying.*

"That's perhaps a bit of a stretch—"

"No, it ain't," he growled, leaning further into her space to impress upon her that he was a stranger. She didn't know him from Adam, didn't know what type of men there were out there, just waiting for a young, sweet thing like her to come along. "You're a lone woman, got no family, no menfolk around to protect you. Changin' your name, tellin' even one person you're married to someone, could give a man the power to do whatever he wants to you. If I were an outlaw, a low-down snake, I could've used that man's word back there as proof to treat you how I see fit. If I wanted to beat you, lock you in a room somewhere, I could. 'Cause I'd be your *husband*, according to you."

Lucy's face was pale and stiff now, and he told himself fear was what he'd wanted from her all along. He needed her to realize the wrong person at the wrong time, could make her a victim of some unspeakable crime.

"I-I didn't think—" she whispered, but he cut her off again, warming up to his tirade. That angry, self-righteous frown of hers was gone now.

"That's pretty obvious. Damn it, girl." He took his hat off, ran his fingers through his hair, perspiring even in the crisp night air, and replaced it with firm, irate movements. "You gave me power back there, and I don't know what you're hidin' from, but is it worth getting stolen away for? You can get yourself killed, or worse, living in the shadow of a bad man, beddin' down like you *were* his wife. Until he tired of you, or the fear that you'd run off and tell, and slit your throat. Men can get away with anything out here. Taking a lone little girl isn't anything. You'd disappear and no one would know where the hell you went, if you were dead or alive. How do you think your daddy would feel, then?"

To his horror, Miss Ricci's eyes were full of tears that she tried blinking back. Her mouth was trembling, her breathing desperate and uneven. She wasn't faking emotion this time.

"Aw, hell," he muttered, and looked around with an anxious swivel, but no one was near enough to see more than just a couple, having an innocent conversation. She was scouring her face as though trying to hurt herself. Choppy breathing escaped from her damp fingers.

"Everything you said may be true, but I *had* to leave, I just had to." Her voice was someone else's, strained and high-pitched.

Seeing her break down in front of him, another thought occurred to him. She looked awfully alone...and awfully young. Couldn't be much younger than his bullheaded little brother. And with the memory of Junior's grinning face, a stalk of wheat the same color as his hair notched between his lips, Ben's anger disappeared.

"Damn it...come here. C'mere."

Half expecting her to run screaming, he gritted his teeth when she stepped into him without hesitation. Her body was shockingly hot, sweaty, and shaking. He wrapped his arms around her, tentative and awkward at the start, then more securely. Shushing her, Ben tucked his chin over her elegant little hat and patted her shoulder blades with a free hand. He kept those comforting, platonic thoughts of his seventeen-year-old brother in mind while he calmed her, and when she made to wrap her arms around him, he smoothly stepped back. He wouldn't cross that line with an impulsive child. She may be a young fool, but he wasn't.

A *sixteen-year-old* young fool.

They avoided each other's gaze.

"C'mon, let's get Reb bedded down, then you and I will find somewhere to get some shut-eye."

Walking into the livery with a weeping woman trailing behind gave Ben no little anxiety, and his jaw hurt from clenching his teeth, waiting for the shoe to drop and someone to demand answers for what he'd done to the poor girl. Inside the large, open barn, oil lamps spread orange light on golden hay, and dusty russet dirt. Miss Ricci was a quiet footstep behind him, her shadow beside his own, bowed and penitent.

"Help you?" an echo asked from the pungent depths of the building. A short, broad man stepped out from a stall, shutting the half-door with a bored, "Two dollars a night, fifty cents extra for hay, another fifty for grain." Dark eyes glittered from beneath the flopping rim of his hat. It was grimed with stall filth, and he smelled of the manure he shoveled.

Muttering at the highway robbery, Ben took out three silver dollars, and the man led them to a middle stall that was in dire need of mucking. The dirty man irreverently counted and bit the coins with chin tucked, lip bulging with chewing tobacco.

"How many hotels you have around here?" Ben inquired, disconnecting the saddlebags before taking off Reb's tack and saddle blanket. He swung the bulk of the leather bags and straps over a broad shoulder.

Tucking Ben's dollars in his shirt pocket, the man slid his eyes in an oily way over Miss Ricci's figure, who had found a curry comb and was making short work of brushing down a grateful Reb. Eying the female's swaying hem, he spat a long stream of brown juice and replied, "Got two on this street, one at that end," he pointed the way they'd come, "and one at that end." His thumb jerked down the street, towards loud laughter, shouts, and tinkling piano music. "One by the train station might be a bit nicer for you sister, here."

Ben didn't appreciate the way this dirty little fellow was eyeballing the impervious Lucy. "My wife," he corrected with a soft bite, "and I are obliged. I'll come by in the morning to get my horse. Make sure you give him plenty of grain, we've got a day's ride ahead of us before the next train station."

He leaned over and scooped up the substantial weight of the ugly green bag, and said with a hint of sarcasm, "Let's go, Mrs. Stone. We need to see if there are any rooms left."

ALTHOUGH SHE PRETENDED to pay the men no mind, Lucy was wholly aware of the conversation and the eyes that followed her around the horse.

Ignoring people was a practiced art of hers, and she continued to do so with aplomb. She'd never felt so physically and emotionally exhausted, and she let the curry's teeth glide through Reb's coarse black mane in a dreamlike state. The lights displayed the blood bay's shining red coat, vivid against the deep black of his legs and mane. There were old wounds from years past, deep spur marks that showed in black crescent parts in the horse's hair, thin over the belly and flanks. The notion that Ben had caused those scars hadn't crossed her mind. He didn't appear to be that type of owner.

When he derisively summoned her, she told herself she deserved it. Her normal fire had fizzled out. He'd rebuked her with such thoroughness after her lies that it was only normal that he abhorred her now. It was obvious in the mocking twist of his lips as he yanked up her doleful bag, and the action was a blow against a fresh bruise.

Close to tears again, she nodded and hooked the comb over the stall's tall wooden wall. Patting Reb on the rump, she trailed Ben out the stall door, and only felt the briefest flutter of amusement when the gelding made to follow them. The livery owner shut the stall door behind her and entered a feed room down the row.

Once the man was out of sight, she tugged her bag from Ben's grip, embarrassed that he was carrying her things when she disgusted him so.

"Thank you, I can manage," she whispered, eyes on the dirt.

He didn't reply, but she felt his displeasure burning a hole through her hat.

When they were halfway down the street, he demanded, "Give me one good reason why I shouldn't haul you over my shoulder and take you to the nearest deputy."

Her pulse regained its fast thrumming. Any defensive re-torts were quelled at the memory of the dressing down he'd given her not fifteen minutes before. Though he might be a decent man to his core, she didn't doubt he'd do exactly as he promised.

Licking dry lips, she said, "It's not just one reason, Mr. Stone, it's a multitude."

Repositioning his saddlebags with a careless shrug, he said, "Explain, then. The truth, if you don't mind."

Pricked by his tone, she snapped, "I'm not of a mind to lie at every instance, sir. I only did so before for my safety."

"Yeah, tryin' to cover your trail from a loving mother worried sick about you, that's a real good reason," he jeered.

"You know nothing about my mother," she spat, but softly, so no one else could hear. "I assure you, it's not love that made her send the wire. It's control, Mr. Stone. In every way, she controls my life with no thought to my own hopes and dreams."

"Sounds to me that you can afford to be that picky. Mamas are always tryin' to do their best for their daughters. Now, people further west, they do what they can to survive. Not many have the money for a train ticket so they can sneak off to God-knows-where."

Desperation and fury at his small-mindedness stopped her in her tracks. They'd made it to the door of the hotel at the end of the street, the one furthest from the train depot that wasn't as nice, but it was beyond her notice. "Don't preach to me about things you don't understand. I told the truth before. I'm going to Texas to live with my father. My mother is not a *worried mama*; she holds the strings, and I'm the puppet. If it were up to her, I'd be sequestered in a finishing school until I moldered, out of sight, out of mind. I want my home, my life back in Dogwood. Please, let me continue my travels so I can get it."

Dark brows had raised over his eyes, and lashes too pretty for such a stubborn cuss made crescent shadows over the blue of his irises. "And does your Pa approve of this, Miss Ricci? A sixteen-year-old train-hopping from state to state all by herself?"

Fed up, she took a deep breath and gritted out, "I am not *sixteen*, Mr. Stone, and I am fully capable of taking care of myself if you would just let me!"

He spread his feet further apart. "You're not lyin' to me?"

She wanted to either shout at him or shake him. Or both. "No. I was in a boarding school in Boston when I was sixteen. And my father was supposed to fetch me on my eighteenth birthday, but he never received the letter." Her very real anger at that deception must have displayed across her face because Ben sighed again and scrubbed a hand from his forehead to his chin. Sensing a crack in his defense, she urged, "I can prove it to you, Mr. Stone. I have letters if you'll look at them. Don't go to the sheriff. Please."

A thin, balding man cracked the hotel door open and peered out at them. "Are you coming in? The front desk is closing, and there's but one room left."

Ben and Lucy shared a look, and she trembled, praying, *Please, please let him believe me.* His eyes examined her expression, her breathing, the way she stood supplicant but proud before him. Finally, decision made, he walked forward. The hotel owner opened the door wider.

"One room will be fine."

"Names?" The middle-aged man sounded tired.

As though announcing terrible news, Ben disclosed, "Stone. Mr. and Mrs. Stone."

BEN SIGNED THEIR names in the registry book at the counter while the owner folded bills and placed them carefully in a small safe in the back room. Lucy watched the money with a keen eye, making a silent vow to repay him as soon as they made it to the privacy of their room.

Their room.

The thought set her teeth on edge. Not because she was afraid that he had designs upon her, oh no. He'd made it perfectly clear that he thought she was an entitled, foolish, and spoiled child. Being alone in the same room with her would be torment for him. She was tight with nerves, and a hot, sick sensation burned in her chest. She couldn't help but lean in close while he wrote his name. The little man behind the counter cleaned his glasses and replaced them on his short, stubby nose.

Ben had paused after signing *'Ben Stone'*, then after that brief hesitation, he scrawled *'and wife'*, lips flat against his teeth. He muttered something low and foul.

The proprietor grabbed one of his many oil lamps from behind the counter, tired and uninterested in what had been written. He lit it, replaced the glass, and beckoned them to follow his stilted figure into a hallway off to the side of a bare-board staircase.

In the dark, narrow hallway stood four small doors, crooked in their frames with a crack two inches tall at the bottoms. From behind one of those doors emitted snores similar in sound to a hibernating bear with a head cold. Crawling in her skin, Lucy strangled the handles of her bag and followed obediently until they reached the last door on the right. Ben was right behind her, his boots brushing against her hem. The door was unlocked and forced open with a squeak of wood against the doorjamb. Light poured into the smallest room Lucy had ever seen. It would have made a perfect home as a cabin in a sleek ship, saving precious room for cargo and passengers. A narrow, lumpy cot was tucked against the wall on the left, and there was just enough room on the right for a washstand that housed a hidden chamber pot behind a ragged curtain, and a washbasin on top. An oil lamp that the hotel owner lit revealed more of the room so that even the spiders couldn't hide behind their cobwebs.

Ben stared at the cot, grim and silent, and she set her bag down against the wall so that she could hug herself. One person could hardly fit on that bed, much less two. And there was no bundle board. Asking for one was out of the question. What married couple used a bundle board? Four feet separated the cot from the wall opposite, and with three people inside, all their shoulders brushed. The owner shuffled outside.

"Here's the key. The room's not much, but travelers can't choose to be picky when it's this or camping outside." His voice warned them not to make any complaints.

As though this wasn't a waking nightmare, Lucy consoled, "Oh, heavens no, this is just fine. Thank you."

With one last grunt from the administrator, they were left alone with their single lamp, a tiny bed, and the awful sawing noises from their neighbor a door across. When their wary eyes met, Ben was the first to look away and dropped his bags on the floor with a muffled thump.

"I'll take the floor. Unless," he turned to her as though just considering an idea, "you want to take the room and I'll lay out my bedroll outside?"

Offended, Lucy put on a brave face and huffed, "Why on earth would you do that, Mr. Stone? If anything, I'll take the floor. The bed is probably riddled with bedbugs in any case."

His beard quirked, and his eyes went from grim to twinkling. "So, you'd leave me to be a feast for the little bloodsuckers, huh?"

Turning red, she shoved her way between their bags in vexation. "No, of course not. It's just that I got us into this-this sharing of rooms, and I'd like for you to take the bug. I mean, the bed—"

Snorting a soft, close-mouthed laugh, Ben shook his head and squatted, unbolting a bag. "I'm just pulling your leg, *Eve*. And no, no man would ever let a lady sleep on the floor when he could."

Blinking dry, tired eyes, Lucy turned her back to him and scrubbed her face before taking in the room one more time. Their shadows were cast eerily against the rough, unpainted walls around them. She glanced up and wished she hadn't. The ceiling was so bowed and low that she could stand on her tiptoes and touch it, which she did. "We'll be lucky if half the hotel doesn't crush us in our sleep."

"Good thing we ain't scared of small spaces," he said, but she couldn't tell if he was amused or not.

To kill the oppressive awkwardness, Lucy snagged her carpetbag from the floor and said formally, "I had promised to show you letters from my father, Mr. Stone. I had managed to save some over the years." She peeked at his stoic expression. His arms were crossed, a looming statue waiting to mete out judgment. She glanced back down, finding a handful of letters in the mess she'd made of her carefully packed bag at the stage office.

The first letter was her favorite. It was one of the oldest, and she read it aloud in a rush, slowing down at the end, at the important part.

"'...and even though you were taken from here, this hotel will always remain your home, Lucy-Lou. When you're out of your lady's school, your mother permitting, I will come by train and whisk you away back to Texas. Be patient, have faith, Minnie and I are going nowhere. All my love, Papa.'" She handed the letter to Ben, who took it grudgingly, but turned it on its back to read the scripted return address.

"This is dated three years ago."

"That's when Mother stole me away and took me to Atlanta." Lucy kept her voice as expressionless as his.

"Got anything newer?"

"I have one from six months ago," she said, handing him a shorter, more abrupt letter. "The most recent ones are gone." It wasn't possible keeping her feelings from slipping out that time.

After a pause at the latter, Ben took the letter to the lamp glow, squinting. "I'm guessin' he's not too keen on you comin' home in this one."

Lucy sighed. The stress of the day was getting to her, and exhaustion sat heavily on her shoulders. "No. There was another fire on the second floor last September, and he was in the middle of renovations. See where he's talking about Melvin Graves? That's the carpenter that was working for him at the time. He was also having trouble with gas installation."

An endless amount of time went by while Lucy handed him letter after letter, and Ben took his time perusing them. Each time he finished a letter, he checked the addresses on the back. Finally, he waved off the next letter she held up, and took his hat off. She said nothing, familiar with the silence of a man thinking, and thinking hard. He finger-combed onyx curls from his eyes. A wide, pink stripe remained on his forehead from the hat band.

With halting reluctance, he stated, "Looks to me like you're tellin' the truth." When she exhaled a relieved breath, he looked sharply at her. "For once."

Stifling a sheepish smile, she made a meal of soberly folding every letter again before stowing them lovingly away into her bag. "So...you'll not alert the authorities?"

"I didn't say that."

No. "Mr. Stone—"

He held a staying hand, and his face was as serious as she'd ever seen. "I'm gonna sleep on it, Miss Ricci. I'm entitled to that, at least. It's not my business to get between a mother's and father's guardianship...troubles. How they raise you is up to them. But," he cleared his throat, "I did see that last letter that wished you a happy seventeenth birthday from a year ago. You'll be eighteen soon?"

"Tomorrow."

"Really." His eyebrows raised. She wondered if everything she said to him would have that same tone of disbelief. It was infuriating.

"Yes, remember? I'd written Papa to pick me up on my birthday but—"

"—something came up," he finished for her.

She nodded, then was overcome with a jaw-cracking yawn that she hid behind a fist.

"Why did you leave a day early?" he asked.

Lucy wouldn't meet his eyes. "I couldn't wait any longer."

IT WOULD BE the first time he'd spent the night with a female in the same room. Even when he was married, he'd slept in a different room like the stranger he was. Now, he really was with a stranger, and he couldn't seem to force himself to get on his horse and ride away without looking back.

Hell, he was practically sleepwalking where he stood.

Knowing he was a fool ten times over, he whipped his bedroll out and snapped it open across the floor in an expert move. Unable to help himself, he glanced at the girl. She was examining the bed with a grimace, pacing along its length like a buyer surveying a horse and finding it lacking.

Fighting a smile, he sat at the end of his bedroll and tugged his boots off, aware of every movement from the woman next to him.

Lucy was now examining the ill-fitting sheets, pulling them from the mattress, inspecting the seams for bugs, then sniffing to check for freshness. She gagged and snapped her head sharply to the side.

Snorting, he threw her one of his extra blankets. "Here. Sleep on top of this. It's big enough to cover up with. I don't have bugs. Might smell like smoke, though."

"Thank you." She draped the hardy travel blanket across the length of the bed and gave him a worried look. "You may have to burn it after this."

"I'll just turn it into a saddle blanket," he chuckled.

"That's a disservice to your horse." Her nose was wrinkled and strange, unwelcome thoughts formed. He likened the sensation to turning over rocks and logs in his mind and finding something not wholly unappealing beneath them, like expecting a bug and discovering a gold nugget instead. She may be a liar, but he was finding it harder and harder not to like her. The more they communicated, the worse it got.

Well, sleep would put an end to that.

They made ready for bed in stilted silence, with faint snores and shuffled footsteps from above their only break from the throbbing quiet. She took her hat off and set it next to the lamp, and he was impressed with the length of her hatpin. Her hair gleamed where it lay sleek at the sides of the middle part. He was grateful she didn't take her hair down. His mouth was dry enough as it was.

When she sat on the bed, the ropes creaked so loud that she shot back up in astonishment. He turned his back to her and feigned digging in his saddlebags so he didn't give in to laughter. The ropes creaked again, just as piercing, but slow and drawn out. He pretended not to hear and settled down on his blankets, hiding his smile with his hat.

LUCY SAT ON the bed with a strident *creak*, leaned over to untie her boots with another *creak*, then gingerly, holding her breath, she lay back on the vociferous cot. Her body was board-stiff, and it was impossible to ignore the moaning and groaning of the ropes beneath her. It must be especially loud for Ben, who was at ear level with the blasted things near the floor.

After a moment of painful stillness, she saw him lift his hat through her periphery.

"You done with the light?"

"Er, yes, I believe so."

He sat up, turned with a lithe twist of his torso, and blew out the lamp, smothering them in the most absolute darkness Lucy had ever had the misfortune of being in. What was worse, a fold in the blanket was digging into her spine. She needed to move. Face damp with nervous perspiration, she shifted closer to the wall onto her side.

Her watch dug into her breast with sharp, stabbing pain. Mortified, she took off the watch and felt around to put it on the washstand, hissing in pain when her knuckles encoun-tered the hot lamp. The watch clattered to the floor beneath the screaming ropes of the cot.

"You alright up there?" Ben asked, whether entertained or irritated, she couldn't tell.

"I'm fine," she hissed back in the dark. She was not fine. She was sweating through her jacket even though it was cold enough to make her shiver, and the sorry excuse for the bed she lay on made such a cacophony with the slightest move-ment, she was sure their neighbors could hear and would be beating down the door at any minute. Unable to stand it any longer, she sat up and began the noisy process of taking off her jacket and corset. Propriety didn't matter if she couldn't even breathe, and she flung the offending clothing at the end of the bed and curled into a ball beneath the smoke scent of his blanket, able to expand her lungs, but afraid to.

"Now I'm afraid to even breathe." Her voice was muffled in the blanket.

Ben started choking, at least, that's what it sounded like. He was holding back laughter, and at her expense!

"That's it, you can sleep on this orchestra made of ropes," she whisper-shouted and made to get up. *Creak, creak, creak.* She stood beside the bed, mutinous and glaring. When she stepped back, she trod on something firm with her stockinged foot, and he chuckled and pulled his arm out from under her.

"Serves you right," she grumbled and gave a feminine snort, close to laughing herself silly at the ludicrousness of the cot debacle. "I am not sleeping on that...*thing*."

What they ended up doing, in pitch black, was yank the mattress from its frame, the latter of which they propped against the corner. The mattress was arranged on the bare wood floor, and when she lay down this time, it was to the soft, muffled music of clothes against blankets.

"Thank you, Mr. Stone," she sighed, closing her eyes and wishing for sleep.

"You're welcome."

Her eyes shot open. His warm voice was close, much closer than before now that they were on the same level. If she wished, she could reach out and touch him. Her fingers clenched and squeezed around his blanket, and she drew it close to her face, breathing in its scent, imagining campfires and popping embers reaching a black sky filled with stars.

Teeth worrying her lip, she took the leap and asked a question she strangely, desperately, wanted to know. "Do you sleep outside often, then?"

Ben shifted, settled, and was still. "More often than inside, I reckon."

"Is it peaceful?"

"It can be. After the drive is over, the cattle's sold, the hands're paid, and you've left town. Most often it's just me and Reb, a little fire and coffee, sleeping with nature."

"Reb?"

"My horse."

It sounded wonderful and lonely. But sometimes, Lucy craved that kind of solitude. "Do you like to be alone?"

"Most times," he admitted.

"I do, too." They were whispering, and she cradled her head with a cupped hand. "In Georgia, I'd ride our carriage horse across our neighbor's pastures just to be alone. My own company was preferable to Mother's and Beth's—that's my sister—and I would get away from all the noise of the parties, the expectations. If I left early enough, the sun would come up, and I'd stop and watch all the colors spread across the sky." She smiled. "It's a shame I'm wretched at painting, or I could have captured them."

"Ain't nothing prettier than a Texas sunrise." He sounded half asleep.

"I agree." Her own voice was muzzy now, and she drew her knees up. "I can't wait to see my first Texas sunrise in three years." Five minutes passed, and her lids grew heavy. She shut them and fought sudden tears. "I am truly sorry about playing you false. For using you. There is no excuse."

There was only silence for such a length that she was sure he'd fallen asleep. But after a minute, he said, "Reckon I know your reasons, now. Lord knows I'm no one to judge. You seem decent enough, just young."

She resented that truth and grimaced in the dark. "I'm not decent. Have you ever acted so despicable that you'd rather do something monumentally dangerous, like traveling alone for days, than face the consequences of it? The things I've done, they're unforgivable. I couldn't face living there for one more day." Memories of forbidden kisses and fumbling made her chest ache, and she pressed her fingers hard into the sockets of her eyes. Self-disgust made her spill ugly truths. "I used people in Atlanta, too. Even though it was wrong. I played with another man's feelings, at first so he'd send for my papa for me. And then, just for spite. He was my sister's beau." Hot tears tracked across the bridge of her nose at her confession. "Can guilt kill you? Like a poison?"

Movement from his bedroll caught her breath. Was he looking in her direction? Or had he turned away in revulsion? Her answer was in the closeness of his voice. "In a way, maybe. Just proves you are a decent person if it's eating at you this way." After a minute, he cleared his throat, loud in the diminutive room. "What happened with the man?"

No longer tired, she swallowed and tried to laugh off her discomfort. "You'll hate me."

"Naw, I won't. It might change my mind about going to the sheriff." He paused. "And after tomorrow, you'll never have to see me again."

Her breathing was rapid and shallow. She wiped her nose and eyes with the neckline of her chemise. "All right." She'd tell him the whole, ugly truth. "It will not...endear you to me. But maybe you will understand why I had to leave."

3

— · —

CHAPTER THREE

ATLANTA, GEORGIA

Three months earlier...

L ucy had never planned to seduce her sister's beau.

Events had spiraled beyond all control after the tumultuous dinner with the Langfords shortly after New Year's Day when Beth had launched the dawning of catastrophe with her big mouth.

"Lucy wants to move back to Texas when she turns eighteen. She wants to live with Papa."

An embarrassed hush followed Beth's unceremonious statement, and Lucy halted, suspended over her pale chicken bouillon, bored beyond measure during this, their weekly supper with the Langfords. Each day, she despaired at the awfulness of three wasted years spent away from the Dogwood Hotel and her Papa.

Her despair transformed to quiet fury, and Lucy glanced up at her older sister, trying and failing to keep from reacting to the proclamation. Beth had been spoiling for a fight all afternoon. Her treacherous words, guaranteed to give Lucy a scolding from their mother, were retaliation for the embar-

46

rassment the younger sister had produced in the presence of Beth's latest caller after church.

"Did you see the size of Katherine Marche's engagement setting? I expect she's thinking twice about marrying Hugh, now," Beth whispered conspiratorially to Peter Langford, her latest beau.

To his credit, he didn't comment.

Having liked the shy and amiable Miss Marche, Lucy rose to her defense. "Katie is perfectly happy with her ring, size notwithstanding. Unlike you, Beth, she has never suffered unduly from cupidity."

"I beg your pardon?" Beth stopped in the middle of the churchyard walkway, halting Peter with her.

Lucy didn't stop, but turned and walked backward long enough to whisper loudly to Peter, "Have a care. Proposing to Beth with her impossible standards may well bankrupt you."

Now, Beth took her revenge in the opulently decorated dining room while warm light glowed on wallpaper and wainscoted walls from a twelve-branched gasolier suspended above crystal glasses, fine china, and white linen. The long cherry table that sat twelve gleamed in the steady light, translucent streaks from the morning's wax barely discernible. The faint hint of lemon scent wavered beneath the aroma of the first course.

Lucy had assumed that Beth's reprisal would be to whisper in their mother's ear behind closed doors, as was her usual wont. Now, in the silence of her sister's hasty announcement, she wondered if the little imbecile had ruined everything.

"What was that?" Aurora asked from the end, an edge of warning cutting across soup bowls toward Lucy.

Before she could deny the claim, Beth chimed in, "She was going on about leaving again to the maid this morning, Mama. I was just telling Mr. Langford."

Beth sat to Aurora's right, a visage in a soft pink dinner gown. Seeing them, practically side by side as they were, was like looking at the same person in different stages of life. Aurora was in her forties, beautiful and slim, and her eldest daughter was even more so. Lucy was never more aware than now how the two were like swans with their graceful long necks and pale hair. She, however, was more akin to the chicken hawk, brown-haired and sharp-eyed.

"I do not go *on* about leaving, Beth," Lucy snapped, her sister's smooth feathers ruffling at the sharp tone. She didn't care. Beth must have crept outside her room that morning when she was confiding in Meggie. The twit was always sneaking and spying; Lucy had caught her at it more than once at the crack of her door.

"Girls," Aurora sighed and smiled at Mrs. Langford to her left. "I must apologize. Having never had a sibling of my own, I find myself floundering when my girls insist on arguing."

While Mrs. Langford soothed her friend, Lucy caught the warning glance from her mother and faced forward in a semblance of obedience. But her jaw was set and firm. The last time she'd brought up leaving when she came of age to Aurora, her mother had been tightening Lucy's corset, the woman's preferred instrument of torture.

"I'll never understand why you enjoy living and associating with such low class, Lucille. The answer is no. I shall never step a foot on that vile soil again, and neither shall you."

Aurora's voice had been as pinched as her face.

That had been months ago, not long after Lucy had read about the new railroad in New Orleans. Since then, her anger built and built, growing in intensity until it was a nuanced entity, whispering invectives as she recalled every constraint, and relived every insult and injustice.

In finishing school, acting meek and easily cowed as the girls were taught had increased her misery. They'd attempted to instill in her the importance of being a spineless, spiritless pretense of the girl she was. That had been more sobering than the helplessness of missing Tony, Minnie, and her hotel family. When had she ever let anyone control the vitality of her spirit?

Never, her conscience whispered.

She'd matured in several ways during her two years in Boston, along with the realization that growing up meant being in control of one's feelings and actions. She could cry and bemoan her mother and sister's cruelty on her bedspread, or she could do something about it. The decision to leave when she was of age had ensued a perceptive change in Lucille Ricci. Her sour attitude metamorphosed into growing competence. She'd made no friends since her move to Atlanta, and that was the first of many things she'd changed. She had already befriended the help, and so she went so far as to chat with the postman, the milkman, and the men at the telegram and ticket office.

At first, it had amazed her how nice and gallant they all were to her, a perfect stranger. Eventually, even an innocent like her soon discovered that above those broad grins were roving, appreciative eyes. All the changes in her body that had made her mother mutter and shake her head demonstrated the opposite effect on the men of the city.

Aurora insisted she was growing fat, but Lucy had fast learned her mother's predispositions. The constant beratement of the shape of her youngest daughter's figure was an indicator of worry. Aurora and Beth were slim with straight edges, sharp collar bones, and flat chests. Their fingers and faces were fine-boned and petite.

Not so Lucy.

She had a wiry strength, broader shoulders than her sister, and hips as well. Her legs were strong and long, and she could seat a horse astride or sidesaddle with impeccable balance. Even now, she looked at her hands, with their square, calloused palms, and long, clever fingers. Scars scattered here or there; burns from ovens, scratches from reaching under broody chickens for their white gold, nicks from a sharp kitchen knife. Aurora had plied caustic creams to erase the offensive patches of skin, but Lucy had thrown them out like the poison they were.

Besides, the baker's boy hadn't seemed to mind when he'd clenched her hands and brought her in close for chaste, furtive kisses.

"Something funny?"

Lucy was smiling into her soup, but at the low murmur of Beth's latest beau, Peter, she wiped it from her face.

Peter Langford III sat across from her, as he always did when his mother accompanied him to their casual dinners. She was surprised to catch him openly observing her. In the past, any eye contact between them had been discreet and careful. Beth was the jealous kind, and quick to notice any untoward behavior between a suitor and her 'odious sister'.

She peeked at her sister and mother, but they were both immersed in the week's latest gossip with Mrs. Langford. Coast clear, she caught Peter's green eyes.

"You wouldn't find it very amusing."

No, he wouldn't find it amusing, but *would* he find it interesting where her thoughts wandered at the dinner table? She doubted he'd tattle to their mothers, at the very least. Peter wasn't a bad sort. Not as much fun as the boisterous cowhands she'd served at the hotel or as amusing as the mill workers that frequented the diner, but what did she expect from a New York lawyer's son? Her first impression of him had been one of immediate dislike. He was a male replica of Beth; slim, wealthy, and beautiful. He was also deep in his mother's pocket. Over time, Lucy discovered that was where such unlikable similarities had ended.

He was, perhaps, Lucy's favorite out of all of Beth's suitors. He was nowhere near as cruel or jeering as Herbert, who happened to be her sister's favorite. Mother hadn't approved of Herb's father, however. It was well and lovely to be rich unless one gained one's fortune in gambling and investing in a dozen downtown brothels. So, Aurora had ordered the forlorn Elizabeth to drop her favored beau in lieu of Peter the summer before. Besides, his father was a lawyer with political connections, and his mother got on famously with the family.

Despite Peter's occasional pretentiousness, he was a kind enough fellow. He never laughed at jokes made at her expense, and she held him in high esteem for that reason alone. If he wanted to dress like a popinjay and was a notorious mama's boy, it didn't matter a whit to Lucy. She could forgive his superficiality and infrequent pandering to her mother and sister because he never once excluded her from an invitation or conversation.

A lull in the women's discussion as their bowls were taken away and lamb and parsnips were served broke Lucy and Peter's eye contact. It was strange enough that Lucy didn't immediately dig into the art on the plate but frowned at it. Thinking.

"Lucille—"

Lucy bumped her knee under the table. Lord, but why did her mother have to shout out of the blue like that? Aurora used Lucy's name with an annoying inflection that made her shoulders tense and feet tap. Girding her loins, Lucy attempted to look as though she hadn't practically leaped from her seat.

"—you have hardly touched your food. Have you resolved in losing some of the..." Aurora paused delicately whilst cutting lamb with limp, fragile wrists, "...inches you have gained since last year?" She took a bite of meat less than a square inch in size, looking for all the world as if she hadn't just thrown down a gauntlet.

Why, that miserable heifer.

Used to dinner-table demoralization, Lucy nonetheless felt that swift prick of anger at the muffled titter from Beth's direction. Mrs. Langford was still sawing at her meat, and Peter had taken a halting bite of parsnip. He wasn't attempting to make eye contact any longer. That, more than anything, brought a creeping heat to Lucy's cheeks.

It would serve her mother right to be humiliated in return, she thought grimly.

Aurora's eyes were unmarred by a single laugh or smile line. No freckles from a cheerful sun dusted her slim, sharp nose. The woman was middling in years and had all the money and notoriety she'd ever striven for after the death of her wealthy parents nearly a decade ago, but discontent was predominant in an otherwise unyielding expression. She'd been born to a good life but had still famously butted heads with her parents. She'd eloped with Papa, yet Lucy remembered nothing but shouts and angry words between them. Then, Aurora had returned to Atlanta after her mother and father had died, an heiress and at the top tier of the social hierarchy—still discontent.

Beth was far too meek to row with. Shouting at the help, unsatisfying. All that remained was Lucy.

Understanding how the gears turned in her mother's mind was far different than accepting them, and a little devil on Lucy's shoulder whispered in her ear. Even though she could choke with embarrassment, she affected an expression of perfect innocence, rose a brow, and cut a man-sized bite out of her lamb.

"Growing bosoms over the holidays does not make one overweight, Mother."

It was Peter that choked—on his wine—and by the grace of God, managed not to spew the ruby liquid on Grandmother's starched white table runner. Mother would never forgive him, never mind Lucy, for speaking of body parts in front of the much-esteemed Mrs. Langford, who had gasped, as her Boston peers would say, in satisfying comportment of offended sensibilities.

Losing her nerve, Lucy shoved the lamb in her mouth. She'd said the word 'bosoms' at the dinner table. Minnie would have washed her mouth out with soap! Even so, it served her mother right, and she refused to be cowed.

"Lucille," Aurora hissed in the sibilant way that proved her shock went beyond mere disapproval; she was incensed. "Apologize to Mrs. and Mr. Langford at once. We cannot have them believe it is acceptable to practice such rough language in this household."

Swallowing her enormous bite of lamb, Lucy dabbed at her mouth with a linen napkin and strove to look collected even though her blood was roiling.

"I apologize, that was horribly crude."

She ignored her mother's face, which was the same hue as the tablecloth, and chose to meet Peter's watering jade eyes. They were watching her, but not in disapproval. Her lips curved, as though they shared a secret.

Dabbing at the corner of his eyes with his handkerchief, Peter waved a hand as though to shoo the apology away. "No matter," he said. "Mama has heard far more alarming words from my mouth at the dinner table. I say, have you seen Howard Bradby's new racing phaeton?"

There was only the briefest of pauses before Beth replied, "Oh, yes, it's exceedingly elegant, isn't it?"

If Beth knew which phaeton Peter was referring to, Lucy would eat her bonnet. She stifled a snort and couldn't help joining in. Anything to change the subject of her bosoms.

"His phaeton is lovely, but his horses are what draws the eye," she said. "Did you see the chestnut thoroughbred he bought from Kentucky this spring? What a beauty."

Beth's eyes snapped in dislike, but Peter's began to gleam in genuine interest. He leaned forward, his tie strings grazing his plate. "Seventeen hands. Howard showed me his papers and what a doozy he spent on that horseflesh."

"They're proud of their trotters, that's sure."

Mrs. Langford leaned over her wine glass toward Aurora to murmur, "I do not find it surprising that he's accumulating these assets since his marriage to Elaine. Her father would be rolling in his grave—"

"Do you mean that pretty red horse he brought to church last Sunday?" Beth interrupted in a false, light voice. Her eyes swiveled from Peter to Lucy, mouth downturned.

Pretending not to have heard her, Lucy drummed her fingers on the table, face lit with animation. "He would not be as smooth as a pacer, but you can see the power in the lines of his legs. I wouldn't mind a fast, hard ride on that one through the countryside."

Peter, in the middle of answering Beth, paused, his jaw slack. He shifted in his seat with a light creak of wood and cleared his throat. "Ah, so you ride, then, Miss Ricci?"

After a quick scan to ascertain their mothers were occupied with their conversation, Lucy conceded, "Only the carriage horses in our stable. I run them occasionally in Mr. Garrison's field, but I've never ridden a racehorse." She poked her food with a fork tine and grinned. "Perhaps I can persuade Mr. Bradby's stable hands to let me take his for a quick jaunt."

Beth gasped. "That's as good as horse thieving, don't you dare. You are so uncouth. I wonder how you ever came to be part of my family."

Eyes narrowed, Lucy asked with false sweetness, "Do you, really? Well, when a man and woman love each other very much...."

Laughter coughed out of Peter, and Lucy joined him.

"I'll tell Mother," Beth hissed, eyes shooting sparks.

Coloring at the threat, Lucy stopped laughing. "I was only teasing. Don't run to Mother at every instance."

"Stop being so common and I shan't."

"Common, yes, I must get that from Papa's side?" She'd only heard such accusations every day for the past year.

"You must, you and he are identical in every way." Said as an insult.

Lucy wasn't offended and shrugged. "Someone should have a bit of him. Heaven knows you are Mother incarnate."

"I'm happy to be just like Mother." Beth's nose was so high in the air that it was a wonder it didn't become stuck in the chandelier. "At least she isn't some Union-loving emigrant like our father. He's no better than a war-deserting carpetbagger."

Parroted straight from the mouth of their mother.

Anger, hot and sudden, intensified Lucy's stare and twisted her mouth. The impulse to slap Beth's haughty face had her half-risen out of her seat, and she whispered, "Papa was a decorated soldier who lost his arm in the Battle of Galveston.

You keep his name from your lips, Elizabeth, do you hear me? And I may be uncouth, but at least I don't talk about my family like you. You're no better than anyone. You're worse, in my eyes, always with Mother fighting your fights, hiding behind her skirts like a rat. You're pathetic."

Beth's blue eyes went wide with shock and humiliation. There would be retribution later, but Lucy didn't care. She didn't dare look at Peter and stood, her chair scraping the parquet floor. Not making eye contact and feeling volatile with indignation, she asked in the general direction of her mother, "I am not feeling well, may I please be excused?"

"What's the fuss about?" Aurora shot a calculating look at Beth, but the blonde's head was bowed.

"Nothing, Mother."

After a tense moment, Aurora acquiesced, "You may, but—"

Lucy, already at the exit, paused.

"—we'll speak of this later, young lady."

Not bothering to nod, Lucy walked out on stiff legs. She didn't want to go to her room, nor to the kitchen where there was usually a warm cup of coffee and pleasant conversation amidst bustling energy.

Tonight, she just wanted to be alone.

The Queen Anne Victorian house they resided at had a wraparound porch, and the best spot to sit at night was the area adjacent to the back parlor. She grabbed her thickest shawl from their elegant coat rack, and stepped into the crisp January air, closing the door behind her so that absolute darkness blanketed her. There was a faint glow of light that illuminated a long, reaching strip of the porch and part of the gardens, touching the length of the yard with hazy gold. A painted white porch swing, unused by anyone but Lucy, sat tucked into a corner, overlooking shrubbery, hibernating flower bushes, and a full moon.

In the summer it would be hot and damp, and mosquitoes would buzz their high-pitched lament around her ears. But tonight, she felt the steam of her breath clouding the air, and the only noise was the rustle of the treetops in the breeze and the slight *creak, crack* of the swing's chains as she reclined against the wood-slatted back. For several quiet minutes, her thoughts were full of trains, stages, and what the hotel looked like now after all these years.

Her musings were interrupted by the swing of the back door as it opened, light spilling out in a rush and washing over the back steps. The silhouette of a man stepping out broke the visibility, then everything was dark again.

Footsteps from polished black boots tapped on the boards, the slim shape of Peter moving leisurely nearer to Lucy. She smiled in the night as he hunched around something in his hands, and there was a quick scratch of a match being lit. Sulfur and singed tobacco burned brightly in the dark, and finally, a long, audible exhalation.

"Escaped, did you?"

Peter jumped and whipped around to look for her.

"I beg pardon!"

He moved as though to snuff out the cigar in his fingers, but she stood.

"Wait."

He paused with the sole of his boot suspended, so she hastened to him. This close, it was much easier to make out the pale blur of his features. His nose and lips were shadows, but his bright forehead and eyes were visible.

Those eyes watched her closely.

Amused, she leaned the curve of her waist against the railing of the porch, her right hand on its edge. In the silence, she studied him. Then, "May I?" She plucked the cigarillo from his hand with two fingertips, balancing it between her first knuckles. Studying his watchful eyes, she took a deep, long drag. The cherry glowed red, revealing their faces to each other, hers thoughtful and wary, his astounded and riveted.

Lucy released the tip of the cigar, and, shaping her lips, blew out two perfect smoke rings, one after the other. They floated white and hazy into the garden, the moon giving them near reflectivity before they separated, wavered, and dissipated over the dead rhododendrons.

Frowning, she admitted, "I always try to get one inside the other, but I never seem to get it right." She flicked the gray ashes over the rail and handed the thin cigar back to Peter. His presence wasn't intrusive, so she made her way to the porch swing and sat, wondering if he'd go back inside.

Wondered if he'd tell. She almost wished he would.

After a moment, he followed and sat next to her, untouching. Ever the gentleman.

He smoked in silence for a while before he asked, "Where did you learn to smoke?"

"At home, when I was fourteen." She drew her shawl around her, chilled and pensive. "My friend Poppy and I would sneak into Papa's office. We would smoke his cigars and drink his liquor until we were both sick. Eventually, Papa figured out where all his drink and expensive cigars were going, so he made the both of us smoke his entire box." She laughed. "It was the worst experience of our lives. But I remember, a couple of times I blew a smoke ring by accident. After I'd recuperated from becoming ill at even the hint of cigar smoke, I'd practice on his butts to see if I could do it again."

Peter grinned. "And so now you are adept." He was the most relaxed she'd ever seen him, perfect posture slouched, elbows on his knees. He rocked the swing back and forth, back and forth. "Do you only partake for the fun of it, then?"

She plucked what was left of his cigarillo out of his hand and drew, blowing a large ring that didn't stick, but grew bigger and bigger until it broke and dissolved. She tsked. "Why do something if it isn't fun?" For a moment, she let the silence grow. "Will you tell anyone?"

He sounded genuinely offended when he denied, "Of course not."

Thank goodness. Feeling more comfortable, she handed the shrinking stub over. "You try it."

Clearing his throat, he said, "Alright." His attempt was a poor one, and they both chuckled.

"No." She turned to him, her knee brushing against his lean thigh. "You have to round out your lips, like so. Then move your jaw forward when you exhale."

He scrutinized her pantomime and tried again. Failed.

Soon they were lighting up another one, laughing and whispering. Finally, when the second cigar was half-gone, he succeeded, making a ring big enough for a fist to enter. Lucy yanked the stub from Peter's fingers and drew hard, blowing a quick succession of misty rings that chased his larger one. It vanished before any had made it in.

"Blast," she whispered, eyes glittering. It had been so close. She leaned back—to find an arm on the swing's back behind her.

"Lucille," Peter murmured.

She didn't look at him. Something had changed in the air, became charged. "Call me Lucy. I don't like Lucille." Something was wrong with her voice. She felt nervous. Jittery.

"Lucy," he corrected.

Why was he staring so?

Swallowing past a dry throat, she turned her face in slow increments. He was so close, so serious.

And very much courting her sister.

Would it be easy, she wondered, to seduce the man right under the nose of her mother and sister? With the way he was leaning so near, she could capture his lips just as easily as the baker's son. A hot twist of pleasure at the thought of Aurora and Beth's white, shocked faces was what decided her.

Lucy turned her face away, then stood for good measure. She opened her mouth to say a brisk goodnight, but he interrupted her.

"Were you accompanying my family and yours to the picnic this Saturday? The church is hosting." He hadn't stood with her but remained seated, and her discomfort waned.

If Mother hadn't informed her by now, then she wasn't going. She leaned against the railing and crossed her arms. "I have plans for this Saturday, but thank you."

His brows rose in the moonlight. "Oh? And what's more diverting than a picnic full of hopeful beaus and friends?"

She scoffed impolitely. "All of my friends are in Dogwood. And beaus? Not with Beth in the vicinity."

A cold breeze ruffled his brown hair when he stifled a laugh. "That's due to your mother, you know. I can name at least five men who won't approach you because of Robert Forde."

Shocked and intrigued, Lucy uncrossed her arms. "Mr. Forde? What do you mean?"

Mr. Forde was one of the only friends she'd made when she'd come back to Atlanta from school the year before. He was a friendly, quiet widower with two young daughters that Lucy had enjoyed playing with at church functions. They had been so quiet-spoken, just like their father, and terribly lonely and in want of a mother figure. She'd caught him stealing glances at her from afar. Impetuous, and entirely comfortable with strangers having been raised in a hotel, she'd taken to chatting with him, tickling the girls, and saving them from splinters or falls.

"You're good with them," he'd say in his soft, shy way while his girls played hide and seek around her skirts.

"Oh, I love children," she had laughed. "When I get married, I want a whole passel of them." Her Texas twang tended to reappear the more familiar she became with someone.

It wasn't long before Mr. Forde began to sit directly behind their pew during church, and Lucy would surreptitiously sneak candied nuts for the girls to munch on during the boring service. She had fallen in love with them and told Mr. Forde so one day when he thanked her for helping to keep an eye on them. So, no one was more shocked than she when, without a single word, he and his girls had moved westward to California. There were whispers that he'd liquidated his home and assets within the week and had vanished from the face of the earth. Church hadn't been the same without his sweet little girls to play with.

Lucy felt cold. Had her mother had something to do with his disappearance?

"What happened?" she repeated, voice tight with worry.

Peter sighed and glanced away. "You can't tell anyone I told you. Everyone believes it a rumor, but I know old Rob's cousin; he's the one that bought the house." He paused, and her feet carried her back to the swing where she perched on the edge, wound tight and heart thrumming.

"I'll not say a word, I swear."

"Well, people started to notice how much he'd stared at you in church. They'd gossiped about it until your mother heard the word. Apparently, she'd approached Robert and accused him of taking an unholy interest in you, but he'd said that he was waiting for you to come of age before asking your hand in marriage." Lucy stiffened at this, stunned. "She wasn't too happy to hear that, you were what, seventeen? And he was all of thirty."

"Sixteen." Her voice was strained. She had turned seventeen not long after his departure. It had been a lonely birthday, she remembered.

He whistled low. "That's a bit worse, then, isn't it? Well, after that bit of news, she'd threatened to get him locked up, said that if he didn't leave town, she'd have him imprisoned and his children put in an orphanage or work mill. He left the next week. That's why no one will look at you twice." His teeth gleamed in the dark. "Well, they look. But they won't do much more."

Feeling ill, Lucy put her hands over her eyes, squeezing them into the sockets until all she saw was white. When she opened her eyes again, they were glittering. Not with tears, but with injustice. "How dare she? That poor man. He just wanted a doting mother for his little girls. He knew I loved them."

"That's not all he wanted, Lucy."

Her eyes cut to him. "Of course not, but if I hadn't played with his children every Sunday, he would not have noticed me. And he was willing to wait until I came of age." When Peter looked like he wanted to argue, she forged on. "And what of Beth? She had suitors at sixteen. Mother introduces them to her in droves and invites them to dinner. A simple no to Mr.

Forde, or even a 'devil take you', would have sufficed. He was so meek and Godly, his children beautiful." Bitter resentment reared its scaly head, but she swallowed the feelings back. Remembering with whom she was speaking, she straightened. Could she have been any crasser, speaking of Beth's past beaus in such a way? "I beg pardon, Mr. Langford."

He shook this apology off in much the way he had the one at the dinner table. "It's different with Elizabeth. Your mother does not introduce you to men, a blind man sees it. You are forbidden."

"After the debacle with Mr. Forde, I cannot reproach men for keeping their distance."

If Lucy needed any more proof that escape from this gilded prison was necessary, this was it. The certainty that her mother would have control over who she married petrified her. Lucy wasn't like Beth and Aurora. She had wants and needs different from theirs; marrying for prestige or money made her feel cold, not whole. She wanted passion, and children, a family for whom to cook, clean, and look after. Her fondest memories were of Minnie in the kitchen, teaching her how to cut biscuits or roll out dumplings, face smiling and laugh warm. Her children would have that with her, she vowed. And Sunday dinners with Papa at her own home, sharing warm glances with a husband that she chose.

Closing her eyes to hold the dream within a tentative grasp, Lucy prayed.

Please, God. Let me have this.

A hand brushed over her stiff shoulders, and she held her breath. Peter had leaned forward, and for the first time since taking her hand in that first acquaintance, he was touching her. He rubbed her back in sympathy, and at first, she held herself still, Beth's subtle presence shimmering between them in a warning. But he wasn't caressing her, just running a smooth palm over and over her shoulder blades, no lower.

Perfectly innocent.

Completely platonic.

And it felt so good, to be touched. She relaxed, and her head lolled. Lucy hadn't had any physical contact or comfort since she'd clung to Papa and Minnie the day that she'd been forced to leave her home. No one patted her head or shoulder, clung to her hand with affection, or had given her tight, squeezing hugs that squashed her flexible ribcage and wheezed the breath from her.

Being comforted now pricked at the hard shield lacquered over tender, girlish sensitivities. Her heart and her throat ached, and she softened, releasing a long, relieved sigh. She leaned back into Peter's hand until his arm snaked around her shoulders and grew tight.

At that moment, Beth walked outside.

"Mr. Langford?" she called, back door opening wide. Her head turned left and right as though she was squinting into the darkness.

Peter jumped as though a fire had lit underneath him. "I'm here," he answered, swift strides eating up the distance between the swing and back door before Beth's eyes could adjust to the dark and she could see just who accompanied him.

Not wanting to imagine the row her discovery would cause, Lucy leaned back into the swing, pressing until she was small and unobtrusive while Peter guided her sister back into the house.

"You know Mother does not approve of smoking," Beth was admonishing before the door shut, blanketing everything in darkness once more.

A moth fluttered around Lucy's ear, and she swatted it away absently. She'd promised not to mention anything Peter had disclosed to anyone, so she sat in silence; angry, confused, and alone.

4

— · —

CHAPTER FOUR

Holding her tongue that next week, seeing her mother at the breakfast and dinner table and not saying a word about Robert Forde, was a feat of mental strength. The pressure of new, condemning knowledge crawled like ants along Lucy's skin and compressed her full lips into an unremitting frown. She refused to betray Peter's confidence and managed to bottle her questions and accusations by ignoring her mother's presence entirely. It worked well for a time until Friday opened its sleepy eyes and the pressure popped the bottled resentment's cork.

"You must wear your periwinkle day dress tomorrow, Elizabeth. It brings out the perfect blue of your eyes."

Beth hated that dress, as Mother well knew. It chafed the back of her neck raw with its rigid collar of rough lace. Lucy would stifle sibling enjoyment when her sister squirmed in discomfort while she reclined in her less fashionable, but far more comfortable, dresses.

Beth nodded as though given a treat.

"And what will you be doing, Lucille?" Aurora asked, stirring one lump of sugar in her tea pale with milk. "I have made a point to the stable hands not to allow your riding of the horses. I was told that you've been running them on Mr. Garrison's property, and I must suggest you never do such a thing again."

Lucy turned her head, slow and accusing, trying to meet her coward of a sister's eye. Beth stirred her tea and must have found the ministrations fascinating because she did not look up. Aurora continued.

"A lady must rest her body and her mind. Such vigorous activities and jolting around cannot be good for one's body, or digestion."

Such a thing was easy for her to say, but Lucy was the fittest she'd ever been from the sport. Whereas Mother had constant visits from the family doctor for persistent urinary tract infections, and something called a prolapse, a curious term Lucy had overheard on accident while tiptoeing past their door to the kitchens. "Loosen your corsets, Ms. Pattinson, please. Or, at the very least, try not to wear them at night when you sleep," the doctor would insist. To Lucy's knowledge, Mother never heeded the doctor's advice.

Aurora was watching her with raised brows, polite curiosity hiding the wont of a good row. What had she asked? Oh, yes. What would Lucy be doing tomorrow now that her preferred pastime had been taken away? The little devil once again sat on her shoulder and whispered in her ear.

"Why, I am accompanying you to the picnic tomorrow," she said, chewing unperturbedly on her thin slice of bacon.

This got Beth's attention, and she expelled an audible huff. "I was not aware you knew of it."

"Why? Because you failed to invite me?"

Mother and Beth shared a look, one pair of eyes pleading, and the other assessing.

Nudge, nudge, went the devil. "If you must know, Peter invited me last week after supper. It would be rude not to make an appearance."

Beth's face wrinkled into a sour prune. "When did you speak to him? I thought you went to bed."

We smoked cigars together, and then he comforted me with a back rub. The thought felt nasty, but it felt good as well, so she ignored her guilt. "I did go up to bed. I passed him as he was going outside for a smoke."

Aurora took a sip of tea and silenced Beth's further inquisitions with a narrowing of blue eyes. "We are sharing a carriage with the Langfords, Lucille. There is no room for another."

Oh, no, you don't, Lucy thought. Why didn't Mother want her to attend the picnic? "I can ride the black mare behind you. She'll look fine with my cream day dress." Her cream dress was the only one she owned that flattered her, and was hidden deep in the closet, away from Aurora's itching fingers that threatened to throw it out.

"This will be a church function, Lucille. You cannot trounce up in that dress, perched atop a horse for heaven's sake." Lily-white hands poured more tea into the tiny porcelain cup and paused. "Moreover, you'll not be attending at all. I never did speak to you of your hideous manners the other night. Consider this your punishment. Stay at home and think of how important it is to this family that you act the lady I spent a significant amount of money for you to become."

Lips twisting, Lucy left her breakfast unfinished and gave into her frustration, clanging silverware, abrading the floor with chair legs shoved back, all in hopes to drown out her mother's words.

"Lucille," Aurora cracked out, better than any whip. "You may begin now and act like a lady should and leave as such."

Mouth working, ignoring the feverish gleam in Beth's attentive gawking, Lucy sat down again but didn't push the chair in. Staring straight ahead, she gritted, "May I be excused, Mother?"

A beatific smile spread over Aurora's lips, showing small, yellowing teeth. Lucy felt her gorge threaten and swallowed bile in response. "That's much better, dear. You may go to your room. I will come by later with the family bible. We can pray together, would you like that?"

She didn't have to tell her mother that she'd rather fall into a pit full of snakes; her face said it for her.

——— ———

LUCY FROWNED AT the letter she'd received from Papa that morning. His recent letters had become different of late, many of which were sloppy and confusing. This one, dated a week ago, was nigh-on incoherent.

Squinting at an entire sentence that was blotted with ink, she tried to make out what he was saying to her. "'Mizz Trudy is a bless...take from me...not like your...a mother did.' What on earth?" She dropped the letter back into the stack that lay in her lap, troubled. There was something wrong with him. She'd noticed his ramblings in letters for the last six months. This was the first one that showed the complete disintegration of his character. His elegant scrawl was chicken scratch on the page, each line more blotted and crooked than the last. Often, the return address would be written in someone else's hand. The postmistress? It didn't escape her notice that any time she invited him to pick her up on her birthday, he never made mention of it in his letters.

Was he ill? Did he decide to take his stationery to the saloon with him and write letters to her there? The image amused her, but her smile slid away as she thought back to all the friends that skirted around the subject of her father. Yes, something was very wrong with him, and she needed to get to the bottom of it. Her pen was flying across a clean sheet of parchment when she felt the wind of her door open at her back. There was a faint clatter of teacups on a tray behind her, and Lucy chewed on the thin tip of her fountain pen.

"Meggie, I'm becoming more and more worried about Papa. His letters look as though a schoolboy wrote them. And he has been speaking of a Ms. Trudy of late. Do you think it's the infamous mistress that owns the saloon near low town?"

A pale hand snatched the letter from her desk, and Lucy turned to gape from her chair. "What—"

"Honestly, Lucille," hissed Aurora, gleaming eyes whipping left and right as she read the confounding letter from Tony. "Is this what you and your father write about? Mistresses, saloons, and the private occurrences within this home?" Her words sizzled between them in a warning. In promise.

"No! We talk of normal things; the hotel, his life, my life, nothing untoward except—"

"Oh, except this one letter that I just happen to be privy to?" Aurora scoffed, a deep line gouging the dry skin between her brows. Her eyes never left the crooked writing on the paper. "I find that hard to believe. And what's worse, you exchange such goings on with our maid."

Lucy took a deep breath, and said with exaggerated patience, "Meggie is my friend, Mother. I often talk with her about my life back home."

"Please, cease your insistence on unnatural relationships with the help. If you tried half so hard to be friendly to our peers, then you would be invited to far more activities." Aurora let her hand fall at her waist, the parchment crumpling in tight fingers. "And *this* is your home, how many times must I tell you?" The last was in a voice that was raised and shrill, so Lucy closed her lips tight and refrained from saying any more. Something feral glinted in her mother's eyes before they shuttered, and a façade of calm washed away the anger to become one of long sufferance.

"Give me your letters."

Lucy felt a prickle of trepidation. "Why?"

Aurora's eyes were glowing a bright, gleaming cerulean in the rosy morning light of the room. After a moment of this stand-off, where mother and daughter had an invisible battle of wills, years of good manners capitulated the younger woman. Lucy handed the stack of letters over with the ease of giving away one's own heart and soul.

"Is this all of them?"

"Yes," Lucy lied.

"Hm." Her mother shifted feet and shuffled through the thick mass of letters and said in a cool voice almost bare of inflection, "It has come to my attention that the reason you may not be moving forward in this significant chapter of our lives is that you are, shall I say, stuck."

"Stuck?" Lucy parroted, eyeing the petite, erect figure glide across the room to the window, where the light was better.

She didn't notice two other figures loitering in the hall, listening. "I am not 'stuck'. What does that even imply?" All she wanted was her letters, but what she sensed she would get instead was a long-winded lecture.

Hold your tongue, bite it if you must, she told herself.

"Oh yes, you are stuck, dear," nodded Aurora sagely. She was now rifling through the contents of the letters, and Lucy couldn't have been more horrified if she'd caught the woman going through her rag drawer.

Lucy stood instinctively and thought about taking her letters from her mother by force. She even held her hand outstretched before her and wondered what Aurora would do if she did take them.

She could do it.

Mother's arms were frail, her fingers more delicate than willow twigs. Taking them back would be nothing. But should she? Minnie would be horrified. There were a lot of things about Lucy lately that would horrify Minnie.

She lowered her hand.

Aurora went on, dumb to her daughter's conflicting thoughts, "Since you have lived here, you've yet to make a single friend your age. And no, the servants do not count. You write to the people of your past as though you still live in that awful town, as if you were simply away on holiday. Well, you are not. You are never going back."

Unable to bite her tongue any longer, Lucy shot, "I beg to differ. I'll be leaving in the spring, and Papa will come here to fetch me—"

"You shall not." Again, her mother's voice began to raise, and her fingers trembled around the letters. She turned around, unsurprised that Lucy had stood, ready to do battle. "You are the daughter of an important member of society, and if it is my wish that you stay, then you will stay."

Grimacing against the heavy, suffocating burden of her mother's dominion, Lucy whirled her skirts around the chair and strode to the doorway with the intent to leave. Beth was there, eyes bouncing between her sister and mother in gleeful absorption.

"I am not finished, young lady."

The old hatred rose, and Lucy bared her teeth like a cornered animal at Beth. "What do you want, tickets to the circus? Stop sniffing around my room like some plague-infested rat." She slammed the door in the lemon-puckered face with enough force to rattle the windows and knock a watercolor painting from the wall.

"Young lady!" Footsteps approached at speed, and Lucy turned her head the barest amount, letting her mother see all the meanness she felt in her heart at that moment from the side of her narrowed eyes. Aurora stopped, and her voice shook. "You are exactly like your father when you look at me so. Don't you understand that this is for your own good? And as you cannot move forward, the only logical recourse is to forbid you to contact anyone from that town again."

Lucy faced her mother fully, shoulders squared. "What!"

"No more letters." Aurora's voice was still unsteady, and her hands were white-knuckling the envelopes she held. The tip of her nose and cheeks flared with color. "I have already contacted every postman in the county with the orders to prevent any more letters addressed to Texas to be sent from this household unless they have come personally from me." She took a step forward and opened the door. Lucy didn't move out of the way, but stood as an immovable doorjamb, nostrils flaring and blowing hard. "No more mail. Do not ask any servants to sneak letters or they will be dismissed, without reference. No more morning rides into town. And for the duration of this month, you are to stay in this house until you understand that I am in charge of this home. Abide by my rules or you'll be sent straight back to the finishing school in Boston."

Battling furious tears, Lucy burst out in a pathetically weak appeal, "What are my letters hurting? You want me to move forward, but where? You don't approve of any suitors, you won't let me get a job and hate my interests, you do not allow me to visit the opera house or theatre because they are 'bawdy' and 'sinful'. My letters to Dogwood aren't doing any wrong. I have friends and loved ones at home; I only write to see how their lives are going."

"You need to worry less about what those people are up to and worry more about befriending the upstanding citizens here."

"They are all pretentious and boring! I have nothing in common with any of the girls my age because they're spoiled and selfish and being in their company makes my skin crawl."

Her mother rolled her eyes heavenward. "Elizabeth makes friends with them very well, and I am fed up with your melodramas and histrionics. You are to stay home today and from every day forward until I deem you are prepared to move ahead with your life here."

Fists clenched, Lucy couldn't control the desperation in her voice. "Move ahead? What does that entail? Marriage to a politician with full pockets? I've not had a single suitor since I have resided here, and when we are out as a family, I am all but invisible to you and your 'friends'. You display Beth like the prize cow and I'm the wallflower in the back." She paused, and asked, testing, "Has no one ever expressed interest in courting me?" Mr. Forde's shy smile seemed to glimmer in and out of her vision as she waited to see what lie her mother would expel.

"Of course not, Lucille," Aurora sniffed, nose pinched. "You are much too young and immature to be of interest to any acceptable man. Become involved with the women of society, volunteer at the church, and you should pique a gentleman's interest."

They look. They won't do much more.

Peter's words haunted her, and she bit her lip. Mother was wrong about men's interests. Not only wrong, the woman was lying out of her ears, something she swore a Godfearing lady should never do. Had she forgotten Mr. Forde, then? Her mother could be such a conniving little liar if the truth didn't suit her, Lucy thought to herself.

A wave of calm masked her outrage, and she made her tone light and casual. "So, I'll not be attending the picnic today?"

"No, you may not attend," Aurora replied firmly. "Church on Sundays is acceptable; the Word should help you curb your temper."

Lucy nodded. When her mother left the room calling for Beth, she shut her door and pressed her back against the molded wood, planning.

LUCY RODE THROUGH shortcuts and alleyways, shooting furtive glances behind her and watching for a carriage with two golden heads perched inside. Public humiliation served as her burning companion home.

As soon as Mother and Beth had departed that morning, Lucy had donned her cream dress with a matching pelisse and was off like a shot. Jimmy the Gardener, their housemaid's brother, had helped ready their black mare in record time, looking through the stable doors with a worried squint at the darkening sky.

"Best you'd hurry, lass," he'd warned in his thick Scots brogue. She'd followed his gaze and cursed under her breath. The picnic would be canceled for certain if the bottom dropped out. She needed to hurry.

The trip to town had proven worse than disappointing. It had felt like a kick in the gut when Mr. Clarence had shaken his head sadly and pushed her last letter to Papa back to her across the counter. Mother had already had words with him the week before.

The stable was warm and quiet, and she gave thanks that no one was outside to see her wilted figure dismount and unsaddle her horse. She took her time to hang up the saddle, folded the saddle blanket, curried, and fed the mare all the while keeping her mind carefully blank. That blankness continued as she snuck through the back door and up the servant's stairs. In reaching the second landing, she paused. Her mother's door to the bedroom suite had opened a crack. Meggie must have cleaned, then forgotten to lock the door.

Stony-faced, Lucy walked at a sedate pace to the cracked door and pushed it open with a shove of two fingers. It swung on oiled hinges, quieter than a sigh, revealing a landscape of thick pile carpet, textured wallpaper, and silken bedsheets beneath a feather-tick bedspread. Every piece of furniture was covered in crystal bottles of perfume, large boxes of jewelry, and family heirlooms.

She ignored those and walked to the desk in a corner, rifling through blank parchment, envelopes, announcements, and invitations. Drawers were yanked open and her fingers flew through papers that looked important but weren't her letters. There was not a single locked drawer, no hidden bottoms, or backs. There were no empty nooks beneath the bottom of the desk, no letters to be found.

The armoire and dresser proved a fruitless search; boxes in the closet only contained expensive shoes, scarves, and winter clothing. The grate of the fireplace held a pile of ashes from that morning's coals, and she crouched down, prodding here and there for tell-tale burnt paper. There was nothing.

Red-faced and panting, Lucy sat on the floor in her dress, crinoline folding incorrectly and making an uncomfortable seat.

What had the witch done with those letters?

Nothing was incriminating within Papa's scrawled words. He never spoke of Mother except for that last post, and only inquired after Beth on occasion.

She despaired because the letters represented home, love, and her future. When Papa spoke of the townspeople, it was as though she'd never left. But of late, many of their friends had moved away, newcomers taking their place. He'd made so many changes to the hotel after the fire of '78 that she felt sharp stabs of jealousy that she hadn't been there for renovations. A grand, new courthouse had been built, made of stone and glass windows. The deputy had replaced the old marshal, who now resided in a cozy townhouse surrounded by his children and grandchildren.

If she tried harder, Lucy could find such people in this town. Friendships that held meaning and cemented her in Atlanta as the old ones did in Dogwood.

And yet, something indefinable resided in Texas, something golden and pure tethered her. Perhaps childhood nostalgia, her best friend Franny who still lived next door above Hobb's General Store. Minnie was there, closer and dearer to Lucy than her own mother. And Papa, with his kind eyes and years of thoughtful correspondence, had never once forgotten her after all these years away.

Sitting on the floor of the grandest home on the street, the nicest place Lucy would perhaps ever hope to live in, she had never felt such yawning scarceness. The paucity of the company her mother kept for a tawdry day-to-day life. Money, politics, etiquette; none filled the emptiness that surrounding herself with her roots ever could. Home was a feeling. It was people who loved her.

Icy rain beat against her mother's window, and she turned a tear-stained face to the gentle, constant tapping.

Tap, tap, tap tap tap.

Lucy scrambled to her feet and wiped the itchy, wet tear tracks from her face. How long had it been raining? It was only five minutes from the park to their home. Beth would have been complaining at the first hint of a raindrop, and at this point, they could be wheeling into the drive.

And she was in her mother's room.

She was straightening up anything out of its place in the room when the door slammed downstairs. Her mother and sister's voices sent her out of the room at a sprint. She shut the door, paused, then left it at a crack. If the harridan had done it on purpose to catch her in the act, it wouldn't surprise her.

"Prod Cook into making some afternoon tea, Meggie. We shall receive it in the morning room." Aurora's cool voice floated from below the stairs, and Lucy gazed at the handrail unhappily. No one's voice had ever set her teeth on edge like that woman's, she thought. Then, "Mr. Langford, feel free to join us until the weather abates."

Lucy's brow furrowed. There was something off about Mother's voice. She sounded...frustrated, or terribly put out. Just the rain, perhaps?

Peter's voice murmured something low, but the words didn't carry.

"Wonderful. Elizabeth and I will change into something drier, please, make yourself comfortable."

Footsteps up the stairs sent her into action. Her room was at the other end of the hall; too far away to reach. She couldn't pretend to meet them in the hall in coincidence; she could feel how swollen and red her eyes were. With the cracked door and swollen eyes, Mother would come to a fast conclusion. Lucy pressed herself inside the hall's linen closet, shutting the door a fraction of a second before footsteps reached the landing.

Beth was whispering to Mother, and she strained to hear.

"—really think he was going to propose, Mama?" She was breathy, excited.

"Of course, he was," Aurora purred. "I spoke with his mother myself. Why do you think Violet was conspicuously absent this morning? At our last supper with them, she confided that she'd finally managed to convince him despite his father's admonitions to put business first. He'd invited you to the picnic with the intent to propose. Grab some towels, dear, before we catch our death."

Eyes wide in the absolute darkness, Lucy clenched the closet's doorknob with strength made superhuman by fear. The knob jiggled once without much force.

"It's locked."

"Now, why would a linen closet be locked?" Aurora sighed.

"Is that why you didn't want Lucy to come, Mama? Because Peter planned to propose?"

"Precisely. I wanted nothing at all to ruin your important day."

Beth walked away from the closet, and Lucy's fingers relaxed. "No, the rain managed that well enough. Maybe she's a sorceress and sent the rain out of spite."

"That impertinent child," Aurora whispered with feeling. "Ever since she was born, she has felt the need to make things difficult for me, and herself as well. Halting her correspondence from that wretched man should force her to see reason. I've never beheld such a headstrong pair."

"Do you still have her letters? What was in them? Is it true that Papa has a mistress?"

Lucy wanted to scream at Beth's prying. The little troll only wanted to meddle so she could rub it in Lucy's face later. Her only life goal was to torment her sister.

"I wouldn't pretend to know the happenings of that man." Mother's voice had turned venomous, and Beth was silenced. "I didn't read the letters." Another lie. Then, she paused, as though wondering if she should confess or prolong some other gratifying knowledge. Lucy pressed her ear into the door so hard the delicate cartilage sang with pain. "I burned them."

Beth gasped and tittered. "You did not!"

"Do not pretend as though I did a deed of evil, Elizabeth. I did it for her own good. Such unnatural attachments to that horrid little town must stop. If I knew where the others were, I would burn them on the spot. Now. Go change out of those wet clothes before we catch cold. Your fiancé is waiting."

More laughter, then they retired to their room with the click of latches and the snick of locks.

For a moment, Lucy stood in the cool, fragrant dark of the linen closet, her fingers biting hard into her cheeks to keep her mouth from screaming at the loss. Her letters. She fumbled with the door handle, and stepped inelegantly out of the closet, tripping on the hall runner.

There was no longer a little devil on her shoulder, prodding her with the tines of its tiny trident into saying and doing disobedient, albeit harmless, things. Now, there was heavy fog around her. A miasma, dark and simmering at her back. It took up all space behind and around her, and she breathed it in, deep and slow, feeling its indifference to what was moral or fair. It didn't care about honor. All it cared about was justice. Revenge. Getting even. A part of herself that Lucy often disliked acknowledging—a mean, secret part—slithered its way out. Her dark eyes narrowed, dry now, swelling abated.

She closed the door oh so quietly behind her and reached in her pocket for the letter she'd failed at sending less than an hour ago.

Within the envelope held precise instructions to her father to come by train and meet her at the station in Atlanta on her eighteenth birthday. Eighteen was an acceptable age by law to make her own choices, and if she left of her own volition, she would not be deemed a runaway. Mother would be helpless and powerless to stop her from going home. She'd made it very clear in the letter that if did he not meet her, Lucy would come home by herself. After all, mail-order brides and women visiting family did it all the time.

And she would leave. She'd do anything to get away from this house and the poison vipers that lived within.

What if....

Lucy turned, calmer, a new idea developing.

She kept her tread on the rug soft and dashed down the gleaming staircase, hand in her pocket on the thick letter that was the answer to her problems.

The morning room was to the left of the entryway, and Lucy breezed in, pretending to be startled when she spied Peter at the window, watching the rain trickle down the panes. He looked behind him, hands in his pockets, and Lucy hid any calculation in her eyes and gave him a soft, slow smile.

"Oh, hello Peter." She put a hand on her breasts, and his eyes followed the daring hint of cleavage for a split second before he caught himself. "You startled me. I thought I heard Mother and Beth come up." She made her way to the window, brushing near him to look at the gray landscape outside. "It turned unpleasant so suddenly."

Peter cleared his throat and nodded. He didn't take a step back, and her skirts played against his pant leg. "Indeed, it did. No one had even the opportunity to open their baskets."

"How unfortunate. And you were to propose today."

He grew very still beside her.

She made her eyes go wide and turned to apologize. "I'm sorry, how very rude of me. It's just that Mother was so disappointed when she came up. I could hear Beth and her laughing, cursing the weather."

"Laughing?" He suddenly sounded different. There was a stiffness to the word that wasn't petulant like a boy's, but hard. A man's voice. His jaw and chin looked squarer, and Lucy took it in, like a hunter would when seeing an otherwise unpromising mutt suddenly point after a hare. She glanced at him, now...with interest.

"Yes," she whispered. "They can be so odious, sometimes. That's why I came downstairs. For a reprieve."

"Is that why you stayed?" He watched her from the corner of his eye, hands clasped behind his back. "You don't look ill."

Her smile hurt and didn't reach her eyes. "Is that what they said?"

"I gather they say a lot of things that aren't true."

By and by, it was the rudest thing Lucy had ever heard him say. And about Mother and Beth, no less! Their eyes met, held, and she started laughing—softly though, so Mother didn't hear. But she couldn't stop it. The anger in his face softened and his lip curled up. Those small changes had a domino effect until they were both facing each other, close enough to see individual hairs in the other's eyelashes. That easy camaraderie from the week before when smoke rings surrounded them slid back into place.

"What else have they said?" he asked, no longer irritated, but curious.

"This and that. Our mothers believe themselves match-makers, you know," she revealed, arms crossed beneath her bosom, hip propped against the sill. "They have planned everything to the smallest detail. Your mother feigned illness, and no doubt my mother walked over to friends to give you and Beth privacy."

His brows, brown and sparse, shot up. "She made it halfway to the reverend before the rain began."

"Poor Beth," Lucy said on a moue. Then, "What do the two of you talk of when you're alone?" Her curiosity was genuine.

Peter opened his mouth, then closed it. Frowned. "I am not really certain. Clothes. Mutual friends. Parties. Our mothers."

Lucy wrinkled her nose. "Funny, when Beth and I are alone, we typically just hurl insults at each other like verbal jousting. Fortunately, when Mother isn't in her corner, I win."

He laughed, and she noticed something else different in him. When he laughed with her, it sounded real. Deeper. Around their mothers and his future intended, he tended to laugh silently through his nose. As she studied him, his laugh faded away, and something strange happened. The air around them charged, changed, and his dark green eyes traveled from the top of her head to the tip of her toes, before making a slow trail back up.

"You're looking very well, Lucy. I'm glad to see that you're no longer bedridden." His teeth showed in a teasing grin.

Bedridden? Those harpies.

"Ha!" she laughed defiantly, "Nothing could keep me abed all day."

He pretended shock. "Miss Lucy! Speaking of beds in a man's company. Tsk tsk."

Lucy covered her face and groaned. "Mother's ears must be ringing. She could hear a church mouse peep over one of Rev Brand's sermons. Particularly if that mouse's name is Lucille."

To her surprise, he laid a hand on her shoulder, cupping it and running his thumb over and over the soft skin of her collarbone. "She does like to torment you, doesn't she?"

Dropping her hands from her eyes, she watched him from beneath supplicating brows, mouth downturned and solemn. He'd touched her back the other night in comfort, and here he was touching her again, but it was different. It was unmistakably a caress. What would it be like to kiss a man like him? She pictured Beth kissing him and felt disgusted. Beth wouldn't know how to kiss. She didn't have an ounce of passion in her. But Lucy was her father's child, and passion pumped harder and faster than blood in her veins. She thought of kisses and what it would be like to make love. When she took baths, she didn't look straight ahead nor cleaned with an impersonal hand. She marveled at the changes in her body, at the curves and textures. The human body was an amazing thing, and she was not ashamed of hers like Beth and Mother were.

Would Peter be ashamed? She remembered that hardness in his jaw, that anger in his eyes. One couldn't feel anger without having a bit of passion. And one couldn't reach over and touch someone the way he was touching her, without a bit of desire to do so.

It's wrong, her conscience warned. He's going to marry Beth. Mother has made plans for him.

She remembered Mother's confession outside the linen closet. Her letters were gone, the only pieces she had of her home in Dogwood burned to ash, and it hardened her heart, leaning her deeper into the warm hand that had made its home on her shoulder.

"Do you consider us friends, Peter?"

His hand slid down her arm, catching her hand and squeezing. His palm was damp. "Unquestionably, we are friends. Why do you ask?"

Lucy glanced up at the small movements upstairs, pressed for time. Peter stepped closer, nearer to her now than when they shared a porch swing. "I have a favor I need done, but I don't know who else to ask that I can trust."

Instead of his eyes shuttering as she'd feared, he leaned his head down, the picture of absolute attentiveness. "Is something wrong?"

Yes, she wanted to shout. "No, but it's quite embarrassing to ask of anyone. Especially you."

"Ask me, I can keep confidence," he teased, his eyes watchful.

She strained to hear if any footsteps clicked down the stairway, but there was nothing.

"Will you send a letter for me? Mother has forbidden me from contacting home, and I'd like to explain things."

Peter dropped her hand and stepped back. "Are you forbidden because it's a suitor?"

Choking back a laugh at his expression, she shook her head. "No! No, it's to Papa, I promise. But that's why, you see? She despises him. Mother has closed off all access to the post office, Mr. Clarence won't even look me in the eye. And I can't ask the servants, she'll have them sacked." Her eyes pleaded with his, hope and desperation turning them soft as melted chocolate.

They looked at each other for a moment, then both glanced up at the crown molding when a thump of something heavy clobbered the floor upstairs. He looked back first, eyebrow raised.

"You went to the post office today?"

She nodded, desperate. *Please don't tell the witch.* "Yes. I went there the second you picked up Mother and Beth. She'd spoken to the postmen already."

Peter sucked in his lips, shifted his feet and thought, then nodded. "I'll send it through Percy; he's my mail carrier. He'll have it sent for a pittance—" He was cut off when a small, cream-colored blur barreled into him, huffing out his breath with the force of her exuberance.

"Oh, thank you, Peter, thank you, thank you! You don't know how much this means to me, I'll bake you a cake every Sunday, thank you—" she babbled, squeezing his waist, and pressing her face tight against his expensive shirt buttons. It felt like the sun was breaking through the clouds and pouring warm, golden light all over her black mood. Nothing but happiness encompassed her body now; no dark mist, no little devil.

She'd be home by spring! Peter was an angel, an absolute saint!

Warm hands pressed her tighter to him, and her whispered thanks dissipated at the pressure of his body against hers. Never had she been so close to a man before that wasn't her Papa, not even the baker's son. It stirred a mixture of skittishness and deeper, more mature feelings inside her. She moved to step back, but his arms tightened further. Her ribs flexed and her heartbeat fluttered, a hummingbird trapped in her throat.

"That's what friends do, Lucy," Peter murmured in her hair, voice deep and rasping. He was sounding less and less like a fop or dandy. Did people change so fast? Or had he been pretending all along? "You don't have to bake a cake, just consider me a friend. You can always return a favor, hmm?"

She did step back, then. Pulse hammering, Lucy looked at him; really looked. Their color was high. His face and body language had altered so that she barely recognized him, and though her own body responded in kind, she felt a wrongness in her chest and stomach.

The sound of a clattering tea tray in the foyer shook off her misgivings.

"Here," she whispered, whipping her letter from its pocket, and shoving it into his outstretched hand. "It's the last letter I'm sending, so you'll only have to do it once. Thank you."

He nodded, eyes boring into hers while he pocketed it, smoothing any lines out against his dark, tweed trousers. She made her escape when Meggie entered the room backward, pulling the silver tray along behind her.

It was when she got to her room that she worried about the possibility of his duplicity. Trusting her sister's beau had to have been the riskiest decision she'd ever made. Just don't get on his bad side, she told herself. Lucy remembered his kindness, his comfort, and the way he looked at her lips and bosom. If he was so deep in her mother and sister's pocket, why would he look at her like that? She'd made her choice, and now there was no turning back. Fear curled her up like a shrimp on her bed until dinnertime.

5

— · —

CHAPTER FIVE

Lucy twisted her hair onto the crown of her head in thick, coffee-colored coils that gleamed in the morning sunlight. She twirled a few wisps of hair at her ears and forehead, softening her stubborn features.

In the Boston school, she'd hated looking like her father; his Italian heritage so prominent in her features and olive skin had been just another line dividing her from her shrewd peers. Her mother and sister, for all their faults, were exquisite from the fine, pale strands of their hair to the true blue of their eyes. However, after spending a year in their company, Lucy could admit that even a flawless exterior was only as pretty as the insides once you grew to know them. She'd rather look like herself and have her spirit than fill her sister's or mother's shoes or walk around in their skin for even a day.

In her hidden drawer behind her jewelry box was a minuscule tin of rouge from Franny. She let her finger linger over the container, looking down her nose from above and wishing before she closed the drawer. Mother could spot the lightest application a mile away. Besides, even Lucy wasn't daring enough to wear rouge at church.

Three short raps on her door startled Lucy out of her thoughts.

"We are leaving in half an hour. Are you decent?" Mother's voice sounded far away through the wood of the door.

Lucy looked down. She hadn't put her thick, itchy jacket on yet, and stood in petticoats, crinoline and skirt, stockings, chemise, and a loose, untied corset. "Blast," she murmured, and just about dislocated her shoulders to reach behind her for the strings dangling over her hump of foldable crinoline.

"Just a moment!"

The door opened a crack, and a narrowed eye peeked in. "Oh, for goodness' sake, Lucille." It was spat as though it were a favored curse, and Lucy fought down a stab of indignation. Aurora stepped in, locked the door behind her with a skeleton key, and briskly marched behind Lucy. "Bend over. Hands on the dresser."

Having heard those frequent orders over the last year, Lucy mechanically followed the instruction and awaited the torture to commence with a patient, indrawn breath. It did not disappoint.

Although slight-of-frame whose only exercise was to step into and from carriages, Aurora could wield corset strings with a damning, painful skill. Within minutes, Lucy's stomach and ribcage had altered from naturally lean and tapered, to an unnatural waspishness, making breathing difficult and pinching.

"Eating breakfast is out of the question now, thank you," Lucy grumbled dryly.

"Oh, hush. Ladies have managed for centuries in the confines of a corset, there is nothing erroneous in the face of proper comportment." Mother walked from behind her where she paused in affront. Lucy's breasts swelled over the top of her corset and chemise in a provocative display. "Perhaps it's best you don't eat breakfast, Lucille. My goodness, when you gained such fat is beyond me."

Gritting her teeth, Lucy glowered. "They are not there because I'm fat, Mother. Some women just have bigger breasts than others."

"Do not say that word! Bust or neckline is sufficient, how many times must I correct you before it affixes in your vocabulary?"

Wishing she could either yank her own—or her mother's—hair out, Lucy decided keeping mum would hasten the painful morning assault.

Her discomfort was forgotten on the way to church. What if Peter confided to Mother or Beth before the entirety of their church peers? She fanned herself with a pamphlet with one hand and chewed on the nails of the other. No matter the consequences if she was found out, she determined that she wasn't a fool for putting her trust in someone she'd considered a friend. Her instincts told her to trust Peter. Friends were hard to come by, and her instincts weren't often wrong. And if he did betray her, then at least she would know never to put her trust in him again. There would always be other ways to get to Dogwood.

Outside the carriage, she watched a young couple stroll arm in arm to church. Her fanning stopped, and her lips parted. The man's dark head was bowed to hear something his young wife was saying. Lucy couldn't see their features from this far, but she imagined he was smiling at the woman. She held her breath when he looked around and leaned down further to kiss the woman on the lips.

A surge of yearning rose from her stomach and made its way to her chest. She longed for that. She'd gotten a taste of it from the boy in town, but it had been watered down from what she really wanted. He didn't know her, had never walked arm in arm with her or told secrets; just traded a kiss for some of his grandmother's recipes. These urges often kept her awake at night. If she'd stayed in Dogwood, would she have had a young man by now? She closed her eyes, ignoring the gentle rock of carriage wheels hitting ruts, and pictured a faceless young cowboy with sun-browned arms and broad, calloused palms. Her imagination replaced the married couple with her and her young man, and she wondered what it'd feel like to have warm lips caress her own before church when no one was looking.

The faceless young man turned into Peter, and her eyes flew open. She frowned.

When the carriage came to a stop, Lucy flew through the door, bounding onto the cobbled road and ignoring the gasps of outrage from Mother and Beth. The sweat from the warmth of the carriage and disturbing thoughts dried instantly in the cool air. Her breath misted before her as she stood in the narrow churchyard full of people, the steeple looming over them all in the crisp gray morning.

Finding a tall man with brown hair was difficult as there were many, so Lucy included a squat, elegantly dressed woman in the search. Ah! There they were. Mrs. Langford had cornered the preacher and was in a deep discussion over some matter or another, while Peter stood, bored, watching the families make their way to the church doors in a crush.

As though he'd felt her relentless gaze, he looked up and their eyes met. He smiled. She returned it in tentative relief, for a man wouldn't smile at someone they planned on deceiving. She had to get to him fast before her mother and sister caught up and met with his mother. Church was a serious affair to the matrons, and once together, they'd all depart inside, and talking was no longer possible.

He met her halfway.

Grasping her arm in the crook of his own, he steered her around the crowd of people until they trailed the outskirts. He was wearing his finest suit and smelled strongly of sandalwood. Lucy noticed his hair was freshly cut and combed close to his head, a side part with bangs pressed into place with pomade. Perhaps he'd chosen today to propose to Beth?

Smiling at familiar faces in the sea around them, she whispered from the corner of her mouth, "Did you manage to send my letter?"

"Mail doesn't run on Sundays, did you forget?" he teased, chucking her under the chin like an older brother.

"Oh, of course," she groaned, rolling her eyes at her stupendous faux pas.

Something passed over his gaze, and he stopped walking. Leaning in close, he asked in her ear, "We're to have supper at your house again tonight. Will you meet me at the porch after? Like last time."

Her first inclination was to demur, but...he still had her letter. She looked up at him and nodded.

A smile curled the corners of his wide mouth and was still there when they reached their mothers and the reverend, their families some of the last to make it in the church doors. He released her arm, and she planted herself behind Beth, thoughts awhirl.

"Miss Ricci, what a pleasant surprise," intoned Reverend Brand as though he were already behind the pulpit. He was a stuffy, middle-aged man with severe features and a tendency to shout about hellfire mid-service.

Lucy managed not to arch her brow. Her arrival was a surprise? She was there every Sunday. "Hello, Reverend." She dipped a small curtsy, but he didn't nod or smile.

"Your mother has spoken to me at length, young miss." He'd never looked so condescending or unpleasant. "I believe you'll find my sermon this morning especially edifying."

Prickles of dislike crawled up Lucy's nape at the forewarning and noticed that Mother refused to meet her eye. That one had had much to say to the Reverend, Lucy bet her last letters on it. It appeared that her punishment was not only to be exacted out in the privacy of her own home but was also to be meted out in God's house as well.

Smiling in that hard, tight way that disproved she could be hurt, Lucy replied to the expectant reverend coolly, "I look forward to it."

When Aurora made as though to speak, Lucy shouldered her way forward, ignoring Rev Brand's disdainful staring that promised a long service with her in mind. It was no secret that the reverend had a strong respect for the beautiful Ms. Aurora Pattinson-Ricci. It would not take much for Mother to persuade him to set Lucy straight, so enamored was he.

Peter followed close behind; she could feel the brush of his fingertips as he steered them to the pew their two families shared. When she paused, he bumped into her and gave her a nudge.

"But you sit by the wall," she said.

"If you sit there today, Rev Brand will find it difficult to see you. Mr. Havers should block your view sufficiently." Mr. Havers was a brown woolen mountain, the pew in front of Peter's usual placement groaning beneath the weight of his immense body.

Lucy gave him a grateful look and allowed him to herd her into the pew, squeezing as close to the wall as she could. To her surprise, Peter followed. When he sat next to her, she smelled his cologne as acutely as though she wore it herself. Their families would be confused and suspicious of the abrupt change in seating arrangements, but Lucy was too relieved to contest it. The man in front of her did block as much room as three ladies.

"I can hardly see a thing," was her gleeful whisper to Peter, a pleased grin spreading wide. He grinned back, but then their family arrived, and they both sat stiff and solemn, staring straight ahead. Mrs. Langford took her place beside her son, and though she didn't say anything, the question was palpable.

Beth glared daggers at Lucy's head before she sat.

True to his word, the reverend preached with Lucy in mind. Never had he waxed so grievously on the sins of disobedient children who went against their parents. If it were up to him, she'd be writhing in the pits of hell with Satan in his brimstone castle. Although she couldn't see the preacher, he was drawing attention her way. Mr. Havers shifted, uncomfortable, the balding pate of his head beaded in sweat. People whispered and seats creaked.

Ears hot and head pounding, Lucy breathed hard through her nose and endured the stares. She'd never felt so miserable during a sermon, the only exception the time she'd come down with food poisoning. Like then, her stomach twisted and turned, as though she needed to purge.

A warm hand encased hers.

Through her periphery, Peter looked sideways at her and squeezed her fingers. She returned it, appreciative and confused, but he didn't let go. He hid their hands between them and stroked the skin that peeked between her cuff and delicate glove. Swallowing, she wondered if she should shove him away as a real lady would. The blush that had pounded at her ears spread across her face and chest, but he didn't stop caressing her and tugged her glove down to massage the plump mound of muscle beneath her thumb. His leg lolled wide, and his foot made its way under her skirt to settle next to hers. She didn't hear the whispers anymore, but a roaring as, like in the morning room the day before, the air between them changed. It was wrong. She knew it was wrong. But it made her feel less alone. So, for the remainder of the service, she allowed him to distract her and keep her in thrall.

"HOW WAS SERVICE, Lucille?"

Lucy was looking at her lap where her hand lay, gloved once more. Normal, and yet not.

"Lucille!"

Flinching, she looked up. "Yes?"

Aurora glared at her child in stupefaction. "Cease your woolgathering. I asked how you liked service this morning."

They were in the carriage headed home from church. Lucy's dazed eyes hardened. She didn't answer.

Thin lips twisting into a smile, Aurora speculated, "I believe everyone enjoyed it. Such teachings rear children into splendid adults."

"I don't think anyone ever really enjoys Rev Brand's preaching. He makes the afterlife sound like masochism."

"What utter nonsense. If one does not sin, then one shan't go to Hell. He's only doing what is proper for his calling, warning the sinners of the torture they will suffer if they don't change their ways and go to Jesus." Mother could have been reciting from a pamphlet the church ladies loved to hand out. The woman was such a self-righteous hoyden, that the indignities of that morning came rushing back and soured Lucy's strange mood.

"Perhaps it's the reverend that needs to be more careful, coveting another man's wife. Lord knows he pants after you enough—"

The blow cracked like a shot in the cramped confines of the carriage. Aurora shook with rage, hand still suspended, and eyes huge. Lucy sat stunned; all three women were stunned. For all her faults, their mother had never paddled their rears much less struck one of them in the face.

Voice reed-thin and trembling like an old woman's, Aurora whispered, "How can you think such things? What do you know of the lusts of the flesh?" Her hands were claws now, and she gripped Lucy's shoulders and shook her in a frenzy. "Tell me! Are you doing things decent young ladies are not supposed to? Answer me. Answer me!"

Lucy had stared, but at the touch of her mother's hands upon her, she shrugged them off and dropped the hand that cradled her face. "You're mad," she whispered. She and Beth looked at Aurora as though they'd never seen her before, then shared a sister's glance. For once, it did not hold accusation, but mutual apprehension.

When the carriage halted, Lucy was off like a rabbit, running, running, before the brake had even engaged. She darted past the house, beyond flowers and shrubbery, and into a small gardening shed in the far corner of their yard. Mother and Beth had never been back there to her knowledge.

What she needed, was privacy.

She slammed the garden shed door shut behind her and sat on a small, round wooden stool, where she held her face in her hands and trembled with emotion.

"If she hated me so much, then why did she bring me here?" she shouted into the emptiness of the little building.

The shed door opened a crack, and someone knocked on it. "Miss Lucy?" came a soft burr. A thatch of fiery red hair peeked in before deep-set hazel eyes settled, worried and downturned, on her.

Lucy's head raised, face wrinkled in misery.

"Oh, lass. What's the matter, noo, why you hidin' in here with the garden tools?" Jimmy's voice was so soft and gentle, it could have been Tony's if not for the Scots accent.

Oh, Papa!

Tears filled deep mahogany eyes and Lucy's chin quivered, losing its stubborn jut. "Nothing, Jimmy. Everything."

Jimmy's arms twitched outward, and his face was so weathered and kind, that she threw herself into his burly embrace. He held her tight to him, like a bandage over a flowing wound, and Lucy felt her shudders abate.

"What happened, sweet? Did ye have a row, then?"

Nodding into Jimmy's shirt, she croaked, "Yes, and she struck me. I imagine I deserved it, but she can be so awful. It's not worth crying about, I never cry. It's quite ridiculous."

"'Spect your bucket's full."

She pulled back and released a weak laugh. "What?"

Orange-haired and freckled as the housemaid—his sister, Meggie— Jimmy had sage wisdom that came with rearing half a dozen children with half a dozen different personalities and problems of their own. "Me wife told me about it. Sometimes she'll cry for no reason 'tall, and worse right after having a wee one. She'll be grand one minute, then the next she'll be crying her eyes out, so I ask her one day what for, and she says to me," he raised the pitch of his voice to a shrill falsetto, "'Jimmy-Lad, I go through one hassle after 'nother during the week, like cups o' water in a bucket, till one day that last cup fills it. Could be a baby cryin', could be the potatoes scorched, and it overflows is all.'"

Lucy wiped her eyes and stepped away. "That's an apt description."

"So, I imagine your bucket is just full, lass." Ignoring the wet spot on his shirt, he shuffled to the back of the shed and moved things around on a high shelf. Finally, he found what he was looking for, and turned back around. He was holding a dark brown bottle with an old cork wedged in the chipped mouth. Jimmy yanked the cork out with a squeaky pop and held the bottle out to her.

Intrigued, calm again, Lucy took it and sloshed it around until a whiff of the contents burned her sinuses. She coughed. "Spirits?"

Jimmy grinned wide, crooked teeth endearing. He made his brogue rough enough to be at home in a Highland village. "Och, aye, and how else d'ye 'spect tae empty yer bucket?"

Through her chuckle, she took a small sip and puckered her lips, then came back for two more large gulps.

"Whoa, slow down, Miss Lucy." He yanked the bottle from her and wedged the cork back in its place. "I don't need the sack for you getting soused on my watch, now."

Shuddering a bit at the afterburn, she waited for her belly to warm, and was shocked when she became lightheaded almost immediately. "What was in that, Jimmy?" she giggled, body loose and tingling.

"Not something you'll find in any old corner store." He waggled a finger at her.

Cheeks pink, she scrubbed her face one more time and gave him a last hug. "Well, thank you for making me feel better. My bucket's a little emptier now. Tell your wife I'll come visit her and the children when Mother allows me out of the house."

There was a moment of silence before Jimmy stalled her. "Miss Lucy, there's somethin' I've been meanin' to tell ye."

Stomach sinking at his uncharacteristic gravity, she dropped her hand from the door latch. "Is everything alright?"

Sighing roughly, Jimmy fiddled with the cork in the bottle without meeting her eye. "I wasnae goin' to mention such things to you, but it's not right, is it, to just leave without warnin'? The, eh, lady of the house has made it plain to Meggie, Cook, and meself that we've been much too friendly-like with ye."

The silence grew for a moment while Lucy absorbed that. "What has she done?"

He cleared his throat and turned to hide the bottle back on the shelf, muttering, "She docked our pay just this week."

The lump that had eased from Jimmy's comforting hug returned. She wanted to speak, but could not.

He turned, glanced at her, then looked away again. His color rose, turning his ruddy, freckled cheeks into burning coals. "Meggie said as not to say anything, but it's not honorable to keep such things secret from you."

Lucy nodded miserably and dashed a hand against her cheeks. She understood, truly. Jimmy was trying to tell her that he'd be ignoring her from then on.

"I'll be leaving come March," he continued.

"No," she croaked. "Oh, no, Jimmy, you cannot, not on my account—"

"Darlin', 'tis not on your account, it's been a long time comin', it has. We've too many mouths to feed." He stood from his stiff lean against the shelves and walked before her. His big, coarse hands clenched her shoulders gently. "I've talked to Mary and Meggie at length. There's work in the mill outside town. It'll be steady work, and we'll have our own house to tenant with more room for the little ones to run amok as they please. Meggie will stay on until she finds work, so you'll not be alone."

Unable to contain herself, Lucy blurted, "I'm leaving, too."

Jimmy's hands dropped. "I'm sorry lass, but 'twouldn't be proper for you to come along..."

"No, no, you misunderstand." This was just what she'd needed, she thought. The path was now paved, the way indisputable. She *would* leave. "I'm meeting Papa at the train station on my birthday, Jimmy."

His wooly red brows rose. "Does your mother know this?"

A harsh laugh was all she could manage for a moment. "Of course not. She's refused all my letters home. I had to send the instructions with Peter. Mr. Langford," she added with a blush when Jimmy looked confused.

"Ah, *that* one." He frowned.

"Yes," she whispered, then shook her head in frustration. "Would that I'd sent it with you. Mother said she'd sack anyone if I'd had them mail my letters. But you're already leaving."

He clapped her back, face serious and voice rough. "You need only ask and I'll help."

She sucked in a breath. "I may have to hold you to that."

Tentatively, she disclosed her plans in full.

"You'll not be travelin' to the train station alone if I've any say," Jimmy said gruffly. "Let me take ye."

They discussed and planned for another ten minutes before Lucy made her way back to the house for a bath. Luckily, she didn't meet her mother in the hall; she wouldn't have been able to hide the disgust in her eyes.

At dinner, she didn't speak at all and picked at her food. Mrs. Langford appeared not to notice, busy as she was gossiping with Mother, who studiously ignored Lucy. Beth attempted to interest Peter in conversation about the latest fashions, what Priscilla was wearing in her hair that morning, or how Mr. Gunham hadn't updated his fabric selections in weeks. But no matter what she spoke of, he'd only nod or grunt, his mind far away. Mrs. Langford slid narrowed-eyed looks at Lucy. Tension at the table grew, and the conversation grew stilted. Still, Lucy kept mum.

"No, no, Meggie. Lucille needs to watch her figure. Skip her dessert for tonight," Mother said during a bit of silence.

Lucy's lips flattened, but she kept her gaze lowered to hide her animosity, even as Mother continued with, "Lucille, stop slurping your water" and "Lucille, do not slouch".

Beth found sport in the game, and with a desperate last attempt to get Peter to talk, chirped, "Monica said Lucy was very unpleasant to her last week. I had to apologize to her, it was dreadful!"

"Is that true, Lucille?" Mother's voice was sharp.

Inhaling a deep, calming breath, Lucy answered through stiff lips, "Monica was being very disparaging of Mrs. Yancey's new ear trumpet. I simply told her when she became that age, she would probably be hard of hearing as well."

"That's not what she said," Beth cut in, miffed.

Lucy bit the inside of her cheek to keep from doing real harm to someone, anyone, with a high-pitched voice and blonde hair.

"Oh?" Aurora said, soft and supercilious.

Now Beth was nodding, eager as a puppy at Mrs. Langford. "She had expressed to Monica that she'd probably be a regular old crone, since she's so criticizing now, just imagine how it will be when she's elderly and thinks no one can hear her."

Peter coughed and cleared his throat, eyes lit up for the first time that supper. Lucy was slowly growing angrier, her fuse lit.

"I like Mrs. Yancey," she defended. "I was only taking up for her."

Aurora's face pinched. "Monica's father is on the city council. You cannot be making enemies with such important people."

The fuse reached gunpowder and Lucy exploded. "Monica is not important just because her father is, and I'll not pucker up to her bottom the way that Beth does."

"You are excused from the table," Aurora barked, and immediately turned to apologize to Mrs. Langford, "I am terribly sorry, passions run high...."

Beth whispered in Peter's ear while Lucy wiped her mouth and laid the napkin on the table. When she replaced the chair, she met green eyes across the table. One of them winked.

SEETHING IN SILENCE on the porch swing passed the time in a blink. The back door opened, once again illuminating the garden, but Lucy did not pay it any mind. She knew who it was.

The door shut out all light until a match flared. A glowing coal and footsteps approached her, then paused.

"Where the devil are you?" came Peter's soft inquiry.

For the first time that evening, Lucy laughed. "I'm on the swing. Here, hold out your hand."

She leaned forward and reached, waving her hand around until she swatted at something. Ungloved fingers enclosed hers and followed her to the swing. The bright red cherry floated in the air between them, and she could only distinguish the shape of his lips when he drew in. He should be inside with her sister, not out here with her. Her jaw and cheeks still hurt from all the clenching and biting at dinner, and she told herself that she didn't care a fig for her sister. It was the chit's own fault for not being able to hold a man.

"May I?" she asked and followed the length of his arm with her hand until she could safely grasp the cigarillo with two fingertips. There wasn't an urge to smoke, just the urge to do something to spite her mother. She drew on it and released, leaving it to dangle between her lips as she dropped her head to thump on the back of the swing. "What a day. What a miserable day."

It was quiet beside her, then, "I brought you something. It would seem like you need it."

He rummaged around in his coat pocket, then his hand brushed against her breast in shocking contact. She wondered if it was an accident and grabbed something smooth and metal from his fingers.

"A flask?" she guessed.

"Yes. Take a draught of that, and I can guarantee you that your day will improve."

Lucy chuckled and handed the cigar back, which he snuffed against the bottom of the porch swing. First Jimmy, and now Peter. What was it about men's belief that alcohol was a cure-all? She didn't mind stealing sips from Papa's study from time to time, but she'd also witnessed people who lived from the bottom of a bottle. But...since he'd gone through the trouble, she uncapped the flask and took a deep swig. Like Peter himself, his liquor was much smoother than Jimmy's. Nonetheless, it still tasted awful. She waited for her belly to warm and took another swig. "Mm, that is good."

A hand grasped it in the black, and she heard him swallow once, twice, thrice, before capping it again when she demurred when he nudged askance. She pushed the swing back and forth instead.

"Is your day better yet?" he asked, hiding his flask in the depths of his coat pocket.

Sighing, she shook her head no, then said aloud, "Not particularly. But your presence is a comfort. Thank you again for your thoughtfulness in church." She moved to squeeze his hand, but it wasn't in his lap, and patted a warm thigh instead. Blushing, she murmured an apology, but his fingers found her chin and turned her to face him in the dark.

"I think you are a brave young lady, and although my mother dotes upon yours, I'm finding it harder to abide the way you are treated in my presence."

Why don't you say anything? she wanted to demand.

Instead, she whispered, "Thank you, Peter." It wasn't his place to champion her.

His fingers went from her chin to feather gently over her cheek, then into her hair. Heart racing, a touch sick from drink and smoke, and his familiarity with her person, she held still and wondered how far he would take it. It was wrong and pleasant in one. She wondered if he kissed like the baker's son.

And then, she was finding out.

Liquor-laced lips were on hers, taking their time, his hand delving in her hair, and she thought faintly that it wasn't like the other kiss at all. For one, his lips were moving, never staying still, and they felt smooth and soft on her own. For another, something wet and slippery touched her lips. Her eyes flared open, then, realization. His tongue. She let him in, breath held as she analyzed the way he tasted and the way he felt. Worried she wasn't kissing well enough, she met his tongue with her own.

He groaned, and stood, leaving her blinking for two seconds before she was wrenched up by her arm and dragged to the darkest corner of the porch. She staggered behind him, hardly believing what he was doing and at the same time, refusing to face the fact that she was letting him. Curiosity warred, and won, against guilt and conditioning.

Peter notched her into the corner of the house and railing and embraced her, hands pushing her shawl from her shoulders, breathing her in.

"I've wanted to do this since the first moment I saw you," he said in a low alto. His mouth dragged over her jaw and to the delicate underside.

"I had no idea." She swallowed, overstimulated. "You always appeared interested in Beth."

Pausing at that, he held her face in his hands. "Mother didn't know I fancied you. I first saw you after a return trip with Father, sitting beneath that tree with those two little girls. You were so lovely, so alive. By the time I was introduced, I'd been warned off by my friends, and my mother was pushing me at Beth. So, I courted her and," he added wryly, "watched men watch you."

Lucy smiled and shook her head. "So you've said. I still do not believe you."

His lips were close. "Believe it." He kissed her again, softly, but she didn't want soft.

She bit his lip, perhaps because he deserved to be punished for not speaking up for her at dinner, or because, even though she had no love for her sister, sneaking around behind Beth's back was wrong. She held his bottom lip between white teeth, staring at him on the cold January night, and his response was immediate and startling.

Pain flashed white as he pulled her hair hard and bowed her neck backward with the force of his kiss. She couldn't breathe, or think, his mouth and body so hard on hers that all she could do was accept it. Fear and excitement warred within her, and she reached for his hair with her fingers but dared not pull it. When he broke away, they both gasped for breath, and his hipbones hurt hers.

"Where'd you learn to kiss, Lucy?"

She shook her head. Her old friend, Poppy, the one who drank and smoked with her at fourteen, popped into her head. The daughter of a whore, Poppy would whisper things that Lucy would only wonder about, until now. To admit that she'd heard how to make a man wild at such a tender age was too shameful, even to Peter.

"I've only kissed one other person before," she admitted instead.

"Who was it?" Jealousy laced his words, hardening his consonants.

"A baker's son, but I won't tell you which. I would die of embarrassment."

Without warning, her arm was in a grip of steel. "Have you done anything else with this baker's son?" Peter's voice was tight as his grip, and it brought to her mind a cherubic child, screaming that he had to share a favored toy.

"No, of course not. I just know things from—from the girls at that school, is all."

His hand relaxed in slow increments, turning from a tight grip to a light caress.

"I just hate the thought of someone else touching you. You've come to mean so much to me, don't you understand?" He kissed her throat while she frowned over the top of his head, nervous pulse beating against his lips. When his hands found the shape of her breasts, she froze and then slid sideways down the railing from him.

"I'm sorry, I don't know what came over me." He sounded repentant and didn't follow her.

"Which part are you sorry for?" She was perturbed, even more so when he changed his mind, and did follow. A shawl, her shawl, was draped around her, and her guard lowered.

"For frightening you. I just don't like that you've been kissing boys."

Scoffing, she rallied, "One boy. You have never kissed anyone? I imagine you've done a bit more than that."

"It's different for men than for ladies," he reasoned.

"Hm, if you want a lady that has never kissed anyone before, perhaps it's best that you're going to propose to Beth." It was out before she could take it back, and she imagined him riding home and shredding her letter into a million pieces. Before she could apologize, he was at her back, pulling her against him with no small amount of strength.

"Don't say things like that," he rasped, his breath hot in her ear. "Don't make me angry, Lucy, please."

Goosebumps rose along her arms and she bit her lip. "Peter, let me go." She hated that it sounded like a question.

"Never." She could feel his smile against her neck, and then, his teeth. He nipped at her and she jumped. Again, his hands roved, but he started talking as though he didn't have her pinned like a hound with a hare. "It is high time for Mother to learn that I'm a man. I've attended college, acquired a position at Father's firm this summer, and the time for letting her lead me around by the pocketbook has come to an end. God, you feel good." He turned her head and this time when he kissed her, there was no gentleness. Confused, afraid, aroused, she let him, her letter burning bright behind her lids. Peter pulled away, and she could feel his stare. "No, Beth won't kiss me like this. How can I marry a woman who doesn't make me laugh? Make me burn? And you're wanting to move away, back to some podunk little town in Texas. What's wrong with Atlanta?"

"Nothing," she breathed after a moment of gaping at him in the dark like a banked fish. "Atlanta is nice, I suppose, if you're wanting to live here. But there's no one here I enjoy being around. The exception being you," she amended when he stiffened.

"Ah. Well, time can remedy that, hm? Have you ever been to New York? That's the firm I'll be working in. There's plenty of people there you'd like." He finally released her and turned her in his arms. "Your nose is so cold. Give me a goodnight kiss and I'll warm you up."

That night, she lay sleepless, staring blankly at the empty black depths of her ceiling and wondering what she'd done.

She'd let Peter kiss her, and a stranger had come bursting forth, saying things that terrified her worse than the biting grip of his hand in her hair. Her plans would crumble between her fingers if he didn't send that letter. And if she angered him, the screaming child in him would come out and toss it in the fire. She scratched at her scalp where it no longer smarted. His strength was not one of a child's, and it was best to remember that.

Feeling as though she'd made the biggest mistake of her life, she rolled over to delve into her many pillows. Sleep did not come easy.

6

— ● —

CHAPTER SIX

A month passed before Lucy saw Peter again.

It was the end of February when Lucy spotted his straight brown hair in the snow-crusted churchyard. Worry held her suspended from a relieved smile, so she bit her lip until he looked up and saw her. He stood beside a man—his father, she realized—and pointed her out with a discreet nod. Mrs. Langford had informed them the month before that Mr. Langford had called Peter to New York on important business. For weeks, the woman's eyes had been red-rimmed, and she'd ceased coming to their weekly dinners.

"She dotes on the boy, that's all," Mother would assuage Beth's fears, but that deep crease had of late made a permanent address between her brows. "She misses him. That is all it is."

Beth would relax, but Lucy knew better. Something was very wrong. She felt it in her gut, which she pressed her clenched hands to any time his name was mentioned.

"Mrs. Pattinson," Mrs. Langford called out, teeth bared in a ferocious smile.

Lucy could feel the tension ease from her mother's shoulders at the first friendly greeting they'd received from Violent Langford in weeks.

"Mrs. Langford how are you," Mother purred, gathering her friend's gloved hands in her own as though they hadn't seen

101

each other in a dog's age. "Your husband and son have arrived home, I see."

Sensing her chance, Lucy ducked through a group of men and moseyed over to Peter. She was choking on her own dread, indeed she felt sick with it from her perspiring back to the churning in her belly. Both the Langford men watched her, their similarities shocking in the snap of the winter sun. Their brown hair had the same wave, and two pairs of green eyes followed her. When Peter's chin raised, she was frightened of a possible rebuff. Instead, his lips curled at the ends.

"Father, do you remember Miss Lucy Ricci?"

The eldest Mr. Langford stepped forward and took her hand before she'd even come to a stop in front of them. "Of course. How are you, young lady?"

"I—I'm wonderful, thank you, Mr. Langford," she stammered, and her eyes met Peter's. The shock from their last alarming night together had dulled until she'd almost forgotten what his fingers and body had done to hers. Instead, she'd cradled the fear that he'd thrown out her letter, mothered it until it was a living thing, a burden that put shadows beneath her eyes and prodded her from sleep. "We've all missed Peter dreadfully."

As she'd suspected he would, Peter softened fully and took her hand from his father's. "Not nearly as much as I did you." The bold words and lips on her hand did more than shock her, and she glanced at Mr. Langford, nervous. The man only gave her a benign smile.

Again, she had the sense that something was wrong. Different.

"Allow me to escort you inside," Peter smiled, and he turned them to the open doors.

"Peter," she murmured from the corner of her mouth, but he interrupted.

"I know what you're going to say, Lucy, and yes, I did mail your letter. The day I had to leave for an emergency to New York."

Just like that, tense muscles and rigid tendons became lax, and Lucy let her eyes flutter closed. "Oh. Thank you, Peter. I've worried so after you left. That I'd done something wrong, that you'd told your mother, or left because of me—"

He stopped them and gave a tight smile to a family of four as they ascended the stairs before them. "It was nothing like that, my dear. I'll explain everything tonight, hm?"

My dear?

"Of course."

This time, he sat between his mother and father, and she was placed firmly between Beth and the aisle. She didn't hear a word of the service.

MR. LANGFORD HAD an important dinner meeting with his friend, the old governor turned senator of Georgia, and Peter accompanied him. Mrs. Langford invited Aurora for a supper at their house while the men were away, and so exulted was she that her friendship was saved, Aurora didn't protest when Lucy pleaded a headache.

Cook and Meggie had gone home early that morning, so Lucy took advantage of the empty kitchen to draw out one of her cooking journals for a cake recipe. The stove was fired up and she pulled the pins from her hair, whipping up a cake mix, greasing a pan, and sliding the batter into the oven with practiced ease. Over the years she'd accumulated a vast number of recipes, the first of them from Minnie, and later, from the cooks of the girl's school. Once reaching Atlanta, she'd had more freedom to wander the more famous restaurants along the city streets. Some recipes she'd acquired from asking, and one, from bribing a boy with a kiss. Lucy had brought out this particular cake recipe gained from that kiss, and she was whisking up sugary icing with a mischievous smile when the door opened behind her.

Whirling, eyes wide, Lucy expected to find a burglar and held up a dripping whisk like one would a knife.

Peter's eyes lit, and he held his hands up. "I surrender, please, don't mix me."

"God's eyes, Peter," Lucy gasped in laughter at the foolish exchange, clenching at her heart with a hand. "What are you doing, sneaking around like a Tom Cat?"

He raised a brow at the comparison and stalked toward her. He wiped her forehead with a thumb, showed her the flour that coated it, and looked at the single illuminated lamp on the work table. "I wanted to see you before business took up all of my time. What are you doing in this house alone, in the dark?" He sniffed, and his other brow rose. "Are you—making a cake?"

The giddiness of the day caught up with her, and Lucy waggled her brows at him. "Come look and see." She grabbed a pot holder from the counter and bent to check the oven. The cake was golden brown, and fragrant spices and heat hit her in the face full force. She brought it out and set it on a dishtowel near the sink. Peter was dipping a finger in the bowl of icing and turning to her with it.

Tom Cat, indeed, she thought, watching warily as he raised his finger, spreading the coating of sugar and milk over her lips. He leaned over and licked her lips with the flat of his tongue. She was at once revolted, amused, and stimulated.

Before he rushed home to avoid her mother, he fed her cake, kissed her, and touched her in ways that made her shy away.

Over the next few weeks, they came together in hidden moments, in dark corners and empty corridors. At the dinner table with their families, he'd catch her eye with a promise in his, and she hid her apprehension with jokes and smiles. She ignored his violent bouts of jealousy and biting fingers any time he brought up her first kiss with the baker's son, which was frequently, or if a man looked at her too long at church.

Because, after all, it was only temporary.

He'd mailed her letter. She'd be gone in two months. What would playing hurt?

Lucy told herself that's what all they were doing, ignoring a deep-down disquiet. Teasing, skirting each other, finding fun in something so suppressed by their lot. Sometimes she liked him, sometimes he frustrated her with hints of small-mindedness or apathy toward the lower class.

As a friend, she made excuses for him. At night, while she nestled deep in her bed, she smiled and imagined Papa's face when he saw how much she'd changed over the years. She might even tell him about Peter. Certainly, she'd send Peter letters. She only hoped that he didn't marry Beth; the girl would make him miserable before a month was out.

HER BIRTHDAY WAS days away, and Lucy had been on her best behavior. Jimmy had left and a new, taciturn old gardener had replaced him. The strain of constant placidity drew on her mightily. Peter was a nice diversion after Sunday supper, but he was becoming more and more demanding, wanting to meet at odd hours of the night which made Lucy shy away.

The struggle to keep her relationship with her mother civil, if not friendly, was a tenuous balancing act. She no longer rose to the baiting and caustic words, and Beth was becoming the only object of Mother's notice. Twice a day at least, she inquired about Peter and Beth's possible nuptials, if he'd proposed, was he acting more interested?

"All he talks about is Lucy, Mama," Beth blurted out finally on a dreary Monday evening that had painted everything gray.

"What?"

"What?"

Aurora and Lucy looked at each other in shock. The silence was resounding in the little parlor.

Lucy hid her trembling hands beneath her book of poems.

"What in heaven's name do you mean by that?" Aurora snapped, clinking her porcelain teacup hard upon its saucer.

Beth shook her head, color high and eyes bright. "Just what I said, Mama! When we walked together at the park yesterday, it was 'Lucy this', and 'Lucy that', he wanted to know what she was like as a child, what was her favorite color, when was her birthday, did she prefer a gemstone—no matter how I steered the conversation, he would find a way to bring her up!" She shot accusing eyes at her sister.

The pit of Lucy's stomach seemed to sour, and her gorge came up in slow, steady increments. She turned a furtive glance at her mother, who was staring at her with dawning horror.

"What have you been doing, Lucy," she whispered, clutching a hand to her breast, her saucer of tea teetering precariously on one knee. "Are you beguiling poor Mr. Langford?"

The unfairness of the accusation, and the shameful truth of it, put force behind her lie. "No!"

Aurora stared, discerning whether or not to believe her, and shook her head. "I have no idea what could be happening between you and Mr. Langford, but you are such a willful child, I would not be surprised in the least if you'd managed to sneak off with him somewhere."

Lucy's cheeks burned, but she held her tongue.

"It matters not." Blue eyes held brown, as though trapping them in a spider's web. "I have contacted the headmistress of a reputable Institution for Young Women in Boston. It's a sister branch to the one you used to attend, you see. Her return letter agrees that you qualify, Lucille. You'll be leaving after your birthday next month."

Eyes full, heart hurting, Lucy found solace in the fact that she'd be gone with Papa by then.

That night it rained, and she sat on the swing in the dark again as she was wont to do during particularly unpleasant days. A voice in the dark startled her.

"Lucy, dear."

Squinting in the dark, she whispered, "Peter?"

He climbed over the railing, slicking back icy, wet strands of hair. "I wanted to say goodbye this time."

"You are leaving again? Where?"

The swing's chains vibrated as he sat and wrapped an arm around her stooped shoulders. "I wasn't going to tell you until I had signed the papers, but I found a brownstone in New York. It's perfect, with bay windows and just a short jaunt to the office downtown."

She found herself relaxing in the crook of his arm while he went on about the house he was buying. She was proud of him for getting out from under his mother's thumb. No wonder Mrs. Langford was so upset of late. For half an hour, she made agreeable noises and asked the appropriate questions, until he sighed, content, and drew her closer to him. "Ah, it's going to be grand, just you wait and see."

A humorless snort was her answer, and she wet her lips. "Not if Mother has any say. She informed me today that she's sending me to another lady's school in Boston. Said, I meet the requirements, if you can believe."

Peter grew motionless next to her, and the squeak of the swing halted. "She said that?"

"Yes. She made plans to send me off after my birthday. Not even a week away. You probably shan't be back by then." In her voice was a bitter kind of humor; he didn't know that would be on a train back to Dogwood before that point. She'd write him an apology in a letter. He'd forgive her for her duplicity, or not. It was beyond her hands now.

Deep down, the thought of not talking to him again was a comfort, though she felt ungrateful and disloyal for the thought.

There was that energy in the air again, the kind that made Lucy still and watchful of his temper.

He growled, "That bitch will have to go through me and Father, first."

Eyes huge, Lucy recoiled from him. "Peter—"

"No, Lucy. I am damned weary of pretending to like your bitch of a mother and sister. She thinks she can send you off at the merest provocation—why did she want to send you off?"

Swallowing and scooting to the edge of the swing, Lucy explained, "Beth mentioned that you've been...speaking a lot of me of late. Mother accused me of sneaking around with you," Peter snorted and mumbled something rude, "so she lost her temper and admitted that she'd made the plans, and written the letters. She'll not let me out of her sight around you now. But you're leaving. So, we won't get the opportunity anymore, shall we?" she tried to tease.

"Won't we?" he asked, soft and dangerous. He was leaning back against the swing still, and snaked an arm around her waist, wrenching her back to him. "Come here. I'll take care of this. Don't you worry. Father's staying behind with Mother, he'll work it out. Come *here*. Give me a kiss to remember. It'll be a long week without you, my dear."

When he left, Lucy touched her bleeding lip, a fine tremor in her fingers. He'd bitten her, marking the soft lining inside the fullness of her lower lip. When she'd shoved him away, he'd chuckled and licked his lips before bounding off into the dark. She wasn't afraid, not with the knowledge of her father arriving in a few days to take her home, but she felt as though she was teetering on the edge of something treacherous. She sucked at her salty wound and worried.

LUCY PACKED.

From the depths of her closet came a sagging carpetbag that her Papa had bestowed upon her at the tender age of twelve. It was hideous; dark green with bright splashes of garish pink cabbage flowers and amber swirls. Lucy loved it because it had been given in love and had often packed it full of things as a child, whether Tony took her anywhere or not. She'd fill it with toys and stuffed dolls, picture books, and tea sets.

Now, nearly six years later, Lucy packed with precision. Every garment was thin and folded tightly, wrinkles be damned. Stockings, blouses, one extra skirt, several cakes of soap wrapped in wax paper, and hidden in the pockets and crevices was something Mother knew nothing about; money Papa had sent with letters over the years. The first year, she'd spent it all on books and pastries, and gifts she'd mail back to Dogwood for her friend's birthdays, weddings, and Christmases.

The next year, she kept it hidden with her letters, squirreling it away like a miser. It took several minutes to sew greenbacks and coins in her dark, heavy skirt hem, keeping the coins apart so they didn't clink together. Some, she shoved deep in her stockings. In the end, there was just enough room for her letters and journals. If she was forceful, she could shove some bread, fruit, cheese, and perhaps some smoked sausage on her journey.

Afterward, she grew still, and asked herself, what am I doing? Papa is meeting me. I'll have plenty of time to gather my things for the trip.

Doubt chased the naivete away. Mother would make trouble for them, that was certain. It was best to meet Papa at the station with her bag on the morning of her birthday, and to hell with Aurora. She was sending Lucy away anyways, what should it matter that she was going West and not East?

Muffled footsteps on the hall rug outside sent her into action. She gripped her bag with enormous eyes and swiped it beneath her bed, its momentum carrying it to the darkest depths against the wall. Quick, surefire raps pounded against the door like warning shots.

"Lucille. We have company. Come downstairs." Aurora's voice was strange. She left before Lucy had even turned the knob.

Downstairs in the front parlor was Mr. and Mrs. Langford. Peter's father stood when she entered the room behind Aurora, but Mrs. Langford remained seated, pale, and looking for all the world like she was ill. But then, she always appeared so when Peter was out of town.

Aurora sat next to Beth, who was dressed in her itchy periwinkle dress, scowling at Lucy with disdain. The atmosphere was strange and niggled at her. She wanted to chew her nails but sat on a straight-backed chair instead.

"We are so pleased you have come to call," Aurora began, frowning at Mrs. Langford's white features. "But I am afraid something is wrong. Violet, are you well?"

Mrs. Langford blinked and pressed her hand to her lips as though she'd be sick. Mr. Langford, however, just sighed. "She's fine and well, Mrs. Pattinson, thank you. You know she has a weak constitution." Said with little patience. He looked down at the settee he'd shared with his wife and continued to stand. "I've spoken at some length with Peter," he began.

Aurora and Beth perked up, riveted. They were probably waiting for an imminent proposal, but Lucy remembered Peter's words last night and felt her heart drop into her stomach.

Don't you worry. Father's staying behind with Mother, he'll work it out.

Oh, God. What had he told them?

Mr. Langford continued. "He mentioned something...disturbing, something to do with the youngest Miss Ricci being sent away after her birthday?"

There was a hush in the air, like the stillness after a cannon had been shot, and Aurora turned her head to Lucy. *Liar,* those eyes accused. Sucking in a breath, Aurora remained calm and answered, "It was a conversation I had with her just yesterday, Mr. Langford. How, I wonder, did your son know of such a recent conversation? Did he not leave for New York just this morning?"

Another hush, and now Beth looked at her.

"He did, indeed."

All eyes were on her, even Mrs. Langford's, now. Accusing.

Feeling faint, face and hands numb, Lucy met Mr. Langford's gaze. "I spoke with him yesterday. Before he left."

"Indeed?" asked Mother.

Mr. Langford's face softened into a genuine smile as he peered down at her. "Peter's had plenty to say about you, young lady. Just last month he was bursting into my office with plans to be made, contracts to draw up. Never before has he been so serious about taking my place in the business one day." His eyes were keen upon her. "I am unsurprised that he's taken such a fancy to you."

Beth and Aurora gasped as one. Mrs. Langford brought out a tissue and dabbed at her eyes, shoulders shaking. Her husband ignored it all and walked to Lucy, hoisting her up from her stunned seat on her chair.

"But, sir—" she began.

"Mr. Langford," Aurora had found her voice. "Your son has been courting Elizabeth for some months now."

Peter's father steered Lucy to the windows. "Yes, yes, he's admitted to me that he allowed his mother to push him at whichever society miss caught her fancy, but it's you—" he patted Lucy's hand, "that he's made clear he wants to wife."

Chilled at the announcement, Lucy stared out the window, not seeing the siding of the house next door, or the withered stems of the neighbor's rosebush.

"But...he's in New York," she said, dumbly. If it was a proposal of marriage, why wasn't Peter there? It felt conspicuously cowardly.

"Yes, buying a house to start a family in," Mr. Langford laughed. His hands over hers became heavy. Smothering.

"He never said anything about..." she broke off and glanced behind them at the colorful statues on the settees. "I thought he was only a friend."

For a moment, he acted confused. "He's neither said nor done anything to imply his preference for you?" When her cheeks grew pink, his smile returned. "Ah, young love. I do admit that he was not intending to be so hasty. Your news of Mrs. Pattinson's plans sped him along, and when he was out of town, of all times. After all, marriage is a big step." It was quite amusing to him, and his laugh came from the belly.

Every kiss, every touch came back to haunt her. The hands she hadn't known had fisted beneath Mr. Lanford's trembled. It was all her fault. She may have been toying with Peter, but it wasn't obvious until now that his feelings had been truer than her own. He'd kissed her like a husband would a wife, and now she was surprised when he took steps to make it true? No matter his predilections—the jealousy, tantrums, and rough hands—he was doing the honorable thing by wanting to marry her. He'd put them in compromising positions, as had she, and although no one had caught them, it came to light now and warranted marriage.

A sob brought all their heads up. Beth stood and rushed from the room, and they listened uncomfortably while her steps disappeared up the stairs.

Aurora stood, wringing her hands. Her voice shook. "Peter wants to marry Lucille, now, after months of pursuing Elizabeth?" If Mr. Langford hadn't distinguished Aurora's opinion on the matter before, he knew it now. No, her mother was not at all pleased.

Mirth dissolving from his face, he turned and raised supercilious eyebrows that gouged the lines in his forehead ever deeper. "From what I have seen, Miss Elizabeth is not madly in love with my son. Disturbing rumors circle that she's still enamored of her last beau."

Though meekened by Mr. Langford's social superiority, Aurora nonetheless defended, "Elizabeth is not 'enamored' of that scoundrel. She said good riddance to him and has not spoken a word of him since. And whether or not she's in love with Peter is irrelevant; love will come in time."

Mr. Langford snorted rudely. "Ah, yes, you are much determined to pawn the eldest off on Peter, whether or not her feelings are in play with such an arrangement. Well, my son's wishes are rather more important to me. If he loves Lucy, as I suspect he does, given his raptures over her, then I'll not force him to marry anyone else." He straightened his jacket crossly and mumbled, "Of all the preposterous ideas."

Aurora's eyes glinted. "I am sorry, but the arrangements for Lucille's boarding school are already in place, she could not possibly marry your son. Elizabeth, however—"

Flinging his hands in the air, Mr. Langford cried, "I don't give a damn if Elizabeth was sent down by God himself. Peter does not want her; he wants the sister. How old are you, dear?"

"I turn eighteen in two days' time." She was beginning to think she was in some strange sort of pantomime or dream.

"There. That is a perfect age for marriage."

"No, she's far too immature, ask Mrs. Langford. The trouble she's been causing these last few weeks alone—"

"A troublemaker, are you?" he chortled, sudden hostility gone. Lucy was coming to understand where Peter's mercurial nature came from. "No wonder our Peter is so enamored of you, he's pressed so far behind his mother's skirts, a bit of excitement here and there...."

"Charles," hissed Mrs. Langford, who had turned an indignant pink.

"Now," he rubbed his hands together, the thrill of business evident in his bright eyes. "Let us begin with the arrangements."

Lucy was chauffeured into the hall, and she stood there for a dumbfounded moment. She was still standing, stunned, when Mrs. Langford let herself out of the parlor while the remaining two adults bartered.

Their eyes met, and Lucy came to an awful realization that if her mother disliked her, then Peter's mother loathed her.

"Why did you do it?" Mrs. Langford asked, swabbing beneath her nose with a limp hanky. "Why did you tempt my boy? He's a good boy, deserving of a sweet young lady like Elizabeth."

"Sweet," Lucy repeated and had the inane urge to give into hysterical laughter.

Ignoring her, Mrs. Langford reached into her skirt pocket. "Peter does not know what's good for him, and his father does not, of a certainty. Here. If you think you know my boy, then have a look at this."

Lucy reached for what looked like a ragged scrap of paper, then held absolutely still. Mrs. Langford smiled and used both her pudgy little hands to tighten Lucy's limp ones around the tattered parchment. Blinking back tears that stung and threatened to shame her, she turned her back on the evil little woman and held her letter up to her face.

The same letter she'd given to Peter to send months ago.

It had been opened and handled a great deal if the poor shape of the creased paper had any say. She looked at her own handwriting with their explicit instructions and wanted to wail.

Papa never got it.

He was not on his way via train as they spoke.

He was probably sitting in his office at this very moment, writing her a birthday letter she would never receive.

"I found it in his room. Oh, he'd read it and had thrown quite the tantrum," Mrs. Langford sniffed conversationally at Lucy's back. "Locked himself up in his room for hours, almost didn't make it to church. But, on the ride there, he'd calmed down. I thought he'd lost a gamble again, so that night, I went through his things and found this under his pillow—his pillow, can you believe it?"

"You never said anything to Mother," Lucy choked. What Peter had done was unforgivable, and she felt the loss of their friendship keenly. For a moment, she'd even believed that marriage wouldn't be so bad....

"Of course not." Venom laced Mrs. Langford's words now. "Your leaving would be the best thing for the poor dear. I never understood why she'd ridden to that godforsaken town for you in the first place."

"To hit Papa where it hurt." Lucy turned around now and realized she towered over the squat woman. It would be nothing to knock her to the floor, but even she had better manners than that. "She took me because she could and because she hates my father. If you wanted me gone, why didn't you send the letter?"

Mrs. Langford's face crumpled then. "Oh, he caught me, Peter did. Swore to me he would send it, but if I meddled, he'd move back upstate with Charles." Her sniffling disgusted Lucy. "After he came in last night and told us of his plans to marry *you*, of all people, I found the letter again. Fickle child, he'd never sent it."

"And you came here with it to stop an unwanted marriage," Lucy finished for her, understanding. Because now, she'd never marry Peter. The warning signs she'd ignored solidified in this last, unforgivable lie. He'd wanted to keep her in Atlanta. It was a neat trap. Even then, had he wanted to marry her? She'd never know.

She wasn't waiting for him to come back to find out.

"Yes," said the old woman—for she did look old. Old and tired. "And I brought this. To convince you to leave my boy alone." Out of her pocket emerged another envelope, this one sealed.

In it was a banknote for five hundred dollars.

That would not only get her to Texas but would set her up independently from her Papa if she so wished.

Pride clashed with feckless temptation for a long minute before her upbringing and fiery temper decided for her. Dark eyes flashing, Lucy sneered down at Mrs. Langford and shoved the envelope back to her. "I don't need your money. If I stay away from Peter, it's because he betrayed my friendship, not because his mother paid me off. Good day." She turned on her heel and ascended the stairs.

At the top of the landing, a snarling Beth met her, eyes bloodshot and wild.

"You just couldn't stand that someone wanted me and not you, could you?"

"You're mad," Lucy said tiredly and brushed past the heaving girl.

"No, you are a slut," Beth hissed. "I'm surprised he asked for your hand when he was getting it for free."

Lucy paused, tried to ignore it, and moved on.

"Mother despises you," was the final shot. "She told me so herself. You're just like our father."

"I know. And you're just like Mother. May the two of you be happy together." Lucy's door shut behind her, and the lock clicked.

LUCY SAT IN the quiet of her room, curtains rustling with a breeze that announced spring into her open window. Outside, life went on, ever-changing, always moving, even as she sat so still on her bed. Her mind stayed carefully blank, unwilling to process the steps she knew she'd take tonight. Not just yet. There would be hours of restless wakefulness to think. To plan.

She felt driven to the edge of that precipice, a tall jagged cliff, a mile-long fall. Every option that made the most sense—for she was a sensible girl for all her disobedience—became blocked by unseen obstacles, popping up here and there to stand shadowy in the paths that were easiest to take.

All that was left was the straight, paved road that led to New York, her mother standing erectly with a raised chin and grasping hand. Peter was just beyond her, teeth biting, hands clenching, and lips lying. Attend school, be a good girl and mind your mother. Be a lady, marry a gentle son of society and never see your Papa again.

In her mind's eye, Lucy stepped backward, pebbles crumbling into an unknown abyss behind her. One more empty step and she would fall into nothingness.

Meggie came and went that night with the requested supper items, but before she said her final "good evening" to Lucy, she was clenched in a swift, back-cracking hug.

"Oh, Miss Lucy," Meggie exclaimed, laughing. The young mistress had always been so impetuous, with her quick smiles and easy nudges, but the sudden gripping embrace caught the housemaid off guard.

"You've been a wonderful friend, Meggie," Lucy declared, voice muffled in the bright orange curls beneath a crisp white cap. "More than that, you and Jimmy have been my light. Without the two of you, I would have gone mad here. Thank you." As quickly as she'd snared her, Lucy let go.

Confused, Meggie looked between Miss Lucy's wide brown eyes. They were large and dark, glittering with something solemn and intense that belied the relaxed smile beneath them. Thinking back, comprehension hit. She grasped her young friend's arms and chirped, "And you've been a light to me, Miss. God willin', I'll be able to visit you one day at your da's hotel."

"Yes," Lucy said, eyes shifting to the side. "God willing."

"Shall I tell Jimmy he's still to come to take you to meet your da?"

Lucy nodded. "Meggie, I need to leave first thing in the morning." She paused. "Papa is...arriving early. I'm to meet him at the station, and we're going straight home from there instead of traveling back here. Will your brother be here?"

Meggie's eyes widened. "It shouldn't be a problem, but I'd better tell Jimmy right away."

Before Meggie left that night, she took the ugly green bag and snuck it from the residence, waddling at its weight.

The next morning, Jimmy had met her on the street with a rented phaeton.

7

— . —

CHAPTER SEVEN

"That was why I ran. And that's the truth of it."

Lucy felt uncomfortably vulnerable after telling Ben, a stranger, the worst thing she'd ever done. In the retelling, she'd heard her selfishness, naivete, and weaknesses. If she could go back, she'd do everything differently. Everything.

He didn't speak. They lay near each other in a quiet that was only interrupted by the rhythmic, sawing snores of the man across the hall. Ben's silence was telling. It also occurred to her how inappropriate it was to be alone in a room with him. If he told the sheriff her identity, they would tell her mother how she'd stayed in a room with a strange man claiming to be his wife. Her reputation would be ruined. Even Peter wouldn't marry her if he knew.

Good, she thought viciously.

The lengthening hush beside her made her suspicious.

"Did you fall asleep?" she asked incredulously.

"No."

It was hard to distinguish his thoughts from his expressionless tone. Her father, when confronted with unpleasant news or unfair treatment from Mother, had acted similarly. His eyes would grow vacant, his words monosyllabic. Was Ben disgusted?

"Are you going to go to the sheriff?" she whispered, trying to stifle her suddenly shallow breathing.

There was nothing for a long time, then, "No."

She breathed out, and her stomach stopped its miserable churning.

"Thank you, Mr. Stone. I'm sure you'll be glad to see the last of me," she said, trying for humor, before he could say it himself and wound her.

"That Paul fellow should be horsewhipped," he said stiffly.

Lucy said nothing for a moment. "It's my fault for tempting him—"

"Don't. He's a coward," was Ben's harsh opinion.

"No more a coward than I," Lucy interjected, not in defense, but self-accusation. "It was no more than I deserved. All that I've done...it's unforgivable."

Frustration made his next words blade-sharp. "You think I've never done something shameful, Miss Ricci? We all do, at some point in time. And we live with it and learn from it, or it eats you up from the inside out."

Swallowing the hard lump in her throat, she turned her head toward him in the dark. "You have?"

"'Course I have. It's part of being human." He let loose a rough breath and turned his back to her on his pallet, his voice fainter and colder. "Five years ago, I turned my back on my consequences. I ran away and didn't look back. Now, I'm coming home to face them head-on. No more running. Sometimes you got to make it right."

The man in the other room must have rolled over as well; there was no more snoring to ease the stifling quiet that throbbed in her ears.

BEN WOKE THE next morning to someone placing something hard on the floor outside their door and tapping unobtrusively.

He'd slept like hell. It had been too dark, too quiet, and chilly from the draft under the door. Worst of all, he'd been lying next to a beautiful woman who'd insisted on sighing and mumbling in her sleep. Twice, he'd woken with her arm across him.

He wondered what she'd been dreaming about.

Slamming the door on those thoughts, he stood from his bedroll, feeling his way around the mattress next to him to the light under the door. The key in his front pocket unlocked the door and revealed a chipped enamel pitcher with steaming water. The hallway was brighter than their room, so he brought the pitcher in without shutting the door.

Lucy laying on his spare blanket in a chemise and skirt froze him, and when she stretched languidly, his breath stopped. She'd slept on her stomach with her legs akimbo, but now she sat up in a panic.

"What time is it?" Her voice was a rasp, her eyes wild and sleep swollen. She reached across the floor for her watch, perused it, then slumped back on the mattress with a relieved groan. "I had a dream that I missed my stage, and that I was stuck in this town forever."

Making a sound was impossible for him. He'd realized that her chemise was thin enough to be transparent, and he could see the shape of her breasts and the points of her nipples plainly thanks to the light in the hall. His face filled with deep, red blood and he hastened to the table and basin. Blood racing thick and swift, he clenched his hands briefly around the pitcher and set it down. He cleared his throat to say something but had become inarticulate.

He composed himself by lighting the kerosene lamp, rolled up his bedroll without looking at her, and set the key on the table, grunting, "Water's hot if you want to wash up. The key's right here. I'll see to Reb."

Halfway to escaping with his saddlebags on his shoulder, she cried, "Wait!", and he paused. He didn't dare look at her.

"I need to pay you my half of the room fee."

Like hell, she needed to. He turned. To his relief, she'd pulled his blanket over her chemise in embarrassed modesty, and he could breathe again. "No ma'am." He shook his head and widened his stance. "I'm not taking your money."

Her dark, arched brows knit. "Yes, you are."

His straight, black brows rose. "No. I'm not."

She frowned at the way he loomed over her, then checked her watch again. "Then I'd like to pay for our breakfast at the diner across the street in, say, fifteen minutes?"

No woman had ever paid for his meal, and one wasn't about to start now.

Her blanket slipped lower.

"Fine," he lied. He'd say anything to get out of that room. "Lock the door behind you." Ben shoved his hat on his sleep-tousled hair and ran like the devil was on his heels.

He returned twenty minutes later, beard trimmed, and face washed from the barbershop two blocks over. He knocked on the door, then tried the knob, nodding with satisfaction that it was locked.

"Who is it?" asked a suspicious voice from behind the door.

Stifling a smile, he replied, "Someone promised me breakfast."

After some jiggling of the lock, the door opened to a tentative Lucy holding her bag and his tightly rolled borrowed blanket. He took the latter, trying not to notice that she was in a fresh, white cotton shirtwaist tucked into the same skirt she'd worn the day before. It was wrinkled, but her face glowed pink from a recent scrubbing and she smelled of fresh soap. Her hat was conspicuously missing today, and her mahogany tresses shone, held back in an intricate twist at the nape of her neck.

"I'm starved," she confessed. She sounded pluckier today and had probably decided to believe his promise not to take her to the sheriff. "Maybe the restaurant will have something on their menu for my recipe book."

Ben arched a brow.

"Oh, it's a hobby of mine. I collect recipes from all over. Growing up I would read all the pioneer cookbooks our general store had to offer, even if I already knew how to cook them. Now that I'm older, it's more fun to learn about the things I can't cook."

"I didn't know city ladies knew how to cook."

Catching the teasing in his voice, she screwed up her face at him. "I am not a 'city lady'. Who did you think was going to cook you the steak and pie when you came through Dogwood?"

They checked out of the hotel, and she continued the conversation all the way to the street, nodding and smiling at sleepy bystanders. Yep. She was feeling braver, alright. He couldn't resist letting her conspiratorial eyebrow waggling charm him from his mulish distance.

It was the first day of April, and there was a snap to the air that cut through the dampness of early morning. Constant windiness brought one last northerly chill that would have inexperienced farmers nervous, wondering if they should have waited to plant. Wispy clouds hurried overhead, promising darker, denser clouds later.

Lucy checked the watch pinned to her crisp white shirt while they waited for two wagons to pass, and frowned. Tendrils of hair escaped her smooth coiffure, and she absently tucked them behind her ears.

"I have an hour before I need to catch the first stage. Are you leaving along with it, Mr. Stone?"

"I've got business just south of town, an old buddy of mine has some horses I want to look at." He thought for a minute. "Why did you take the train this far west instead of just goin' straight through to Houston?"

"The train coming to Jackson was the earliest one, and I couldn't afford to wait until Mother discovered I was not at home." Her cheeks filled with a sheepish blush.

Fighting the urge to shake his head at her foolhardiness, Ben dropped it. There was no point beating a dead horse. "I plan on taking the next train to Tyler, then Reb and I will ride the rest of the way home."

"Oh." Her chatter tapered off after that, and they reached the diner in dismal silence.

They opened the door, the smoke of frying bacon fat and the murmur of early customers a welcome change. They sat at a simple wood table with mismatched chairs close to the window, and Lucy stared out of it, a solemn profile with her chin perched on her fist. Their admissions last night, easier spoken in the weight of pitch black and muzzy-headed exhaustion, resurfaced. It was an enigma to him, the ease of telling a stranger the hard truths you wouldn't even dare admit to your own friends or blood.

Looking at her profile now, eyes serious and empty of mischief, brought forth the forbidden image of her on the mattress that morning. If she had bunked with any other man.... The thought conjured feelings he refused to examine.

"Still feeling honest?" he inquired.

"What?" Her brows were the most expressive part of her, like they had a mind of their own, particularly now when they puckered together. Maybe when she was forty or fifty, she'd get one of those little wrinkles that grooved deep in between them.

"Why would your mother wire that you were sixteen?" If she wasn't lying, and the letter hadn't been falsified, today was her eighteenth birthday.

Lucy turned her eyes back to the window, mouth downturned. "I think I know why she wired that I was sixteen. The authorities are more likely to get involved if it's with a child that ran off as opposed to an adult." Her eyes followed a portly man wearing a derby hat. "If I were in Atlanta right now, Mother would throw an obligatory birthday party where my engagement to Peter would be announced."

That name again. Peter the Peckerhead. Wishing he could snap her out of her strange mood, Ben asked, "And if you were in Dogwood right now?"

Ah. There it was. Her mouth curled up at the corners. "Minnie would bake a cake for me and wouldn't let me in the kitchens. Papa would take me on a trip to a theatre somewhere in a bigger city, maybe Houston. Or a circus if there was one nearby."

His leg jiggled under the table and he looked around for their absent waitress. "Well, I can't bake a cake that wouldn't poison someone, but I can buy you some hotcakes."

The mischievousness lit her eyes again, and her chin stopped sulking on her fist. "Oh no, you don't, Mr. Stone. I'm paying for breakfast."

As though summoned, a tall, rawboned young woman left their neighbor's table with a coffee pot in hand and stopped at theirs. "What'll you have?" She looked ill-tempered and harassed, but Lucy managed to smile.

"Hotcakes, one scrambled egg, a ham steak, and coffee, please."

The waitress didn't write it down and turned to Ben expectantly. "And you?"

Ben frowned and crossed his arms. He didn't like rude waitresses, especially not ones that were rude when it was a customer's birthday. If he'd had the time, he'd be inclined to get their breakfast elsewhere. "Same as her but triple it."

The woman left in a whirl of skirts and a raised nose, disappearing into the kitchen.

Glaring after her, Ben muttered, "She's about as pleasant as a thorn in my side. Didn't even give us any coffee."

Lucy took her gloves off, smirked, and leaned in close with a whisper, "It doesn't matter if she curses your mama and spits in your eye. Never insult a waitress."

"Better spit in your eye than spit in your food?"

She nodded, eyes twinkling. "Precisely." For a long, comfortable moment she maintained eye contact she laid her gloves on the table, holding his gaze until his temperature started coming up, and his knee jiggling stopped. Then her smile drooped, and her eyes hit the table. "Mr. Stone, I never thought to ask, and I'm so sorry." Her voice was low and worried. "I know I'm pretending to be married to you, but I never did think, do you have a wife somewhere? Or a lady you're courting? I'll never forgive myself for insinuating that we'd made vows when—"

"Whoa." He patted her ungloved hands. "I don't have anyone back home, stop your frettin'." When he caught her examining the brownness of his fingers against hers, he snatched them back and crossed his arms. "My luck may be changing though," he tried to tease. "I think our waitress was making cow eyes at me."

The waitress took that moment to arrive with hot plates of food, slapping them down in petulant silence and spilling coffee across the stained tablecloth. The woman looked between the quivering faces of her customers, frowned suspiciously, and left without saying another word.

Lucy quietly laughed into her napkin while Ben took a scalding drink of coffee. They resumed comfortable chatter while the sun made its way over the town, lighting up the street and its burgeoning activity. They argued over which was the worst about traveling; hard seats on a long train ride, or the rough ride on a stagecoach. She denied his claims that the mosquitos there were so big in Louisiana that they carried small children off. He didn't believe that she'd once seen an alligator the length of the room they ate in.

"You gonna ask for recipes before we leave?" Ben wiped his trimmed beard with a napkin, going along the grain so that the black and brown hairs lay sleek and obedient.

The hotcakes were rubbery, the eggs had been overcooked, and the ham steaks over-salted, but she'd warily cleaned her plate as though not wanting to appear impolite. Considering he'd had thrice the same thing that she'd had, he knew good and well that the food hadn't been good. He couldn't resist picking at her.

"There's no time, unfortunately." She glanced at him with big, worried eyes. "I need to wait for my coach. I would not want to be late."

He put a silver dollar on the table, ignoring her whispered objections until she had no option but to give embarrassed thanks. When they stood, they looked around in silence, neither making the first move to leave. The waitress ignored them as she disappeared into the kitchens, and more people filled the room, mostly men grabbing a bite before opening shop.

Lucy cleared her throat and suggested casually, "There may be time to say my goodbyes to Reb."

There wasn't time, and they both knew it. Ben hefted his bags over a shoulder, plucked his stained hat from the back of the chair, and settled it on his head, hoping the brim hid the gladness in his gaze. Damned if he wasn't making cow eyes at *her*, he scoffed to himself. "Figured you'd give my horse more appreciation than you give me."

A sweet smile spread across her face as she picked up the Dreadful Bag. "He *is* a fine example of horseflesh."

They left the smells of breakfast at the diner, and made their way down the line of boardwalks, brushing against each other occasionally while crossing busy streets. Old-timers loitering on shaded benches smoked pipes and gave them squint-eyed nods as they passed. Young women followed their mamas in colorful skirts, with little hats or bonnets that matched.

For a while, they were just one of many couples strolling along. For a moment, they *were* husband and wife. Ben wouldn't allow himself to imagine another life where brown or blue-eyed children trailed along behind them while they walked arm in arm. After today, he'd never see her again. A soft, tender spot inside of him seized, and it must have been his conscience because then he started to wonder. What would happen to Miss Ricci if she didn't have anyone to protect her during the rest of her travels home?

Well, she may just learn the hard way that running off was dumber than facing the consequences of her actions in Atlanta, he thought cruelly. If that opinion wasn't straight from his father's mouth and into his head, Ben didn't know what was. Teeth gritting, he forced himself to think of his

Mama. She'd have walloped him with the rug beater for even thinking of letting the girl go off on her lonesome.

He gnawed on the thought of following Lucy discreetly from town to town until she'd boarded the next train. It wouldn't look like an accident, a coincidence of fate that they had to share a train car again. He'd already told her he was taking the Jackson train to Tyler. Riding south to follow her, jumping on a train from New Orleans to Houston would add days to his trip.

Ben looked sideways at her, watching the graceful, long strides she took, her slender profile and perfect posture. She was a lady, he a vagrant. A drifting cowboy without even a home to call his own. She deserved one of those fancy townhouses, sipping tea and eating those tiny cakes that never filled him up no matter how many he'd pocketed in the kitchen at his stepmother's house.

When they reached the open doors of the livery, he was torn, stuck between saying "to hell with it" and continuing with his plans, or following the lonesome miss like a dog after a bone.

Reb nickered softly at Ben when they approached the stall, and Lucy touched the horse's silky soft nose. He placed a blanket and saddle atop the strong equine back while she nuzzled against the hapless gelding's jaw.

"Goodbye, old Reb," she murmured, lifting long lashes dreamily. "It was a pleasure to meet such a handsome and masculine horse as yourself."

"Not much masculine about a gelded horse," he shot, aware of the sweat trickling down his back beneath his sturdy work shirt. Shocking her was impossible, and she lifted a taunting brow to prove how unimpressive his wicked statement had been.

"Do not listen to him," she whispered in Reb's ear. The ear slung away at the tickling breath and twitched back up.

The way she kept looking at him, serious and intense, had him experiencing an inappropriate pang. It was weak and unwelcome, so he turned away from her and retied his saddlebags with hard jerks that swayed the whole horse. Was that what had happened with her sister's beau? He could just imagine it. Lucy, looking up at that city-soft mama's boy with those big eyes, and what could the poor fellow do but fall over himself to do her bidding? The antagonism he felt at that image was far more welcome than the other, more amorous responses to her. It grounded him and cleared his mind.

"Promise me something, Miss Ricci."

At the lack of inflection in his voice, she stepped away from Reb's head.

"I need you to promise me not to get friendly with any more men, you hear?"

Those eyebrows flew high, and her mouth opened defensively. He maintained eye contact and she halted at his gravity.

SHROUDING HER FACE of emotion was difficult when one was completely offended. Not get friendly with any more men? What a thing to say.

"Any *more* men?" she repeated casually.

He positioned his feet wider. "Yeah. No more smiling and carrying on conversations with strangers of the male variety."

The conversation was getting more and more absurd. It was becoming difficult not to laugh in his face. Unable to help herself, Lucy frowned at her left hand, flipping it over back and forth. "Have we become married in truth without my notice, Mr. Stone?"

The grim press of his lips didn't even twitch, and he glanced behind her once before crossing his arms. His sapphire eyes burned into her until she dropped her hand. "In fact, don't get too friendly with anyone, Miss Ricci. There's women out there too that are just as good for nothing, steal you blind at the first inch you give. You've gotta be smart. There's nice folks out there, yes, but mostly, there's buzzards and criminals. They'll steal from you or hurt you, then mosey on to supper without blinking or thinking twice about it. Understand?"

Oh.

"Bossing people around, trying to scare them, is that how you show you care?" she chided.

Ben's neck darkened in a flush, and he turned back around to fiddle with Reb's cinch, pulling it until the gelding swung his head around for a nip. "You need to be scared. If I had a sister out here, on her lonesome, I'd hope she was being smart and keeping her distance." He paused. "You have a gun on you?"

Now she was beginning to feel like a fool. Her smile dropped. "No, I did not bring a firearm." Lucy perked. "I do have a knife—"

"A knife isn't going to scare a fly. You feel threatened, you pull out a gun. People will take you serious, then."

Lucy fumbled with her watch. "There's no time to buy a gun, I have five more minutes to say goodbye, then I need to get on my stage."

Swearing under his breath, too low for her to make out, Ben went to the other side of his horse and shoved his hand into a saddlebag. She watched with wide eyes as he approached and thrust the cold metal of a derringer into the palm of her hand. The weight of it frightened her. This was a weapon that could kill or maim. Or, as Ben intended, keep her safe.

"You know how to handle a gun? How not to shoot your own foot off?" He had the gall to sound angry about it, and she wanted to stomp his instep for being so cantankerous.

"Yes," she snapped, glancing at him resentfully. "I'm not a complete fool. But I've only shot rifles, never pistols."

"If you're lucky," he said, "you won't need to use this. Bringing it out and aiming should do the trick. But if you're real unlucky, just get close enough to someone, cock it back, and shoot. Aiming isn't as important when you're only a couple of feet away."

To hide her disappointment, Lucy gingerly opened the two-shot chamber and counted the bullets. One was missing. What had he used that shot on? This had not been the goodbye that she'd envisioned. There'd been no witty rejoinders, fond smiles, or even, dared she'd hoped, a lingering hug. Instead, he'd pushed a gun on her and ordered her not to be stupid around strangers. She couldn't help comparing the way that he cared to how Peter cared. Ben was neither polished nor charismatic. He was blunt and negligently amusing. He was also much too bossy by far. She frowned. And yet, he was still far more trustworthy than Mr. Langford.

She stowed the gun away in a corner of her carpetbag for easy access.

"If you come to Dogwood one day, I'll be sure to return this to you, Ben." She'd said his first name in a surge of bravery but couldn't quite bring herself to make eye contact. "Thank you. I really must go, now. Thank you for everything." She forced a smile, but he was glowering at her bag.

A coach rattled by outside, and she whipped around, her nightmare of being left in this town forever still fresh in her mind. Thankfully, the six-horse team slowed to a halt outside the stage office, and she swallowed around the lump of anxiety that had threatened to choke her.

A large, hard hand on her shoulder startled her, and she glanced up at him, looming like a dark shadow at her back. "Promise me you'll be safe, you hear?" He squeezed her shoulder, then gave her a gentle push on release.

"I promise." She licked her dry lips and turned for one last look. Ben was checking Reb's hooves, unaware.

Why was it so hard? Saying goodbye to a stranger shouldn't be so difficult. *That's the problem*, she mused. *He doesn't feel like a stranger*.

The task at hand reemerged, dragging behind it a new apprehension and respect for the dangers around her. She exited the warm, straw-insulated livery and made her solitary way to the stage office, eyes shifting side to side. This time she didn't smile or nod at anyone. The muscles in her arms and back strained with tension when she made it to the end of the line on the boardwalk. The coach had fresh horses and drivers, who loaded piles of luggage to the boot in the back.

The Stuarts arrived, along with a fussy, flushed baby. She nodded to them, but they were in bad tempers, hissing words to each other under their breath while their son squirmed and cried. Embarrassed, she found her ticket in the depths of her bag and clutched it. The wind teased more of her hair from its pins, but her hands were full. She stood in line, hair everywhere, feeling conspicuously young and alone.

Inexorably, her eyes were drawn to the broad-shouldered man riding his blood bay. Ben stopped by a lanky, middle-aged man with several days' scruff, and leaned down over the pommel to have words with him. Lucy squinted at them when the tall man glanced at her, nodded, and gave Ben a few words of his own before walking off. She frowned after him, wondering at the strange exchange, and looked askance at Ben.

His blue eyes were riveted on her, and he tipped his hat her way, relaxed in the saddle like it had been made specially to fit around him. A fierce urge shivered through her at his lean-waisted sentinel, one that fired signals in her mind and body. It was the kind of impulse she'd not felt with Peter; if she had—if only she'd felt this way, hot and crawling in her skin—marriage would have been far more appealing.

This was how it was supposed to feel around a man. Just the steadiness of Ben's regard caused hot pulses to swell in her, raising her temperature. Had it been his worry about her safety? Or had it existed on the train, this feeling? Either way, it was an inopportune moment for her to have such realizations. If it had been a different time or place, Lucy knew that she would have pursued this man. Now, however, her journey home demanded full attention.

Even so....

That little devil on her shoulder peeked out of hiding. It didn't have to nudge her much to bring her hand up. Lucy pressed her fingertips to her lips, maintaining eye contact with deep blue, and waved. If she was a fool for blowing him a kiss, which his stern glower communicated over several yards away, then so be it. It didn't keep her from flashing him an impish smile before handing her bag over to the new driver and alighting into the coach.

Perhaps he wouldn't forget her after all.

BEN CALLED HIMSELF a dozen foul names for letting a girl dressed in women's clothes tie him up in knots and wrap him around her little finger.

He followed the stagecoach into the next town after having a word with the driver. Reb stayed some ways back from the thundering dust cloud of the coach while he stewed.

The conscience was a funny thing. Sometimes it didn't make a lick of sense. He'd be in Texas hours ahead of schedule if he just went on and didn't look back. The voice that knew between right and wrong whispered in his ear that he wasn't much of a man at all if he left the young lady to travel alone. If he were ever lucky enough to have a daughter, and she did a monumentally stupid thing like run away and journey four states alone, he'd hope someone with sense would step up and help her out.

What he'd never told her was that his father's ranch was a four-hour ride from Dogwood. If he could manage to wrangle his mother's old stone cabin from the elder Stone, he'd only be two hours from the Dogwood Hotel. From her.

Maybe he knew better than to open that can of worms, and if he was smart, he'd never tell her. He knew what it would lead to. No woman he could remember had ever looked at him like Lucy Ricci had before she'd blown him a kiss and rode away. It brought up feelings no trail boss should have for a young lady, one so high above him he'd have to climb for days to get to.

Six years ago, he'd been skinny and clean-shaven; not quite the catch his brother probably was now, but he'd been judged "respectable enough" by his stepmother's cousin, Mrs. Simms. She and his stepmother had thrown her daughter, Abigail

Simms, in his path so often, that he couldn't get a bit of work done. Ben hadn't been stupid, and at twenty-two, he had no notion of settling down with a pale, quiet girl that never spoke.

John Stone had words with him one night and changed all that. No one ever said no to John. Five months later, he was married to a stranger.

Bile collected, and Ben spat out that and the memory that came with it. Reb's ear twitched. The wedding night was something he hated dredging up. Abby had been so uninformed of the marital act, so sheltered, that she'd grown hysterical midway through consummation and he'd been unable to continue. For days after, she'd acted terrified of him, like he was some devil there to drag her down into Hell. Sleeping in separate rooms hadn't calmed her nerves, and any time he turned a corner and she was there, she'd break into tears. It was enough to put anyone off marriage.

He'd tried to talk to her, to apologize to her and suggest an annulment after dinner one night, but she'd started crying. He'd left the room, got on his horse, and camped out near the southern fence line, full of self-loathing and confusion. Later that same night she'd run away to town, showing up at her mother's townhouse with bruised and blistered feet. Mr. Simms had ridden to the ranch that night demanding answers. John didn't take well to threats and had brought out the shotgun, then waited on the porch until Ben showed up the next morning. Ben had never felt such humiliation. Simms' lawyer had arrived not even a week later, demanded an annulment, and wrung as much money as he could out of the Stones for the physical and emotional damage caused to poor Miss Abigail Simms.

John Stone had been irate, his wife shocked, and the town whispered "wife-beater", and "rapist" behind Ben's back. The annulment was the talk of the county for months, and people loved whetting the stone on the blade of gossip over the Stones' good name. Ben hadn't been able to handle the heat. Despite John's roars that he needed to get a lawyer and man up, he gave the Simms all the money he'd made since the age of seventeen and signed the legal papers without even looking through them. Then, with his twelve-year-old brother Junior crying for him not to leave, he'd fled the state.

It took him five years to grow a backbone and make right with Junior, who undoubtedly hated Ben now for leaving him with the old man. As soon as he flashed a stack of greenbacks to John, Ben would collect his rights to his mother's home and would move his little brother with him. Hopefully, he didn't make it too late.

Following Lucy was a deterrent from his true purpose. She was someone he didn't owe any of his time to, and yet here he was, unable to turn his back on doing the decent thing. His old man would call him a damned fool, and spit at his feet. Junior was older now. Lucy's age. Ben couldn't imagine what kind of man his brother had turned into and whether he was kind, or hard and angry.

And if his brother was more like John than Ben, well, he could only blame himself.

8

—·—

CHAPTER EIGHT

The man across the rocking stench of the coach's cab stared at Lucy without even the decency to pretend he wasn't. Before she'd promised Ben the morning before not to be friendly, she would have smiled at the man and initiated a conversation. Now, she looked out of the curtained window of the stagecoach with a set, stubborn expression, pretending an unwelcome leer wasn't eating holes through her clothes.

The stranger had swung into the stage at the last stop. The first thing he'd done was curl a lip at the smell. "What in tarnation is that? Somethin' die?"

The Stuarts had absconded moments before, their poor, motion-sick baby the source of the smell. Poor Little Will had begun the trip with raucous crying the day before and ended it in projectile vomiting over his mother and the seat they'd shared that morning. She'd felt horrible for the poor dear and had given the ruffled family sad farewells at one of the nondescript waystations. Lucy had felt close to them after bundling with Mrs. Stuart and Little Will the night before.

Any introspection at their exit had been squashed with this new passenger's arrival. Beneath the sour, biting scent of drying vomit came another pungent odor from his person. She dubbed this man 'Buffalo Jo' in her mind, even though he'd introduced himself as Bobby Jo Canton. Buffalo hunters were one of the smelliest customers they'd had at her Papa's hotel,

135

though they were few and far between now. They would come into the diner smelling of sweat and rot from the skinning and work they did with the valuable hides. Mr. Canton may not have smelled of the particular decomposing odor of a buffalo hunter, but his stench was caustic to the sinuses.

Her response to his entrance in the close quarters of the cab had been a reflexive jerk of her head before she grew wise and pressed her nose as close to the open window as possible. The wind was fierce and smelled of rain, and she gave a quick word of thanks to the heavens.

"Careful sticking your face out the window. Wouldn't want that pretty little nose whacked off," chuckled Buffalo Jo.

She managed a thin smile, but inside she desperately wished for the Stuarts and their vomiting child in lieu of present company.

"Where ya headed?" The man leaned forward. His nose and the tops of his ears were peeling, and the shoulders of his filthy jacket were snowcapped with dandruff. "Hey, you never did give me your name."

Cornered, Lucy shifted minutely away from his breath. "Mrs. Stone. I'm meeting my husband in New Orleans."

He blinked, then laughed. Large gaps between brown molars flashed, and she glued her eyes back to the scenery, swallowing.

"You ain't married. How old are you, fifteen?" His eyes narrowed and moved down her erect posture, which bounced now and then in the seat. "No sirree, you ain't old enough for that. Still in the schoolhouse, probably."

"I am eighteen," she gritted. "And yes, I am married."

"Where's your ring?"

Lucy couldn't help raising an acerbic brow at him. "I am not keen to wear my valuables while traveling. It's with my husband." It was distinctly chilly in the compartment, and she crossed her arms tight, thankful she'd put on her jacket. The cold air around them didn't stop the sweat gathering in the hair at her temples and nape. Her underarms and back prickled with it.

Her companion shifted around, getting comfortable, spreading his legs wide so that his foot nudged hers. She smartly tucked hers back.

The green carpetbag was tucked neatly in the boot of the coach, the gun along with it.

Oh God, let me get to the train station soon.

Her prayer went unanswered.

It took four slow, crawling hours. Bringing cards out to pass the time, or even a book, was impossible since she didn't have her bag. Instead, she had only her thoughts. Ben's words repeated over and over in her mind. *There's nice people out there, but mostly there's buzzards and criminals. They'll steal from you or hurt you, then mosey on to dinner without blinking or thinking twice about it.*

It wasn't hard to imagine Buffalo Jo hurting her. His idea of small talk was personal questions that dug under her skin like splinters wiggling about, looking for a vital organ to stab.

How'd she like being married? he'd ask. Was her husband a big man? Why'd he let a good-looking thing like her travel alone?

When she was unresponsive, he took a swig from a small, stained canteen around his neck. After an hour, spirits swirled in the air with his breath, and his questions became more intrusive and disturbing. Did she know what happened to white women when renegade Indians robbed a stage? Outlaws would kill a person outright, but she was comely enough that they'd consider her a good trade to some Comancheros. She'd wish for death, then. If she wanted, *he* could keep her company until she made it to her husband. They could bundle up together, nice and cozy-like.

By their next rest stop, Lucy was shaking with tension and sweating through her jacket. When he opened the door for her and held a dirt-grimed hand out to help her down, she didn't have an excuse not to take it, but she ignored it anyway. The thought of touching him made her want to mimic Little Will and empty her stomach of that morning's breakfast. Her bladder was fit to burst, and she waited until the revolting man walked into the woods to find a tree before skulking in the opposite direction. Relieving oneself in skirts and a corset in the wilderness was not a graceful thing, and she bumbled about, scrabbled at tree trunks and scrubs, and lit the air on fire with curses.

When she returned, Bobby Jo was still missing, and she beelined it to the driver, who was stretching a long, potbellied torso and wind-milling his arms to get the kinks out.

It didn't take much to bat her lashes and convince Tucker, the driver, to let her ride on top for a spell. When the old driver's hangdog eyes slid to Bobby Jo, and he asked if 'that man was botherin' her', she laughed and said it was more the smell of the interior after Little Will's illness than the passenger inside. She argued that the smell of baby sick was triggering her own motion sickness and that sitting on top might clear her head.

Tucker stroked his bristly face and paused. "Alright, Mrs. Stone. Just pray we don't get bushwacked on the way there."

"I'd rather get bushwacked than sit in that coach another moment, Mr. Tucker," she fervently admitted.

Snorting, Tucker helped her alight onto the driver's bench, told a scowling Bobby Jo to get inside, and followed behind. He took up the reins to Lucy's left and waited for Rex, the shotgun, to climb up beside her. The small-statured man didn't seem a bit bothered, and Lucy breathed a sigh of relief as they moved forward.

It didn't occur to her to peer behind them long enough to see the speck of a rider on a familiar gelding following carefully behind.

DUST ROILED AROUND the wheels of the stagecoach as they creaked to a stop. Tucker set the brake with a worn, gloved hand and tied the reins with a groan. Rex jumped down as sprightly as a man twenty years his junior in his hurry to help Lucy down. She gave him a grateful, tired smile. The youthful lines of her face were set in weariness and coated in a fine layer of dirt kicked up by the hooves of the team. When the door of the coach swung open, she ignored it and took her bag from Mr. Tucker with heartfelt thanks.

He tipped his hat to her fondly and directed her to the train depot so she could buy a ticket. Thunder boomed and rumbled, matching Lucy's stomach for the ferocity of its growls. Thick, heavy clouds churned, boiling temperamentally in the low ceiling of the sky.

Her leaden feet took her to the train station, and she clutched her sorry carpetbag without making direct eye contact with people. In Dogwood, old-timers told her good morning, friendly women stopped her on the street for a chat, and the children begged her for candy. In this city, no one knew her. A man tipped his hat as he rushed past, and a woman gave her rumpled travel clothes a quick perusal before dismissing her to enter a shop.

Lucy felt her nose start to sting and took a deep breath.

She needed to buck up!

This was only temporary, a means to an end. If she kept mucking through fear and self-pity, she'd never make it to Papa. Firming her resolve and thrusting out her jaw, she managed to find her way through the confusing roads and alleyways of the town to the open space housing the depot, oily black train tracks an unexpected comfort.

When she entered the ticket office, she felt more like herself. The man behind the counter had a toothpick in his mouth and an attentive expression. He lifted his brows. "May I help you, ma'am?"

"Yes, I would like a ticket to the next available train to Houston, please."

His toothpick wobbled behind closed lips as he checked his rosters. "Next one is the night train, coming through this evening at seven. You have luggage?"

"One bag. I intend to keep it with me." She hefted her bag for him to see, vowing that she'd never let it leave her sight after the unfortunate incident with Mr. Canton. The ticket clerk scribbled on an empty ticket.

"It's a long trip, ma'am. You want a bed in a sleeper car?"

"Er, how much more will that cost, sir?"

They reviewed prices, what they entailed, and the estimated time of the arrival to Houston, Texas. She agreed on a third-class ticket, a bottom sleeper berth in a Pullman sleeper car, and two meals provided by the porter. She counted out the money while he wrote, then paused.

"Name, Miss?"

Hesitating for a split second, she made up her mind. "Stone. Mrs. Evelyn Stone."

A deep voice behind her asked, "Aren't you gonna buy me one, too, darlin'?"

Eyes widening, she whirled, and a smile broke huge across her face. Ben stood in the doorway, an immense presence, and even more travel-worn than she. His clothes were wrinkled beyond imagination, and his bandana lay limp and sad at his neck. Saddlebags were held close to his person, and his hat was tipped forward to hide his expression.

"Mr. Stone!" She dropped her bag and greeted him with the enthusiasm of a stray finding its long-lost owner. Her arms wrapped around him in a brief but heartfelt hug, and she felt her loneliness melt away like frozen snow slush in wake of a spring sun.

Ben's eyes were warm and crinkled at the edges, but he disengaged from her clinch to step past her and order another third-class ticket with a top sleeper berth above hers. The man wrote another ticket, and Lucy hid behind Ben to conceal her pink cheeks.

When they walked out, she looped an arm through his after he'd untied Reb and ignored his raised brow. Nothing could curb her good humor, except for the fact that she was weary, rumpled, and smelled like she'd been pressed between two sweaty men for hours. What she wouldn't give to be dressed in her cream-colored gown, with a daub of perfume and some candlelight. He'd never seen her at her best, and it stung her pride.

She smiled through her insecurity. "I thought you'd be in Texas right now. Weren't you taking the Jackson train?"

"Change of plans."

"What plans?"

He took his arm from hers in the guise of shifting his saddlebags closer, and she felt her cheeks warm at the subtle reminder that they were practically strangers. She reached back with the arm he'd abandoned to pet Reb's curious muzzle.

"Calvin wasn't home, so I decided to take this train. My Pa's ranch is closer to Houston than Tyler anyway."

"Oh." She tried not to sound confused. The decision to travel south to a different train instead of just taking the one in Jackson didn't make sense, but she kept her opinion to herself. His business was his business, not hers. Still, she couldn't help digging. "Where did you stay last night?"

"I camped out by a waystation."

"*Our* waystation?"

He shrugged, and she looked at him narrowly.

His hair and beard were ungroomed after two days' travel, his blue eyes squinted ahead. She wondered if he was lying about his friend not being home. And had he truly stayed the night outside like he'd said, or had he gone to a saloon and had a few drinks to while the night hours away as her Papa had often habituated?

The thought of him sitting in a saloon with a painted lady on his lap brought on an unwelcome barb of jealousy. It was a unique phenomenon. She hadn't thought she was jealous by nature. Her wants and needs were peculiar; the things she coveted were less physical and more nostalgic. Lucy craved the feeling of hearth and home, a father swooping a child up on his shoulders, and the sight of a busy, well-loved bakery.

Now, she was aware of a pair of older women walking by, and how one of them glanced at Ben's broad shoulders and slow, gliding walk. Her lips tightened, and though she knew the absurdity of staring at a stranger in a challenge, it didn't stop her from doing so until the lady's wandering eyes skittered away.

Ben was saying something.

"I apologize, what were you saying?" she asked, blinking at her own bewildering behavior.

"Got some dirt in your ears?" he asked, leaning down as though to check.

Lucy ducked in mortification, thinking she might die in fact if he *did* see the state of her hygiene. Flushing, she defended, "I'm sure I have half of Mississippi in my ears after being on that Godforsaken stagecoach."

"Sounded about like my trip," he chuckled. She didn't look up at him while he led them to a livery, still burning at the possibility that he'd seen dirt in her ears. He gave the horse to an eager teenager with simple, curt orders and an exchange of silver. They left and crossed the busy street, and this time he took *her* arm. She was cognizant of how he maneuvered her unconsciously around road apples, in front of horses rather than behind, and away from strange men. It softened the edge of self-conscious anxiety, and she relaxed, discerning the hard bunch of his muscles in his bicep as he helped her onto a general store's wooden deck.

"Need anything from in there?"

For a moment, she watched, immobile, while he took his hat off and beat it against his leg, fine dust floating off behind him. Large fingers splayed through his sweat-dampened hair until the matted locks released their grip from his skull. She looked away, guilty and ashamed of her fascinated staring, and cleared her throat. "I could afford to get a few things. Do you need anything?"

"Naw, I'll get what I need in Houston. I'm gonna go order us our baths before they run out of time slots. How about I meet you here in twenty minutes?"

The prospect of a bath sounded heavenly. "That would be perfect! Here, let me give you some money for the bath—wait!" Ben was already stepping off the deck and crossing the street.

That confounded man!

"More stubborn than Minnie with a cold," she swore, burning holes into his broad back with her disapproving gaze. There was nothing more that she could do. When a man got something in his head, you couldn't beat it out. With no other choice, Lucy sighed and entered the store. Her brows went up high at the prices, so all she grabbed was a small tin of mint toothpowder. A display near the front advertised 'everything for a dime', so she used the remaining time to peruse the selection. An indigo ribbon that was almost the exact shade of Ben's eyes shimmered on its spool. She fingered it and then moved on. Several dime store books caught her eyes, and she grabbed two about rustlers and outlaws that she hoped would interest the hardheaded man across the street.

The kindly store owner wrapped the thin paperback books in brown paper at her request, and she took the meager gift and toothpowder outside. She may as well wait outside in the open air before she broke and bought some of those tempting peppermint candies in their glass jars.

For five minutes, she watched from the boardwalk as darkening clouds above roiled and twisted, making the air heavy with humidity and the scent of rain. Thunder rumbled, deep and resonant and never-ending, reverberating through her ribcage and stomach. People in the street glanced above, hastening for shelter.

Someone bumped into her in a wave of liquor fumes and body odor.

"I beg your pardon," she said. That's what happened when one lollygagged in front of a busy store. Lucy stepped away from the wiry man, endeavoring to skirt around him without making eye contact.

"Hold on. Wait, wait, wait."

The man's voice was familiar, and she stifled a groan.

It was Buffalo Jo.

He held up a hand, smiling drunkenly. All the vile things he'd said on the journey came to the fore and she quelled the urge to wrinkle her nose. Why, he was soused!

"Ain't you that pretty little thing from the stage?" He laughed, and a couple of women stepped around them, muttering to each other in haughty tones. Mr. Canton didn't notice.

Unafraid in the presence of onlookers, she stiffened her spine. "Excuse me."

"Naw, I got somethin' to say to you."

Ignoring him, she compressed her lips and continued on her way. Her eyes scanned the road and in front of shops, hoping to find a familiar cowboy hat and sure stride. A hand clutched her shoulder and turned her. Her mouth opened in shock at the persistent man's gall.

"It ain't polite to turn your back on someone when they's talkin' to you," he claimed. She shrugged his hand from her person and gave him a cold stare and raised brow. "You're a liar," he continued. His breath, if possible, was worse than before, and she teetered back a step. He looked pleased with himself, had probably stewed on insults he could have given her all the way to their last stop.

"Is that all?" Lucy couldn't resist asking, then bristled and took another step from him when he opened his arms wide, swaying side to side.

"You said you was married. I don't see no husband." He looked around in question. Several people paused in their strolling to watch the strange banter, wondering if they should be alarmed and come to the rescue. "Nope. No husband a'tall. Ain't that just like a woman—"

"Why don't you look behind you, hand." A menacing shape had stalked up behind Buffalo Jo in the darkening shadows. Ben's voice was deep and calm, the timbre of the thunder around them, but his eyes glittered ominously when the drunk whirled around. Lucy caught glimpse of a knife gleaming against a muscular thigh, and Mr. Canton must have seen it, too. He muttered something placating, and stumbled off the porch, falling into the dirt in a surprised heap before rising and fleeing.

Ben's eyes followed the man while he sheathed his knife at his waist, tucking it back under his vest. His gaze was fixed until Buffalo Jo disappeared between two Creole-style buildings, then slid to Lucy. She felt something stab deep at her chest, down into her solar plexus, then lower. That tight, hot sensation from the morning before resurfaced. Her lips parted so she could get enough air, too stunned with awareness to care that she'd been saved...again.

"Who was that?" It was almost, but not quite, accusatory.

Raising her chin an inch, Lucy said, "He's the reason I sat with the driver on the stagecoach."

Ben made as though to step down into the street.

"Wait!" she cried and pulled him back with a clutching hand in the crook of his elbow.

They looked at each other for an uncomfortable moment until, panicked by the hint of violence she sensed in him, she handed the brown paper package to Ben.

Glassiness metamorphosed into quizzicality while he held the wrapped books in a rough hand. Her pulse beat along the paths of her veins in long, avid pulls at the brush of his hand against hers, and her nostrils flared, soaking up his scent and heat.

"What's this?" he asked after a long, tense moment.

She wanted to say it was for the bath, but all she managed was, "Nothing."

"It's your birthday yesterday. You should be getting presents, not giving them."

Hopeful that he'd forgotten his pursuit, she shook her head. "Nonsense. You've given me two presents. You chased Buffalo Jo away and now I get to enjoy a bath."

A laugh exhaled out of his nose. "Buffalo Jo? Is that his name?"

"That's what I called him in my head on the journey here. He smelled like one of those buffalo hunters we used to serve in the diner."

When Ben smiled, it was genuine, reaching his eyes first. He nodded that they should get moving and wrapped an arm around her shoulders. "Why don't you tell me about it on the way to the hotel? We have rooms on loan until five, then we'll have just enough time for dinner before we get on our train."

Lucy tried not to become too distracted by the heavy weight of Ben's limb on her shoulders, and regaled her trip to him, enjoying his quiet laughter and the way his shoulders shook without sound.

In the hotel, his room was across from hers, and he reminded her to lock her door. For a moment, she stood quietly in her small, private room. The lamp was lit beside the bed, and she moved to put her bag on the bed and checked the time slot Ben had given her for her bath. A note on the pillows caught her eye.

I checked for bed bugs just in case.

She smiled so wide it hurt her face, then grabbed the note. Lucy folded it once, twice, then placed it in the tube of one of her stockings amongst some of her hidden money. Then she sat on the bed and worried.

THERE WAS A communal bathroom at the end of the hall. Wanting nothing more than to wash days of travel grime from his skin, Ben gathered a bar of soap, his last set of clean clothes, and the room key. He stepped into the carpeted hall and locked the door behind him. From the corner of his eye, he glimpsed an attractive woman waiting for her turn at the end of the hall. He did a double-take.

"Shit," he breathed.

It was Lucy, leaning against the wall by the door sporting a 'Do Not Disturb' tag dangling on the brass knob. She looked bored, body svelte with hips thrust forward, back arched, and shoulders pressed flat on the wall behind her. An arm full of folded clothes was pressed tight into her bosom while she stared at nothing, eyes glassy and out of focus.

After two or three seconds, she looked up and saw him. She smiled.

"Shit," he repeated grimly. He'd thought she was a damned fool two nights before but was coming to the realization that he was the fool. She was wedging herself like a splinter under his nail and hadn't even realized it.

A man was almost hurt because of her today. Ben had been so close to dragging that bean pole of a man out into the street for a fight. Somehow, his knife had come out before he'd even grasped what his hand was doing. Fists weren't good enough for that fellow; he'd wanted to dig his knife deep into that pickled liver. It scared him. He shouldn't have been so ready to gut a man just for a bit of heckling. Now he was stuck well and good in a quagmire of his own making. He'd follow Lucy until Dogwood. Hell, he'd probably walk her to her Pa just to make sure she'd made it safe. It was enough to make him sick. The faster he got her home, the better.

Thoughts heavy on his mind, Ben walked the length of the hallway, reveling in the silence of the upstairs. From outside was the faint, constant sounds of the town life; men shouting, horse and buggies clattering down the street, and the constant tinkle of a saloon piano.

"This should be your time. You been waiting long?" he asked, stepping in behind her and leaning a shoulder on the faded floral wallpaper.

Curiously, her cheeks pinkened and she looked at the toes of her boots peeking from her skirt hem. "Yes." Her voice quavered, and her lips trembled and twitched, fighting a...smile?

"What's so funny?" he murmured, enjoying her crisp profile, dark lashes, and smooth forehead with its sleek mahogany brows. The pins in her hair had loosened. The coils drooped, gleaming in the hall's unforgiving electric lights. She released her lips from between her teeth, and he had to look away because they were damp and shiny.

"You'll see," Lucy said after she'd composed herself.

He couldn't imagine what would have had her in such a tizzy. "You're being—"

The bathing room door opened and cut him off. A young man with damp hair stepped out, saw that he'd kept people waiting, and paled. The young woman that followed close behind, however, went bright red. She didn't look at either of them as she grabbed her husband's hand and they took off down the hall.

Eyebrows high on his head, he said without thinking, "Good thing you're not in the room next to them." His neck went hot. It wasn't the first time he'd said something inappropriate in her presence. Years of living around cowpokes had made talk about sex commonplace, but Hell, even Junior knew not to talk about it in front of womenfolk.

Lucy covered embarrassed giggles with her hand. Her face and ears were similar in color to the fleeing wife's, which made him chuckle. They both laughed as quietly as they could, meeting each other's eyes. Hers were watering.

After a minute, she gasped, giggles tapering off, to say, "I like your gold tooth."

Self-consciously, he rubbed his mustachioed lip. "Got in a fight a few years ago. If you've ever had a chipped tooth, you'll know every drink of water hit like lightning. A doctor put this over it for me." He showed her the gleaming canine, lifting his lip around his other teeth. Might as well let her have a good look.

"You look like a dashing pirate," she soothed.

He scoffed.

"I always thought it made me look like one of those crazy miners that lived up in the hills." Growing uncomfortable at her appreciative staring, he waved her at the door. "Bath's free now, and we have a train to catch. The man at the front said the food's real decent."

She nodded. "I'll be quick."

Lucy disappeared into the bathroom, locking the door behind her. He tried not to imagine her naked once he heard splashing. He was able to keep his thoughts pure for the first five minutes. After that, wet limbs and loose hair flooded his mind until he hid the state he was in with his pile of clean clothes.

THE CLOCK DOWNSTAIRS chimed five times while Lucy finished final touches to the loose plait of hair that she'd twisted into a figure eight at her nape. It was in a damp, sorry state, but she was clean and smelled nice, and her scalp no longer itched from dried sweat caked with dust.

She worried that she needed to send a wire to Papa so he wouldn't worry, but a quick rummage through her funds squashed that idea. Her father had never beat her before, but he may just whip her good now. Her hand closed over her remaining money in a fist. She'd take that whooping, and if it was the price of his forgiveness, she'd take it with a smile.

There was a hollow knock at the door, and Lucy picked up her bag and gave a sigh of farewell to the room she'd never even managed to sleep in. It was five o'clock now, and there would be people clamoring to come in. Her key jiggled in the lock, but when her hand moved to turn the knob, it met resistance.

"For goodness' sake..."

"Don't open that door 'till you're sure who's on the other side," came a voice through the wood.

The man was crazy. "Saying that defeats the purpose—"

"You can't just open hotel doors unless you know who's on the other side," Ben instructed through the door. The knob held firm no matter how hard she wiggled it. "I thought you were raised in a hotel. You're supposed to know these things."

Wanting to laugh, she rolled her eyes and quashed a smile. Dryly, she asked, "Well, alright then. Who's there?"

"It's that stranger from the stagecoach, come to take you to my hidey-hole."

The smile she was stifling broke free. "And I'm sure he'd say his exact plans in just such a way. Now let me out, I'm starved."

The door opened and Lucy couldn't help but give a suspiciously sober Ben a stern look adopted from her least favorite teacher, Mrs. Swanson. She couldn't hold the frown for long and laughed aloud. "You are deranged."

He offered his arm and led her down the hall to the stairs. "You can never be too careful, Miss Ricci."

She made a humming sound of agreement. "Little did you know, I would have known immediately if it was the gentleman from the coach."

Ben quirked a brow, shifting his right arm that was full of the ever-present saddlebags.

Her look became sly. "I would have smelled him through the door."

9

— • —

CHAPTER NINE

The porter led them to a dark green Pullman sleeper car. People settled in the several tiers of the sleeper berths, and Lucy gave her ticket to the smiling man that showed she was to sleep in Bottom Berth 8.

It was a cozy little ensemble with white sheets and dark curtains that closed over the open space for privacy. Already an older woman was snuffling in the bed across hers. She and Ben ignored each other's gaze while the porter directed them to the curtained-off alcove with chamber pots at the end and instructed them that he'd wake them come first light.

Weariness settled over Lucy's shoulders after bidding the porter goodnight, and she gave her mattress a quick poke. Ben was frowning doubtfully up at his berth, and she elbowed him.

"Shall I get up top, then?"

He froze for a fraction of a second, then ran a hand across his eyes at the innocent innuendo. To hide her faux pas, she gave a melodramatic sigh.

"I must insist on getting the top berth. What if I'm below and the ropes break with you in the bunk above me? You'd crush me in my sleep."

"It's fine, I'll take the top—"

Much like he enjoyed doing with her, she ignored him midsentence and threw her bag in the topmost bed, then climbed after it with much puffing and maneuvering of skirts.

"See?" she panted once she was comfortable, wiping a tendril that had escaped after brushing against the thick curtain. "You would not have been comfortable up here, Mr. Stone. I, however, feel like a robin in its nest. Goodnight." She yanked the curtains closed in his amused face.

"Goodnight, spitfire," came his reply not thirty seconds later from directly under her.

She stopped unbuttoning her blouse and closed her eyes. What she would do to be down there with him so that he could say it in her ear. Though she was dog-tired, it was hard to fall asleep knowing that Benjamin Stone was laying beneath her.

All night, she tossed and turned, her thoughts switching between amorous thoughts of the man below and worries about her father's anger when she arrived at Dogwood.

WHEN THEY WOKE the next morning, Lucy and Ben were both sluggish and reserved.

A friendly new porter showed them to a diner car, and they sat across from each other at a table just big enough to hold two cups of coffee, cold biscuits, and a motley of preserves and jellies. They ate quickly and without complaint. Ben's coffee was black and oily with one sugar. Lucy's was pale with three sugars. The conductor bid them good morning and notified them that their stop in Houston was on schedule for 9:30 am.

"I can hardly believe it," Lucy proclaimed, mouth soft and eyes wide after the conductor left to converse with the other passengers. "I may well be home by tonight. We're almost there."

"Appears so." He took a swallow of his coffee and looked outside.

Lucy had never known such a closemouthed person. Her thoughts were eating her alive, but he spoke not a word.

"Tell me more about you. We have over two hours before we never see each other again." She knew it was a dramatic statement, meant to get what she wanted, but she couldn't force herself to care.

He'd kept his hat off for once. His hair curled around his ears, hiding the tops from her view. "What do you want to know?"

"What's your middle name?"

His eyes grew wary. "Ricardo."

She made a show of serenely stirring her coffee. "Do you have Italian blood?" Her question was unaffected, and she offered him a polite smile.

The booth he sat in creaked when he sat back. "No. My mother was half-Mexican." He paused, then asked, "That matter to you?"

"Why would it?" She tried hard not to let defensiveness sharpen her words. "That would be very hypocritical of me. I asked because my father is full Italian, and I wondered if your family hailed from Italy. Does that offend *you*?"

Ben raised his hands in entreaty, eyes big and shocked as if she'd drawn the derringer in her bag. "No ma'am!"

The spoon in her coffee clattered and she gave her hand a frustrated wave. "Well, you should have seen your face, Mr. Stone! Have I ever judged another person in your presence? My, but you must have a low opinion of me. I was only curious about the name."

"Keep your hat on, spitfire," he whispered, leaning forward, and glancing at curious passengers around them. "It matters to a lot of people."

"Not me," she grumbled, frowning into her coffee, tepid now. Then his words sank in, and she grimaced. He'd spoken of his mother in the past tense. "I'm sorry about your mother. It was uncouth of me to pry." Maybe her death was the reason for his journey home.

"She's been gone a while now, eighteen years or so, there's no reason to be sorry." He clasped his hands and looked down at them. "I reckon she'd like it if I talked more about her."

"Why don't you?" Lucy put her chin in her hand and propped her elbow on the table. "Did she look like you?"

He picked at a gouge in the tabletop. "She was a lot smaller than me, and her temper ran hotter, that's for sure. But she was a fair woman. She only chased me around with anything she could lay her hands on when I deserved a good wallop."

Lucy laughed at the thought of a youthful Ben running from an irate mother. "Don't you know that running just means your whooping will be worse?"

"When you've got an angry mama hollerin' in Spanish things that would make your hair curl, you ran for your life and came back when her temper cooled off." He laughed around the rim of his coffee mug and asked, "Your Papa ever tear your hide?"

She grimaced. "No, but I think that will change in the near future. It was Minnie who would get after me with a wooden spoon and beat me half to death with it." She tried not to think of how sorely disappointed Minnie would be in her when she made it home.

"Who's Minnie?"

"She's the woman who helped my father raise me. She's the diner's cook, and she's closer to me than my own mother."

There was a moment of silence.

Then, he nodded and grunted, "That wooden spoon why your nose ain't so stuck up in the air like the other ladies? You don't whine like no city miss."

It was almost an out-and-out compliment, and it made her laugh. "I suppose so. Minnie taught me to be hardworking, and Papa taught me to be kind. I imagine this is the result of their rearing." She gestured down her person and grew still when his gaze ran the length of her.

He cleared his throat, clasped his hands behind his neck in a stretch, and glanced out the window again. "You think about what you're going to do when we make it to Houston?"

"I have enough money for a stage home."

"If I were you, I'd wire your Pa and wait for him in a hotel."

The thought of waiting made her want to shout, "No!" She said carefully instead, "Wires are too expensive. It will take less than a day's travel to get home on a stage."

Ben was looking at her now, shaking his head, and it spiked her temper.

That blasted, infuriating know-all! He was the kind of man that tried to think for a woman, and it drove her endlessly mad.

"It's safer to wait," he was saying. "You'd get plenty of rest that way, and I'm sure he'd appreciate word as soon as possible. It might even give him time to cool down before he made it to you. I'm sure he's chomping at the bit right now."

Attempting not to grind her teeth, she lied, "I shall give it some thought."

For the next two hours, they went back and forth on safer things. He asked about her sibling, and it didn't take long before he had an idea of just how she felt about her older sister, Beth. She asked about his and was pleased when he told her about a younger brother about her age, named John Junior. There was a wealth of affection when Ben talked about Junior. He went on at length about a young, troublesome little boy that followed his shadow and tried to mimic the way he rode, dressed, and talked. When he asked if she'd ever been in a fight, she covered her face.

"No, but I did chase a group of girls away from Poppy O'Connell when I was thirteen. They were surrounding her, taunting her." It had been the year before her mother had taken her away, and she remembered that day vividly. Ben leaned forward, and she looked at him, arrested by the complete attention his eyes gave her. His beard was thick as a beaver pelt, so dense she couldn't see the skin through it. It was just long enough to hide the natural planes of his cheeks and the cut of his jaw beneath it. What would he look like clean-shaven? And what would he think if he knew all about Poppy?

Telling him the crucial bits wouldn't hurt his opinion of her friend too terribly much. "Poppy was new in town. They found out what her mother did for a living at the saloon down the street. Her daddy was a gambler and had abandoned them to settle a debt with a saloon owner a few states over. Her mama was poor, Irish and condemned for it, and was tired of working in factories, so I guess she stayed in the...saloon profession to get by and feed her child. She didn't know anything else." Lucy shrugged and glanced out the window, wondering how much closer they were to Houston. "It wasn't right for those girls to tease Poppy just because of what her mama did. She couldn't help it, and she still went to school every day so she could make something of herself."

There was a strange light in Ben's eyes now. "You befriended her."

"Oh, yes. Besides Franny, Poppy was my best friend. Oh, we would get in a heap of trouble. We'd smoke Papa's cigars and drink his spirits—" she paused, remembering telling Peter this exact secret. There was no censure in Ben's eyes. Only knowing amusement.

"I reckon you were something else. Look at you now. Traveling alone without a care in the world."

Lucy shook her head. "Oh, I do care. Very much."

"Not many girls your age would have the gumption." For the first time, grudging respect crept into Ben's voice. It made her warm inside, eased some part of her that had grown tight and worried of condemnation, and she nodded with passion.

"Yes, Mr. Stone. I know what I want out of life, and it isn't in Atlanta or Boston, and definitely not in New York." Her chin squared. "I'll admit it wasn't well planned, but maybe there was a reason I sat beside you on that train."

When red crept over Ben's tanned neck, it made Lucy's fingers twitch to touch it. "And here I was thinkin' you were sent to make me lose sleep."

Laughing, Lucy swatted the table close to his hand. "I apologized for that! Lord, you have a long memory."

For a long while, they teased and picked until the conductor announced that the train would be making its final stop in a quarter-hour. Something desperate moved around in her ribcage, a fish placed in a too-small bucket, swimming round and around in tight circles. Should she dare make another overture? Desperation wasn't attractive, even amongst friends. She was far too attracted to him to be just friends, though. And he didn't even seem to realize it. Sometimes he was downright closed off and crotchety. Being his friend would become exhausting over time, surely. And if he were to court some other woman, Lucy may just howl with grief and despair. She never wanted to witness it.

So, with this new enlightenment in mind, she stood and nodded once to herself. Theirs was a friendship that could never be. He was an older man with a chip on his shoulder, and she was young, just out of school. He wasn't even attracted to her.

Yes, it was best that they cut ties.

"LET ME GIVE you my address," Lucy said. She tore a sheath of paper out of one of her precious journals, dug for a pencil long enough that she started muttering under her breath, and pulled it out with a flourish. "Aha!" Her hand flew across the torn paper in a large, flowing script. Then she tore the paper in half at the bottom and handed him the address as if it made no never mind to her.

What he should have done with the address was fling it out the window and let it flutter away with the wind. Instead, he pulled out one of his little dime store novels she'd given him from his jacket pocket and tucked the slip of paper away into the flimsy pages with the reverence of a hundred-dollar banknote. When she glanced up expectantly at him, holding the remaining empty piece of paper, he showed his empty hands.

"I don't have an address yet. I still need to buy my house and land."

Her hopeful eyes skittered away, and she murmured, "Of course," in that God-awful city accent.

"I don't want you to get ideas about—" he stopped, at a loss for words, and motioned a hand between them. "—this."

"*This?*" Her voice grew cold.

"Don't get all het up."

Her lowered lashes obscured her eyes, but her eyebrows pushed together mockingly. "Het up? If anyone is 'het up' it's you."

Ben sat straighter, her tone pulling an answering challenge within him.

"What do you think I'm going to do, Mr. Stone?" she taunted, but her eyes were dark and flashing when they met his. "Show up on your property with my father and a shotgun? Friends exchange addresses all the time."

"It isn't proper, Miss Ricci." Grinding his teeth, he prayed for patience. "After I escort you to Houston, I'll send a wire to your Pa so that he can come get you. It's the right thing to do."

"I don't need an escort, and I already told you, I'm taking a stage home, not waiting around any longer."

He snorted and leaned back on his bench leisurely even though his shoulders were tense. "I'll just have to let the law know, in that case."

Hurt suffused her face. "Why would you do that?"

Ben leaned forward again, impatience sharpening his words. "Because you do impulsive things and you're gonna get hurt. I'm trying to help you."

"I am not a child, I am a woman, and I am fully capable of making my own decisions." Her words were uppity and precise and it set his teeth on edge. "You're just bigoted against me because I lied to you, and you're pushing me away because...because you're scared to be my friend!"

His neck felt hot and he tugged at his collar. "We can't be friends, Miss Ricci."

"And why not?"

"Because you've been givin' me calf eyes since the first minute you met me, and it's not gonna happen, that's why."

Her mouth opened and closed, but no words came out. He couldn't look at her big, hurt eyes for one more minute.

He stood just as the porter opened the train car's door and announced, "Next stop, Houston! If you will gather your belongings, we will disembark within five minutes."

The train had slowed without their knowledge.

Lucy stood and kept her gaze averted, and soon he was following her erect spine down the aisle to where they'd stowed their bags.

Ben knew something was wrong the minute Lucy reached into her bag and tried to gingerly hand him his 41-caliber derringer. She was solemn and unsmiling, and her lack of playfulness added five years of maturity to her face. It disconcerted him enough that he tried to argue with her, as though she were his brother. But through every insistence that she keep it—he had other guns—she simply ignored him, placed the two-shot gun carefully on an empty bench, and walked into the narrow hall.

He didn't like this new, hurt Lucy. He missed the old one already.

He told himself tough shit.

They would never be more than traveling companions, never be friends. They would never be a couple. Sure, he'd expected her to be downtrodden, maybe like a little hound pup scolded with a roll of newsprint. What he hadn't counted on was a cold, yet polite, stranger. Was this what being married was like? He hadn't been married long enough to know. Tip-toeing around each other, speaking in monosyllables when one was angry with the other, acting like acquaintances instead of friends. It was just another reason not to marry again.

Still.

Jamming his sweat-stained hat hard on his head, he stowed the gun carefully into a pocket of his saddlebags and followed the steely, slim back of Miss Ricci.

Just two days ago she was blowing kisses at him.

Now she didn't even look back. He'd never understand women if he lived to be a thousand.

They disembarked the train with the help of the conductor, following the line of men and women in colorful skirts and plain trousers, hats, shiny black shoes, and scuffed boots. Lucy was the only bareheaded woman, but she held her head up and stared straight ahead, a girl on a mission.

Above them, heavy black clouds rumbled and flashed with occasional lightning. The air picked up, whipping one woman's hat from her head. Water drops misted across them, bringing with it a current of cool air.

Ben shrugged his saddlebags onto his shoulder, right elbow upraised, watching his companion warily.

Lucy paid him no mind. Her eyes were bright and keen on the tall buildings in the distance. Downtown Houston had buildings six and seven stories high, finely made with brick and stone faces and real glass windows. The streets weren't made of dirt like the little towns scattered to the four winds. At each street corner was a finely made signpost engraved with the proper street names. Ben thought Lucy would do well in a city, dressed in fine clothes, escorted on the arm of a rich, well-dressed man about town.

The Grand Central Station didn't have much of a board-walk, but they were protected from the increasing rainfall and walked beneath a great steel awning that kept them dry. To their left was a fenced area with trees and shrubs, and to the right, a tall, white building with canopied windows was the focal point for most of the passenger's attention. *Shelter*, it seemed to shout.

"I'll finally be home today, Mr. Stone," she said softly at his side. She hadn't cracked a smile since the diner car.

"I have to get Reb."

Jolted out of her reverie, she acknowledged this with a distracted nod and a wave of her fingers. She was asking directions from a man her age in a porter uniform, her mind elsewhere, as he made his way further down the tracks. When he led a grateful Reb down the ramp, she'd disappeared.

"Just like a woman," Ben sighed to his horse. "Give them a crowd and a distracted man, and she'll disappear quicker than a penny in a low town."

His pride dictated that he not ask around for her, and decided she would pop back up in due time. First thing first, he thought. He needed supplies; his were depleted. Attaching his saddlebags to the saddle, he made his way around the fence, keeping the brim of his hat low. An oilskin lay folded in one of his bags, and he brought it out, wondering if Lucy managed to keep dry wherever she went.

A dry goods store was behind the tall white depot building, and he tied an unimpressed Reb in the rain to get the supplies he needed for a two-day ride home. Canned goods were essential, and he might as well grab another canteen. His old one was in sorry shape. A crack of thunder made his fingers pause over a can labeled with a painted depiction of pinto beans with chunks of bacon.

The man watching him from the counter chuckled. "Storm's gonna be a fierce one, yes sirree. You traveling a ways, young man?"

Ben blinked at being considered a "young man", but after a glance at the clerk, he decided anyone would look young compared to that walking ruin. He grunted, "Day and a half. Maybe two. Depends on the weather, I 'spect."

"Well, you stay on the main road, and you'll be all right. It's when these whippersnappers take to those cut roads that gets them in heaps o'trouble." He mumbled under his breath as Ben put an armload of supplies on the counter. The old man squinted at something out the window. "Speakin' of whipper-snapper, that young fool needs to use that brake before he gets somebody killed. Would you look at that?" Ben gave a cursory glance outside, then did a double-take. A stage coming in fast jerked to an abrupt stop across the street. Two young men jumped off after setting the brake, laughing and shoving each other. The group of people that exited it were scowling and harassed. An old lady shook her parasol at the driver.

"Just get younger and younger," the man sighed, counting the goods with a gnarled finger, tallying the cans up with a slow scratch of a pencil against a yellowing notepad. "They drive too fast and can't stay on the main road."

Ben thanked him with a nod, grabbed the burlap sack of goods, and stepped out into the gray, wet world. With the rain came lower temperatures, and Ben was glad for his slicker and the jacket underneath.

"Ben!" a voice cried over the relentless rain.

Lucy was running across the street to him, soaked through with hair falling apart from its pins. He took his hat off and held it over her face.

"It's quite alright!"

Something was missing. "Where's your bag? Somebody steal it?" he asked crossly, looking up and down the street for the culprit.

"No, no, it's on the stagecoach! They had room for my bag and just so happened to be traveling North toward Dallas. I'm going to take a second stage to Dogwood from Huntsville." She sounded breathless, as though she'd run a mile, and he had trouble absorbing what she was saying through the din. "I should be home by supper."

He heard that time. Surely, she hadn't already purchased a stage ticket, and no way in Sam Hill was she taking the coach that had just rolled in.

"What are you talking about? Aren't you going to wait for this storm to pass before you get on the first stage you see?" His voice sounded angry and he didn't give a good God damn if that forced little smile melted off her face. He was upset because that's what fool women-children did. They made stupid, last-minute decisions and angered everyone that gave a damn about them.

If looks could kill, he'd be limping home right about now.

"No, the driver said he was used to bad weather, as long as I didn't mind getting wet." Wonderful, now her voice was all prissy again. "He said that he takes shortcuts and will shave off thirty minutes—"

Ben was laughing now, right in her shocked, affronted face. It was not a polite laugh. "Bless it, woman, how you manage to stay in trouble amazes me."

Brown eyes flashed sparks at him now. "In what way do you mean, Mr. Stone? It's a perfectly reasonable plan."

"If it wasn't looking like a hurricane, yeah, maybe. Look at that." He motioned at the treetops bowing at the strength of the wind. "I say wait the storm out, what's one more day as long as you're safe?"

Lucy shook her head in disbelief. "It's just a little rain. I wish you would have a little more faith and stop treating me like a child."

Talking sense to her was like arguing with the brick wall behind him.

"Miss!" shouted a masculine voice through the drudgery. They both turned to the young driver, who was hailing Lucy with an upraised arm. Water streamed off his floppy hat. "We'd best get going if we're going to make good time."

"Coming!" she cried, looking increasingly like the world's most beautiful drowned rat. Ben glared at her, hating her spirit for once, wishing she was more cautious, knowing that this foolhardy decision was because she was so close to home. She was becoming reckless again. She should send for her father now, so the man could meet her here and safely escort her home.

Her independence was foolhardy. Ben had a sickening suspicion he'd escalated it by rebuffing her offer of friendship on the train. He slapped the hat he'd held over her head against his leg. Reb shied away, nostrils flared.

Lucy turned back to him, chewing her lip and wiping wet hair off her forehead. Her eyes met his and flinched a little at his obvious frustration. "I truly do appreciate all you've done for me, Mr. Stone. You've been a friend, despite your denial of such a title, and made traveling less...scary. And lonesome." Her throat flexed as she swallowed. "You don't know what your kindness has meant to me."

They had to shout in the rain to hear each other.

It was his turn to swallow. "It wasn't a big thing. And I wouldn't call what I've been to you, *kind*."

Her hand, that capable, tough little thing with its long fingers and burn scars, grabbed his arm and didn't let go. "It meant something to me. I'm so grateful to you. I hope you get your land and make up with your brother. And be careful." She reached up on her tiptoes, paused, and wavered for a protracted amount of time before gently laying her soft lips on the section of his cheek bisected with skin and beard. It made his heart thrum like an angry thing.

He hated her at that moment. He hated himself more.

She turned around, got on the stagecoach, and was gone.

She did not blow him a kiss.

And she didn't look back.

10

— · —

Chapter Ten

Lucy was rigid with terror.

The storm had worsened the further north they went, thunder loud and cracking, lightning illuminating the whole world in jarring series of flashes. The coach had been riding most of the day without stopping, hellbent for leather, despite the protests of its passengers. Many times, they went off-track onto smaller, winding roads that tipped the coach alarmingly to the side. They were now on one of those such roads.

"We should be stopping," cried the woman across from Lucy. "How can they even see in this weather?"

"They ain't worried about a little rain, they're just trying to make the next waystation before sundown," the nice, steel-haired rancher to the woman's right consoled.

The nervous, small man to Lucy's left trembled. As he'd taken his seat hours before, he'd introduced himself as Harry Wimer. He had a stutter and small spectacles that magnified the way his lashless blue eyes darted frantically around the bleak interior of the coach.

"At this speed, the coach could crash. They-they need to slow down before we have an accident!" Harry Wimer's voice was high-pitched, afraid.

"Oh, merciful God, spare us," prayed the rancher's wife on Lucy's bench. "Please, please—"

"Everyone just calm down," soothed her husband. Belying the calm advice, he rapped on the ceiling of the coach with enough force to make everyone jump. He stuck his head out of his window, shouting in the stinging rain and wind. "Hey! Pull over or slow down. You're scaring the ladies." There was no need to mention the frightened man next to Lucy, who was now desperately leaning over her to look out her window into the dark gray blur of the landscape around them. They were off the main path, and the trees were so close that many branches scraped the side of the coach with sharp, jolting raps.

All this time, Lucy hadn't said a word. She sat white-faced in her corner and hoped for the best. She worried about Ben and hoped he was holed up somewhere dry. They'd hit the worst of the storm an hour ago, but it was steadily worsening. The wind and the hard, driving rain made even the heavy leather curtains over the windows flap wildly, spraying them all with water. Everyone was soaked head to toe. The young driver had ignored all the cries of the passengers so far; his response was to whip the horses harder.

"Slow down, you goddamned bastard," screamed Harry Wimer out of Lucy's window. She shrank further, watching him with wide eyes as he grew further unhinged. He ignored her, breathing fast and shallow at her window as though he couldn't get air.

Their world tilted, and everyone screamed.

The stagecoach had momentarily gone on two wheels.

Mr. Wimer fell to the floor, and when he clambered back up, the whites of his eyes showed.

Lucy's entire body had drawn tight when the vehicle righted itself, and everyone seemed to hold their breath as the interior of the coach was illuminated with a blinding flash of lightning. The following crack of thunder was so loud that her stomach and eardrums trembled from the reverberation.

The horses screamed.

Their stagecoach gained speed despite the driver and shotgun's cries to 'Woah', and the other two women screamed above the cacophony when the coach overbalanced yet again.

After that, things happened quickly.

The hysterical Mr. Wimer made to dive out the door and had it open when, reflexively, Lucy grabbed him around the waist. She thought faintly that she was mad, but instinct warred against her better judgment, and she was helpless to control her impulses.

He would die if he leaped from the coach at this speed!

The driver screamed, "Tree!" and the coach veered sharply to the left.

Harry Wimer, in the process of ripping Lucy's death grip from his person, tumbled out the door...and she along with him.

She felt a moment of weightlessness, of two precious seconds where she was flying while raindrops fell against her face and eyelids. There was enough time to blink them away before she catapulted onto the ground, cartwheeling across the road and into the leafy muck on the side of the narrow trail. Her breath whooshed from her with the strength of a body hitting wet sand and rock with extreme force. She was vaguely aware of the sound of equine and human screams, and splintering wood. The noises continued, seemingly forever, growing further away until all sound ceased with resounding abruptness.

Rain pattered on the leaves above Lucy while her mouth gasped like a fish; open, closed, open, until finally, her seized lungs functioned, and she took a huge, whooping breath. With it, came the agony in her hip, shoulder, and head. There was sandy dirt in her mouth and ears, and wet leaves coated her left cheek.

The silence of the aftermath was ringing.

Lucy blinked, wide awake from adrenaline, but disoriented. *They had crashed, they had crashed, oh God, they'd crashed.*

She was on her back, cradled in damp earth. She tried to get up, but once she'd eased to her knees, her skirt twisting around her legs in a vise grip, pain like she'd never felt stabbed sharply up her left hip to her shoulder. Her head felt tender, and her brain sloshed where before it had been tethered. The felled tree that the driver had swerved to avoid rested not ten feet from where she'd come to a stop. The bark was black with wet, and the spring green leaves were shining, the only bright thing on the trail that was much too narrow for a full-sized coach and four.

How they'd managed to last this long without wrecking, she'd never know.

Shouts behind her grabbed her attention.

"Help me! I-I think my leg is broken. Is anyone there? Can anyone hear me?" The small man, the one that had successfully dived out of a moving stage—and had taken her with him—was somewhere behind her on the trail.

Putting a hand to her tender head, Lucy winced, then called, "I'm here!"

She blew out a shaking breath. First things first. Could she stand? With the man's broken leg firmly in mind, she put tentative weight on her right leg, which felt normal and strong. Her left leg, however, was problematic. When she put weight on it, the twinge in her hip sharpened. Gritting her teeth, she breathed through it until it withstood her weight enough to take a limping step. There. Nothing was broken, merely sprained.

A quick look around revealed several broken, rotten pieces of wood from the branches of the felled tree. She made her halting way to one about the length of her armpit, grabbed it and thanked God it wasn't too rotten, then limped to the man with the broken leg.

He was in the middle of the pathway, rocking back and forth over his right leg. His glasses were missing, and his thin hair was all over the place. The poor man was white as death, and his lips were blue. When she made it to him, he looked up at her, looking for all the world like he was about to cry.

"Why wouldn't they slow down?" he asked her.

"I don't know, sir, but I think you may have saved both of our lives by jumping out of the coach. For that, I thank you." Her left cheek felt raw, her brain like mush.

He blinked several times as though he couldn't see her, which he may very well not have without his glasses, but he finally took a shuddering breath and said, "Yes, it was a very rash decision. But when I felt us go on two wheels, I knew I'd rather face my chances with a few broken bones in the road than be one amongst a pile of bodies in the aftermath of *that*."

He pointed toward the scar in the wood to the left of the trail.

"Those poor people," Lucy gasped. "I had better check on our friends. I don't like that I can't hear anything. Not even from the horses."

Using the filthy stick as a cane, she lurched to the edge of the trail that dropped off in a steep decline to what looked terrifyingly like a creek bed.

"Oh, no," she whispered. Luggage and clothes littered the leaf-covered ground. Several clothes items were tangled in shrubs and trees. Her eyes saw bodies on the ground, equine and human, without absorbing them.

The throb in her temples intensified, and she felt the faint urge to vomit grow and grow until her mouth filled with thick saliva. Lucy took deep breaths to control the impulse to purge, covered her mouth with her dirt-grimed hand, and stared wide-eyed at the tragedy.

Then, steeling herself, she moved.

The first body was the driver. He appeared to have been run over and was beyond help. She moved to the next. It was the shotgun; Lucy could see the angle of his neck from several feet away and couldn't bring herself to get any closer. The hitch had splintered and broken, but not before dragging the last two horses along with the momentum of the coach, which lay fifty feet from the path on its side in a flooded creek.

At the edge of the violently rushing water and cypress roots, the middle-aged woman lay on her front. Lucy dropped her makeshift walking stick and hopped to the prone figure. The woman didn't respond to gentle prodding or shouts, so Lucy ran her hands over the woman's face. She was warm. A soft prod to her neck revealed a strong pulse, and Lucy shouted once in relief. The man on the road yelled something in response, but she ignored him and attempted to drag the woman away from the water. Satisfied that Lucy had made the woman as comfortable as possible in leaf litter, she turned back to the stagecoach.

It had made its final resting place on its side in the angry brown swirls of the current. The yellow-painted wheel had stopped turning, and the door that she'd flown out of mere minutes before hung on one hinge. The elderly couple had to still be in there.

Lucy didn't think.

She took deep breaths and waded into the floodwaters. It was hard, made more difficult by the fact that her dress material, corset, bustle, and petticoats weighed up to thirty pounds when not soaking wet. Now, she felt the pull of them, the significant weight of her tangled skirts against the power of the current. But she was strong and young, and her veins were coursing with adrenaline and the instinct to get to the people inside before they succumbed to drowning.

A flash of lightning showed a brief glimpse of the pine trees above her lashing back and forth in the powerful wind. Spooked, more determined than ever, she beat on the bottom of the coach.

"Can anyone hear me? Is anyone inside?" The coach was more than halfway submerged, and she struggled to clamber on top, notching herself between the step and the wheel. Her arms shook and she bared her teeth, using all the strength she had in her arms to escape the sucking force of the water and crawl her way to the top of the coach. Cursing her skirts, she raised her uninjured leg and managed to hook it over the bars of the step and shove her body onto the coach.

"Can anyone hear me?" she tried again.

No response.

She stood on the coach's side wall and pulled the coach door open with its awkward single hinge. She grunted with the effort. With the door out of the way, the dark opening of the cab gaped ominously. There was a square of gray light shimmering on the surface of the water that had infiltrated the coach's interior. There were no people standing, hopeful and waiting for rescue.

Just water.

Lucy felt a shiver of pure fear, and her arms shook with cold and shock as she lowered herself across the doorway and reached into the water with a hand. Something soft slithered against her fingers in the murky depths, and she reflexively yanked her hand back out of the water. She was crying, and reached in again, this time grabbing what felt like soft fabric made buoyant by water.

It was a skirt. Gritting her teeth, she pulled with all her strength, using both arms now. Her stomach dug into the wooden doorframe while she pulled and pulled, endlessly pulling until lightning flashed just as the rest of the old lady floated up. The side of the woman's white face surfaced. Lucy screamed and drew away. The body floated for one awful moment, then sank back into the watery grave of the coach.

Sobbing desperately now, Lucy scuttled off the stagecoach and back into the water. Something sharp snagged her, ripping into the material of her right sleeve, but she didn't acknowledge the cutting burn. She waded toward the bank, tripped, then swam the rest of the way, climbing up the steep bank of roots and sand on her hands and knees. Once she'd crawled two yards away, she stopped and vomited. Mud coated her hands and skirts. Horses squealed and neighed nearby.

With the purging came clear-cut comprehension, delayed but sharp.

Three of them had survived, and she was the soundest.

She had to find help.

Reminded of the others, she shoved images of pale skin and blank eyes from her mind. Two people needed her. Then, she would go get help.

She looked around her for a moment and took slow, measured breaths. To herself, she murmured, "You can do this. Now, where are we and how close did we get to the waystation?" The wind was slowly dying down, but the downpour was heavy and plastered her hair to her head. Rain rolled into her neckline with a sodden, itching insistence. She wiped her face, distracted, and tried to stand. Shudders from shock wracked her body and putting weight on her leg became more painful, but she ignored all of this.

The other passenger, the woman she'd laid beside a tree with a thick canopy, was stirring.

"Ma'am," Lucy called and hobbled as swiftly as her injuries allowed to the moaning lady on the ground. "Are you okay? Can you hear me?"

"I can hear you," was the slurred reply. Her eyelashes fluttered, then opened, squinting against the occasional drop the canopy above her couldn't shield. Lucy cupped her hand over the woman's brow, and her heart seized with happiness at the signs of life.

"Our stagecoach wrecked," Lucy continued and swallowed past thick emotion. "It was pretty bad. What's your name?"

Despite the news, the lady's eyes remained vacant, unfocused. "Julia Turner. I'm visiting my daughter. She's getting married."

Biting her lip, Lucy mopped Julia's face of moisture. "Julia, can you stand? We need to get to the road so someone can see us, do you understand?"

"Yes, I understand," Julia said, then closed her eyes and promptly lost consciousness.

"Damn," Lucy cursed when shaking and lightly slapping Ms. Turner's face did not rouse her.

Helplessly, she regarded the steep hill with dread. She listened for hoofbeats or the clatter of a buckboard on the path in the hope that someone would come upon them.

There was only an awful silence.

JUST BEFORE DARK, the rain stopped.

Dark gray clouds moved fast in the distance, and residual thunder grew fainter as the storm found another stretch of land to torment. It was marginally lighter outside, wispy steel-gray clouds straggled behind the storm, hiding the setting sun and deepening blue of the sky.

Lucy comforted a dying horse.

The poor creature was an old chestnut mare, long-legged and brawny with lean muscles. Two of her legs were broken, and she laid on her side, big stomach heaving as her ribs flexed and showed in relief. The mare's companion lay dead beside her, a mousy gray gelding, splattered with mud and pine needles. The remaining two lead horses were gone; they had somehow come untethered from the others during the chaos and had absconded.

Wet and cold, Lucy stroked the neck of the mare, soothing her with words that didn't make sense.

She'd managed to drag Ms. Turner up the slope to lay beside a silent Mr. Wimer. He hadn't responded to the fate of the others, but he had dug a handkerchief out and struggled to keep the rain from their unconscious companion's face. On her way back to the bodies of the driver and shotgun, she'd had to stagger past deep ruts in the soft sand from the stagecoach's tumultuous journey from road to trees. Grooves from the wheels showed their sporadic journey after the driver had either lost control of the team or turned them purposefully to their death.

Unable to face the condition of the driver's mangled body again, she'd circled him and approached the shotgun's form at a creep. He was so still. Not a twitch, no gentle movement of exhalation. She'd never seen a dead body like that before. There was the occasional outlaw that was posted in front of the undertaker's shop with a sign around his neck, but it had been different. Those men were killed on purpose. Someone had already checked their pulse, straightened them up, and wiped away the blood. This man's death seemed more real, more raw and weighted. No one had washed him, and silty mud covered his clothes as though the ground was impatient to swallow him up. Breathing hard, she'd placed her fingers against the harsh angle of his neck to check his pulse.

His neck was rock hard and cold as an ice block.

She'd flinched away, a coward, and had spent precious minutes rocking in the dirt with her face between her knees, despairing in the silence.

Now, she comforted the horse and forced the fear away.

As a child, adults had explained that if children ever get lost in the woods, they were to stay where they were until someone came to find them. With night approaching, it would be unwise to walk into the dark looking for help in an unfamiliar setting. Their best bet was to wait.

Unsure which would arrive first; nightfall or rescuers, Lucy crouched in the grass and leaves with the horse, wishing for Ben's pistol. Her little knife and bag were either in the boot of the coach or strewn across the woods. She couldn't formulate the courage to check the coach.

Thunder pealed, faint and constant in the distance, and she laid her head on the damp, warm neck of the mare. If the rain returned....

Lucy's head shot up, and her pale face slackened with hope. That wasn't thunder. Those were hoof beats!

Rising from her crouch with a grimace, she struggled up the bank to the path and squinted up the road. It was a rider, and he was coming in fast.

Waving her right arm, voice stuck in her throat with acute gratefulness, Lucy planted herself in the middle of the road until the features of the horse and rider came into view.

It was Reb and Ben.

THE ONLY TIME Ben had ridden Reb this hard was when he was trying to reach the front of a stampede to turn it. His thoughts were chaotic, filled with bone-deep fear.

Reb had floundered after a couple of mile's hard ride, but Ben let him trot for a few minutes before urging him on again.

An hour ago, he'd reached the waystation in a small, non-descript town. Following the stage had added an extra day to his journey home, but he couldn't shake the resolution to look out for the young woman he still denied that he cared for. Once he made a decision, it was set in stone. After purchasing a pack mule and waiting out the worst of the rain under an abandoned barn off the main road, Ben had jumped from waystation to waystation, asking about the stage. They were making astonishing progress—dangerous progress—and worry ate at him until he quickened his pace, praying for dusk. He'd make certain the stage had come into the last checkpoint and bedded down for the night, then he'd give those young drivers a talking-to that they would never forget.

But they'd never made it to that last stop. The folk that managed the stage line appeared unconcerned, but Ben didn't want to stick around and wait. He'd asked about the shortcuts and trails the coach could take, and retraced Reb's footsteps in the rain, anger hiding his fear.

He wasn't at it for a half hour when he spied two horses tethered to each other rooting around in the brush off the main road, searching for fresh grass. Reins trailed behind them, and Ben's heart began racing. They were the lead horses from Lucy's stagecoach. He caught the horses and followed their fresh tracks up the main road before the rain could swallow them, and thanked God loudly and expressively when he passed a homestead. A large family with several men lived there, and Ben left his mule and the lead horses in the woman of the house's care while the menfolk loaded up a buckboard and trailed behind at a slower pace.

"You might want to check the trail that runs along the crick," the woman's husband offered after grabbing the three animal's reins. "Darrel likes to take that way when he's in a hurry. I've seen him come flying by on my way to go fishin'. It's about half-mile up the way, you gotta look careful or you'll miss it."

Ben had shouted thanks then dug his heels into Reb, frantic at that point. Sure enough, tracks showed the way, and Lord but it was a narrow path. He pictured the stagecoach crashing into the trees and exploding into splinters, killing passengers, killing Lucy. It turned him cold.

I'll strangle him, Ben thought. *I'll kill that driver with my bare hands.*

They were nearing a corner in the road going on five miles in when he saw the felled tree. His curses rang out, and he leaned lower over Reb's neck when he saw a shape limp onto the trail. A person with skirts. The woman waved an arm like one possessed, then she was scrabbling over the trunk of the tree and hopping along the matted stripe of grass in the center of the path. Reb saw her and his ears swiveled forward.

Relief came swift and debilitating, making Ben weak, bowing him over the saddle horn like a fist in the gut.

Thank you, God. It was Lucy. She was alive. She hadn't died.

"Lucy!" he heard himself bellow.

She was getting close now, and he reined back, dismounting and running before Reb had even slowed to a trot. He caught a glimpse of her face, the left half covered in bruises and raw scratches. Her hair was dark, wet, and completely down, matted against her head and back. She was crying and mouthed his name just before he caught her. He clenched her full against his body in a hard embrace.

She was talking but all he heard was roaring.

"What the hell happened?" he croaked.

"—I'm so happy you're here, how are you here, I thought we'd have to be here all night until I could find some help." Lucy was shaking hard, holding him in a death grip that surpassed his own. He splayed a hand against the back of her head, stroking her tangled hair.

"Sh," he shushed her. "Hush, I'm here now."

"Those poor souls," she was saying in disbelief. "Some are dead, Ben." Her voice steadied, and she pulled back. Her eyes were wet and pink-rimmed, her nose red and lips blue. "They'll never see their families, or hug their children."

He pulled her back into his chest, helpless against it. Her shock was wearing off. He could feel her falling apart against him, shaking and gasping for air. "You're alive. You're alive and that's all that matters to me. You're hurt, let me see. You have bruises."

"I'm fine. The others, Mr. Wimer survived, and so is Ms. Turner but she's in bad shape. I can't wake her. And the drivers, I couldn't pull them to the road by myself."

Taking a deep breath, he tried to calm his heart. It was still pounding as though trying to jump straight out of his chest right into Lucy's reddened fingers. He stepped out of the embrace and took his oilskin and coat off, draping it around her shoulders. She winced. Her left shoulder was tender, and her right arm had a long scratch on it, the sleeve bloody. His blood ran cold.

"Is this from a nail?" Lockjaw fever was just about one of the worst ways a person could die.

"I scratched it climbing down from the coach after we crashed. I think it was the step on the side that got me. I wasn't thinking very clearly."

Ben drank her in, the way she was standing and cradling her arm at the hurt shoulder. He wanted to strip her, see every bruise and mark, and make sure she was well enough to satisfy him. His jaw worked and a pulse flickered at his temple.

Gruffly, he said, "Let's go check on the others. Then we're going to get you dry and warm."

The story of what happened came gradually.

The man and woman that survived were on the side of the road, one conscious and in pain, the other in the dangerous sleep that didn't bode well after a head injury. The gouges in the road explained what words couldn't, and hatred for the driver didn't ease even after Ben saw what was left of him. It was obvious that Lucy had attempted to pay her respects by laying an article of clothing over his face, arms crossed and over his chest. The shotgun rider was similarly positioned some feet away.

After a terse warning to Lucy to cover her ears, Ben put the poor mare out of her misery, and his face twisted as it always did when he carried out this particular task.

"Christ," he uttered when he saw the coach. The red paint was vivid in the gloom.

"There's...there's an old couple in there," Lucy said behind him. He looked at her and didn't like what he saw.

"Sweetheart, get back up there with the other two, all right?" His voice was gentle.

Eyes swimming, she nodded and limped back to the path. His eyes followed, discerning that she was fine and wouldn't just drop dead before returning to the job at hand.

He pulled the couple out gently, one at a time, with constant glances up the hill to make sure big brown eyes weren't watching. He carried the bodies with no little effort in their waterlogged clothing, and brought them to the other bodies, settling them on the ground beside each other.

It was a damned shame.

Matt Kershaw made it to the site with two extra men in tow just before darkness fell. Lit lanterns hanging from the buckboard cast weak orange light over the path. The men whistled under their breath and murmured sadly at it all while Ben tried not to glare at the youngest fellow keeping eyes on Lucy. She was cleaning blood from the unconscious woman's head. Besides shallow breathing, there was no other response from the lady.

The men had questions, and Lucy answered them, but her voice quavered and she looked like she'd collapse at any moment.

Alright. Enough was enough. He'd helped all he could. It was time for her to get some seeing to. Ben offered Lucy a hand after motioning to her to stand and caught Matt's eye.

"She needs doctoring." The other two passengers needed it worse, but they shared a man's look, and understanding passed between them.

"Yep, these two are too hurt to sit a horse. Take her to the missus. Sally will have her seen to."

"Appreciate that. I'll drop her off, then fetch the doctor and the sheriff."

Matt approached Ben and clasped his shoulder. "I'd sure appreciate that. Maybe you could stop on the way back and get another wagon for—" He broke off and nodded toward the dark woods where the bodies lay.

Ben nodded curtly and led Lucy to Reb.

Lucy put her foot in the stirrup gingerly with gritted teeth. Her hip was smarting, that was obvious. Ben tried to lift her into the saddle, but she wheezed, "My ribs." Frustrated and helpless, he steadied her good arm while she slid behind the saddle sideways. It was going to be a damned uncomfortable ride for her that way.

"Can't straddle him?" he asked low, concerned.

She didn't meet his eye and jerked her head to the side. "No, my hip feels like I fell on it from a runaway horse. The last time I did that, I couldn't sit a horse for a week."

"We'll go slow then." He mounted, careful of her on the back. "Hold on with your good arm."

They had traveled in silence for an hour when she asked, "Why didn't I die, do you think?"

The answer was that he didn't know. Maybe God had pitied her. Or maybe He knew what it would do to Ben if she'd died.

What he said instead was, "You're too stubborn, I reckon."

For a minute, she was quiet again, then she relaxed against him and pressed her forehead hard between his shoulder blades. She covered his warm hand with her cold one and kept it there until they reached the homestead.

11

—·—

CHAPTER ELEVEN

L ucy rolled over on her injured shoulder in her sleep and came awake with a gasp. Her entire body screamed with pain, particularly her shoulder, ribs, and hip. She sat up on the pallet graciously made by Sally Kershaw and hunched over in pain. After Ben had dropped her off the night before, she'd taken a bath drawn by the kindly farmer's wife, dressed in a borrowed nightgown, and fell asleep as soon as her head hit the pillow. She recalled waking once when Ben kneeled by her sleeping form to check on her. His hand had brushed against her face, and she'd snatched his fingers.

"Thank you for coming after me, Ben," she'd whispered.

"Get some rest, sweetheart," was his response. Something pleasant happened inside her chest when he called her sweetheart, so she fell asleep smiling.

And woke up screaming, she thought wryly.

She pulled back the sheet Sally had tacked across her corner for privacy and glanced at the nearest window. It was dark out, with a tinge of gray. Early morning. Now that she was awake, her mind reviewed the events of the last twenty-four hours, and her aches settled into the background.

She had to stop thinking about it.

Shoulders squaring, Lucy stretched the stiffness out of her muscles, gasping on the occasion that her ribs would twinge. Standing was a feat, but the thought of going home gifted her with mettle. Even so, she couldn't ignore the deep purple bruises that stood out, vivid along her hip, which suffered the impact of the wreck the most. It was swollen with edema, and she pressed on the fluid-filled curve of her hip.

The dress Sally had loaned her last night was seven years old, a faded yellow calico with printed flowers, worn at the elbows, cuffs, and hem. It fit her well enough, but she'd had to leave the borrowed corset on the bed. Her ribs smarted too much. The house was quiet, and Lucy was despairing. She couldn't get the back of her dress buttoned up. Her left arm would lift a few inches before the joint stiffened in agony. A peek past the sheet showed it had grown only minutely lighter outside. Movement outside caught her eye, and she breathed with relief.

Ben was leading the pack mule and Reb, loading them up with saddlebags and supplies beyond the side of the house. Glancing left and right, Lucy snatched a blanket from her pallet, wrapped it around her shoulders like a cape, and scampered as noiselessly to the front door as she could.

The Kershaw's porch was narrow, but it reached across the entire front of the house. She limped along its length, glimpsed Ben again, and tried to catch his attention.

"Pst! Ben," she whisper-shouted, glancing around for anyone going about their chores.

He caught sight of her immediately and stopped fiddling with the ties. He grabbed the reins and hastened her way, leading the gelding and mule behind him. The porch didn't have a railing, so he leaped up beside her.

"What's wrong?" His eyes, bright compared to the dark shadows beneath them, studied her.

It was her fault he hadn't slept well. Yet again, she should have listened to him. If she had listened to him, they wouldn't have had to witness the tragedy from the day before. Guilt threatened to cripple her for the hassle she continued to put him through on this journey, and for a moment, she said nothing. She just drank in the sight of him, remembering clearly how she'd felt when he turned that corner on Reb.

Ben was always rescuing her. Discontent with that reality didn't make it any less the truth.

"Nothing's wrong." She forced a smile, but something tied to the mule grabbed her attention. "Is that my bag?"

Stiff and crusted with dried mud was her ugly green carpet bag. It looked deflated and half-empty, but her eyes grew big with wonder.

"Yep. I borrowed a lantern and found it in some brush last night. Most of your things scattered, but I found some of your clothes, your hat." He shrugged as though it didn't mean anything. She gave him a tremulous smile and brought her palms together, her heart full. It did mean something; it meant the world.

"Thank you. I thought it was lost forever." When he shifted his weight, uncomfortable, she swallowed her pride and lowered the blanket. "Will you do my buttons up? I didn't wish to wake Mrs. Kershaw, but my arm can't reach...they've done enough as it is," she finished lamely.

His Adam's apple slid up and down, but otherwise, he didn't give a reaction. "Hold these."

Closing her fist around the reins, she turned and let the blanket fall around her hips. When his fingers brushed against the small of her back, her eyes fluttered shut and she held her breath, waves of goosebumps erupting over her arms and chest. Aware of every touch, she wished for the hundredth time that she looked her best. Her night braid swung to her waist, and she wondered if it settled against his wrist, wondered what he was thinking.

All too soon, he finished.

"Done." He cleared his throat and took the reins from her.

"I look a fright, don't I," she blurted, trying to tease.

They were both surprised when he admitted, "You're beautiful."

It was her turn to swallow. Doing so was like gulping down a hot coal. Her sinuses and throat burned. She wanted to tell him what he meant to her. She wanted to reach up and kiss him. But instincts again warned her. She knew that those weren't the ways to approach him. A wild mustang was less flighty and suspicious than this man. She couldn't handle rejection from him, not now.

The sound of a screen door flapping open interrupted the charged air, and they moved away from each other.

"There you are. I was scared you'd left without saying good-bye." Sally stepped out, wearing a calico dress with an apron cinched tight around it. The worry in her expression was real. "There's a bite to the air. Come inside, dear, I'll make us some coffee."

"We'll be headin' out right after breakfast, ma'am," Ben said. "If we're going to get to her folks before dark, we'd best leave soon as we can."

Lucy's heart soared. When the woman's face fell, she stepped forward and grasped her new friend's hands. "Thank you so much for your hospitality. I'll never forget you."

"Oh, any Christian would do it," Sally brushed off the gratitude, but her cheeks were pink and her smile was genuine.

Breakfast was a simple affair; coffee, bacon, fried eggs, and buttermilk biscuits. Lucy felt the peace of the warm kitchen seep right into the roots of her. The cast iron stove was small, but it had fresh coats of blackening, and it radiated a heat that warmed her skirts against her legs. To keep her mind off the day before, she asked questions about the homestead, what animals they had, and what they planned to plant come spring. Sally surprised her by hustling across the kitchen to grab several labeled packets from the little corner pantry.

"Here, take these. These are seeds from last season's harvest. Keep them dry until you decide to plant them."

Delighted, Lucy hugged Mrs. Kershaw with the strength of her appreciation.

When they left, Lucy perched behind Ben on Reb, she gave the little farm a lingering glance and murmured, "I'd like to have a home like that someday." Ben looked back to see what she saw. There was a homely little cluster of buildings and tilled earth with the evidence of green sprouts hardening off. Nothing special or particularly nice. Before he could say anything, she asked, "What happened to Mr. Wimer and Ms. Turner?"

Ben faced forward and answered, "We brought the doctor to them, and they were taken to the next town."

"Will we have time to stop and see them?"

There was a telling pause. "Don't think so. It's best we move right on through. We have to make it to Dogwood before dark and still take it easy."

"We don't have to take it easy, I'm perfectly fine," she lied.

His answer was a disbelieving snort.

FOR HALF THE day, Ben walked Reb slow and steadily northwest. Occasionally he'd take backroads and cut through fields, keeping an eye out for angry property owners. There was no one. The weather was mild, the clouds that passed overhead wispy and non-threatening. There was no wind, so they weren't cold. If it had been summertime, mosquitos would've swarmed them with a sanguinary vengeance, leaving round welts that itched like blazes over every inch of exposed skin.

As it was, the weather was mild, the scenery beautiful with branches bursting into new growth down every tree line.

Now and then, Lucy shifted and her breathing hitched. And every time, he asked her if she was well. Her answer was always 'yes'. She was so silent that he grew worried. Something was wrong. She was normally a chatterbox, chirpy as a mockingbird, always with something interesting to say, and always with an opinion about everything.

Unnerved by the hush, he asked, "What's on your mind?"

Her arm tightened around his waist, and her body swayed against his with Reb's careful steps.

"You don't want to know," she said without inflection.

Ah, hell.

"It doesn't do any good to think about it." He resented this concern for her. The emotion was welcome as a snake in his bedroll, if only he could snatch it by the tail and whip it away.

"How can I not?" She was incredulous.

"It happened, there's nothing you can do about it, you gotta move on."

"In a week, maybe, in a month, certainly, but it *just* happened, Ben. All I can see are those people. The ones that didn't make it. It was such a needless happenstance. I just don't understand." Her voice rose and fell and her hand gestured against his stomach.

"Then talk to me about it. Don't just sit and wallow in it, let me know what you're thinkin'."

So, she did. For an hour she raged against the driver, wondered at why she'd been compelled to grab Mr. Wimer the way she did, and, after several minutes of hesitation, she told him about the old woman in the stagecoach.

"That was the worst part," she shuddered. "It was like a nightmare."

He knew what she meant. He had, after all, pulled the bodies out. The strongest stomach couldn't help but turn at such a job, collecting the dead from a fatal accident.

"The thing that haunts me is my mother," he heard himself admitting. Lucy grew statue-still behind him, her interest palpable. "I was going on ten when she died. We were alone at the ranch and Pa was in town with his buddies. I remember I was riding my horse bareback in the corral when I heard her scream. At first, I don't know, I thought it was a wasp or something that got her. She hated flying things. But then, she just kept on screaming. I got off that horse and ran so fast it was like my feet didn't touch the ground."

The arm around his waist grew tighter, but she remained silent.

"She'd been gardening in the flower bed and come up on a nest of copperheads."

Lucy's head pressed like a brand against his shoulder blades. For years after it had happened, he hadn't been able to talk about it without choking up. But he'd had nigh on eighteen years to make peace with it, and he covered her hand with his to let her know the wound was an old one, he was fine.

Taking a bracing breath, he continued, "I've seen men bit by a copperhead since then and live to talk about it. Mama, though, she had a bad reaction to it. At least, that's what the doctor said. She was gone not even an hour after she was bit." He remembered running after her to the kitchen where she grabbed the first paring knife she could find, and slit the wounds open, bright red blood dripping across rag rugs on the floor. He'd shouted, begging to be told what to do. "She told me to get water from the rain barrel, but by the time I'd come back with a full bucket, she'd hit the floor." She'd seized and was incoherent, and nothing he could do would rouse her. He'd cried hard, had watched her, unable to help through snot and tears, begging her not to die.

"Pa found me by her later. I told myself she'd fallen asleep and waited for him to get home so he could fetch the doctor."

"What did he do?" she asked, her voice thin. Her hand was unconsciously stroking his stomach, and he closed his eyes, brief and hard.

"He shoved me away, picked her up, and rode hard back to town with her."

Her inhalation was sharp. "He left you there alone?"

Ben smiled with humor he didn't feel. "He tried. I got on the horse that was still in the corral and followed him. That's how I know what the doctor said; I sat outside the door and listened." He'd meant to keep this next part to himself, but he found himself continuing, "After, when my Pa caught me eavesdropping, he smacked me good. He said it was my fault she was dead, I should've known to suck the poison out of her."

John Stone hadn't said it; he'd screamed it directly in Ben's snot and tear-covered face. He'd never seen his father so angry before that point. John had given him a last look of contempt, mounted his horse, and rode off into the night.

Ben hadn't followed that time. The doc, having heard, came outside and laid a hand on his thin shoulder. He had stayed the night with the doctor and his wife that night, the latter of which coddled him and gave him a warm bed and hot milk, all through which he accepted with the numbness of fresh grief.

"He said that to you?" Lucy exclaimed in disbelief. "What a horrible, evil thing to say to a child."

Her hand clenched in a fist against his vest, and he was grateful the stroking had stopped.

"I reckon he was just heartbroken," Ben said, indicating with a shrug that it meant nothing to him now.

"Heartbroken or not," Lucy shot, "I'd horsewhip him now if he was in front of me."

Laughter rumbled through his chest, warming it up when before it felt cold, hard. He stopped when that hand went back to stroking. It was wrong, but he didn't stop her.

"I'm sorry about your mother." Her voice was soft now. "Will you tell me more about her?"

Smile returning, he said, "Mama's mother was from Mexico near the border and taught her all she knew. She made food so hot steam would come out of your ears."

Lucy laughed, her head bumping against his back.

"I remember walking into the kitchen in the mornings and listening to them gossip, rolling out homemade tortillas on the table. I helped, of course," he chuckled. "If I didn't work, they wouldn't have let me stay. Helping them fry tortillas was better than mucking out the stables."

They traveled this way for some time, the hours melting away as he shared his better memories to keep her bad ones at bay.

AFTER SO MANY hours of constant riding, Lucy's head began to pound, centering behind her eyes, which felt tight and achy. A familiar sensation swirled topsy-turvy in her belly, and she let go of Ben to cover her mouth.

"Stop, stop!"

He pulled Reb's reins and turned in the saddle, but she was already slipping from her perch, her brow beaded with sweat.

Oh, no. It was happening again. She was going to be sick in the bushes. She ignored his queries and stood still, which helped a bit. She remained motionless, ignoring Ben's concerned watchfulness. He didn't ask what was wrong anymore; it was quite obvious.

In a hesitant voice, she asked, "Would you mind terribly if I walked for a while?"

He dismounted, the reins slack in his hand. "I'll walk for a spell with you. It'd do Reb good to rest."

To keep her mind off her queasy stomach while they walked, she asked, "What do you want out of life?"

"What sorta question is that?" Ben scoffed, scratching at his beard and then smoothing it flat. "Next you'll start wanting me to recite poetry."

"Just answer it, please." Her chin went up, and though she knew she was growing haughty, she couldn't seem to prevent it when he peeved her. If she didn't keep her mind busy, she'd grow sullen and morose, and that was an uninspiring way to pass the time.

"I don't know, I reckon I want what everyone wants."

Lucy wrinkled her nose and gathered Ben's spare flannel jacket she had borrowed around her against the chill. "That's impossible. Everyone wants different things. I want to write a cookbook, have a home and family of my own one day. Papa wants to have the nicest hotel in the county. My best friend Franny wants to sell her clothes to rich women and swim in gold as a result. And Minnie, she wants to be a grandmother. Are you wanting to be a grandmother, Ben? What? You said you want what everyone wants."

"You sure are nosy, you know that?" he said without heat.

Sensing a victory, she smiled at him, batting her lashes in exaggeration until he did a double-take and groaned aloud long and suffering.

"I'm not interesting."

"You are to me," she countered.

"You must've hit your head harder than I thought," he quipped, and she broke into laughter at his obstinate bull-headedness. She sidled closer, whining and urging him with the point of her elbow in his side.

"All right, all right, you win, keep that thing away from me." He nudged her arm away, pretending to soothe a sore spot over his ribs. She grinned fiendishly. "What I want is to buy the house I grew up in from my Pa—"

"The house your mother..." she trailed off, her smile dying.

"I don't think of it like that anymore. That house had more good memories than not," he assured. "Mama was practical. If she were around, she'd shake her head at me if I abandoned her home because of its last hour."

Lucy nodded, soothed.

He continued. "With the house, I want to buy enough land to train cow ponies for other ranchers and cowpokes during trail season. A well-trained quarter horse can herd scared cattle without shying away, and on a trail drive, a man is only as good as his horse. Be less stampedes and accidents that way." He shrugged it away, as though his dream were insignificant. Inane.

"That could save lives, that's a noble plan." Lucy nodded smartly. "I imagine there's good money in that type of business, too. Papa would approve of it for that reason alone. Me, I wouldn't mind watching you train horses. What does it entail?"

For another hour, she was his avid listener while he educated her on training horses from colts, teaching them subtle signals and cues with knee pressure, balance, and rein control. There were endless tricks to taming all sorts of horse personalities, and because Ben was interested in it, so was she. She asked a hundred questions and he answered without rancor or impatience. It truly was his dream.

Ignoring sharp, stabbing pains from her leg to her hip and up her back, Lucy was saying, "I've always loved palominos. They're so beautiful with that golden coat and cream mane and tail, but you're right. It's much better to have a smart, friendly horse than a pretty one—Hey! I know that house." The sight of a house on a nearby hill hidden between large live oaks had her craning her neck. "That's Joe Ebson's place. We're almost there!"

They mounted Reb and passed more familiar landmarks. Dogwood's city limits were less than a mile away.

Lucy was almost home.

12

—•—

Chapter Twelve

The ride into Dogwood wasn't the celebratory homecoming she'd imagined. The town was nestled at the foot of a low, sprawling hill dotted with oaks and conifers. The center of the town was visible from the steep road they descended, proudly displaying the brick courthouse that had replaced the clapboard building previously built in the town's infancy.

Painfully aware of her sorry condition and precarious perch on the back of Reb as they rode into Dogwood, Lucy kept her bruised face turned away from curious stares and familiar shops. Even with her eyes downturned, she noticed that the town had doubled in size in her three-year absence.

She directed Ben down the street that housed her father's hotel, taking in all the beloved clapboard buildings, noting which were further dilapidated, and which had fresh paint. When she caught sight of the grand, white building with its familiar porch, balcony, and round attic window, she pointed to it and cried, "There!"

It wasn't until they were sitting in front of the building, looking at the bold print on the sign, that the unbearable relief of having made it home hit her, the force of her alleviation pricking her eyes.

We did it, she thought, covering her mouth. *We made it.*

It was finally over.

The travel, the uncertainty, and the strain of running away, all of it sat hard in her chest. She hadn't forgotten the reckoning she'd have with Papa and Minnie. It also sat heavily that Ben would ride out of her life as soon as he dropped her off at her father's porch steps.

"Ben?" Lucy scrubbed her damp face and cleared her throat. "Would you stay a while, so I can give you a proper goodbye? Don't run off as soon as I touch dirt."

He touched her hand. "Wasn't planning on it. Someone promised me steak and pie."

Heartened by his teasing, she took the arm he offered and slid down Reb's sweat-covered rump. Her eyes drank in the changes of the building, three years of burning to stand *right here* in this very spot, doused as efficiently as a pail of well water. She was, strangely, not as euphoric as she'd imagined. The toils of the last week had scraped her raw, like sandpaper scouring a whittled figurine until it came away wholly transformed from the shape it had assumed before.

No longer was the hotel and its clapboard face bare. It was white—not with whitewash—but with real white paint, gleaming brightly in the afternoon sunlight over the railings of the covered front porch and balcony above. On the eave between the balcony and front porch, a long sign advertised in bold, black letters: **DOGWOOD HOTEL**.

A week ago, she'd have laughed aloud with pride.

Wariness, however, was wont to creep up on her, stealing these little moments of joy in case the happiness was false, a trick.

"What's wrong?" Having noticed her hesitance and dwindling smile, Ben finished tying up the animals at the railing, the horse and the mule drinking their fill from the trough.

No one came out with arms open, no one looked at her besides the censorious side-eyes of passers-by at her bruised and bedraggled appearance.

"The diner's not open, and it's not a Sunday. And the curtains are shut over the front door windows. It looks dark. And empty." Where were Papa and Minnie?

"Might be he shut it down when he found out you'd run off."

A horrible idea occurred to her. "What if he's not here?"

"Only one way to find out."

Blanching at the thought, Lucy ascended the sturdy wooden steps to the front door and tried it. Locked. There was no sign explaining why the hotel was closed, no 'Closed for Construction' notice of any sort, not even a 'Closed Until Further Notice Because My Daughter Fled Like a Thief'. It did not bode well at all.

They looked at each other, and she knew that expression on his face a little too well, having been on the receiving end of it in the past few days. Doubt and pity all blended into an awful amalgam set to force a saint into a fine temper. Firming her jaw, she jerked her chin.

"To the back."

They snaked their way into the dark, narrow alley between the hotel and Hobb's General Store, the tense silence a living, breathing thing between them.

All this way for nothing, that hush accused.

Well, damned if she hadn't prepared to face the consequences of her actions. But she'd expected at least some form of welcome; perhaps not hugs and laughter, but at least the greeting of the round end of a wooden spoon on her rump.

Instead, there was nothing.

The back porch was much the same, albeit also painted and furnished with a porch swing and several rocking chairs. The back door, thankfully, hadn't been replaced. Lucy surprised Ben by hiking her skirts to step on a chair and reach behind a porch rafter, but her hip twinged, and she paused, abashed.

"Will you reach up and feel around on that board for me? There's a key hanging on a nail."

After a moment's fruitless searching, where Lucy shot a swift glance down his frame from broad shoulders to thighs, he lowered his hand and shook his head. Disbelieving her rotten luck, Lucy shoved her hands into the drooping hair Mrs. Kershaw had helped her pin and winced at its sorry state. On a whim, she strode to the back door, thinking to yank on the knob and bang on the thick boards in anger. The knob turned with ease.

"It's unlocked," she breathed, and her moment of astonishment became motion.

The interior was dark, and it smelled like a combination of new wood and old dust. There were no lingering aromas of homecooked food from the kitchens, no inviting smiles from anyone behind the empty concierge desk, and no faint thumps from customer activity upstairs. It was as though she'd barged into someone's deserted home, the renovations modifying the space just enough to make it foreign. Most disturbingly of all, it was empty. No Papa, no Minnie. Ben hadn't taken one step across the doorway before she was yanking open another door to her immediate right, revealing the hidden stairway that ascended into the family's quarters.

Her heartbeat whooshed in her ears when she reached the second landing, and she reached for the brass knob that led into Tony's office. It opened, and another shock assailed her. His office was now a bedroom. The furniture she'd recalled from one of the nicer suites at the front now replaced the area his desk and broad-backed leather chair had stood.

"Lucy." Ben's voice interrupted her observations. He nodded to the door at the very end of the hall.

It had been Aurora's suite, with the best view of the corner street from an expensive bay window. From beneath the door, a shadow moved across the hardwood floor. They shared a glance, and Lucy's urgency dwindled.

This was it, their eyes said.

Her feet carried her to the end of the hall, and she balled a hand. It hovered in the air for an indeterminate moment while she was hit with a wave of uncertainty. Oh, but Papa would thrash her. It would serve her right if he sent her back to Georgia for being such a fool. Small noises behind the door proved someone was indeed in residence, and her fist wavered, lowered.

Ben leaned past her with a hard fist, knocked right in front of her stupefied face, and folded his arms without sympathy at her look of pure horror and betrayal.

"What," a voice barked.

It was her Papa's voice, rough and unhappy. Her glower melted into worry.

"I'll be at the livery," Ben said in a soft baritone. She watched him stroll to the stairs, and the fierce longing to either follow him or trounce him held her motionless.

"Who's there?"

Inhaling, she turned the knob and opened the door a crack. "Papa? It's me."

He didn't deserve such a feeble greeting after what had to have been days of torment, but it was all she could manage.

She should not have been surprised at his sudden and violent reaction. Slouched in his chair behind an ornate, dark-stained wooden desk, at the sound of her voice he jack-knifed out of the chair and was around the wide desk corner. He wrenched her bodily into his arms, and she grunted and flinched, her ribs protesting. He didn't appear to notice.

"What in God's name were you thinking, Lucy? Do you know how I have worried? I have wired every goddamned town across the southern states to find you, and none have had any word. I feared you dead!"

"Papa, you're squeezing too hard." Her voice was sharp, and he stepped back. She bent over a little, cradling her midsection. *Now he notices*, she thought as her appearance dawned on him.

"Poppet, what—" he couldn't continue, and they stared at each other, finally drinking in the changes of the last three years. Her bruises were florid at her temple and cheekbone that bore scratches from being scraped across several feet of road, and she regretted not thinking to straighten up. Tony found his voice again. "Were you set upon? Oh, God, if something happened to you—"

Raising a hand to snip that heinous idea in the bud, she denied, "No, no, it's nothing like that. Yesterday, my stage from Houston crashed during the storm. This, is the result." Her hand gestured, her mouth wry, but her eyes revealed the lingering misery.

For a moment, the years vanished and he cradled her face with his hand in the paternal concern she'd missed, his murmur soft. "It must have been a terrible wreck."

"Four people died, it was awful." Her chin wobbled. "I've missed you so much, I missed being home. Every day, I've missed it."

Two things became alarmingly clear.

Firstly, her father was quite drunk. He weaved where he stood.

Secondly, something was very, very wrong. Those letters, there had been hints of it in his writing. Had he written to her while drunk? But why? What was going on?

Tony whirled away from her, his right hand massaging the back of his neck, and his head dropped back with a guttural groan. "Why didn't you write? All of this could have been avoided if you'd sent a message." The accusation was apparent.

"I did, well, I *tried*," she hastened. "Mother forbade me to send you any more letters in January, and I tried to send one with my plans to come home, but it was...waylaid." It was a struggle to keep her eyes from filling and to hide the weakness, she accused defensively, "I thought you would be happy to see me, Papa, I'm here now. I'm home, all is well, Mother can't do a thing—"

"Damn it, girl, the hotel is bankrupt!" His shout echoed in the empty room.

If he had backhanded her, she could not have been more dismayed. She blinked in rapid succession, and whispered, "What?"

"As I said, belly-up. We'll be evicted soon." He motioned to the mounds of notice papers on his desk, one that in the past had been so conspicuously neat. His back was still to her. "I've got creditors breathing down my neck, Mr. Brewster considers me more enemy than friend these days." The quick swipe across his forehead showed her what a blow that was. His voice softened, and the Italian accent from a past life emerged. "*Perdonami, amore mio*, you should have stayed with your mother."

Lucy was aghast. "How can you say that to me? She stole me away, against my—*our*—will, then sends me off straight away to some boarding school East of nowhere." When he said nothing at all, frustration replaced hurt, and she rounded the desk to see his face. He was looking out the window, mouth down-turned and hair akimbo. "Why did you paint such pretty pictures in your letters? Why didn't you tell me the truth?"

Ignoring her gaze, he shook his head, sat down with a flop, and reached in his desk drawer for a tin of cigars. He was thinner, graying, with a hard, round paunch. The sleeve around his amputated arm flapped, where before, it used to be tailored to fit. The cigar was clipped and lit with unsteady fingers, and this time, the smell of the smoke made her feel sick. All this he did familiarly one-handed.

Finally, "I didn't want you to worry. I was afraid you'd probably do some fool thing like try to come to the rescue."

She flinched at that.

"There's nothing you can do that I haven't already done. I partnered up with Trudy, got the loan for the reconstruction, and made some changes. It all just went to hell after that."

Lucy turned and leaned on the edge of the desk, the way she used to when she was a girl. "What happened?"

Massaging his eyes, the cigar still clamped between two fingers, he admitted, "Trudy fired Minnie."

"What? What!" Disgust and heartbreak wrenched the words from her like laundry through a press. "And you let her? How could you? When?"

"Trudy didn't think it fit the rest of the hotel, having Minnie in charge of the kitchens. Wasn't a good look." Shame broke his words up, but she didn't give a damn.

"How could you do that to her?" Voice shaking, she stood and motioned, much like he had, to the past-due bills and notices on the desk. "And this is what you have to show for it. She was what kept this family together. Minnie was what kept this hotel running. Who did you have replace her, hm? Some old lady that wasn't worth her salt at cooking, but because she was a little lighter, Trudy found her acceptable?"

His silence said it all.

Lucy's eyes grew hot and irritated, and it was a struggle to swallow. Tony looked at her as though he'd never really seen her, and he slid bloodshot, sagging brown eyes from the bruises on her face to her clenched fists.

"We had to close the diner. People stopped coming. I tried to hire Minnie back, but she refused, and no one else would work for a woman of—" he paused, and Lucy shot him a reproachful glance while he found an acceptable word, "—ill-repute. After a month, we could only afford to hire one person to clean the hotel. Trudy didn't want a part of it anymore. She asked me to buy out her side of the partnership, said the hotel was sinking and she couldn't let her saloon go down with it. After that, I had enough to pay taxes, but I'm four months behind paying the loan."

"What can we do?" Her voice quivered.

"There's nothing left to do but just let it go. Sell what we can, and let the bank take over." His pause was longer this time, and when it broke, it was with the sureness of a gavel. "You'll need to go back."

It was as though he'd told her to go back to prison, and the words hit like a knife in the back.

"How did all of this happen?" She swallowed and now it was her turn to stare out the bay window, not seeing the people scurrying like ants, with their own busy lives and their worlds not falling around their ears. "This mess. It started three years ago when Mother took me away, and I never knew why. Why couldn't she just leave well enough alone?"

He didn't answer immediately. Then he braced himself and stubbed out the cigar. "Your mother found out about that friend you'd been accompanying about town. The whore's daughter. Women from town were writing to her, and you know your mother. She was forced to act."

Understanding dawned, and venom tinted her words. "Oh, yes, I bet it was torture for her. All the common folk expressing a worry for me. It must have galled her, knowing that if she didn't come fetch me, my reputation was at stake. Well, not mine so much as *hers*." She tried to force out a laugh.

A sob broke free instead.

And once they started, they wouldn't stop.

Tony rose from the chair and his hand dropped to her shoulders to comfort her. Lucy, with a sudden flash of red-hazed rage at him, shrugged it away and turned her back.

It wasn't Lucy he saw in that familiar movement, but Aurora, and all the times he'd been rebuffed in just such a way. Nothing had satisfied that woman as much as making him feel less than a man.

"I need a drink," he said colorlessly. "I'll be at Trudy's after I wire your mother that you're home safe. We'll talk in the morning."

He left the door cracked behind him. Lucy dabbed at her eyes with the borrowed dress's cuff and sat in his chair, still warm from his body. He'd left her there, after a week's hard travel and covered head to toe in bruises, to visit a saloon. She sat alone and absorbed what he'd revealed about the hotel, about Minnie, about why Mother had taken her away. That recurring darkness, the void of black inside, replaced her tears and kept her company.

BEN TIP-TOED UP the stairs, and it was just as eerily quiet as the first time he'd taken a step in this empty hotel. The place he'd imagined from Lucy's stories didn't fit the bill. He'd known from her pale, worried face when she'd walked through the door that it was as different for her as it was for him. His brow lowered and his ears listened for a murmur of conversation, or sobs of homecoming; hell, an angry shout would be welcome. Anything besides the oppressive quiet of a building with too many rooms and not enough people.

Her bag sagged in his hand. One of the handles dangled.

Had Lucy and her father left?

He reached the landing, and finally, a whisper of a sound broke through the heaviness. From the end of the hall, he saw the top of Lucy's dark head bent over a desk. She was shuffling papers. Some scattered to the floor. They were ignored.

He cleared his throat.

Lucy's head shot up. She looked haggard. Her hair lay bedraggled and limp halfway down her back, her hand-me-down dress wrinkled and stained.

"I sent for a doc. He should be along shortly."

"I do not need a doctor."

"The hell you don't."

She scoffed and went back to shuffling papers. "I cannot afford a doctor, Ben. If these bills were dollars, I'd be a rich woman. Do you think the doctor will take payment in late notices?"

He opened his mouth, but the question appeared to be rhetorical as she sat back down in her father's chair and continued her diatribe. She looked as though someone had tied her up and dragged her through a ditch.

"If I were a lawyer...." She trailed off and dropped her hands, blinking away what he imagined were white spots from the pressure. "Blast it, if I were a lawyer none of this would look like gibberish."

Ben rounded the desk of towering papers she'd indicated, frowning down at her. They were both dog-tired and she was in here, more melancholy than ever. She was home, she should be jumping for joy. The legal papers that littered the desk gave his stomach an ominous lurch.

He asked the obvious question. "You and your Pa have words?"

"Did we ever. It looked like he'd been drowning in spirits for days. He certainly had no compunction telling me how irresponsible *I* was." Her eyes remained downturned, but her jaw moved forward, jutting for a telling second. Then, she gave a quiet, self-deprecating laugh. "My actions had quite the result. How everyone must despise me."

That strange urge to protect her seared hot, an iron bar burning in his solar plexus, and he shied away from the emotion. "Stop feeling sorry for yourself." He was far too aware of his rough voice, and he took his hat off, twirling it round and round while he thought of what to say. "Sometimes people say the worst things to the ones they care most about. 'Specially when they're scared. I imagine if my daughter was traipsing across the Mason Dixon, alone and penniless, I'd drink myself mean.

When Lucy ducked her head, he crouched down in front of her, knees wide and wrists draped over them. He caught her eye with his.

"He cares about you. You can both talk forgiveness tomorrow, yeah?"

He'd never been so close to someone that he could see the tears fill up in their eyes, making them large and limpid. Watching Lucy's fill up now, feeling helpless as a lamb, he'd do damned near anything to make them stop. She was so beautiful when she cried, lips swelling and trembling with the anguish of the growing pains of youth. She smelled of sunlight, horse, and laundry soap.

He was still watching her lips when they spoke. "Do *you* forgive me, Ben?"

If she hadn't looked at him as though the answer truly mattered, as though everything hung on the balance and all it would take was a single word from him to make her fly, or have her plummet into the earth, he probably wouldn't have done it. As it was, he was eye to eye with her, close enough to feel the tickle of her breath in his beard. All he could see were silky eyelashes, spiked and damp, and they were lowering, resting above her cheeks for several seconds before raising again at half-mast. The blacks of her pupils expanded, dilating within the ring of rich mahogany brown.

Did he forgive her?

There was nothing to forgive, not when he could count the freckles on her nose. And when she licked her lips and they reappeared from behind her teeth, all wet and shining, he couldn't think.

He rocked forward on his feet, and she met him halfway.

The touch of their lips together, warm and shockingly lush, halted both of their breathing. He went back on his heels to retreat with the full intention of breaking the kiss, to escape from the slick feel of lips his body decided that it liked too much. Almost too much to stop.

It was supposed to have been chaste.

Comforting.

A dry peck with closed lips. He didn't account for her to kiss like a woman.

He also didn't account for her mouth to refuse a disruption of the kiss; it followed.

Lucy's hands were everywhere. One delved into the hair at his nape, the other brushed over the beard he suddenly, fiercely, wished was gone. For a moment he allowed the heat to swell, a moment of insanity while her lips parted over his, once, twice, until he was suffused with her taste and hot wanting.

The impulse to fling her away and mount her wasn't exactly the dash of cold water it should have been. For half a second, he allowed an explicit series of events to unfold in his mind's eye, a lightning-quick fantasy. Her wide eyes as he threw her to the floor, a flash of skirts, creamy thighs, and that darker, mysterious place he could plant himself deep in—

He snatched her snaking wrists in a hard hand-hold, forcing her away from his person with a quickness that nearly planted him on his backside. The chair behind her screeched against the hardwood. She'd somehow ended up on her knees between his. Blood pulsed, rapid and swift in his ears. Breath coming hard, he shook his head at her bemused glare.

Yeah, well, she may be angry that he'd stopped, but he was furious with himself that he'd ever started.

"No," was all he said, with painful finality.

"Why?" she challenged. At least she wasn't crying anymore.

"Because you're just a girl," he lied because being a bastard was better than admitting the truth. "You're young, you got a long life ahead of you. And play-acting a woman is only gonna get you in more trouble."

She ripped her wrists from his hands and stood. He followed. "Play acting? How could you accuse me of that when you kissed me back?"

It was unlikely that he'd forget it for the rest of his life. She made a valid point, and he felt boorish and simple, which only riled his anger more. There she stood, more tempting than any normal man could resist. This time, he thought before he spoke.

Gentled his voice.

"It's not right, Lucy."

Her eyes glittered and flashed, not with tears. "Why not?" she cried, arms widespread. "You must know how I feel about you."

Such a declaration sucked all the air from the room, and they stared at each other with gape-faced stupefaction. It was becoming normal the more time he spent around her, this sensation of being walloped by an iron mallet with tremendous force. She couldn't say things like that, damn it. He wasn't made of stone, despite the telling namesake. If she felt any way about it, it wasn't real, he told himself.

He was a convenient body, in the right place, at the right time, a handhold to cling to when trial after trial assaulted her.

Softly, he repeated, "You're young."

It was her turn to shake her head, and she did it as though the perplexity of the two words were beyond her grasp. "I cannot believe this," she breathed, walking with her arms crossed tight beneath her breasts to gaze unseeing out of the bay window.

"Find you a young man, a banker, or a lawyer maybe. Someone from town or the city that can give you the things you're used to. That you deserve." He tried to ignore the narrow look of challenge she sent him because it made him want to lash out. *Listen to me and do as I say*, he willed her.

"You act like you're ancient. You're only twenty-eight."

He ignored this. Ten years difference was a lot. Wasn't it?

"Spend time with your Pa at the hotel," he continued as though she hadn't spoken. "See your friends. Soon the boys'll be beating down the door to come call on you, and you'll thank me."

She deserved better. Better than that Peter fellow, better than him. One day she'd see that, and then she wouldn't think of either of them again. A spot of growing up would do her some good.

Lucy didn't thank him. She ignored him, holding herself together by a force of will and hardheadedness. What she needed was a lie-down, a bath, and some food, not in that order. What she didn't need was to stand in front of that window all night like death warmed over.

He tried one more time. "Live your life a little before tying yourself down."

Her response was silence, unbudgingly cold.

Cursing, he plucked his hat off the floor, jammed it on his head, and walked out of the office. At the stair landing, he paused and looked back. Her silhouette against the weak light of the window was still. She hadn't moved an inch and appeared as lifeless as a dressmaker's mannequin. He wasn't close enough to see her body wracked with tremors, to hear her breath sawing in and out, desperate for air.

Disgusted with himself, he disappeared into the dark stairway.

13

—.—

CHAPTER THIRTEEN

T he bed smelled of three years' worth of mold and mildew, and the blankets were damp. On the floor, crates, buckets, old lamps, and a variety of cast-off items lay in a pile of rubble.

Once Lucy had politely declined the doctor's services the evening before, she'd ascended the stairs to her old attic bedroom, ignoring the creak of boards that should have filled her with familiarity and comfort. At the top step, she'd stood frozen and peered around.

Her room was filled with old junk.

The attic space was long and narrow with a sharp pitch. Near the railing of the stairwell, positioned at one end of the attic, were piles and piles of discarded things; crates full of old lamps and knickknacks, old, broken furniture, and an ancient butter churn. Lucy touched the latter softly, a wealth of childhood memories of churning butter for Minnie on the back porch suffusing her. All the things she held dear, stowed away in the attic, forgotten.

If she stayed here long enough, would she disappear along with the other unwanted pieces of the past?

It became a blur after that disturbing notion. She'd watched as though through someone else's eyes as her feet strode to her old bed, groaning and sunken, laden with more piles of memories, thrown out and forgotten. Her arms in the too-short sleeves had lashed out, her hands ripping at the pallets and boxes until every item went crashing to the floor in a heap. The result had given her a brief flicker of satisfaction, making a mess for the sake of the destruction, and there it was. Her bed. The corners of the crates left deep grooves in her mattress that didn't fade, and her quilt was gouged in two places, revealing vulnerable cotton batting.

It had been dark in the attic. The small window had no longer filtered light, and the sounds of the night were muffled and eerie. Not bothering to find a lamp or candle, she'd peeled back the blanket and curled into a ball. Her shoes were on. The bed smelled. It was probably filled with several generations of bedbugs, and she wished for them. Lucy had hoped they'd come teeming out to cover her skin and drain her of life. They'd find her corpse months later, having forgotten about her until then, and shake their head sadly that she'd died at such a tender age.

You're young, live your life.

His words had crept up on her, a ghost in the dark. Had he said that mere hours before? It felt like a lifetime. If he'd meant to be noble, it was wasted on her. She didn't want nobility. She wanted him to reciprocate her feelings, to drop everything for her the way she was beginning to think she would for him. After all that time planning and traveling, she'd made it home, and found it wasn't a home at all. Would she abandon everything now that it was nothing? Ben had but to say a word, and she'd tail after him, get on the back of Reb, and his dreams would become hers.

In the dark quiet of her dusty attic room, Lucy relived the moments before he'd rebuffed her.

He'd crouched before her, and that cottony swell of affection for him had lightened the immense pressure of fear on her chest. Everything about him had been particularly dear to her, so she'd perused his close face shamelessly. She knew him, the way he ate, how his hard body softened in slumber, the sleepy way he looked first thing in the morning. His eyes were pale in the setting sun, his skin dusky, and the black silkiness of his hat-matted hair and luxurious beard transfixed her. She hated the way it hid the bones of his face.

When she'd licked her lips with him knelt before her, his eyes had watched, burning into her from within and from without.

When he'd kissed her, she couldn't breathe. She couldn't think. Her heart had beat like a wild thing, and her blood had rushed into her brain so fast she'd been intoxicated, drunk on his taste and a thick surge of ardor.

You cannot make him feel something for you that he doesn't, she'd reflected. It was as though God had whispered it, elemental and true.

You can't force someone to love you when they weren't ready, Lucy.

But...he kissed me.

Look at yourself, you're a mess. It was not desire; it was pity.

It didn't feel pitiful.

It was a friend's kiss until you made it more.

For hours, she'd lain there in her childhood bed and had conversations with her truest selves, her deepest wishes versus her sensibility. Beneath it all, the raw wound of her drunken father, the bankrupt hotel, and the lost Minnie lay quiet and dormant. She couldn't face anything more. Instead, she'd stared at black nothingness until dawn came and exhaustion blanketed her, soft as soot, with dreamless slumber.

A VOICE WOKE her from a dead sleep. For fourteen years, she'd been roused in just such a way, her name trailed by the sounds of the stairs creaking under a slight weight.

Lucy blinked her salt-crusted eyes open and rubbed them with the knuckles of her right hand. Her body ached all over, even stiffer than the day before. The owner of the voice registered, and the events of the evening before flooded back.

Dismayed, she eased the blanket from her and swung her feet to the floor.

It was Minnie.

The slim, coal-black woman was skirting the wall of castaways at the railing in disgust. Her hair was now more than halfway gray.

"What in heaven's name…" she was muttering, gaping at all the things she'd once overseen. Her eyes, black and shrewd, moved from the scene at the stairwell to the pile of rubbish that had been shoved to the floor the night before. Her full mouth flattened at the sight of such a mess. Then, she found Lucy and froze.

For an endless moment, they watched each other, three years an invisible gap between them. Minnie pulled a damp handkerchief out of her soiled apron with long, wrinkled fingers, and dabbed at her sharp little collarbones with it.

"It's hot as blazes in here, child," she said and stepped over the scattered objects on the hardwood as though they weren't there to wrench the small window open.

A breeze cooled the room in a slow trickle, and the muffled noises of town life sharpened. Light skewered Lucy's eyes, and she turned away.

"What in the world happened to your face," Minnie gasped, and those three years disappeared like smoke out the window. Her face clouded with righteous maternal rage. "What kinda trouble you in, Lucy Lou?"

Lucy couldn't answer. She couldn't speak. She hid her face in her hands and shuddered. Through her fingers, she garbled, "Oh, Minnie, it's gone all wrong. How could it have gone so terribly wrong? I'm so sorry, I didn't know—"

"Hush, chile," Minnie soothed, planting herself beside Lucy in a familiar, heartbreaking clutch.

Reduced into child-like wretchedness, Lucy sobbed and let it all out.

She told Minnie all.

Everything came to the fore; her treachery, her manipulations, running away, and meeting disasters along the way.

She did not mention Ben. It hurt too much, and she was already bleeding. Minnie was quiet and listened with occasional soothing murmurs. Finally, the whole wretched story told, Lucy drew back.

"Why didn't you tell me what Papa did, Minnie? How you must hate us—" she was trying to say.

"Now, I done told you to hush up," Minnie snapped, fingers trembling and terribly gentle in the rat's nest of Lucy's hair. "I loves you more than my own self, that ain't never changed. You can't control what your Papa does, you were in Georgia." And may as well have been in Egypt, said Minnie's unspoken conviction.

"Not even Mrs. Hobb said a word."

"Well, you weren't s'posed to know, now were you?" Minnie reasoned, patting Lucy's bowed shoulders.

They clung again for an endless amount of time, and still, it wasn't enough. Lucy eventually pulled away and wiped the snot and tears with her filthy sleeve, ignoring the disapproving noise from the other woman. She needed answers, answers that Tony hadn't given to her satisfaction.

"What happened, Minnie?" she asked.

The whites around the older woman's perceptive black eyes were yellowed, and they met Lucy's without artifice. "It's been a whole lot different after you left.

"Your mama spirited you away, and Mr. Ricci—well, ain't a day went by that he didn't struggle. That first month, I couldn't get him to eat a decent meal. Just stayed shut up in that office of his all day long. At night...." Here she paused and frowned at a crack in the plaster over the young woman's shoulder, a line creasing between her brows. "Well, he'd drink himself to sleep, most nights."

"So, the condition he was in last night wasn't a recent transformation."

Minnie didn't respond to that and brushed lint from Lucy's hair and shoulders.

"The first letter he got from you woke him up some. He started makin' plans with Mizz Trudy and the bank. He was fixing the hotel up for you when you came back, see?"

It fell into place after that.

Lucy saw what Minnie withheld. Tony, melancholy and drinking himself into a stupor every night. Then, a swift, expensive change of heart when he partnered up with his mistress the saloon owner, borrowed money on credit from the bank to renovate the hotel, and forget about his whole family deserting him. Would Lucy have done the same thing if she'd been him? Maybe. Maybe not.

What she would never have done, was fire Minnie, the heart and soul of the hotel.

After a moment's pause, when Minnie had finished relaying the somewhat modified news during Lucy's years away, Lucy whispered fervently, "I'll never forgive him for firing you. You are not expendable."

Without hesitation, Minnie fired back, "I forgave him a long time ago, so you don't have no say-so to be angry about it, not when it was done against me."

Lucy shook her head. "I cannot believe that. I wouldn't blame you if you had never entered the hotel again."

"Believe it. Lawd, but you need to be cleaned up."

"Minnie." Lucy clasped brown hands and halted the woman's journey up from the bed. Minnie sat back down, quietly attentive. "Papa's already given up. He wants me to go back." Her voice broke at the last, and it echoed in the quiet of the attic space.

Minnie was shaking her head. "You ain't no quitter."

"I don't want to go back, but—"

"Fight!" Minnie cried, startling her into silence. "You gotta fight, girl."

She couldn't!

"Every time I try, something gets in the way, it's not that easy—"

"You're here, ain't you?" Minnie stood and waved her hands over Lucy's sad, bruised state. "A stagecoach crash couldn't stop you, and now that you made it home, you just gonna quit? That ain't the child I raised."

Glaring now, Lucy stood, too. "How could you know me anymore, Minnie? I told you the things I did, I'm no better than Mother and Beth."

Laughter cackled out of Minnie, who took advantage of Lucy's current position and yanked the bedclothes from the bowed bed. "Whoo, ain't that a hoot! Reckon I know you better than you know your own self. How many times I had to pull you away from that stove 'fore I gave up and let you get burned? Every lesson you learned was learned hard. Ain't never raised no stubborner child than you, Lucy Lou. And ain't no one prouder o' you than me, best believe it." She whipped dust from the sheets as though she didn't notice Lucy's face collapsing. "So, if I gotta wallop that sense back into you, I will."

This time, when Lucy cried, Minnie didn't embrace her, but grabbed her by her shoulders and squeezed. "Growin' up sho is a lonely thing. But you ain't got to be alone no more."

An idea sprouted. "I could—I could stay with you, Minnie. I could help you start and run a business—"

Minnie looked scandalized. "What in Lawd's name you talkin' about?"

Lucy blinked. "I can't go back, but I can't stay here. Papa said the hotel is bankrupt. He'll move in with Trudy, and I couldn't possibly live in a saloon."

"Well, you can't stay with me. What would people think?" Minnie shook her head at the very idea.

Struggling not to feel hurt, Lucy said, "I don't give a fig what people would think."

"You should if you gonna run a business, girl! No, you ain't movin' in with me, you're gonna stay right here at the hotel and get it back runnin'."

Lucy didn't think Minnie understood, and repeated, "Minnie, I don't have any money to pay help to get the hotel running again, and I can't do it by myself."

"Who said you was doin' it by yourself? I'm gonna help you, 'course."

As though enjoying stunning Lucy again into silence, Minnie hooted with laughter, eyes shining with merriment.

"I couldn't ask you to come back," Lucy choked. "Not after what was done to you. And without pay."

Minnie drew up. "You're my little girl, in my heart you are. And you couldn't stop me comin' back. My daughter moved to Kansas with her husband to be with his Exoduster family. Jon works day in and day out at Mr. Rankin's farm, and I barely even see him as it is. You just leave it to me to help you, punkin'."

Love replaced all the fear and uncertainty of the last twenty-four hours, and Lucy felt hope bloom. Then, it was replaced by a deep-rooted fear, and Lucy looked at the window over Minnie's fuzzy salt and pepper hair. "We don't deserve you. What if, after working here again, you don't like the person I am anymore?"

Huffing at the ridiculous sentiment, Minnie turned back to the discarded sheets on the bed. "Just be the best you that you can be. If *you* like you, I'll like you just fine."

For the first time in twelve hours, Lucy gave in to a watery smile. "I'm so glad you're here."

Minnie's broad, white smile flashed. "I couldn't get here fast enough after that big fellow came to our farm this morning. Jon thought I was plumb crazy."

Freezing from her crouch over the mess on the floor, Lucy asked very carefully, "Big fellow?"

"Some drifter that says he knows you, says you made it home." When Lucy stared, obviously waiting for more information, Minnie's gaze grew speculative and sharp. "Black beard, cowboy getup, red horse, and a mule?"

Eyes shuttering, Lucy looked down. Ben. He'd be gone, then. He'd left the hotel this morning without a goodbye.

Minnie continued, "Nosier than the reverend's wife, that one. Asked a whole passel o' questions."

"What kind of questions?"

When Minnie had finally disclosed that she didn't work at the hotel anymore, and admitted that the diner had closed months ago, he'd asked if that had been a large source of income. Thinking that was none of his business, she'd remained close-mouthed, which was just as bad as fessing up. After that, he'd pestered her about how the hotel was doing. Minnie had stalwartly denied knowing anything, and soon he'd become agitated and rode off.

Lucy drank this in like a trickle of cold water when she was dying of thirst. It wasn't enough. She wanted to pepper Minnie with questions. How did he look? What precisely had he said when she refused to answer him? Which direction did he ride to? Did he say if he was going to come back?

Regret sat heavily on her shoulders that she'd allowed him to leave as he had. She should have never said anything after their kiss, should never have admitted her feelings. With the knowledge that he'd cut ties and left without a farewell, she was equal parts anguished and bolstered. For now, she tucked her feelings for everything Benjamin Stone in a corner of her mind and brought important things to the forefront like Minnie, the hotel, and how the hell she was going to get them out of this mess.

Because now, she'd be damned if she went back to Atlanta.

THE FIRST THING she did was visit Hobb's General. The floor plan and shelving in the roomy store had been completely rearranged, but everything else was the same. Mrs. Hobb crowed over the changes in her daughter's oldest friend, but Lucy didn't have time for a long reminiscence.

"I need to get the hotel back in business. We're in debt. How do I get out?"

Mr. and Mrs. Hobb had been shocked at the proclamation. For all they knew, the hotel was shut down for more renovations.

"Good," Lucy declared. "I hope everyone thinks that. As it is, Minnie and I are going to get the diner running. How is Papa's credit in your general store?"

Lucy left with a wealth of information from a helpful Mr. Hobb, and a large order for Mrs. Hobb to gather for the up-coming reopening of their diner. The next place she went, was a tiny storefront with a smallish sign proclaiming, Hartfield and Sons, Attorney at Law. Then, she visited the bank, heart on her sleeve.

When she made it home that evening, starving and exhausted, Lucy ascended the stairs and knocked on Tony's door. He was in, and furious.

"Where have you been? I've looked everywhere for you."

"Papa," she interrupted crisply, "I have a proposition for you."

Silenced by the confidence of her words and the busy way she glided past him and puttered with papers on his desk, lining them up this way and that as though she knew exactly what she was about, he stuttered, "I beg your pardon—"

"Minnie will come back, but only if she and I take over management."

Shock registered, blanked, and lit up his face. He wasn't smiling. "What do you mean?"

"We'd like to try our hand, co-manage the hotel if you will. But I'd like Minnie to manage the diner specifically, which should be a large source of revenue."

"Where did you say you've been?" he asked, still immobilized at the doorway.

"Mrs. Hobbs, then the attorney's office, then the bank. If there's enough change and improvement at the end of next month, you can sign for a payment deferment until the end of the year. I, of course, can't do it for you as I'm not the owner of the hotel, but the bank owner seemed to think that my plans weren't entirely without merit. With Minnie manning the kitchens, me the dining room, and you the front, we should get everything in tip-top shape and running the way it used to."

Tony shook his head, and his brow grew black as a thunder-cloud. "I told you last night, Lucy. I'm done with this hotel. I don't want a part of it."

Fire flashed in Lucy's eyes as she whipped around from her shuffling to look at him. "Then sign the deed over to me, why don't you? I'm not giving up. You can go to Trudy's and live there for all I care, but this is my home. It's all I've ever known."

"You don't think I've put my heart and soul in this god-forsaken building?" he roared, sudden as an Atlantic squall. She flinched. "This place survived The War, it survived my marriage to your *puttana dal cuore freddo* of a mother, I'm tired. Damn it, I'm *tired*."

Lucy's nostrils flared. For a moment, they'd never looked more alike than now.

"If you let this place go, Mr. Brewster is going to contact Mother to see if she'd be interested in buying out the loan with her money." Tony narrowed his eyes at the emphasis of 'her' in the last. "You're both still married by law. And it was her father who gave you the funds to build this place." Trying to control her breathing, she shrugged her shoulders and played her trump card. "Who knows? Mother may just renew her interest in this place."

She'd never seen her father stand so still. He was like an ice statue until his lip curled and his teeth bared, the one in the front still gray, still slightly crooked. "She'd have this place torn down within the week."

"What do you care?" Lucy snapped. "You're *tired*, you're giving up. What does it matter if it's torn down?"

What mattered was Aurora getting her greedy, self-right-eous hands on it, Lucy thought grimly. With a growl, Tony stomped to his chair, yanked his coat on without a glance in her direction, and left. Lucy listened. He slammed out the front door. Then, seconds later, he walked in full stride below the bay window.

In the direction of the bank.

LUCY STAYED UP late that night with Minnie and Mrs. Hobb, cleaning up the cyclone of a mess that was the kitchen.

Hours before, Minnie had opened the door and gasped, with Lucy right behind and unable to hide her dismay at the changes in the kitchen she'd grown up in. There seemed to be no rhyme or reason; the prep stations and pantry were a jumbled mess. Wet flour had hardened like plaster over most of the worktable and countertops. Whoever had locked the kitchens when the diner had closed had not bothered to clean up from the workday before. Old vegetables and empty meat wrappings lay scattered at the mercy of flies and gnats, and coffee had been left in the pot on the stove, molded over and thick as tar.

Something in her lifted its head sleepily and saw that the once clean, perfectly functioning kitchen had turned into a veritable pigsty unfit to serve food to patrons. She bristled with repulsion, and for a split second...Lucy turned into her mother.

"What," she bit through her teeth in cold disgust, "in heaven's name has happened to the kitchens since we have been away?"

Mrs. Hobb had chosen this moment to come in behind them, pad and pencil out and at the ready. She was a robust woman with the stature of a mountain man; most men had to look up at her to talk, and it was as known as the moles on her face that it didn't bother her a whit. Her face was speckled with a smattering of skin tags and large brown moles, but she had such a broad grin and boisterous nature that most overlooked them with time.

She had grinned then, looking back and forth between the mess and quietly steaming Lucy. "Looks like we have our work cut out for us, huh? Well, nothing for it but to get to work!" And with that, they'd pushed back their sleeves, and worked their fingers raw with scraping and scrubbing.

When they were finished, the double cookstoves were coated in fresh blackening, spoiled food and opened jars were poured into slop buckets, too fouled to even give to the slop boy to deliver to the pigs down the road. Everything was inventoried, surfaces shone with cleanliness, walls were scrubbed of old grease, and Mrs. Hobb wrote several lists for restocking.

While they worked, they caught up. Years' worth of conversation made the enormous chore fly by, laughter made weariness and aches fade away.

Tony may have changed from the gentle and sober Papa of the past, but Minnie and Mrs. Hobb were still staunch and no-nonsense. The two women were their same old selves, and because of it, Lucy felt for the first time since she'd returned that she was home.

That night, Lucy knocked on Tony's office door, Minnie in tow. When Papa had looked up from his empty glass to see stoic Minnie in the doorway, he had covered his eyes with his hand. Minnie took a deep breath, guided Lucy into the hall with orders not to eavesdrop, and shut the door firmly behind her. Lucy didn't know what the two had talked about, but the next morning, Minnie and Tony had nodded to each other in passing with hesitant, but mutual, respect.

News spread like wildfire that Lucy was back.

She used the town's curiosity.

People were anxious to see what the Dogwood Hotel's darling looked like all grown up. She put a sign up on the front door that said 'OPENING SOON: Join the Dogwood Hotel family in the reopening of the Hotel and Diner! Thank you for your patience!'. Inquisitive folks stopped to read it. Some peeped into the darkened windows. They remembered the food after Minnie's impromptu departure, but most importantly, they remembered the food when she was working. Rumor had it that she'd returned now that Miss Ricci was back, and wouldn't it be nice to have a decent plate of food in this town?

At first, Lucy was overrun with work, and she wondered if she wasn't in over her head. She swam in the endless laundry of linens and bedclothes, dusting, polishing, and waxing the miles of wood accents, beating rugs, and scrubbing around the modern plumbing of the renovated bathroom.

She was outside churning butter one evening, dead on her feet and grateful that for a moment she could sit down when Tony stormed out the screen door. He was already across the length of the back porch and glaring at the vulnerable white part in her hair before it slapped shut.

"You are working yourself to death. Stop."

Grinding her back teeth for a quick, satisfying moment, she said, "No. We can't afford a laundress. I cannot hire any more help until my first week in the diner. And that's only if we do well. We're reopening in two days and everything must be perfect."

When this 'new' Papa wasn't apathetic, he was belligerent. She could do with less of both. He took in her steel-straight spine for another moment, then turned his back. He hopped down the stairs and crossed the backyard. Before he got out of earshot, he yelled, "I'm having a couple of Trudy's women help you."

Trudy was in love with Tony, madly so. While the saloon owner's brassy hair and braying laugh might grate on Lucy's nerves, she wasn't so heartless she didn't see it. Trudy was also strangely, cautiously deferential to Tony's favorite daughter. To the saloon owner's reckoning, the bad side of Lucy was worse than the bad side of Tony.

Though Lucy was not wont to admit it, Trudy's rough-around-the-edges women were an immense help. That next Monday, the Dogwood Hotel opened its doors.

Waiting on people after three years' absence was like putting on worn and comfortable slippers. Lucy's smile was bright, and she topped off mugs with freshly made coffee while chatting with the people at the tables like they were old friends. Some of them were her friends. People newer to town had heard of the scandal of the youngest Ricci's departure from Dogwood for the whole town to witness and were downright curious about the hotel owner's mysterious daughter.

Though a visage of calm in the dining area, Lucy nevertheless rushed into the kitchens, terrified to find an overwhelmed Minnie...only to discover her oldest friend humming over the cookstove, dredging and flipping and plating with flying arms and nimble fingers.

Much later, she climbed the stairs to her attic room at the end of a successful night's work—once again back to normal and cleared of refuse—and smiled. A flash of muddy green caught her eye, and her smile faded.

Lucy pulled her old, grimy carpetbag from beneath her bed by its broken handle. When she opened it and looked inside, warped journals and the occasional crusted article of clothing mocked her. No matter how much she'd searched in the past few days, it remained empty of the one thing that she'd cherished.

It had been the scrap of paper with Ben's handwriting from the hotel they'd shared.

Her last memento of him had been rolled lovingly in a stocking but was gone now, resting somewhere on the side of a cut road fifty miles away.

14

CHAPTER FOURTEEN

Ben took his sweet time riding to the Stone Ranch, denying that he was a coward all the way. He'd stopped at the nearby town, and wired money in from his account. The wad of greenbacks burned a hole in his pocket. For years he'd saved up. It was a substantial amount of money, and carrying it on his person had him pricklier than a cat in a hound dog's pen. It was never smart to carry this much cash, so he held his rifle across his lap and his eyes on Reb's sensitive ears.

He'd spent the night at his mother's old house.

It stood, sad and forlorn among the crumbling outbuildings. The barn had lost most of its roofing, and the bunkhouse leaned precariously to the right. His old home, two-story, but on the small side, had good bones. The roof was intact, the foundation was still sturdy, and there didn't appear to be much water damage. Ben had scrubbed at his beard. It did need work, though. The porch was sagging, the door hanging on a hinge, and many of the shutters over the windows had fallen off. Instead of being disheartened by it, Ben felt a rush of inspiration.

Someone had tried to take off with the old wood stove, but it had been scraped halfway across the floor before the thief had given up. Ben would have lived in this house years ago, but his father had stoutly forbidden it.

That's why, when Ben had written him a few months ago about returning to buy the house and land, he'd been almost shocked when John had written back and agreed. The letter had necessitated that they discuss the terms face to face.

Ben sighed. That meant John would have plenty of time to plot some sort of asinine condition. Luckily for him, there was a lawyer a town over who'd agreed to look at any legal documents before Ben signed.

For the hour it took to get to the big ranch from his mother's land, Ben thought of Lucy. His back eventually lost that crawling sweat it tended to get when he thought of a meeting with John Stone.

He'd found the woman, Minnie, easily enough before he'd left Dogwood. After asking the woman questions about the hotel, and getting worrisome reticence from her, he'd been more unwilling than ever to leave. Saying goodbye to Lucy would have been impossible. He probably would have kissed her again. This time, he might not have been able to stop. He was no saint, but it wasn't in him to do that with an innocent without an intention of marriage. And marriage...it made him sweat more than a meeting with his father.

The Circle S was a big, sprawling ranch, and he passed multitudes of cow patties that littered the ground, evidence of thousands of heads of cattle. His Pa was one of the more modest cattle barons of the area, but he turned a good profit and kept with tradition.

In the distance, Ben spied a group of riders on their way to the main house for supper. None of them saw him, and he felt the unwelcome weight of lonesomeness. He hadn't seen any of them in years and hadn't written to anyone except Tia and Frank, Sol, and Junior. Junior never wrote back, whether by his own choice or not, and it stung. He had to remind himself that he'd left his brother a twelve-year-old boy who used to follow around in his footsteps close enough to share footprints. Why should he write back?

Still. It wouldn't have hurt him to send at least one letter. Maybe cuss him out, call him a good-for-nothing bastard for leaving him the way he did. Ben's only solace was Junior's mother. No matter how much dislike he held for his father, Junior's mother was damn good to the boy, and for that Ben was grateful.

The sun was settling down by the time he crested the hill where the main house was. It was an immense two-story structure, white with a lot of windows and a wrap-around porch with several balconies. There was fencing all around the house, separating it from the barn and other buildings that housed the ranch hands and livestock. A dozen tiny cabins dotted the copse of pines in the far distance, golden light filtering from the windows and gray, wispy woodsmoke trailing up from the chimneys.

Ben took his hat off, letting the gentle breeze part the black hair he'd acquired from Rosa and caress his scalp. He'd just have to grab the bull by the horns. Make his deals, hope to God his father put him out of his misery quick, say a polite goodbye, and hopefully ride like Hell out of the man's life for good. Even as he thought it, he knew it was a pipedream.

Reb stumbled over a wagon-wheel rut in front of the big house, and Ben solicitously dismounted. The horse was strong but middle-aged and tired from a week's worth of hard travel. He patted the blood bay's withers and walked to the barn for some grain and, if he was being honest, more time. He met a tall, gangly young man on his way out. They both stopped, frozen.

Junior.

His little brother was taller than him now, rawboned with a jutting Adam's apple and golden stubble that grew in patches all over his face. The thatch of white hair had turned thick and golden with age, no longer cut in the bowl shape that his mother was so fond of.

"Little brother," Ben greeted, unable to hold back a smile.

"I ought to be mad at you for leaving the way you did, Ben," Junior drawled. His voice had deepened out of the crackling sound of adolescence. He drew closer with a wide, long-legged step. "But I reckon I understand why you did it."

Junior embraced Ben in a swift, back-clapping hug that was returned fiercely.

"Well, dadgum, lookit what the cat dragged in," a voice hooted to their left. Another tall, wiry man with flopping brown hair and a Texas-wide smile loped their way. Ben's smile spread into a grin.

"Sol! I barely recognized John Junior, and here you are, ain't changed a bit."

Sol was the oldest son of the dirt farmers a little way down south. He came from a family of twelve, and as far back as Ben had known him, sent most of his pay to his family. After his mother had died, Ben spent as much time with Sol's family as he could. They were boisterous, hardworking, and funny as hell.

"You back to stay?" Sol asked, clapping him on the back with the force of his exuberance. There was uncharacteristic caution in his hazel eyes.

Feeling lower than a snake, Ben grew serious. "I'm done drifting. I made some money, wanted to try my hand at horse training."

Sol's eyes lit up, but Junior looked away.

"I'm hopin' Pa will take up my offer, and let me buy the eastward land."

"Your ma's land? You gonna fix up that little house you grew up in?"

Ben's grin returned. Sol knew his friend's mind like he knew his own. "That's the plan."

"It'd almost be better if you just built a house," Junior said, shoving his hands in his pockets. "No one's lived there but some squatters for over fifteen years," he pointed out.

"You know that was Mama's house," was all Ben said before changing the subject. "Think you'd want to help me get on my feet for a year or so?"

Junior's hangdog expression perked, and the three went into the barn together, and for a moment it was like those five years disappeared.

BEN SAT IN front of John Stone across an imported desk, surrounded by taxidermied animal heads, mounted guns, and maps and memorabilia from the Civil War.

His father was an older, softer version of Junior. Soft in the middle, but hard in the eyes and creases of his face. In front of him on the table were written documents drawn up by his lawyer, areas marked 'X' for them to sign at the bottom.

"So. You want my old property, hm?" The derisive amusement in John's voice was a cat scratching a chalkboard.

Nodding, Ben affirmed as politely as he could. "Yes, sir. The house and some of the property around it."

"And why should I do that? You're not just going to leave with your tail tucked between your legs when the going gets tough again, are you?" That ever-present scorn returned.

Striving to remain professional, Ben shook his head. "I'm here to stay. I made more than enough money over the years as foreman to pay what the land and the house amounts to—"

A fist slammed on the table, and Ben clenched his jaw shut. He should have known John couldn't stand to have a civil conversation with him.

"Don't presume to know how much that property is worth, boy." John was already fuming, but he slicked back his thinning gray and blonde hair with two hands, then grabbed a fountain pen and ink. "I've spoken with my lawyer, had some papers drawn up. The only way I'll allow you to buy that land, house, and other buildings outright is if you follow a few other stipulations I had in mind."

Unable to stop his sarcasm, Ben said, "Figured that."

A meaty finger pointed at him. "Watch that tone, boy. I'll throw these papers in the fire faster than you can blink."

Ben said nothing. He neither moved nor changed his expression. Inside, he was burning and hating. Outside, he wondered if he wore that hollowed-out mien Junior had sported outside by the barn.

Satisfied he wouldn't hear any more lip from his oldest son, John grunted and turned papers around smoothly, pushing them in front of Ben. "I want this amount for the property. I won't go down on it, so don't bother asking, hm?" Ben didn't even blink at the exorbitant amount. He'd known his father would give him a ridiculous sum, and had saved more than enough money to cover it. "Now this paper, this explains that once you buy the land, you'll no longer be a part of my will. Everything else, the ranch, the other properties I own, my stocks; they'll all go to Junior when I die. If you don't agree to this, I won't sell you a goddamned thing."

Pride, anger, and no small amount of hurt that was shoved back into some dark hole and covered with a lid of indifference made him ignore the warnings of the lawyer in town. He gave the document a swift read and signed it without hesitation. John smiled with cruel satisfaction.

"Good, good. This one explains that in addition to payment, you'll be foreman, without pay, for the cattle drive for the next year, and help with the roundups in the next five years. If you get the steers there in one piece, maybe I'll just have you lead the drives every year. Might even pay you," John chuckled.

And Hell would freeze over, Ben thought.

He took half an hour to read through the documents, line by line. Plenty of it was worded in an ambiguous, misleading way that had Ben's lip curling. He started crossing out things, a few smaller details John had failed to mention. Then, he wrote down some of his own prerequisites in the margins while his father scowled.

"I'll agree to the terms except these three things." Ben pointed to the lines he'd marked out. "In addition to helping with roundups, I get to cull a few of the steers for meat every year, starting now. I want a hundred head along with the house and property, immediately." John glared down at the new sprawl ruining his neat legal contract but didn't deny any stipulation. Ben continued. "I'm going to need a few men. You gonna give me any trouble if a few decide to come along and help me out?"

Laughing with an edge, John raised his hands. "As long as it's not Parker, he's foreman this year."

Ben scribbled that in, ignoring when his father bent to watch with hawk eyes. "One more thing. I want you to let Junior come stay with me whenever he pleases."

John's humoring smirk melted. His pale blue eyes grew flinty. "You're not takin' my boy from me."

"No, I'm not. I want you to give him the option to come see me any time he—"

"Like hell he will!" John roared up from his seated position and stood in a decidedly threatening pose over Ben. "You left him here, cryin' every night like a goddamned baby, and you think you're just gonna waltz in here and take up where you left off? It took me years to make that boy a man. Years! He was so far up your craw, it made me sick. He talked like you, acted like you, I thought I'd never get my son back. No." He shook his great head and barked a laugh. "Hell no. You want to see Junior, you ride your sorry ass over here and see him that way."

The door burst open, and a blonde-haired body barreled in. "You're gonna let me go with him," Junior shouted, eyes red-rimmed and lips downturned in such a way that sharp creases appeared at the corners of his mouth. It was frightening to see such a childlike expression on someone nearing manhood. Ben stood, fists clenched, but it was as though he wasn't in the room. Father and youngest son faced each other, battling it out with their stare.

"Do you really think your mother and I are going to allow you to hole up with him?" John whispered. Deadly. Threatening. "She'd fall in her sickbed and never leave. It's not up for discussion."

"Yeah? Well, how bout I take another trip to Dallas?" Junior's eyes had a manic glow that seized Ben's heart. Something was wrong. Very wrong.

"That's enough," John growled, eyes darting to Ben.

"You let me go with Ben, or I will. I'll leave and you won't see hide or hair of me this time."

John, so hard and imperious, tougher than nails and meaner than a snake...took a step back. Straightened his jacket. Cleared his throat. "You better stop those threats while you're ahead." Tried to be gruff. But it was clear to everyone in the room that Junior had won. Looking for a semblance of control, he pointed a finger at Ben again. "He stays with you, you're responsible for him. Anything happens to him; I'll kill you myself."

If Ben had swallowed grit straight from the river bottom, it couldn't have been harder to speak. Finally, he managed, "I'll have my lawyer look these papers over. I'll bring them back tomorrow and we can have them signed. Junior, I'll pick you up tomorrow—"

"I'm goin' now," Junior interrupted, and was out the door, stomping down the hall to his room.

It was silent as a tomb in the office. Ben stacked the papers, rolled them up, and stuck them in the inner pocket of his jacket. "What happened in Dallas?"

John went to a sideboard and opened a decanter of bourbon. "Mention Dallas again and you can kiss your Mama's house goodbye."

In fifteen years, John hadn't mentioned Rosa. Ben turned on his heel and strode out the door. God, but he hated it there.

The next day, he returned with the documents, more things crossed out, more things added, and John eventually acquiesced and wrote his signature. Ben thumbed out the money he'd grudgingly carried in his pocket for the better part of a week, slapped them on his father's desk, and got the hell out of there. Junior tagged behind, ignoring his weeping mother with a stubborn frown.

BEN PARKED THE buckboard in front of Hobb's General and set the brake with a boot heel. He couldn't resist a lingering glance at the white clapboard siding of the building next door.

Was Lucy in?

What was she doing?

Disgruntled that a month-long absence from the female hadn't stopped the constant wondering, and had only made his curiosity worse, Ben jumped from his buckboard and stomped up the stairs. The store's windows were large and painted in neat words advertising dry goods, canned goods, farm fresh eggs, and more. He needed to know if they sold fresh meat, and had a place for the butchered steer he'd brought. It was strapped to the boards, packed in ice, and wrapped in tarpaulin. When Sol and Junior had asked where he was taking the meat, they accepted the logic of selling it to the butcher shop in town. What made them narrow their eyes was when he refused their company and took off before they could argue.

It was obvious he was a man with a secret, and he'd glanced behind him a dozen times to assure his brother and best friend didn't get the idea in their head to follow.

The door opened and the bell above it tinkled gaily. The store was crowded with rows and rows of neat shelves, but the high ceilings made it less claustrophobic. Mirrors were perched in corners and above shelves to dissuade all but the stealthiest of shoplifters. Cast iron skillets and laundry tubs hung at the highest points of the walls, and in one corner clothing had its own section. A headless cloth mannequin wore a pretty green and white flower-printed dress with a ruffled white apron housing deep pockets.

The harsh scent of cleaning solution was softened with the factory smell of packaging: brown paper casing with wax interior, burlap, the woody odor of pallets and boxes. Easing into the comfort of the bright-lit room, he wandered around for a moment, fingering a shaving kit in a kind of stupor. Would she recognize him if he shaved? The answer was yes, and no.

"Good morning!" a cheerful, booming voice called from behind the counter. "Can I help you find anything?"

Ben looked up expecting the man of the establishment and was surprised to see the mountain of a wife instead. Mrs. Hobb was a large woman, not with fat, but with the big-boned structure found in Vikings, boat dock workers, and bouncers in fancy bordellos.

"You wouldn't want to get on the wrong side of Mrs. Hobb," Lucy had said once in passing. "I once saw her throw Mr. Lentz bodily from the establishment. He'd called her a not-so-nice name after she refused him any more credit. Even Mr. Hobb is terrified of her."

The memory made Ben smile, and he left the aisle with the shaving kit.

"I'm hopin' you can," he replied, taking in the bracing size of the woman, but still thinking of Lucy. "I've got a proposition, if you've a mind to hear me out."

"Well, well," Mrs. Hobb raised her pale brows. "It's not too often I'm propositioned by young, strapping men these days. Now, in my youth—" she broke off, pretended to think, "—no, not then, either. That's right, I was doing the propositioning." She let loose a deep belly laugh that shook Ben's teeth in his head, slapping the countertop and entire face turning ruddy with the force of her hilarity.

Some people's laugh was contagious, whether the joke was amusing or not, and he was unable to hide a quick grin. He was becoming more and more curious as to what kind of man Mrs. Hobb had managed to marry.

Clearing his throat, he smoothed his beard and tried to remember the business at hand. "Do you sell fresh beef? I've got a load of meat outside—"

Still smiling wide, she interrupted, "We deal with the butcher across town. He brings a load daily, and we keep it on ice out back. Do your dealings with him, he won't cut you a raw deal, give you a fair price."

Nodding, Ben shifted on his feet. "Well, the thing is, I'm not lookin' to sell."

"Not look—"

"I want to do a friend a favor," Ben cut in, tone sharpening. She may be used to cutting people off, but he'd say what he came to say. "I hear the Dogwood Hotel opened up the diner. I'd like to make weekly donations. I'll bring a steer a week for a while, and I'm wondering if you'll house it for the Ricci's at no cost. What they don't use, you can sell and keep, no charge. Would you be willin' to do that?"

For once, Mrs. Hobb was rendered speechless. Her thin lips parted. Closed. Frowned. The faint mustache above them trembled. Finally, she asked, "Why?"

Sweat gathered on his scalp under his hat, and Ben whipped the offending thing off to comb through his hair. It needed another cut. "Just tell Lucy it's an anonymous donation. Don't tell her it's from me.'

Mrs. Hobb's great breasts bounced with her sudden laugh. "Mister, I don't even know who *you* are. And she don't take kindly to handouts." Her smile grew sly. "But I'm even stubborner than she is. I'll accept your deal, young man, on the instance you tell me who I'm doing business with."

"Ben Stone." He replaced his hat and tipped it at her.

Small blue eyes registered the name with no surprise, and her sly smile gentled as much as it could on a woman like her. "Hm. You can bring your buckboard out back, on the westward side," was all she said.

"Thank you, ma'am."

He'd made it to the door before she hollered a word of warning. "If you fancy her, you might want to act quick. That girl has caused quite a stir, has half the men in town panting after her."

Ben froze, hand stuck motionless to the door handle.

"It makes for good business, I imagine. But you know as well as I that they ain't there just for pie."

Mrs. Hobb didn't laugh this time.

She didn't sound one bit amused.

Ben's hand tightened hard on the handle, feeling the cold metal bite into a calloused palm. In the reflection of the window next to the door, a deep scowl crawled across his face. Mrs. Hobb tried not to grin as he gave her a cursory nod and left, but she knew. That boy was in a whole heap of trouble if he thought he could keep away from that girl, not with feelings like those on his face for the whole world to see.

BEN WALKED INTO the diner after entering the hotel that he'd sworn to himself that he wouldn't step foot in. He'd nodded to the middle-aged man at the front desk who was tall and lean and looked an awful lot like Lucy. The family resemblance was acute. One of the man's arms was amputated at the elbow, solidifying Ben's suspicions. Mr. Ricci's bone structure jutted and edged where Lucy's was fine and curved. He'd given Ben a passing glance, saw the direction he was headed, and with a rueful head shake, turned back to the papers out of sight.

No doubt he was only one of many men in this place since Lucy's arrival.

The smells from the kitchen had hit him on the boardwalk outside before he'd even reached the front door. He'd only meant to walk past the front door, to see what the flyers posted had said. Fragrant frying meats and stewing greens with notes of bacon had set his saliva glands off, flooding his mouth and stirring his empty stomach. It growled loud, hollow, and demanding.

His feet made the decision for him and stepped across the threshold before his mind even knew what it was doing. Unlike the first time he'd meandered his way through the dark halls, the foyer was well-lit. The gas lights had been turned on and glowed across the gleaming wax of crown moldings and creamy wallpaper. The banister at his left shone without a speck of dust, and conversations from the dining area at his right filled the space with a comfortable feeling of life.

It had to be Lucy's doing. She'd given the building a heart-beat.

The dining room was full to the brim with customers. He'd expected there to be young men and was annoyed to see that he was right. The room was medium-sized with a large window overlooking the veranda and Main Street. Square tables decorated with gingham tablecloths, tin salt and pepper cellars, and tiny vases of flower sprigs took up most of the space. Legs sprawled and lolled in spaces between them, hats hung on the pegs of the chairs, and eyes watched as the solid wood door swung open. A slim back in a blue shirtwaist tucked into a navy skirt backed out, arms held aloft. One hand grasped a coffee pot, and the other a heavy tray of plates heaped with food. How Lucy kept the tray balanced, Ben had no idea.

Her head was bare, mahogany tresses shining in thick coils. Her cheeks lifted in a smile and she called something out to someone in the kitchens. Cheeks pink, forehead sweat-damped, bruises gone; she was so lovely his saliva-filled mouth went dry. Ben wanted to snatch her over his shoulder, food, and coffee smashing to the floor while he took her away, primordial style. While she delivered the food to an elderly couple, he took advantage of her distraction and strode to the only available table. It was tucked in the corner to the right of the swinging door and hadn't been bussed yet. Another woman exited the kitchen as though reading his mind, and whisked the plates and mugs away, rag wiping crumbs from the tabletop cursorily before vanishing from where she'd come.

He sat.

Then, he wondered why he was torturing himself.

Lucy sailed across the dining floor as though she'd been doing it her whole life, which, according to her, she had. She topped off mugs, chatted, and laughed, skirts brushing against the knees of those many wide-spread legs. He watched the men watch her. They lusted, but there were no pats on the bottom, no brushes against her cheek, no feet disappearing under her skirts. They may lust, but they respected. If not her, then perhaps the shotgun that her father probably kept behind the counter. Coffee pot empty, tray laden once more with dishes, dirty now, she glided through the maze of tables and glanced at his corner.

Preoccupied, she nonetheless called out to him before she disappeared into the kitchen that she'd be right with him.

Ben's fingers clenched into light fists, and his thighs bunched to stand, to leave...then there was a crash from the kitchen and she was busting back through the kitchen door before it had completed its swing.

He held stiff, suspended from his stand. She gaped at him, then that devastatingly slow smile spread across her face. It made his knees weak, and he sat back down. Half the diner watched them, eyeballs jerking back and forth inside prying skulls. Ignoring the joy in his chest was becoming impossible the more he encountered this woman, and he tried to hide it while slowly taking off his hat, and hanging it purposefully on the peg of the chair next to him.

You gotta stop looking at me like that, he pleaded internally. His hands trembled, and a wet stripe on his back pasted shirt to skin.

As though she'd taken pity on him, she wet her lips and composed her face into polite attentiveness. But her hands told a different story. They wiped and wiped against her skirts, wringing the pleats that shifted as she inched to his table.

No sooner had he wished she'd say something than he was taking it back when her mouth opened.

"You left without saying goodbye." Her earlier pleasure had curdled into a challenge. Those mobile dark slashes of her brows drew together, accusing. She didn't look away from him when she pulled out a notepad and flipped it open. Her pencil held poised over the paper, as though she would write his defense to that statement instead of his order.

"What? I was comin' back." He couldn't stop his smile, didn't even care if his gold tooth flashed in the light of the gas lamps on the walls.

"A month later!" Chagrinned, she looked around and lowered her voice. "A month later, Ben. And how do you expect I felt, not able to say goodbye, not knowing if I'd ever see you again."

It had been cowardly, he knew it. And he couldn't bring himself to admit that he'd never planned on coming back until Minnie had admitted to financial difficulties with the hotel.

"You gonna yell or get me steak and pie?" He told himself he didn't know why he sounded angry.

Lucy's eyes glinted dangerously, looking about as intimidating as a peeved kitten. "Both," she sniped and turned to the kitchens.

She came back with a white mug, studiously ignoring him when he stared. The hem of her skirts tickled his shin, and just that whisper of sensation had his pulse throbbing, strong and steady in his temples, his fingertips, his groin. He relearned the length and thickness of her lashes while she filled his mug with black coffee. Color rose across her cheekbones, slow, like the blush of sunrise.

Ben's thoughts turned to kissing.

"You're pretty busy," he said before she could disappear into the kitchen. Brown eyes finally met his, and he couldn't stop the sarcasm from creeping forth. "Never seen so many young fellows in one place."

Except in whorehouses.

"Everyone missed Minnie's cooking."

Said breezily.

She lifted the porcelain lid of the sugar dish she'd brought to his table, and as though she had every right, measured one spoonful and stirred them in his mug. A lifted brow dared him to say anything. That she knew how he took his coffee unsurprised and infuriated him.

"So you're not cooking the steak yourself? That's good to know." Pretending dubiousness in her kitchen prowess would only anger her further, but he couldn't help himself. Riling her up made him smile with inane satisfaction, and her eyes widened in affront.

Sure enough, she was properly insulted and defended her abilities in the kitchen, impassioned. She was in the middle of preserving her pride when she saw his expression, and he laughed outright when she retaliated to his teasing with an impressive shove to his shoulder that rocked his chair back on two legs.

He'd never felt so many hateful stares.

Later, she set a steak down in front of him, still sizzling from a hot pan. It was over an inch thick, dark and crusty outside, tender and pink inside. When he took that first bite, it just about melted in his mouth. He'd deliver a steer a week for the rest of his life if this was the result. While he ate, she finished billing the remaining customers, giving them heartfelt farewells to come back and see her soon. Several times she pocketed the glint of silver coins. A couple of men gave her side eyes as they tipped their hats and left, and he was still shaking his head when she helped bus an empty table next to him.

"What? Is your steak not done enough?" She sounded worried.

Ben snorted. "Steak's perfect. I've just figured out why you're always so dad-gummed nice to strangers."

Amusement penetrated her careful expression, and she wiggled her eyebrows at him. "Makes for better tips."

Chewing the last bite of the best steak he'd ever eaten, he leaned back in his chair. Speaking of tips.... He dug around in his jacket pocket.

"If you think you're paying for your dinner after all you've done for me, you're not as sharp as I thought you were." She'd stopped clearing the table. Her eyes were solemn, and when the same woman from before entered the dining room, she looked up. "Patsy? Can you finish up in here for a moment?"

Lucy plopped in the chair across from him. Now that most of the patrons had left, there was a weariness in her eyes. She rolled her shoulders as though to ease the tightness.

Frowning, he asked, "How long you been at this?"

"We open at six every morning," she sighed, passing a hand over her left shoulder for the briefest moment. "We opened Monday, and people are so wonderful. Apparently, the cooking had left something to be desired after Minnie…left. As soon as they found out she'd returned, all our regulars came rushing back."

"The good service doesn't hurt, either."

A wealth of vulnerable gratitude suffused her face for a moment, softening any tension she'd held around her eyes and mouth. "Thank you, Ben."

He shifted in his chair uncomfortably. "It's Saturday. If you've been at it since Monday, you must be dead on your feet."

"I look it, don't I?" She laughed.

"No, you look—" he stopped himself.

That was close. He'd almost called her beautiful.

He took a sip of his coffee and pretended he hadn't said anything. But she'd heard. Instead of looking tired, she looked alive and alert, perched on the edge of her chair, always studying him. It made him nervous. She'd learn that there wasn't much to him, nothing interesting or special. Hell, everyone he ever knew ended up being disappointed in him.

"Ben," she started, and he tensed for a terrifying moment, hoping she wouldn't bring up that day in her father's office. "I wanted to thank you for all your help and guidance on our journey home—"

He relaxed. It didn't last.

"—and I would like to pay you for all the time your services were needed—"

"You are payin' me. With steak and pie."

"Be serious." She hadn't appreciated his glib interruption. Well, too damned bad. "What you did for me cannot be repaid with a dinner. Or a hundred dinners. If you'll give me your address, I'll send it through post."

"You're thankin' me right here. You don't need my address." She didn't need to thank him. He had a split-second fantasy of her thanking him with her lips, clinging to his shoulders, and not talking for once. His fingers twitched.

"Yes, I'd like to send compensation." Her chin tilted mulishly.

"No."

"To the money, or the address?"

"Both."

Oh, she really didn't like that. Lucy squared her jaw along with her chin. "I'd like for us to remain friends. Why won't you let me write to you?" she asked after a long silence. When he said nothing, she pulled her notepad and pencil from her apron pocket and slid them his way.

He could feel her eyes, and it made him tense and hot in his own skin.

Jaw hard, he said, "I'd like some of that pie, now."

She shocked him by knocking over the salt cellar in her haste to stand, eyes narrowed. "Of course." She slid around her chair and stalked like an angry cougar to the kitchen. The pad and pencil lay on the table.

Furious with himself and with her, he yanked the offending thing to him and wrote the town's address on the unlined paper, his name boldly scrawled across the top. Lucy reappeared and slammed a small dessert plate with a pathetically small piece of pie slapped haphazardly atop it. It fell onto its side from the force of its presentation. Ben smacked the pad of paper on the table in front of her with equal force, address facing up like a bad jest. Her pencil fell onto the floor, clattering by her skirts.

Ben ate the sliver of buttermilk pie in three bites while she slowly picked up the notepad. His neck prickled, and he wiped the facial hair clean around his mouth with a laundered napkin, then washed the pie down with the last swallow of cold coffee.

If she didn't quit smiling at him, he was going to snatch that paper right back.

"Would you like a bigger piece?" Her voice was contrite.

"Quit acting like you feel sorry," he grumbled. He finally met her eye. "And if you send me money, I'll send it right back and change my address."

Her smile blinded.

She said nothing when he left a five-dollar piece, but he shot her a stern look of warning when she squirmed. She held her notepad against her breast, right over her heart. The urge to kiss her was back, but with an undercurrent of anger. If he were to kiss her right now, he'd be rough. Punishing. He'd bruise those lips on purpose, teach her the consequences of plaguing a man.

The burn of her scrutiny followed him when he left. She hadn't acted victorious, but it had been a close cousin to it. If he had been privy to her thoughts, he imagined he'd hear crowing. Mrs. Hobb's words worried at him on the trek home, and he prayed for the strength to stay away.

15

— • —

CHAPTER FIFTEEN

I t took two weeks of working herself to death— practically bringing in customers from the street when they were slow, waitressing, cooking, and cleaning, desperately trying to make enough money to help Papa with the bills—before Lucy allowed herself to think of Ben.

He was always there in the back of her mind, like some insidious entity in the corner she refused to look at or she'd go mad.

That night in bed, Lucy lay awake. She stared up at the shadows of the rafters against the pitched ceiling. It was humid, but the open window allowed a breeze to keep her skin from growing damp. Her mind raced. It had been an awful day. She'd rowed with Tony first thing that morning after she'd found him in a stupor in his office, still drunk from the night before. Work thereafter had been busy and overwhelming, and her arm pulsed from a burn. She'd been clumsy, still angry at Tony, and had spilled boiling coffee on her arm in her rush to keep up with the customer's needs.

Worst of all, she'd managed to visit her elusive friend, Franny, with abysmal results.

Her childhood friend had remained introverted and shy. She was still her best friend, and one of the most remarkable pen pals who had kept Lucy sane while she'd been sequestered in the girl's school. Every attempt to visit Franny

239

since her return had been refused with every sort of excuse. Already frustrated from her monumentally bad day, Lucy had barged upstairs at the Hobb's General, Mrs. Hobb clomping at her heels.

"Franny!" Mrs. Hobb bellowed in a warning. "Company!"

"What?" called a soft voice.

Franny rounded the doorway of the parlor and into the foyer. Lucy had to hide her shock.

Oh, poor Franny.

When puberty had first hit her friend, it became woefully obvious that she'd inherited her mother's skin condition; moles and skin tags popped up on her skin seemingly overnight. And now...Lucy barely recognized her best friend. Not in any letter had Franny disclosed that her condition had worsened. Her face was now completely covered in spots and small disfigurements. Franny blanched when she saw Lucy.

Hiding her devastation behind a tentative smile, Lucy breathed, "Franny, you don't know how I've missed you."

Franny had turned away, murmured an excuse, and disappeared into her room down the hall. Lucy felt sadness that her friend was no longer comfortable with her. Too many years apart, too many changes. Mrs. Hobb had laid a hand on Lucy's shoulder and steered her back downstairs with an apologetic squeeze.

The shame, so fresh on her mind, jolted her out of bed. She groaned into her hands and imagined how much Franny was suffering because of Lucy's meddlesome nature. Pacing didn't help, so she thought of Ben. If only she could talk to him. He never came back, and he'd never written to her, probably too busy, or too proud.

Lucy knew that if she never made that first leap, neither of them would go anywhere. Ben was set in his ways, immovable as stone: a blocky, irritating stone that you could push and push, and it still wouldn't budge a centimeter. The thing about stone, though, was that it could be eroded over time, drip by drip from rain, fissuring from the weaseling of slender roots of shrubs.

It was impossible for her to give up once she decided something. And waiting around for Ben to give in wasn't an option.

Pulling the chair out from her writing desk, she lit her lamp, pulled out one of her two-sided writing parchments, and thought of what she could write about. Just be friends, she thought. Nice and friendly. Otherwise, she'd scare the suspicious man away like she had Franny. The challenge stiffened her shoulders, and she bent at the waist. *Dear Ben*, she wrote.

She'd just have to erode his will with her own.

BEN WAS WORKING the horses he'd bought two days before when he saw the dust trail from the direction of his father's ranch.

"Aw, hell," he muttered, climbing the fence of the round pen with practiced ease. He met Junior halfway across the yard.

"What do you think he wants?" His brother ran a jerky hand through his hair, then strained his neck to squint and make certain. It had taken Ben weeks to stop Junior from acting like a downtrodden dog from being kicked around as a pup for too long.

Sol donned the shirt hanging over the corral, buttoned it over walnut-brown skin, and joined them in the middle of the yard. Ben had never met a man that hated working in a shirt as much as his friend.

In the distance, Frank and a couple of other part-time hands loaded up fencing materials in the same buckboard used to bring beef to Dogwood. His father's mouth had puckered when Frank volunteered to help out at Ben's ranch. He was a middle-aged, weathered man that had pretty much raised Ben after John had remarried. He was wiser and more skilled than any cowboy in the county when it came to wrangling and herding steers. The white-haired man rode with fluid grace, roping cattle with the ease of decades of experience.

Ben peeled the leather gloves from his hands and tucked them in his back pocket. Here it was, a month after forking over thousands of dollars for property worth half that much, and John Stone was riding in like a maniac after seven weeks of angry silence.

"What's he want, Ben?" Junior repeated.

"Guess we're gonna find out."

John Stone's body may have softened after years of too much money and excess dinner parties, but he could still ride like the wind. He was on a flashy thoroughbred stallion whose foals sold for thousands of dollars, and he rode him like he was on some nondescript cowpony. Ben shook his head, hoping the horse didn't break a leg in a hole. John stopped his horse sharply but remained seated. He glared around at the barren house, restored barn, half-built bunkhouse, and smaller outbuildings.

They still had work to do, Ben admitted to himself. There was a freshly installed pump that they'd build a well-house around soon, and the roof and front porch of his mother's house was newly replaced.

"Looks like you've been busy." It wasn't a compliment. John looked at Junior, and his eyes softened. "Your mother misses you, John Junior. Hasn't stopped crying since you left."

Junior shuffled his feet. "I see her every Sunday after church," he muttered at the dirt.

John's voice hardened. "Yeah, and then she has to hear from everyone in town how you rabble rouse every Saturday night. Keeping company with whores and gambling away your trust. If you're gonna gamble, boy, be good at it." He turned to Ben. "Thought you'd teach him better than that, but can't say as I'm surprised."

As their father well knew, Junior had been visiting whorehouses long before Ben had come back around, getting lays for free as half the youngest whores thought themselves in love with the golden boy. But he kept his mouth shut. What his brother did on Saturdays behind closed doors was his own business. He'd turn eighteen this month and wasn't about to listen to advice from a brother that had been absent for most of his teen years.

"That what you came for?" Ben asked instead. "To tell Junior his Ma misses him?"

"Naw, I rode over to give you this." John reached into his vest pocket. He threw a folded, white square of paper at Ben, who caught it reflexively. He leaned over his saddle horn and narrowed frost-blue eyes. His teeth had begun to brown at the gum line. "Didn't you learn your lesson the first time?"

Ben loosened his fist from around the unfurling parchment. It was a letter, folded up tight to fit in the front pocket of a shirt. The address written in an elegant script was Ben's. The return address proudly stated it was from Miss Ricci from Dogwood, Texas. His eyes sharpened on the timestamp. "This was delivered a week ago." His enthusiasm from seeing the delicate penmanship was tainted by his father's self-righteous smirk. "And it was addressed to me. Why'd you have it in the first place?"

"It must have been a mistake," John argued. His shrug was too off-hand. Ben didn't believe a word.

"Next time, don't accidentally pay for my mail. I can still afford the post."

"Next time?" John bristled. "Next time, I won't pony express any love letters for you, boy. I'll burn 'em." He spat in the dirt, turned his tired mount, and galloped off. Clumps of grassy dirt sprayed the three men left behind.

Sol and Junior looked at Ben, puzzled, then Sol chuckled. "Well, what is it?"

"A letter," Ben hedged, smoothing the wrinkled little letter with work-grimed fingers.

Lucy hadn't forgotten him, then. She'd written him a week ago, and curiosity ate at him. What did it say? Had she found him out, discovered who the anonymous benefactor was that sent meat every week? And how long had his Pa had this? He checked for tampering, but couldn't tell for sure in its wrinkled state.

"Who's Miss Ricci?" Junior asked, peering over Ben's shoulder. "Is it really a love letter?"

Ben stuffed his letter in his back pocket, and whirled away, hustling to the barn. Junior ran to keep up.

"Hey, isn't Dogwood where we send that meat to the butcher?"

Sol's long legs ate up the ground until he was on Ben's other side. "Uh-oh, he's smiling," he chortled.

"I'm plumb amazed. I thought for certain you were a woman hater."

Ben stopped smiling long enough to glower at his idiot brother. "What damned fool notion made you think that?"

Junior shrugged and defended, "Well, in all the time you've been back, you haven't taken up with any whores or widows. You're not even wooing the neighbor's daughter, and she's right pretty."

"She's got eyes for *you*, or haven't you noticed," Sol said, then smiled slyly and weaved behind Ben, who ignored them to saddle Reb. "I bet it's a shy school teacher or a preacher's daughter. No!" He snapped his fingers. "A librarian. You must've got one of those books you're always reading from her. Now she's writing you telling you to bring them back, or else."

Ignoring Sol's gleeful heckling was easy when one was floating on a cloud. Cuffing the back of his brother's and friend's heads was tempting, but he was too full of anticipation to get angry. If the idiots wanted to laugh at him, let them laugh. They wouldn't be laughing tonight after Ben kept mum about his mysterious pen pal. If it was up to him, he'd never let his skirt-chasing brother and meddlesome friend within a mile of Lucy Ricci.

Mounting Reb, Ben called out, "Make sure those horses in the round pen get put up."

He zipped out of the barn and into the fields toward the little water hole downstream from the creek.

The gilly hole was about a thousand square feet altogether, deeper at one end than the other. Clusters of cypress tree stumps stuck out like bony knees at every bank. The mosqui-toes weren't so bad today, so Ben tied up his horse, plucked the letter from his pocket, and plopped against a leaning tree he grew up rope-swinging off of. He opened the letter with tightly reined enthusiasm.

The letter was an entire page long, the neat cursive written in black ink. Holding the far edges carefully so he didn't dirty up the paper, he read it with painstaking slowness.

Dear Ben,

I have attempted to allow you time to write and tell me if your endeavors to begin training horses were indeed fruitful. However, we both know that patience is your strong suit; not mine. Hopefully, you will not mind my forwardness in writing this letter.

As of this moment, I sit at my desk in my room. The pile of junk some good-for-nothing set in my attic space has made a new home in my sister Beth's room (oh, but to witness her expression if she were to ever visit and discover it). I've lit the lamp beside me, as it is one-o-clock in the morning and quite dark outside. Why am I up at this ungodly hour, you ask? Papa and I rowed this morning, which was beyond unpleasant, and we both said things that keep me awake still. Subsequently, the day became worse, and I burned the skin right off my arm after a nasty coffee spill. Later, I visited my childhood friend, but even after several years of correspondence, I was, alas, treated like a stranger. It gets worse. Minnie informed me that she cannot come in the following week, as her husband has fallen ill. I sent her on her way with a smile, but inside I'm wondering if I've not placed the noose around my neck. We can manage without her, I suppose. I am handy with an iron skillet.

Perhaps, while I cook, you could don an apron and take orders at the front. Do you like yellow ruffles? Perhaps not. They would clash terribly with your angry scowling.

Sometimes I feel so alone here I could weep. Did I truly believe that everything would go back to normal when I returned? Something elemental is missing. The things that used to make me happy no longer do so. Oh, listen to me go on. One really should not write when one is feeling so maudlin.

I wish you well and hope to see you soon. I still owe you a larger piece of pie.

Your Friend,

Lucy

Dear Miss Ricci,

I would have written a week ago, but my Pa picked up my mail by mistake. So he says. He's nosing around, more like. How was your week without Minnie? It's best I don't show up in no apron. All your customers would be runnin for the hills. Not too good for business. The ranch is comin along. The house needs the most work. Porch was like to fall off the back of it. The barn is in good shape. We had to tear down the bunkhouse and rebuild. Junior may be moodier'n a hornet, but he's got some carpenter skills to do any man proud. I bought some horses a few days ago. They'll make someone some right fine cowponies. And when I get to feelin lonely, I step in the roundpen and it all goes away a little while. When work slows down, I'm sure I'll get a hankerin for some of Minnie's cookin.

Ben Stone

Dear Ben,

I understand the mix-up. Your father sounds like the perfect counterpart to my mother. She exceeded at 'misplacing' my letters. Some even managed to fall into the kitchen stove by mistake. Mother recently sent a lovely missive bemoaning how I have made her 'a laughingstock in the women's circle', and that if I darkened her doorstep without a proper groveling, she'd be forced to turn me away. What codswaddle. As though I would ever be so desperate. I could lose the hotel and beg in the alley without once considering it.

As to the week without Minnie, it was a most horrible few days of my life and we shall not speak of it further. We managed to survive the stampede of slavering customers when she saved our hides and returned several days early. I'm still of a mind that you in an apron would be grand, if not for business, then for my spirits.

I think your farm sounds lovely, lethally sagging porch notwithstanding. Is it in any way similar to the Kershaw's homestead? Their home keeps a special place in my memory. When you step in your round pen, it sounds like your version of sanctuary. I have similar feelings when I write letters and cook.

Your Friend,
Lucy

Dear Lucy,
...sometimes I have a powerful worry about Junior. The more Pa shouts at him to come home, the more the boy drinks and spends money in town...

Dear Ben,
...he sounds as though he's going through a difficult time. Too mature to let your father treat him like a child, too immature to act like a full adult. He thinks such antics will prove him to be a man, perhaps. I am concerned about Franny, as well. I don't know how to get through to her...

Dear Lucy,
...I sold half a dozen cowponies, so our next build is the well house. It keeps Junior busy and out of trouble. Pa's been at my throat about our contract, helpin brand and

wrangle and mend fences. Knew I shouldnta signed it. Waves it under my nose every time he needs a job done...

Dear Ben,
...this has been quite an odd week. On Monday, a man asked my father to court me. I know him not-at-all. No, that is a lie. I know that he orders the same meal with every visit. Fried chicken, greens, home fried potatoes, and cornbread. Coffee, black. Papa denied suit, of course. The man has not come back.

Then, yesterday (which was a Friday), another man proposes to me right over pie! Well, not truly, it was a jest, all in good fun. He couldn't be much older than myself. He said if my cherry pie was this good, he ought to marry me for it, or something to that effect. His friends thought him terribly clever, even though his pie was blackberry, not cherry. What a fool.
Sincerely Yours,
Lucy

Ben had chosen to read this latest letter in the cool shade of the barn. His relaxed slouch against the stall door in the barn's breezeway became alert halfway through the letter. Shoulders squared and lurched off the stall by the letter's end. Reb poked his nose out, whiskers of hay dangling from his lips, but he was ignored.

Her cherry pie? Didn't she know the implication of what that horny toad had said?

Ben's ears turned red, hot with blood and indignation. He pictured Lucy blinking wide, innocent eyes while a table of idiots had a good laugh at her expense. The young man was probably only half-joking with as good-looking as Miss Ricci was. Serving pies with a smile and not even noticing the eyes following her every move, roving over her every curve. It made Ben want to strike something.

His booted foot slammed into the wall of Reb's stall. The gelding reared his head and rolled a reproachful eye.

"Damned fool."

Whether he meant Lucy or himself, he didn't know.

Hell, they were both fools. Sending each other letters like they had a right to. Like it wouldn't hurt anyone. That was a falsehood. It was damaging him right now. Every week, he walked on pins and needles, on edge and fidgety until he received her next letter. He went into town every day, no matter how busy or exhausted. Once her letter was in his hands, he was euphoric, his manic grin drawing eyes from town and his ranch alike. He'd reread every letter a hundred times. He would write a return letter, send it, and the whole process would begin again. Anxiety, euphoria, obsession, sleepless nights, and endless days.

He thought he was doing her a favor by keeping his distance. One of these days, she'd meet a nice boy with a nice family, not all twisted up like Ben on the inside. They'd get married, have a passel of babies, and Ben would take lengths to never step foot in Dogwood again. The thought of her under another man made him flush hot with rage. He'd thought about it particularly long and hard the other night, punishing himself for his other...thoughts. Adrenaline had coursed through his veins with the images of Lucy with a young buck, wrestling around in bed with a stranger that wasn't Ben. Only five minutes of this, and he'd ripped away from his lonely bed, barging out of the house half-naked until he reached the barn. Once there, he'd lit a lamp and pitched hay, cursing himself the entire time, until it was two in the morning and he was soaked with sweat.

Now...now he was thrumming with repressed rage once again. He wasn't surprised about the possessive anger. What scared the hell out of him was the sharp feeling of nausea in his stomach. It burned up from his gut to his chest, and he paced, rubbing a fist against his diaphragm, gritting his teeth, breathing hard out of his mouth.

She thought she knew him, maybe she even reveled in it, the way he sent images of his daily life to her. Did she feel as though she owned him? Look at him. Of course, the dad-gummed female owned him. Neat as a noose, she'd used her letters to maintain his attention. Sol may be the one to send the delivery of beef to Dogwood once a week, but Ben had remained firmly in that hotel, heart, and soul for weeks now.

And he was currently so jealous he could barely see straight. He'd never felt that way before, as though he could plow a fist through a man's face with enough force to see it emerge, bloody with bits of tooth and brain, on the other side. Another man had joked about Lucy's 'cherry pie', her virginity, and laughed about it with a group of other men. Knowing that another man had thought of her in that way, spreading her legs and taking her the way a man takes a whore....

This time, he struck the wood of the barn door as he strode out, legs eating up the distance between the barn and the house. Three heads popped up at the explosive sound and uncharacteristic sight of Ben charging across the yard. The anger in his stride was palpable. Sol and Frank looked at each other, worried; they'd seen the letter in his hand. Junior started climbing the round pen, a gleam in his eyes that was proof that he'd noticed the slip of paper as well.

"Junior," Frank snapped.

Junior stopped climbing. There were only three men he would listen to, and Old Frank was one of them. It didn't stop his attentive glances from stealing to the activity in the house, however.

Inside, Ben was refolding Lucy's creased letter and tucking it away in his bedside table's drawer. He grabbed the unused shave kit from Hobb's General from the washstand and stamped back downstairs.

It was time for secrets to come out.

Then, the letters would stop. The torment would abate, and he could focus his energies on where they were needed most. His ranch, his brother, and the upcoming cattle drive next spring. He couldn't hide who he was anymore. It was time for Lucy to hear his piece, to know about his previous marriage and the scandal behind it. There were parts of himself he'd kept from her, his shameful annulment, and one other.

Ben looked in the shaving mirror in his barren kitchen.

The beard had to go.

Without thinking too much about his actions, he used slender scissors to clip thick black hair away. Piece by piece, his beard fell away, drifting over his old boots and into the dirt of the wooden boards of the kitchen. He used a straight razor with a simple wooden handle, shaved away the black hair of his mother, and revealed a face that became more and more his father. Lean cheeks with deep, grooving dimples. Squared, cleft chin. He'd kept those Stone dimples and cleft burrowed deep, hidden for years behind his beard.

It didn't do to look like the man he hated.

The difference was shocking, even to him. He'd bet his best pony Lucy wouldn't even recognize him. His hair was shaggier. The skin he'd revealed along his cheeks was a shade paler than his cheekbones and the bridge of his nose, having been shaded for years from the sun by hair. His color was still high, and he was sweating through his work shirt. He was stripping when a pair of boots walked into the open doorway and stopped.

Shock rolled off Junior. "You shaved your beard."

Ben didn't answer. His thoughts were of the letter upstairs. While he scrubbed with a rough bar of soap and the cold water of the washbasin, Junior took another step into the kitchen.

"Where you going?"

"None of your business." Ben stomped upstairs, found a collared dark blue cambric shirt, and donned it. Junior, having followed, watched with wide eyes while he buttoned the cuffs, the front, neatened the collar, and buckled on a belt.

"What happened? Who sent the letter?" There was a note of fear in his brother's voice, the youthful worry that the anger in Ben's straight spine had to do with him.

"Nothing happened. I'm goin' to town. Stay here with Sol and Frank. I've got to take care of some business."

"I'll come with you."

Ben shook his head and flew down the stairs in hard, bouncing steps. Junior was at his heels all the way to the barn, so he turned a hard stare at the boy. "No. I don't want company this time."

"Oh, c'mon!" Junior burst, ignoring Ben and digging through tac. "You think I'm wet behind the ears? You get a letter today from that woman and suddenly you're ridin' off, mad as I've ever seen you. I'm going with you."

"The hell you are." A muscle ticked in Ben's temple, and he snatched the reins Junior had chosen out of the meddlesome boy's hands.

"The hell I ain't!" Junior tried to snatch it back.

"Some things ain't your business, John Junior. If you want to go somewhere, go to your ma's and eat one of those fancy dinners. God knows that would get Pa off my back for a week." He knew it was the wrong thing to say the minute it came out of his mouth.

Shadows appeared in Junior's eyes.

Then steel.

"Fine. I'll see you when you get back." Junior turned on his heel and stalked off. A few seconds later, a ringing sound from the chicken coop caused a ruckus of a dozen squawking hens.

Unwilling to let the cantankerous moods of his little brother deter his goal, Ben saddled Reb, mounted, and rode toward Dogwood. Half an hour later, he was too distracted to notice a golden-haired man slinking behind him on a chestnut mare.

"JUNIOR, THIS IS a bad idea," Sol repeated when they rode into Dogwood two hours later. They'd watched Ben canter into the town minutes before. "He's gonna tear your hide when he finds out. Mine, too, come to think of it."

"I just want to see what kind of woman has my brother in an all-fire hurry, that's all." Junior was squinting through horses and wagons, looking for a worn black hat and a dusty blood bay. "Besides, we've been working all day. It's time we had a decent supper."

Junior needed to know what kind of female had caught the attention of Ben, whom he'd thought would've sworn off women for good. Ever since Abby had pulled her stunt with her father and that blood-thirsty lawyer, Ben had been as flighty around females as a feral cat.

"What you reckon, Sol?" he asked. "She'd have to be older. Experienced. Maybe not Ma's age, but a spinster widow in her thirties. Maybe even homely. Can't be too educated, either, but one of those good church goin' gals."

Sol was listening, but resentfully, and made a face. They should be breaking in those new horses, not sniffing around in the boss's love life. He'd seen the boy leave, guilty as a stray dog circling a chicken coop. "What makes you think some ignorant pudding face older'n him is his type?"

"'Cause that type is safe. There he is! Come on."

Junior stalked behind Ben, past a livery, to a butcher shop, while Sol trailed behind in an aggrieved hunch. They tied their horses to an empty hitching post. "Hey Sol, don't you deliver beef to this place?"

Sol's face curved into a smug smile that Junior itched to wallop. "Sure do. 'Pears he's taking care of some business. Unless the butcher has a daughter."

Ten minutes crawled by. Junior grew bored, hooked a finger around a wedge of chewing tobacco from a tin, and stuffed it deep between cheek and gum. Ben reappeared, waving good-bye and shutting the door behind him. Junior spat a stream of brown tobacco juice into the dirt and motioned for Sol to follow. The taller man rolled his eyes.

They followed Ben all over town. He stopped at G.M. HOOVER'S CIGARS & TOBACCO. No woman there. Then he took a trip to the bank. Then the courthouse. All over the damned creation, they went. Each time he exited a build-ing, Junior cursed. He was mumbling about ill fortune and 'make-believe women' when they saw Ben pause in front of a building sporting the DOGWOOD HOTEL.

"Thank you, lord almighty," Junior sighed when he saw a window painted 'Diner'. "I'm starvin'."

Sol had been uncharacteristically quiet during their misadventures, but his eyes were shrewd on the painted sign above the window that said 'Rooms and Dining'. Next door was the general store. But whatever his friend had in mind, he kept to himself until Junior made to follow inside.

"Wait," Sol said. Understanding was dawning in his hazel eyes.

Junior shrugged off the staying hand and cajoled, "Might as well come out with it and get a good dinner for once. I'm tired of Ben's cooking, and so are you." He spat the wet clump of tobacco in the dirt and clomped up the stairs.

Ben was sitting in the corner of the room when they darkened the doorway to the diner. Junior wound his way around tables and plopped down at the table beside his brother, who stiffened in his chair at the sight of them. The fresh-shaved face turned a ruddy brown color back to his ears and Ben's eyes became blue slits. Junior ignored the warning signs and doffed his hat with a huff.

"I give up. I can't make heads or tails of who your mystery woman is. You dragged us all over town for nothing. Might as well pay for my supper."

When the blue gaze sliced Sol's way, the man was already raising his arms in surrender. "Don't look at me. I just followed him to keep him out of trouble."

Ben's lips were so compressed they barely moved. "I ain't payin' for a dadblamed thing, you horse's ass. What the hell are you playing, following me out here like it was your business?"

"You looked fit to kill, and I just wondered if you needed help, that's all," Junior defended. Ben was ignoring him and had stood up, changed his mind, and sat down again.

Junior's eyes widened in delight.

"She's meeting you here, isn't she? She write you to set up a time? Hellfire, this is too good." He craned his scrawny brown neck toward the front door and missed Ben's glare.

BEN WANTED TO kill Junior in the worst way.

His hand was even reaching toward that neck with the prominent jugular when the kitchen door swung open and a woman in a sky-blue dress backed out. He dropped his hand and his mouth filled with cotton.

Lucy wore a ribbon in her hair that was tied in a tail down her back. Her face shone from the warm kitchens, her tray loaded with full plates. Would she notice him when she looked over? He stroked the smooth skin of his face self-consciously and met Sol's eyes. His friend saw what his fool brother didn't, and gave him an apologetic grimace.

It was too late now to get the two meddlesome cockleburs out of his hair. All he could do was wait for Lucy to recognize him.

16

— · —

CHAPTER SIXTEEN

Lucy couldn't remember a time that she'd worked so hard in her life as she had these past few weeks.

She balanced four white plates on her round tray loaded with steaming food straight from the skillet and slapped a smile on her face. The table she served was full of bachelors, and a pretty smile made for extravagant tips. It paid to be extra friendly. They didn't need to know that her feet were aching, her hands felt raw from washing all the linens the day before, and she had another blister on her forearm from the oven.

Murmurs of assent and approval eased the tension in her face somewhat after she served the men their hot food, and they were tucking in when she felt it.

A quiver along her back, an itchy nape.

Frowning at the sensation, Lucy tucked her round tray under her arm and stopped halfway to the kitchen door. That small frisson of awareness pulled at her, and she cocked her ear to the side.

"She late or something? Let's make a deal; while you wait for your sweetheart, I'll ask the pretty waitress for some supper."

It wasn't the man's words that caught her attention; the timber and cadence did. He sounded so like Ben that she turned her head. A group of three cowboys, one blonde, one brunette, and one black as pitch. The one with golden hair had spoken. He raised his arm and gave her the full force of his angelic features. Blue eyes the same pure shade as Ben's looked her up and down in interest, but the shape was off.

What was happening to her? she wondered. Pining away so hard for a man that she was imagining him in the faces and voices of others. She'd been standing still for several awkward moments and dropped a mask of pleasantness over her frown. Turning on her heel, she instinctively mirrored the young heartbreaker's smile with one of her own, but something was still...wrong. Off. The brunette was tall and rawboned, hiding the third man behind his cap of glossy brown hair.

"How can I help you gent—" She broke off as the full force of the black-haired man's gaze met hers. Familiar almond-shaped eyes dared her to recognize him. "Ben!"

For a mortifying moment, she thought she'd mistaken him when the young Adonis gaped. But the man had Ben's sapphire eyes, and soft black hair curled over neat ears. The same thick neck met broad shoulders in muscular chords. He'd shaved his beard off, and to her delight, the dense thicket had hidden two deeply creased dimples. Why, he even had a cleft in his chin! Heat crawled from her dress when she noticed his mouth. The bottom lip curved sweetly.

For months she'd convinced herself she was happy to be simple pen pals, living vicariously through letters that couldn't come quick enough. The realization of how immense that lie was hit her with a wallop, and her throat worked. She was so hopelessly infatuated with him it frightened her. He was here in the flesh, and with awful insight into her inner workings, she was afraid she'd probably latch on to his leg if he tried to leave again, kicking and screaming like a madwoman.

The second thing she noticed was incandescent happiness. Her smile stretched so big it hurt her cheeks. "What are you doing here?" Lucy's tone proclaimed pure pleasure that he *was* here, and he didn't look offended. "And you shaved!"

She saw that flash of gold amidst the white row of his teeth before he tamped his lips shut. It shamed her that she couldn't stop looking at those lips.

"Got tired of my own cooking." Ben's warm voice sent shivers into the deepest parts of her, and for a moment, her vision tunneled and everyone disappeared; the patrons, the friends that had accompanied him, everyone. Lord, it was hot. With trembling fingers, she plucked the buttons of her bodice away from her damp skin. His eyes followed.

"Will you be staying the night? I can have a room set up for you."

It was astonishing the things that a beard could hide. She watched the bulge of his jugular bob as he swallowed. "Hadn't thought that far ahead, if I'm honest."

"Well, you must stay. We have so much to catch up on."

His dimples deepened, and the sweet mouth curved. And simultaneously, they both remembered they were in a room with a dozen others, and two of them happened to be following every word.

"Oh," she breathed, breaking eye contact with Ben and meeting two sets of very curious eyes. "I am so sorry! You must be Ben's brother, and—" she bit her lip and glanced at the tallest man.

"Sol Williams, ma'am," he said, tipping his head and giving her an endearingly broad smile. Wild humor glittered in his lively hazel eyes.

"Of course." She chuckled and glanced at his suddenly quiet brother. "So, you must be Junior."

"Yes'm." There was no hint of a smile now on the youngster's face. The light appeared to have dawned, and he watched her warily and fidgeted with a piece of the tablecloth. Junior couldn't have been much younger than she, Lucy mused. The young man had the beginnings of a patchy mustache, the hair so fair it was almost white. Even so, his bravado from earlier had dissipated as though in the presence of a schoolmarm.

Self-conscious, she blabbered, tucking a piece of loose hair behind her ear. "It's so strange. It feels as though I know you two after reading about you in letters. I'm Lucy Ricci. It's nice to meet you both, finally."

Sol was laughing before she'd even finished speaking. Junior swiveled on his rear and asked Ben accusingly, "This is who you've been all-fired up about? This is the mystery letter writer?"

When Junior jerked and grabbed his shin, hissing oaths, Lucy shoved a knuckle against her twitching mouth. The betrayed cant of the young man's brows warned her not to laugh. His strong reaction worried her if she was being honest with herself.

"Can I get you gentlemen some coffee?" she asked to distract them.

"Too dadblamed hot for that," Junior muttered, not looking at her again.

It was. Shirts stuck to men's broad backs, and dark crescents ringed beneath arms. Several people fanned themselves with their hats. The open window let in a passing breeze, but it was no more than a whisper of air once it reached their corner.

"How about some cool glasses of lemonade? We keep a pitcher in our icebox."

The men nodded at that, placed their orders, and she burst into the kitchen short of breath and wide-eyed. "Patsy, can you take over? I have a visitor."

The middle-aged woman watched Lucy hasten to untie the knot in her apron without moving from the work table, hands covered in sticky biscuit dough.

"Ben came." She announced, her mouth unable to cease smiling, and she blushed when the women clapped, laughed, and voiced congratulations. She'd talked about Ben since the first day he'd written back, and the kitchen staff was now as embroiled in her fixation with Benjamin Stone as she was.

While touting the men's orders, Lucy smoothed her hair and wiped her sweating face with a dampened rag from the reservoir.

Minnie turned from the stove with sparkling eyes. "You look like a lady goin' courting."

"Men go courting, not ladies," Lucy huffed, filling glasses with the pitcher of lemonade from the squat little icebox. The pan beneath the ice block needed emptying.

"Things change," Minnie mused, pursing her lips to hide her smile.

"I wish I had some petroleum jelly for my lips." Lucy sucked and bit them distractedly, longing for a mirror.

"You goin' up two flights of stairs up to your room for that little lip shine?"

"No."

"Then hush up and go courtin'." Minnie swatted Lucy's bustled bottom toward the door.

Carefully, so she didn't embarrass herself and spill the drinks, Lucy exited the swinging door and made her cautious way back to the table in the corner. "Here you are."

The three mumbled 'thank you ma'ams', but her cheerful smile wavered at the thick tension in the air between Junior and Ben. They had an air about them like a long-suffering parent and his sullen child. Clearing her throat, she motioned to the chair closest to the wall between Ben and Sol.

"May I?"

Her eyes locked on Ben's, who looked up from his clasped hands, stood, and pulled the chair out. She glanced at those hands, the ones she pictured in her daydreams of him, and felt an incredibly inappropriate surge of feminine interest. She sat and hoped they didn't sense her longing, then came to the helpless realization that she *was* courting him. Absolutely shameless, that's what she was. But how was she supposed to keep away from him? She met sapphire eyes beneath straight black brows and looked at the smooth skin along his jaw. There was no way she could resist the pull to him.

Fight, Minnie had said.

Oh, she would.

"So, how'd you two meet?" asked Sol, smacking his lips after a deep drought of lemonade.

"We rode the same trains to Texas together," Lucy said, ignoring the intensity of Junior's stare.

Ben leaned back in his chair with a creak, spreading his legs wide beneath the table. She could feel his boot brush her hem. "She sat in my seat, and woke me up."

"It was an accident," she assured Sol, laughing.

Lucy told the story of their adventures, with a few playful interjections from Ben. Sol made a perfect audience, laughing, groaning in places, and giving solemn headshakes. Junior, however, made disparaging comments about Ben. When she mentioned how he'd flayed her alive when he found out she'd run off, Junior had sneered, "He's one to talk."

When she relayed the horrors of the stagecoach wreck, Junior rolled his eyes at Ben's rescue. Her irritation grew, and, sensing this, Sol steered the conversation to something that caught Lucy's attention.

"Ben ever tell you 'bout the time the two of us thought we were goin' to be hanged for horse thieving?"

"What?" She widened her eyes at Ben who stopped cutting into his pork chop.

"We were about fifteen, and found a horse in Sol's crops." Ben shook his head at the memory. "Figured it was a mustang."

Junior snorted, sawing at a steak. "Ain't no mustangs out here anymore."

Sol spoke over him, mouth full. "We caught it and took it home, but we hid him so my parents wouldn't decide they needed him to plow or something boring like that."

"We kept him hid in the woods for two days before we got word the neighbor's prize stud had escaped his pen," Ben said.

"Uh-oh." Lucy smirked at him. "Is that when you decided to come forward and tell all?"

"Heck no!" Sol was laughing and pointed at Ben. "He was so all-fired scared we'd get into trouble, we kept that horse a secret for two weeks before one of my sisters found us out. Kathy can't keep a secret for sh—for anything. We couldn't sit for a week."

For the remainder of their meal, Lucy laughed at tales of a young, mischievous Ben. She imagined a quiet, skinny young boy with charming dimples and a fear of getting in trouble, then doing the troublemaking anyway.

Even so, no matter how Sol tried to keep the peace, Junior would pop the bubble of good humor, reacquainting the tension at the table. Lucy was confused and looked between the two brothers. If it had been her sister Beth monopolizing the conversation with her petty jealousies, Lucy would have struck her down with a hot rejoinder by now. Ben...he just sat, becoming more still and coiled as time went on. Soon, it was mostly Sol and Lucy conversing.

Feeling as though Ben's visit was quickly becoming a complete disaster, she addressed Junior, "I hear you're a pretty good carpenter."

"Is that so?" Junior moved his half-eaten food around on his plate. "I haven't heard much a'tall about you. Why is that, Ben?"

"Watch your mouth." Ben had woken up and sat forward, forearms on the table, eyes pinning his brother.

"I just think it's funny, that's all."

"You got somethin' to say to me, say it."

Junior scowled. "I shouldn't have to say it. Don't you remember the last time you got involved with a female?"

Ben seemed to swell, eyes hard blue flecks. Lucy froze. *Female?* There had been another female? Well, surely, he would have had other women in his life. He was nearing thirty, after all. Sol sighed beside her and broke through her internal reasoning.

"Hey, Junior—"

Junior looked at all of them, the deep red of his face and wild eyes acknowledging that he'd gone too far. Throwing his napkin on his plate, he defended, "If he's sparking her, it shouldn't be no big secret."

"And I don't remember that being any of your business," Ben cut in softly.

Sneering, face sour, Junior scraped his chair back. "Yeah. You're right. The last time you divorced and left me with the old bastard wasn't my business either, how could I forget?" He stood and left without paying.

Divorced?

As though she'd been struck across the cheek, Lucy recoiled and looked wide-eyed at Ben. His face was blanched of color.

Sol whispered an oath under his breath and laid money on the table, donning his hat while he stood. "I got 'im, Ben. He thinks the world's owed to him these days. He's still got some growin' up to do. Ma'am." He tipped his hat to her and followed the path that Junior had taken out the door.

The joy she'd felt when she'd seen Ben at that table slipped away, and pride was threatening to rear up and soothe her hurt feelings. Hot, angry words lay upon her tongue, ready to lash out at the smallest provocation. She tamped them down in disgust. Prideful squabbles had never helped her before.

"Divorce?" It was the one word that couldn't be squashed. She didn't know of anyone who'd ever had a divorce before. It was unheard of in these parts.

"Annulment," he grated.

So there had been a woman. He had been married before. She pictured a beautiful, regal woman in his arms. This woman had all the things that Lucy did not. The pain of it set fire to her chest, and she massaged it with a hand. Ben's jaw worked, then he stood and held a hand out to her.

"Can we go somewhere private?"

Without hesitation she grabbed his hand, squeezing it with all the strength of her feelings. The hardness momentarily eased from his face—Lord, his much *different* face—at her small show of belligerence. She'd done a good job being meek and polite in front of his friend and brother, but she was itching to come out and say a thing or two to him.

Lucy released his hand at the curious stares of her patrons, to whom she gave stiff smiles and gracious goodbyes. All the while, Ben was a prickle of awareness at her back, his steps light and careful. She led him through the foyer and down the darkened hallway. Her father wasn't at the front desk, and she exhaled hard out of her flared nostrils. That was a fight for another time.

The back porch was occupied by a couple of gentlemen in rocking chairs, sharing a smoke after a good meal. She nodded at them and took a right. At the end of the porch, the alley began, and they found a modicum of privacy in the darkness between. She ignored the faint smell of compost and horse manure and turned to Ben.

Her breath seized again at the look of him. He was massaging a shoulder, looking the most unhappy she'd ever seen, aside from their post-kiss. Even so, the sharp edge of his jawline and squared chin made her fists clench with want.

For a moment, she watched him, then, impatience shortened her temper. "Well?"

"Just hold on," he shot, pacing, shoving hands deep inside his pockets. She hadn't seen him so wound up since she'd gotten on the stagecoach in Houston.

Another minute went by, and she declared, "I forgot talking to you is like pulling teeth."

He gave her a dirty look before he stopped pacing and gathered himself.

Finally, he explained, "I got your last letter today. I came into town to tell you...hell, I don't know, to tell you everything. Junior beat me to it. He followed me. That boy can scent a commotion a mile away, just stands to reason he'd follow me and stick his nose in my concerns."

Crossing her arms under her breasts, she knitted her brows at him. "Why doesn't he like me? He was fine at first, but once he realized who I was...." She trailed off.

"He likes you, he just—"

"Ben." Who was he trying to convince? She'd seen it. Her blank stare proved it.

Ben sighed. "Like Sol said, he's angry at the world. Angry at me. He's probably scared what happened five years ago will happen again."

And there it was, the root of it all. Lucy uncrossed her arms and stepped closer. "What *did* happen?"

"Something that's going to change the way you look at me," he warned. His eyes were solemn, his mouth firm. "So you better listen hard and listen good while I say it."

Challenge strung her body tight.

"Nothing you say is going to change how I feel," she vowed through gritted teeth.

He shook his head and turned his back to her. She felt faintly sick, as though she'd purge and add another unpleasant smell to the alley. When he spoke again, she forced herself not to react.

"Five years ago, almost six, I was married."

The silence was deafening. Helpless anger and possessiveness rose up, but for once she kept her mouth shut.

"Junior's ma, Loretta, arranged a marriage between myself and her cousin's only daughter." His body was tense. It was his turn to cross his arms. "Her name was—is—Abigail. Abby was nice enough, I s'pose. She smiled a lot, didn't talk much. She was real quiet. I didn't even know much about her when we spoke words in front of the preacher.

"She was sheltered. Her pa was one of those bible thumpers, and I don't know what her ma told her about the wedding night—" he broke off and took a deep, shaking breath. "Hell, I scared her. It's like she thought we'd just lay in bed side to side, and that's it. When I...." he cursed low and savage, "Damn it, why is this so hard?"

Lucy heard him try to laugh.

She'd never felt less like laughing.

"I believe I know what happened. She didn't know about the...physical intimacies of marriage?" It was harder than she'd thought possible to ask.

He nodded, the silence once again heavy, suffocating. "She didn't know a thing. I didn't do much, couldn't. I'm not one to keep goin' when the female next to me starts shakin' and cryin'."

A white-hot poker in her ear would have been more welcome to Lucy than those words. She swallowed her grief.

His hands interlocked together behind his head, knuckles standing out, white and full of tension. "What I wouldn't do to have never married her.

"She ran away. She didn't talk to me, or even Loretta—Junior's ma. Just ran off in the night barefoot like one of those books Lorretta likes reading. When she made it to town to her ma and pa, it didn't look too good on me. Her pa wanted to kill me, God-fearing man or no. He tried to have me arrested and thrown in jail, and wrung of every penny."

Furious, Lucy skirted Ben's tense figure. She wanted to see his face. "Did you fight their allegations? Pay a lawyer, had a doctor check her to ascertain that you hadn't assaulted her in any way?"

His lip twitched, but he still didn't meet her eyes. "Pa would like you. He did all of that and more. The family refused to have another man 'abuse her modesty', and denied the physician."

"Codswallop!"

"It didn't matter. The doctor could have cleared my name in the court, much good that would do; but by that time, half the town hated me. Since Abby's folks refused the doctor's services, and the proof of my innocence or guilt, the judge acquitted me of any charges. They were madder'n hell. The tales her mother spun, everyone thought I was a monster. I felt low. Lower than a snake. All the women would act real scared when I walked into a mercantile. They'd all leave without paying. That's when I left town. I signed the annulment papers, got on Reb, and hightailed it out of there like a yellowbelly."

"Oh, Ben, that was just rumormongering at its finest. It's based on hysteria. Ignorance." She was so enraged he finally looked at her.

His hands dropped and disappeared into his pockets.

She wasn't finished.

"Some of the town's finest, most upstanding women can turn into harpies when given a bit of gossip. You must pay them no mind. Don't give a group of vicious hens the power to bring you to your knees. The real villain here is that girl's mother."

"Addy's ma?" Ben shook his head. "That girl's mother rivals my brother's for coddling. She's no 'villain.'"

A blanket of darkness was falling over them, the shadows deeper in the corners of the alley. Summertime night sounds fought to be heard over the movement of the townspeople. Cicadas had quieted and were superseded by trills of crickets rubbing hind legs together, playing their instruments. A cat yowled in the distance. Lucy's head was mostly shadow, nodding in assent.

"Yes, she is. Girls count on their mothers to ease them into the idea of marriage and...all that it entails. If Abby was that naïve, enough to flee so drastically, it only reveals the flaws on her mother's end. Not yours. You said that you stopped—" she couldn't manage to go further. It seized her throat to think of him having carnal knowledge of another woman.

His inhale was rough. His face was in complete shadow beneath his hat. "I stopped before I'd even started. It was clear enough she was terrified. I'm not a monster."

"I never thought that," she rushed. "Just from the day you brought me home—" She broke off.

The tension between them changed, thickened. That evening he had taken that tentative step over the line they had both toed since the first day they'd met. But she, she had met him more than halfway and would have dragged him to the floor if he'd allowed it. Shame and embarrassment swirled in the pit of her stomach, and she clutched at the edges of her apron.

"I never apologized for that."

"There was nothing to apologize for." Ben said it carefully, as though she were fine china.

Like his first wife.

Her jaw clenched. "I don't wish to be handled with care. You offered a kiss in friendship, and I tried to take it further. It was inappropriate for the moment."

Ben started laughing. It didn't sound very nice.

"What?" Her brows nearly met. He thought her apology was funny?

"Friendship?" he asked in disbelief.

"Yes, what else could it be?" she challenged.

"Lucy." The admonishment was there. A warning. Don't get too close or he'd turn her away. Lord knew he was afraid of the truth. And it was obvious now, after his confiding, why he had to be so careful.

I am not his first wife, she thought, and her head began to swim with anger. She had apologized but hadn't meant it, for a kiss that he apparently hadn't intended.

"If not in friendship, then for what other reason, Ben? Pity?"

"Christ, no." Good. Now *he* sounded angry.

Someone lit a lantern on the porch, and they both turned to look as the gray of dusk turned into a fuzzy umber, and the shadows became more pronounced. Whoever had lit it went back inside, and it was quiet once more. When she looked at him again, he was watching her. His hat was in his hand, and his hair was a mess. She longed to brush it from his forehead. She could see the angled edge of his jaw, the curve of a cheekbone, the crescent shadow of his lashes.

"You look so different now," she whispered, stepping closer as though under a spell. "I never imagined that this was what was under your beard."

He didn't stop her when she lifted a hand to his cheek. A five o'clock shadow was visible, but his skin was still smooth beneath the light stubble. She saw his nostril flare in the hazy porch light, the other half of his face lost in the black of the alley. Both of her hands were on his cheeks, unmistakably a caress. Her thumbs met in the center of his chin, sinking into the groove. They followed her other fingers up his cheeks, whispering over the dimples along his cheeks.

"I didn't know you had dimples, Ben. Did you know as a girl I always wished for them?" Her smile flashed, but he remained staid. In the obscurity and absolute privacy, it was easy to admit secrets. "Your letters kept me sane these months past. I'm not ashamed to admit I visit the post office every day.

Mrs. Pritchett and I have become good friends. I miss you dreadfully. You cannot know how much your presence here means to me." Her hands had found their way around his neck. When her nails ran the length from collar to nape, he grabbed her wrists. Could he sense her excitement? Stepping closer, Lucy locked her fingers together. Her breasts brushed against the front of his shirt.

The hands gripping her wrists squeezed. "You just gonna ignore everything I just told you?"

"I haven't ignored anything you have said," she reasoned calmly, chin tilting up. She could feel the tickle of his breath on her forehead.

"Then what are you doin'?" His voice was strained.

A sudden notion had her unlocking her fingers in fear. "Do you still love her?"

"Who?"

"Your ex-wife."

"Hell no!" He burst out, and pure joy and relief suffused her.

"Then why do you never want to touch me? She must have at least been very beautiful." Lucy was choking on her jealousy, and it was truly awful. She'd never cared enough about another man to care. Not like now. Now, she wanted to find that little miss and berate her for all Ben's pain was worth.

"She was a little mouse, you'd never even know she was in the room most of the time," he said. He slapped his hat against his thigh. "And I can't touch you, Lucy. You know what would happen."

"What would happen?" She spread her arms, chest thrust out, and taunted, "I'm to never show you the depths of my feelings and pay for your first wife's sins?"

"We'd have to marry."

"And you're afraid of marriage."

"No, I think you think you want marriage, but you'd run scared after one week on the ranch."

The whites of her eyes flashed briefly in the dark, and then she was nose to nose with him. "I would not!"

"Oh, 'cause you've never run away before?" Ben's sarcastic barb hit, and she made a sound similar to that of an agitated mountain lion.

"I am not your wife!" she cried, and shoved his shoulders, hard. He didn't move an inch, but he grabbed her and crushed her against him. His hat fell against their feet, and his breathing was wild. This close to him, she smelled shaving soap and heat.

Fingers still wrapped around her biceps, he lowered his face into her middle part, breathing deep. Finally, he said, "You're so young, you still don't know what you want."

Lucy struggled at that, hating his words, but discovered that his strength was five times that of hers and grew still again. Her breathing was harsh from the strain, and her eyes pricked that he was pushing her away yet again.

"You're wrong. I know exactly what I want, and I don't have to be thirty or forty to know it."

"Yeah?" he scoffed. "What is it you think you want?"

She was beyond weary of his condescension, but her body was so interested in his proximity that she pressed even closer, stomach to hip, face to neck.

"I want..." but she broke off because he pulled back. His lips were visible, bare of any facial hair, and they held her enthralled.

"You can't even say it," those lips whispered. Gripping fingers loosened on her arms, drifted down, then up, so slowly she felt every touch all the way to her toes.

"I can say it," she breathed, feeling drugged. "I will say it. I want you. I don't care about your past; I want you now. On your ranch, in your life, every day and not just glimpses through letters."

"What else?" He took that last step closer to her, voice gravely, his head canting.

Fierce longing stabbed through her, and she gasped inaudibly with it, helplessly dipping her gaze to his frowning lips. "I want to wake up every morning and see your face next to mine. I need it. I don't eat, I can't sleep, you're all I think about and it isn't going away."

The groan that vibrated through him could be felt clear to her bones when he crushed her to him, bowing down until his face pressed hard into her neck, scraping her with indiscernible stubble and hot breath. "That what you need? Maybe I need it, too," he growled against her skin, which promptly erupted into goosebumps.

"Most of all, I want you to kiss me," Lucy whispered, squeezing her eyes shut. His answer was to trail his lips up swiftly from her quickly pulsing vein to the soft part of her lips. The kiss wasn't the chaste meeting of mouths from that day in her father's office.

Ben no longer restrained himself. She wanted to be kissed? He gave her what she wished for. His mouth was lush, the kiss almost messy in their eagerness. Fingers delved into her hair, loosening her ribbon, and the heady taste and feel of him made her senses swim like too much drink. Thinking was impossible. This kiss was all sensation; no analysis of previous kisses or worries that she was doing it wrong. Nothing could be wrong about this. Every second was torture and bliss in equal measures.

Now and then they parted for air, but each time they'd come back simultaneously, their need for each other identical and urgent. Her hands found purchase around his neck and into his rough-silk hair, and she drew his tongue deep into her mouth, suckling it greedily, wishing to devour him into her body.

Her feet left the ground, and half a second later, he flattened her against the wall of the hotel. Rough hands parted her legs through her skirts and shifted her to cradle lean hips. When his hardness pressed, fervent and rigid against her, she dropped her head back and moaned. That hot mouth left her lips and dropped to her throat. The instant his tongue touched her sensitive skin, she reflexively pressed his hips deeper into her with raised calves, opening her legs wider, and made small noises in her throat. Roaming hands lost any finesse, hers and his both, and she squeezed handfuls of his hair to force another kiss from him while he skimmed over her hard-corseted waist and up onto the softness of her breasts. She groaned in response, biting and licking his sensual lower lip.

When she grabbed his hand and forced him to squeeze her breast harder, he finally surfaced, breathing labored. Beautiful blue eyes glazed over, he gripped her hands firmly in his. "Enough."

Lucy fluttered her eyes open, mouth tender and swollen. She wondered if she was cross-eyed. No kiss had ever made her feel so staggered. Swallowing pride and sense alike, she met his gaze soberly.

"Ben, I love you."

Those words were surprisingly hard to say, something she couldn't take back and keep safe within herself, and she held her breath. His response was to watch her, searching for something, until he eventually took a step away from the cradle of her hips, helping set her back to rights on the ground. She swallowed, trying not to feel hurt. And failing.

"Where are you going?"

Hair tousled and shirt wrinkled, he brought her hand up for a tender kiss on the knuckles.

"I think I'd better find your Pa."

If her heart had been hammering before, it now took flight, beating like hummingbird wings.

"What will you say?" She watched him pick up his hat, afraid to hope as he dusted it off.

"Don't rightly know," he sighed, donning his hat. "But I can't take any more letters like that last one. I can't keep my hands off you, either. And I can't be your friend, not with the way I feel. It's marriage, or it's nothing at all." Soberly said, almost apologetically.

Lucy felt as though she'd won something priceless, and her smile nearly cracked her face.

"I thought you'd never ask."

TONY WAS IN his office when Ben knocked.

"Come in."

Ben entered with the hesitation of a gladiator entering a lion's den. He was still reeling from the kiss. Shock at Lucy's passion kept his mind in the gutter, and he was hard put not to go back downstairs for more shocking discoveries. The last two times, he'd forced them to stop. How far would she go if he didn't pull the reins? He was half afraid, and half titillated that he knew the answer. This meeting with her father should quash some of those urges.

It was obvious Tony was drunk. If his rumpled clothing and slanted tilt in the chair hadn't been proof enough, the empty bottle of whisky on the desk was. He was looking through ledgers, squinting at them, and scratching at a thinning pate of hair.

Not one for social niceties, Ben cut to the heart of the matter. "Mr. Ricci, I'd like to ask your daughter's hand in marriage."

Tony didn't even look up. He laughed. "Two in one month, that's a record."

Clenching his jaw with enough force to almost crack a molar, he gritted, "I'm the man who brought her safely to you, sir. We've been corresponding ever since. I reckon she feels the same way, if you'd like to ask her."

Finally, Tony looked up. He squinted harder. "Come closer. What did you say your name was?"

Taking a steeling, deep inhale, feeling like an idiot, Ben strode to the desk. "Benjamin Stone."

Thick eyebrows shot up, and his right hand reached for the bottle, then dropped it on the floor dispassionately when he realized it was empty. "Oh. That one. I feel as though I know you already, young man. Mr. Stone this, and Mr. Stone that. I cannot get a moment's peace without your ghost popping up.

No man can is comparable, so my daughter says." Tony's words were only a little slurred. Not too drunk to cloud judgment, it appeared.

His words, however, embarrassed Ben. He could feel his ears glowing like coals in a metal grate.

Brown eyes assessed him now that he was closer. Tony sat straighter. "You're not quite what she described. You're not a young man at all, are you? What do you do, Mr. Stone?"

For an hour they talked. It was akin to a business transaction, releasing important property from one business holder to the next. Will you have to funds to take care of this property? Clothe it, house it, suit its needs? It was more uncomfortable than asking for Abby's hand; hell, his father had dealt with every detail of that marriage. All Ben had to do was show up and say 'I do'.

"I have one last stipulation." Tony held a finger up. He was no longer slurring, and his eyes were a modicum clearer. "My daughter is not a soiled dove, and I don't need the town thinking this is some shotgun wedding. Six months should stop any traps flapping, and give her time to cry off. And I'll thank you to keep your hands to yourself until then. Do we have an agreement?"

The delay of any wedding bells didn't trouble him, but he had his doubts that he could keep his hands off her. Regardless, fierce elation coursed along his body. The two men shook hands, and he made his departure.

When he opened the door, he froze. Lucy's back was to him, and she was silently doing a jig of celebration. When she turned around fully and saw him, she stopped and stood still. Shutting the door behind him, he knew in his heart that if he hadn't loved her before, he damned sure did now.

With a whoop, he picked her up and twirled her. She kissed him, closemouthed and smiling.

TONY SMILED TO himself as he pulled out a sheet of foolscap and began a letter to his bitch of a wife. He wished he could see her beautiful eyes grow wide in horror at the news of their youngest daughter's upcoming marriage to a common cowboy. Perhaps it wouldn't ruin her life in the same ways she'd ruined his, but it would put a damper on any of the harridan's plans to take his daughter away from him again.

17

—·—

CHAPTER SEVENTEEN

Tony insisted on taking Lucy for a buggy ride the month after her engagement. It was a crisp morning, surprising for mid-Summer in Texas, and the sky was a piercing blue. They enjoyed the sunlight and spoke of safe, comfortable things while riding in the rented buggy down a well-tread dirt road.

Lucy wore a creamy ruffled shirtwaist tucked into a navy travel skirt. In homage to the memories of riding with her father as a young girl, she'd worn an old bonnet he'd gifted to her years before. A giant blue ribbon tied into a winsome, girlish bow beneath her chin. When he'd helped her into the rig, he'd beamed, and for a moment it had been as though those three years of absence and heartache had never been.

As a child she had bugged him, incessant as a mosquito in his ear. "Where are we going, Papa?" "We there yet?" "How much longer, I need to use the privy."

Now, she relayed what she'd been taught by tutors in the girl's school. Aurora's name was conspicuously absent from their conversation. Tony spoke of renovations, the troubles of building on a business, and the occasional oddball that would come into the hotel.

"Are you going to tell me where we're going?" she asked, not for the first time.

He was holding up a piece of paper, and Lucy caught a quick glimpse of a roughly drawn map before they took a fork to the left. This road was less traveled and bumpy, and houses dotted the countryside next to it. Some of the cabins were so immersed in the woods around them that their windows stared like black holes from trees and overgrown vines.

"Do you think those houses are haunted?" she mused to break the silence.

"I'm not certain, shall we stop and find out?"

"I'd rather not."

They smiled at the comfortable banter. The land was hilly, and the hardwood trees around them were full of bright green leaves, swaying proudly in the breeze. She estimated them to be two hours northeast of Dogwood.

"How far are we from Huntsville?"

"A few hours ride in a buggy like this. Roads are pretty rough out this way."

"It's beautiful."

Papa's homemade map reappeared, and they took another left. The houses disappeared and the road become rougher and riddled in potholes, a thick central stripe of grass leading the way to...where? After fifteen minutes, the trees thinned out to a clear-cut stretch of land with a carpet of summer grass. Cattle grazed here and there, but they were sparse. The road became a driveway, and it wound its way up a low, sloping hill.

A modest two-story cabin stood between two live oaks at the crest, chimney reaching high next to a lazily swaying weather vane. Smaller outbuildings peppered the cleared acre behind the house, and a barn stood sentinel beside a round pen at the base of the hill. It housed half a dozen curious horses, each with their ears pricked at their advance. Several called greetings to their buggy horse, and the tired mare neighed back, picking up the pace.

"I think this is it," Tony muttered, studying the scribblings on his paper with a worried frown.

Lucy practically stood now, admiring the beauty of the fields around them. The yard needed flowers, particularly the weed-choked flower beds that encircled the front porch, bordered with natural stone. The house was a quaint little thing, and would perhaps be lovely if only it had a fresh coat of paint. As it was, graying clapboard siding and newer raw wood were its only decoration. It was small, but the lines were squared and even, with real glass windows instead of the black, empty spaces and drooping shutters of abandoned homes during the trek there.

Wherever *there* was.

"Where are we?" Her father's refusal to illuminate the destination of their journey was more than suspicious, and she was tired of the tight-lipped secretiveness. He hadn't even wanted her to look at his map.

"What do you think of it?" Tony was being far too sly.

Their rented mare heaved up the winding drive, and Tony stopped the buggy in front of the house. A rooster crowed on his coop that leaned on the side of the barn, and she smiled when he jumped from its roof to herd the hens away from some unseen danger.

"I think it's positively lovely," she finally answered. It would have been even better than the Kershaw's farm if it had a garden in the back. She looked to the west and noted that no trees or homes hindered the view of the horizon. Sunsets would be spectacular here.

Tony observed her, speculation glinting in his eye while he set the brake with his good arm. "It's a nice little place. Now, let's see if it's the right one."

A man walked out of the barn, his stride as familiar as his dusty old hat.

Lucy sat back down abruptly.

"Ben," she whispered, her mouth opened in an 'o' of astonishment.

This was *his* land, the home he'd traveled so far to buy from his father. She looked back around her with fresh eyes, and everything now held a golden hue to it, every wall, door, and step became priceless and all-important. This was her future home. Papa had taken her to Ben's home for the first time. She could put flowers in those beds if she wanted. She could paint the home a cheerful white, and grace each window with black shutters and flower boxes. Something that she'd only ever felt for her father's hotel, and Ben himself, surged through her and had her rising to her feet again.

Possessiveness.

Homecoming.

There was an undeniable need to own this beautiful place and put her stamp on it. But more than that, she wanted to own the man. Eyes big, she didn't wait for Ben to reach them and clambered from the buggy, heedless of her uncooperative skirts.

Ben wore work clothes, the trousers tucked haphazardly into his boots, and the sleeves from his worn shirt were rolled up to the elbow.

"Ben!" she exclaimed, not giving her father another thought. "This is your land!" It was an absurd accusation, and the men glanced at each other.

"I reckon it is."

"Why didn't you tell me we were coming here?" Laughing, she bent and tossed a pebble at Papa, then patted her hair and quailed at the sting of a sunburn on her nose. She had tossed the bothersome bonnet from her person miles back and wasn't completely certain where it had landed. Oh, she must look a fright. She stopped her fussing and perused her intended. His face remained cleanshaven, and she marveled at the strong lines and curving lips.

Shifting from foot to foot, he doffed his hat and twirled it.

Oh. He was nervous.

"Well, Mr. Stone, if you don't mind, I'd like to have a look around." Tony was businesslike and firm.

"Sure. Let me unhitch your buggy in the barn."

"I can help," Lucy announced.

She didn't care if Tony quirked a perceptive brow. Time alone with Ben was few and far between. For weeks since their engagement, he'd only come to town twice, each time with Sol acting sentinel. No matter how the sight of Ben set her aflame, he remained stoic amidst the public or his best friend. There had been no opportunity whatsoever to catch him alone, no cornering him in the shadows and stealing kisses. She'd thought that the knowledge that she'd be his wife would put a damper on carnal urges, but it had been kerosene to the spark.

I'll get him alone today, she vowed. Four weeks was far too long to have kissed those lips. The way he stood, legs far apart, thighs thick and shoulders broad—it was too much. Pink climbed up her throat, and she tugged at the tight scalloped collar choking her.

Ben called Sol from his duties to show Tony around the property, and Lucy hopped back into the buggy and rode the short stretch to the barn with Ben.

IT WAS QUIET in the barn, the air charged like the moment before lightning struck.

It made Ben nervous. Too aware. Lucy sat hip to knee to him, having inched closer once her father had turned his back. He'd closed his eyes, which had been a mistake. Any time his eyes closed, he saw her in her father's office, or the alleyway, lips wet and begging him not to stop. He was hotter for her than a stud for a mare in season, and it was only getting worse. Spending time away from her may remedy the inevitable, but he needed to keep his vow to her Pa that she'd remain innocent until their wedding night.

Now, he was alone with Lucy again, and the temptation was excruciating. Empty lofts and tack rooms invited, and all he could smell was her sweet skin mingling with the scents of dried hay and horse manure.

"Ben?"

They had stopped in the breezeway of the barn, sitting still in the hush. The reins creaked in his tight fists. He released them and turned his head to her, stone-faced. "Maybe you shouldn't have come here."

Her face fell, slack with hurt. "Why?"

His jaw bulged. "Because now all I can think of is kissin' you. Right here." He dropped the reins and flattened her bottom lip with his thumb.

When an anticipatory smile replaced fear and she leaned into him, he released her and got the hell off the buggy. He was going crazy. Could pent-up urges cause insanity? He went around to help her down, but she was already halfway there, beginning the unhitching process.

"Why don't you?" she asked, and he stopped fumbling with the horse's chest harness.

Why didn't he kiss her? Because she didn't deserve to be flung onto the pile of hay in the stall next to them, that's why.

"It wouldn't be a good idea."

Her face poked out mischievously from beneath the mare's neck. "I think it would be a marvelous idea."

Struggling for stern, he said, "*No.*"

Pretending to think hard about it, she acquiesced, "Alright, Mr. Stone. No kisses. May I barter instead for a hug?"

"You getting lessons from your Pa's lawyer?" It was impossible not to laugh at her. Delight in her teasing made his body loose, relaxed. Smelling a victory, she led the horse to the nearest stall, motioning him to her.

"A lady does what she must." Once Ben took a step into the stall and was out of sight of the yard, she wrapped her arms tight around him. "I missed you dreadfully. You don't come to town often enough."

Delving his face into her fragrant hair, he wrapped his arms around her tight. *She's mine*, he marveled. *I can hold her like this every day until the day I die.* She whispered something, and he pulled back. "What did you say, darlin'?"

Lucy looked up from his chest. "I said that your hugs are the best. They're like a tonic. We should sell them in little bottles and cart them around the countryside."

Laughing, he lifted a dubious brow. "I doubt any farmer would want one of my hugs as a cure for a toothache or diphtheria."

"Hm, just women then."

Her face withdrew again, and her arms pulled him almost as close as two people could get. Hugging was distinctly different from kissing, both equally intoxicating, though dissimilar. If his hugs were medicinal, hers were heaven. Sinking into her hugs at the end of every day would be a cure-all for every mortal grievance.

Ben had no idea how long they'd been there, wrapped in each other's embrace. A distant call alerted them and they broke apart with the haste of new couples.

"Lucy, you in there? Come on out, now."

Long, delicate fingers wove through his.

Swallowing, he asked, "Want to see the house?"

"I thought you'd never ask."

They left the barn, and he motioned to the house. "Is it what you expected?" Damn it to hell, he couldn't remember the last time he'd felt such uncertainty. His shirt stuck to his lower back, and his heart galloped.

"No. It is beyond any expectations." At least she was smiling when she said it.

"Would you like to have a look-see?"

"I would love to."

BREATHLESS, SHE ALLOWED him to pull her across the grassy yard and up the front porch steps. She fervently wished her Papa wasn't there when he cleared his throat and Ben released her hand like a burning skillet handle.

The flower beds were barren except for choking grass and weeds bordered by lopsided rocks, but the boards of the steps and porch were new. The porch itself was bare of any chairs, tables, or rugs. Not even a dog graced its planks. She'd remedy that by her first week of marriage, she vowed.

"My father and mother built this house after I was born," Ben said, opening the plain wooden door and letting light stream into a nearly empty sitting room.

A fireplace took up half of the wall on the left, and the only furniture occupying the space to the right was a dining table and four chairs. Two mismatched armchairs sat close to the only window in the room, and they looked thinly cushioned and uncomfortable. The floor was dull with a layer of dust and grime, and cobwebs tried to hide in the corners of exposed beams in the ceiling. Behind the table was a door opened ajar, revealing a work table and the kitchen. Eyes brightening, it was Lucy's turn to lead Ben, and she paused in the doorway to absorb the details of the room.

It wasn't the grandest kitchen she'd ever seen. The hotel and many of the bakeries she'd been in, not to mention her mother's kitchen in the Queen Anne Victorian house in Atlanta, had all sported fine, large kitchens, every available space occupied with pans, shelves of jars, or counters.

Ben's kitchen—the kitchen she'd soon be cooking in—was small but airy, with two windows on hinges to allow light to stream in across the room. The worktable was smaller than the dining table and had a single painted, earthenware pitcher on it. There was a brand-new stove that made Lucy itch to try her hand at cooking in it; a large black beast with several doors and drafts and a long, black pipe climbing the wall behind it. Adjacent to the oven was a long stretch of countertop full of large buckets, cast iron pans, and a dishpan. Things sat higgledy-piggledy and she quashed the urge to organize right away.

It's not your kitchen yet.

To the immediate right was a small, cozy pantry and larder, shelves sad and mostly empty with jars that looked frightfully out of date. Hooks for aprons and kitchenware sat rusty, but firm, in walls that dearly needed a fresh coat of whitewash.

To Lucy, it was an area full of potential, of beauty, a place where she'd cook for her husband and future children. At the thought of children, she self-consciously stopped gawking to face Ben. He'd been watching her expression, thumbs hooked into his pockets. He was truly too handsome for his own good, and the way he stared at her as though her opinion meant everything to him did funny things to her insides.

"It's perfect," she murmured to him with complete truth. And if it wasn't perfect now, then it would be by the time she was finished with it.

"Want to see the upstairs?" He rocked back and forth on his heels twice, then stopped when Tony shouldered past them to squat in front of the stove and peer inside to check the dampers. Ben's face was carefully bland, but Lucy wasn't blind to the tension in his arms and fingers, wrapped in a death grip over his pockets.

"Yes, please."

They went up narrow stairs at the back of the house, and there were three bedrooms—two were quite small—and a linen closet that was even more diminutive. One of the smaller rooms didn't have beds or furniture, and one was Junior's room. Lucy managed not to balk at the pungent bite of old sweat that tended to cling to teenage boys before snapping the door shut again. The master had a large bed with a sturdy wooden headboard and a view of the land in front of the house from a large glass-paned window. It needed curtains, an armoire, and finer quilts and pillows for the bed. The floor was more wood and would need rag rugs to stop the chill when winter arrived.

Though the bed was made, the blanket on it was uncomfortable brown wool, and there was only one pillow. She wanted to tease about having to fight over the one pillow but refrained. She could feel her father breathing down their collars.

"The view is lovely," was what she said instead, pressing close to the new glass. He murmured in agreement, then grew quiet. After a minute of tense silence, Ben cleared his throat.

"I want to show you something else. Feel like a walk?"

They left the house and walked across the yard. Tony was held up by Sol again, and Lucy breathed a sigh of relief. She snagged Ben's hand firmly, teasingly, and he intertwined her fingers in his. She marveled that just the touch of his skin upon hers could make the landscape around them blur. Every brush of his thumb against hers made her swallow hard, and she looked sideways at him. The breeze blew his hair to the side, and she saw glimpses of vulnerable white scalp.

"Your home is perfect, Ben," she said over the rasp of grass parting at her skirts.

He squeezed her hand in response. "It'll be your house, too, soon enough."

"Not soon enough for me," she teased.

Eyes crinkling, he rebutted, "Is that so? Can't wait to make your mark on it?"

"I have some ideas in mind." She peeked up at him in an effort to be mysterious. He only laughed.

Ben introduced her to Frank and his wife, Tia, when they passed them, and then pulled her toward the edge of the woods. A rough, narrow trail, invisible in some places, wound from the tree line to a slender ribbon of a brown creek. Lucy chatted about it, asking questions about if it dried out during droughts, and if it had any fish, and she could tell she sparked Ben's interest in the latter.

"You fish?"

Scoffing, Lucy elbowed him. "Of course, I fish. I could probably out-fish you by a mile."

His straight black brows rose incredulously. "I doubt a city miss like you could catch more than a tree branch."

She wrinkled her nose. "You forget I was raised in the country for the first fourteen years of my life, Mr. Stone."

Their banter back and forth lasted another five minutes before she noticed the treetops clearing ahead. Titillated, she released his hand while they ascended the steep incline until they broke into Eden itself.

"Why, it's a perfect little gilly hole," she cried in delight. There was a bend in the creek that widened to a perfectly round swimming hole, wide enough that the sun broke through the trees.

He grinned at her reaction. "My ma taught me to swim here. Sometimes I'd bring your letters and read them under that." He nodded toward a small lean-to.

Charmed immeasurably by the image of this rough cowboy sitting beneath a lean-to to read her letters, she admitted, "I would read yours over and over almost every night in my room. Especially when I'd had a rough day."

A frog leaped from a cypress stump into the water. It occurred to her that they were very alone. The heat in his eyes revealed that he'd thought the same thing.

Slowly, as though sudden movements would scare him away, she stepped into him, twining her arms up and around his neck. Ben didn't stop her. Standing on her tiptoes, she focused on the scar above his lip.

"You never did tell me how you came by that scar, not the full story."

"Happened when I chipped my tooth."

Lucy smiled and met his eyes, leaning closer. "That wasn't a horse incident if I remember."

Shaking his head slowly, eyes burning with the effort to keep his hands off her, he said, "Got in a fight."

When her eyebrows shot up, he chose her moment of stillness to pull her flush against him, slanting his head down to part his lips over hers. The questions she'd planned to fire at him dissipated like fog before the hot, blinding light of the sun. Her neck bowed backward a bit, so she opened her mouth over his with a prayer he wouldn't shy away.

He didn't.

A hand fisted gently in her hair, the other cupping her bottom and hip boldly, pressing her hard against him until her senses sang. His mouth opened over hers, and his taste was dark and erotic, their tongues gliding sensually, slowly over one another. Her hands roved over his back, feeling the pliant, yet firm musculature. She thought about how it would feel when he was lying on top of her, and dipped the fingers of one hand beneath his waistband at the small of his back, tightening the embrace even further. She felt keenly the need to crawl him, to envelope him inside of her, and take over his body and mind.

She didn't want to wait until their wedding night.

She wanted him right here, right now, in the sand.

He pulled away from her just as she tightened her hands around his neck to pull him atop her. Blinking up at him, she asked, "Why did you stop?"

His inky hair had fallen over his brow in a rakish way that made her want to rub her face into it.

"I have to stop, Lucy." He sounded as out of breath as she, but there was a note of finality to it that she didn't dare contest. "What kind of man would I be if I brought you out here and," he made a sweeping gesture of helplessness, "and took you, even after I gave my word to your Pa not to?"

They'd gone over this before, and her body denied the sense he made. Her hips pressed back into him, and Ben gave an involuntary answering nudge against her. But she leaned her forehead against his deep, powerful chest, nodding through a soft, plaintive groan.

"You're right. It isn't honorable or at all dignified to go further. I suppose I can't fault you for being the man I fell in love with." Her lips smiled against his shirt, and she gave him a wicked kiss just over his heart. "Though the sooner we are married, the better."

He chuckled weakly and disengaged from her arms. "Gettin' harder to stop, that's for sure."

She wished he wouldn't say things like that. It made her want to tempt him again. "What do we do now?"

He glanced at the lowering sun. "Let's head back."

They hurried up the trail and groaned as one. A dark, one-armed silhouette on the hill paced.

"I bet your Pa thought we gave the fish something to look at."

Laughing, Lucy pinched his hand. He dutifully yelped.

"Hardly."

An hour later, after eating a meal with Tia, Frank, and Sol, Ben gave her grave news while helping her step into the buggy.

"I'm leaving tomorrow to buy some more horses to train for the trail drive come spring."

She didn't release his hand. "Oh. How long will that take?"

"No more than a month. It depends on how good the stock is. If it's bad, I'll have to go somewhere else to search. I don't want to take more than one trip; boarding up half-wild horses ain't easy."

Her glowing mood was gone and she waved goodbye to him, wanting him so much it hurt. She wished she'd given him a goodbye kiss to remember. Not likely with her father watching her every move like a hawk. Reminded of him, she leaned against his sturdy shoulder.

"Thank you for taking me to him, Papa. It was lovely."

He wrapped his arm around her and kissed the crown of her head. "Think nothing of it, poppet. I know you love him. He'll make a fine husband for you."

They pulled into the hotel at dark, voices hoarse from talking. Despite Ben's looming absence, she was in a wonderful mood when she ascended the stairs that night. Visions for what she'd improve in Ben's home kept her enthralled, particularly in the kitchen.

When she descended the attic stairs hours later for a midnight snack, she paused. Tony's office door was open, spilling light in the shape of a rectangle into the dim hallway. She knocked on the doorway.

"Papa? You're still awake?"

Tony was pouring bourbon into a glass, hand trembling. A thundercloud of an expression sat heavy, digging grooves into his forehead.

"I received a letter from your mother," he said, voice like acid.

"What does it say?" Her own voice sobered distinctly. Aurora hadn't written again after that last scathing letter renouncing her for running away. If Aurora was writing now, something must be horribly wrong.

A quivering hand gestured toward the opened letter on the desk. Lucy strode in and snatched it up. Her blood *whoosh, whoosh, whooshed* in her eardrums while she read it. Then, she crumpled the parchment up with a violence that startled Tony into sitting erect. A bit of his animosity drained while he watched Lucy pour another glass of bourbon. With a slow smile, Tony raised his glass to hers, but she was already draining the amber liquid. She gasped, coughed, and poured another one. Within the hour, they were laughing like fools, tears of hilarity shining in their eyes.

Aurora and Beth were coming to visit.

They'd be there before the month was up.

And...they were bringing Peter.

PART II

18

— · —

Chapter Eighteen

Aurora, Beth, and Peter arrived on a Friday.

Lucy was tightly wound; her teeth ached from clenching them all day. Her stomach was in knots, and if she'd only picked at her food before they'd arrived, she scarcely ate a bite at all now.

Minnie hovered, anxious as Lucy. She remembered all too well how the eldest Ricci woman had treated the youngest daughter, ignoring outstretched arms and spitting insults at a child who couldn't understand them.

Tony had stayed holed up in his room, drinking since the evening he had read his wife's letter. He wouldn't share any more spirits with his daughter, even though Lucy had asked, only half teasing. Two conspiratorial drinks between them had been the limit.

It didn't make a bit of sense that the three were coming to Texas, particularly with Peter in tow. The letter her mother had sent had been brisk and to the point. She was coming to tie up every loose end in Dogwood before retiring permanently at her Atlanta home. Have their rooms ready for them by this day. Peter Langford would accompany them.

But, why?

Surely Peter couldn't have conformed to her mother's plans to marry Elizabeth. Beth was an heiress, but the Langfords were already rich. The two families had to have made up in some way, but still...Lucy couldn't think of any possible explanation as to why they were coming.

What 'loose ends' could Aurora possibly have in Texas?

Was it a ruse?

Would they kidnap Lucy and bring her back to Georgia?

Was *she* the loose end?

Inane possibilities swirled around in Lucy's mind until she was sick with them. She'd never go back to Atlanta, no matter what her mother promised or threatened her. She'd never let Aurora matchmake her with some stranger, or be led by the nose to some finishing school. That old trapped feeling, a mixture of resentment and insecurity, suffused her normal cheerfulness into something darker, quieter. By the time the stagecoach pulled in, bags piled obscenely high atop it, Lucy was pale and shadowy-eyed in front of the registration desk.

Three heads, two in various shades of blonde, stepped out across the street, two men behind them in rough clothing dragging half a dozen suitcases. Lucy remembered her lonely green and pink cabbage flower carpetbag. She thought of Ben tossing heavy saddlebags over a shoulder, bicep bulging and shirt growing taut. He had no idea that the man she'd been involved with was here now, and quiet anxiety set her teeth on edge.

Would he be furious when he found out?

She had no address to which to send him letters. All he'd told her was that he was leaving the state to buy prime horse-flesh.

Seeing Peter again after discovering his betrayal made her want to scream. He was a past that she had rid herself of gratefully, like mud from her shoes. Now she'd have to atone for the things she'd done to him. And with him.

Her mother and sister drew closer, chatting with each other, motioning at the face of the hotel. Tony stepped up beside Lucy, and reached for her hand, clenching it gently. The fact that he'd come out of hiding to lend support relaxed her somewhat, but it would almost have been better if he was absent. He hadn't seen his wife since she'd left with Lucy and all his money three and a half years before. He hadn't seen Beth, either. Even now, his eyes roved over the changes that time had transformed in his oldest daughter.

Peter, tall and slim, held the door open for the women. They looked marginally travel-worn, but it had taken them the entire week to get to Dogwood, with several stops in luxurious hotels along the way, Lucy imagined. They wore clothes Lucy had never seen before, new and complicated in design, with waists cinched in at eighteen inches in circumference. Both women were tiny and doll-like, Aurora a touch older. Her face was beautiful but hard, and she didn't meet her estranged husband's eye. Instead, she looked around at the hotel with pursed, frowning lips, and ice-blue eyes. A tiny, jaunty green hat perched at a fashionable angle matched her dress to perfection.

Unable to look at her for long, Lucy glanced from her mother to her sister, who was dressed in pale pink and looking as perfect as a rose blossom. Beth watched Tony with wary eyes, not making a sound or smiling. She stood a few inches behind Aurora, ever the pretty little coward.

Lucy thought yellow suited her far better than pink.

And Peter...he wore a dove gray suit and a tall top hat that added several extra inches to his already considerable height. Remembering their trysts, their kisses, and naughty words from the past, Lucy peered up at him miserably. He was examining her as though one would a bug. From head to toe, his gaze judged her, pausing at the fresh crop of freckles on her nose, and found her wanting.

So.

It appeared that their friendship was no more. It was better that way, she soothed herself. If she had acted disgusting, then he had been neck-and-neck with her. No matter his disapproval, she knew the truth of it. He had lied and had sent his parents to entrap her, without even the mettle to ask her himself.

No.

They were equally despicable.

When he made another pass over her, she narrowed her eyes at him, daring him to continue the impudence. His glare snagged on hers and caught. For long moments, they seethed at each other, a battle of wills that turned his neck ruddy and her cheeks pink.

Neither smiled.

The silence became so strained that they eventually looked away. Aurora and Tony were locked in a similar battle, and Beth couldn't seem to decide which couple to look at. Finally, a burning set of crystal eyes focused on Lucy.

"*What* are you wearing, Lucille?" Aurora's eyes slid over the blue dress Lucy wore. "You'll not be so provincial during our stay, I gather?"

Standing straighter, Lucy took a bracing breath. "I imagine you are all exhausted from your journey. Your rooms are made up and readied. Papa, will you show Mr. Langford his suite?"

"Have you lost all of your training in etiquette, young lady?" Aurora snapped. She turned to Tony. "Mr. Ricci, may I introduce you to Peter Langford III." For a moment her eyes rested on Lucy before adding, "Elizabeth's fiancé."

Lucy became very still.

Tony's brows raised, and he offered his right hand. "Fiancé, you say? Two daughters betrothed at one time, how first-rate. Pleasure to meet you." His sarcastic words slurred only a little.

A hint of a frightening expression darkened Peter's stiff features before he hid it. "The pleasure is mine, Mr. Ricci," he said, wooden as a fence post.

Peter was Beth's fiancé? No wonder he was in such ill humor. They were a miserable pair.

Aurora's lips pursed, drawn together tight, and she sniffed. "I have a great many things to say to you both, but I find I am simply too exhausted to list them to you this evening. I shall be in my room. I expect you to meet me in my study in the morning so that we may talk."

Her study? That was laughable.

Papa took an audible, bracing breath.

Lucy would be busy in the morning. Saturdays were their busiest days of the week, and she needed to be up with the cock's crow to get the kitchen prepped for the breakfast rush. She managed to keep her mouth shut, however, and stood alone after the women left and Peter was ushered upstairs. It was no surprise that she felt as she always had around them.

Small and unworthy.

LUCY SAT IN an empty stall in the hotel's backyard stable, rubbing the smooth ears of Mama Kitty, the stray she'd adopted since her arrival. Mama Kitty purred loudly, almost drowning out the sounds of humming, chirping nighttime insects. Her newest litter of kittens nursed at her teats, eyes still closed to the world around them. The ache in Lucy's chest abated with the balm of quiet shadows and late-night introspection. She had tossed and turned in bed before fleeing outside in her night rail. She'd moved like a ghost, avoiding every creaking board and squeaking hinge, a longtime talent of hers.

She kneeled in the dry comfort of fresh hay, scared to death. When Ben found out the man that used to spark her was staying in the same building, he would be furious. Would he cry off? Wash his hands of her? No matter what, she'd have to tell him the truth. If only he were here now. Tony would let Ben stay in the hotel, free of charge, and her misgivings would ease inordinately. Keeping Ben and Peter separated, however...

"What in God's name are you doing out here?" a masculine voice cracked from the dark behind her.

Swallowing a scream, Lucy whirled and fell on her backside, legs tangled in her billowing nightgown. "Peter?"

His dark silhouette loomed in the doorway, shoulders rounded and somehow menacing. "What are you doing out here?" he repeated. "Are you meeting someone?"

As though the time away had never happened, she fell back into the habit of appeasing him. "No! No, I couldn't sleep. I came out here to pet the kittens."

"The...kittens?" Again, it was so familiar. The accusation in his voice melted away as he decided to believe her. He took a step into the stall and crouched beside her. His knees cracked.

"Yes, see? Mama Kitty is black, but all her kittens are white and black spotted. You can just see them if you look hard enough."

For a moment they strained in the dark. Even if he hadn't seen them, suckling sounds and tiny mews could be heard from below. After a moment, he surprised her by sitting on his backside with her.

"You could not sleep?" He was still guarded, his words harsh.

Playing with the tip of her braid, Lucy sighed. "Not with Mother in the same building as me, no."

And you.

He didn't say anything more. She fidgeted. If he was just going to sit there like a stump, then why did he come out there?

"How was your journey here?" she asked dully.

He didn't answer long enough that she thought he never would, then, "Dreadful. Boring. Infuriating."

"Adequate synonyms to describe Mother and Beth." She couldn't help laughing, and watched his shadow head turn to her in the dark. When he said nothing, simply pointed the black void of his face at her, she began to feel prickles at her nape and along her arms. The last time she'd seen him, he had kissed her so hard he'd split her lip. Would he expect more kisses? It made her uneasy. Everything about his trip there did. It felt like a farce for something that they wanted to get their way with. The air around them crackling, Lucy decided that directness was the only cure for their mutual animosity.

"You're engaged to Beth, then?"

Peter snorted into the air with violence, making her jump. "Father forced the issue. He found that you were unacceptable."

Anger brought her from her lounge back to her knees. "I was unacceptable? *I?*"

"Yes," he sneered, "*you*. Mother told me everything."

"And what did your dear mother have to say?" she ground.

"That you laughed at my proposal. That you seduced me to torment your sister. Then, before you fled like a coward in the night, you stole all the money from your mother's safe to bring back to your drunken father."

Lucy was laughing before he'd finished the first allegation. "What a heap of lies! And you and your father just believed them, did you? No doubt she and Mother schemed all day to think of this one."

"Are you calling my mother a liar?" Said stiffly. *Watch it*, that voice said.

Too furious to care about the danger of his temper, she crowded nearer, eyes slits in the dark. "I'm telling you that those are all false accusations, Peter Langford. But you were all too willing to believe it. And who are you to accuse? That's the real question. I could tell you what your mother followed me from the parlor to say, but you wouldn't listen to reason. You never did before, why should you now?"

Lucy made to stand up, but a hand squeezed her arm and forced her back down. Her knees hit the hard-packed earth beneath the straw, and she gasped in anger and pain.

"Let go of me," she growled, wrenching at his vice-like grip. He only gripped tighter until she bowed forward, grimacing. Fear was fast replacing her pique.

"What did she say to you?" he whispered, breath fanning her hair from her ear.

Heart racing in flight instinct, she nonetheless raised her chin. "I'll tell you when you've released my arm."

He didn't move away for several seconds, cheek to cheek with her. "Fine. Then tell it. And I'll know if you're lying."

No, you wouldn't, she thought to herself, fuming while she rubbed the feeling back into her arm. "After your father proposed for you," she paused to let that sink in for a moment, "they ushered me out so that he and Mother could conduct business. She wasn't happy. Tried to foist Beth on you but your father wouldn't hear it. Your mother followed me into the hall. I was of a mind to accept you at that point, but then...she showed me the letter."

"What letter?" he snapped, quick as a viper.

Guilty as one, too.

"You know what letter. Honesty, remember? You kept the letter I asked you to send to my father." She wasn't angry anymore. Her words revealed all the hurt she'd felt inside when she'd learned of his betrayal. "I thought we were friends, Peter. How could you keep it?"

Peter was breathing hard, almost panting. He wiped his hands on his trousers. The fine gray ones that cost more than the hotel made in a week that he sat on the filthy stall floor in. "I was going to switch envelopes. Put a different return address on it. But...I read it and realized I couldn't let you go. Not without seeing if you felt the same way about me that I did about you. If you had accepted my proposal, you'd never have made that godforsaken trip here!"

"But Peter, you barely knew me at all. You lied to me. How could you base a marriage on a lie? I would've found out eventually."

"Letters get lost in the mail with some frequency—"

"Ah, more lies, then!"

"Damn you—" His hand raised high as though he'd slap her, but then it lowered slowly. Reluctantly. They were both breathing fast, now. Lucy's throat pinched, and she blinked irritated eyelids. "Goddamn it, I won't hurt you. Don't shy away from me."

After swallowing with some difficulty, she managed, "Shall I finish?"

His shadow head nodded.

"After she showed me my letter and what you had said when she'd discovered it, she offered me money to go to Dogwood after all."

"You took my mother's money?" It was his turn to rise to his knees.

"No, blast you, will you listen?" she cried. "She offered the money, and I turned it away! I am not as despicable as all that. I told her I would go to Dogwood of my own accord because you had betrayed me, and not because I was compensated for it!"

Peter lowered his head between his knees, back hunched, scrubbing his styled hair with rough hands.

"And I did not *steal* money from mother," Lucy continued derisively. "Papa sent money over the years, and I saved up. I want nothing from that woman. Her presence here, it's like—like a waking nightmare," she struggled to explain. "I'm sure she came here to flaunt your engagement to Beth under my nose." As though she cared. But she wouldn't tell him that. It was best not to poke a hibernating bear.

His laugh was humorless. "Oh, she came for that, but also to stop your engagement to this 'Stone' fellow." He stopped, and the quiet was so heavy Lucy wanted to shout. "It didn't take you long to move on, Lucy."

Ah, so he believed that she was telling the truth about not stealing her mother's money, but now he was upset about her entanglement with another man. Striving for patience, she murmured, "I met Ben on the way to Dogwood. He's a good man."

Growling, Peter stood, startling the cat from her nap. "It's absurd. You've just met the man. I've known you for more than a year. How could you jump from one man to the other?"

Affronted, she stood alongside him, dusting the hay from her night rail. "That's not fair. You're engaged to my sister, are you not? One sister is as good as the other?"

"Christ, the things you say make me want to take a horse-whip to you!" he practically shouted. He stabbed a finger in front of her face. "If you marry this man, it will be the biggest mistake of your life."

"You're wrong."

"How? How is marrying this man any better than marrying me?"

She shouldn't say it. She shouldn't. But he needed to hear it, even if it hurt him. "Because I was never in love with you," she choked, hating to hurt him no matter his faults. "And I love Ben."

Peter's finger lowered, and she could feel his stare, feel the hate radiating from him to the marrow of her bones. Without a word, he stormed from the stables. Exhaling unevenly, she leaned against a post of the stall and dropped her face into her hands. Eventually, she scrubbed the silver tracks from her cheeks and disappeared into the quiet darkness of the hotel.

IT WAS ATLANTA all over again.

The next morning, Lucy was up before daybreak, losing herself in the busyness of the kitchen and dining area. When customers arrived, she turned on her smile and was able to temporarily let go of all her worries. That was, until Peter strolled in and sat at a corner table. She took his order with a stiff smile, and he ate, sullen in his corner. Watchful. When he was in these moods, it made the hair on the back of her neck stand up. Made her clumsy. She tripped on two different men's shoes and had a hard time listening to orders.

Minnie's worried eyes would light on her every time she entered the kitchen. When Ben visited, Lucy would glow, dancing around the tables and teasing the women in the kitchen. With this other man here, this 'gentleman', she was on edge, snapping out orders and forgetting which plates went to which tables. Constantly, she would rub her neck, feel around for her pad of paper and pencil, and frown down at orders with a faraway look.

Halfway through the breakfast rush, one of the maids that cleaned the hotel rooms entered the kitchen with a harassed frown.

"Miss Lucy, Mrs. Ricci is wantin' to see you. I'm to bring her a tray of tea, but I done forgot what she asked for—"

"I know what she likes, thank you," Lucy soothed, then took off her apron and handed it to Patsy. "Could you please take over? I'm sorry, I'm afraid I won't be back until lunch. If I'm lucky."

Lucy carried a heavily loaded tea tray full of most of her mother's favorite pastries on the best china. Papa was staying at Mizz Trudy's place, so she shouldered the cracked office door open, assuming her mother was nosing around.

Aurora sat in the chair, delicate spectacles perched on her nose as she perused every ledger she could. A frown line cut deep between her brows and deepened further when she glanced up.

"Your father is bankrupt," she said.

Lucy spared the ledger a glance and set the tea tray on one end of the desk. "That one is outdated. See there? Six months ago. We broke even with the late charges a few weeks ago, and now most of the money made goes to Mr. Brewster and those that we employ."

"Those that *we* employ?"

"Yes, *we*. Papa and I work together to keep this place afloat. Now. You wanted to see me?"

Ever one to be in control, Aurora ignored Lucy's hastening and poured her tea. Then, she buttered a scone and took a delicate bite of the flaky crust. She made a face and dropped it as though she'd found a hair.

Praying to God and all His heavenly angels for tolerance, Lucy went to the window and leaned against the trim. The street was alive with people walking around, enjoying their day, probably happy in their ignorant bliss of no Aurora in their life to muddle things up.

"Lucille."

Bottling up suppressed rage, Lucy crossed her arms beneath her bosom and gritted, "Yes?"

"Do not stand so, heavens, have you forgotten every speck of comportment?"

Lucy dropped her arms and stood straight. "What did you wish to talk about?"

Aurora sighed. "I cannot have my daughter working like a common waitress or maid. It isn't done, Lucille. I am not surprised at your father, but you? Surely you can do better for yourself than menial labor."

With patience she didn't feel, Lucy interjected, "I find nothing offensive about honest work. The hotel is doing so much better, and the townspeople respond well to a friendly face and good food."

"Please." Aurora waved away her daughter's coaxing. "I have heard quite enough about this farce of a hotel."

Fists clenched, Lucy turned, shoulders bunched up tight and words quick. "And I have heard enough of your scorn for every slight I have made against your unmeasurable standards."

"Watch your tongue—"

"No!" Her shout rang against the walls, reverberating with exasperation. Mother and daughter's eyes protruded with equal ire. "I will not watch my tongue. Why should I? You want me to pretend that I care what the people of Atlanta think?" She sliced her hand through the air. "I care not at all! If anyone has tarnished my name, it wasn't I. You've done a fine job of that yourself. Really, Mother, you told Mr. Langford that I stole from you?" Lucy's face wrinkled in a disgusted grimace. "That was low, even for you. I've never been a thief."

Aurora stood, mouth small. "What are you blathering about?"

Lucy crossed her arms again. Hate was a tame word for how she felt about rows with her mother, and right now, she was ill with it. "Peter told me everything."

That she used his Christian name no longer made her mother blink. "Everything? We haven't been here twelve hours and already you've had an opportunity for a private conversation with Mr. Langford?"

"You forget that we are not strangers to one another." Contempt dripped from Lucy's words.

"Oh, yes, how could I forget that you seduced him from beneath your sister's nose." Aurora's own words could freeze brimstone. "How it must irk you to know that he's engaged to Elizabeth."

Fingernails digging in her clenched biceps, Lucy kept her tone light. "On the contrary, I'm quite happy for the two of them. Perhaps we could all have a double wedding, Mr. Langford and Beth, and Mr. Stone and myself."

At this, Aurora's nostrils flared. Her corset creaked with the deep breath she took, and when she spoke, her words were tight, as though spoken through a tautly drawn coin purse. "There will be no marriage between you and this *Mr. Stone*, Lucille."

"Yes. There will be."

"I forbid it."

Nose stinging, throat tight, Lucy hissed, "You come here, unwanted, and make demands you have no way of mandating. Go back to Atlanta, and let Papa and I live our lives in peace!"

"Have you neglected to remember whose money started this hotel, child?" Aurora had finally succumbed to irrationality. She was shaking, face blotchy, nose bright red. "Mine! My money! My father took it from my inheritance and that is how this foul building was borne. If I so wished, it could be torn down to nothing."

She would, Lucy despaired, eyes pricking and voice gone. She'd convince Mr. Brewster and lawyers to demolish it out of spite, someway, somehow.

Aurora gave Lucy a contemptuous once-over and pointed a trembling finger to the door. "Now. Go to your room and dress in something appropriate for a lady. If I see you wear one more apron in my presence, I will burn every one of them in the backyard."

And dance around the flames, Lucy thought. For a long moment, they waged war against wills. When tears began to fill her mother's eyes, Lucy turned on her heel and exited. The door slammed behind her.

19

CHAPTER NINETEEN

Aurora dragged Beth and Lucy all over town for house calls, accompanied by Peter. It was decidedly miserable. There were a thousand other things that she could be doing besides drinking tea and coffee with the southern gentry of the growing town. Dusty old money or crisp new money, neither mattered to Aurora except for the power that their money could buy.

Their argument resolutely swept under the rug, Aurora went on as normal, roving eyes once again judging and finding everything lacking. Beth was the slight shadow in the corner that people forgot about, an ornamental parasite that glowed with a mother's praise.

Peter, however, surprised Lucy. It appeared to her that he was finding it just as hard to keep up pretenses. He sat on uncomfortable settees and chairs, ankle crossed elegantly over a knee. He had two expressions. Near-fatal boredom, or a brooding sulk that made an appearance any time he glanced at Lucy.

She ignored him.

It was best for him. He needed to move on. The sooner she married Ben, the better. If only Ben would hurry and come home to her.

"Yes, Beth was tutored by the finest teachers the South has to offer. We even had several travel all the way from

Boston just to grace our home for the summer," Aurora boasted self-importantly to Mrs. Brewster, the banker's wife.

Lucy closed her eyes long-sufferingly so that she wouldn't roll them. When she opened them, green eyes were watching. After a week of being in each other's tense company, Peter looked more relaxed that day.

It was about time, Lucy thought unkindly. One could have a stick up one's behind for so long.

"Mrs. Brewster, we are of a mind to throw a party this Saturday evening. Would you care to join us?"

"Oh, why, I'd be delighted." Mrs. Brewster bestowed Lucy with a warm smile. "Mr. Brewster and I have admired how well you've done with the hotel, Lucy, dear. It's been the talk of the town since you came back. Tell me, how was your time in Atlanta?"

Aurora's brows pinched to the middle. "It was difficult for her—" she began.

"Atlanta was a brief adventure," Lucy cut in with a forced smile. "I spent more time in a boarding school in Boston, thanks to Mother's connections. When I returned to Atlanta, I spent most of my time visiting the local restaurants and bakeries."

Aurora stiffened, then hid it with a sip of her tea.

Mrs. Brewster leaned forward, intrigued. "Is that where you learned those new recipes? My favorites are your breakfast pastries."

"Oh, those recipes were a chore to acquire."

"How did you convince the owners to share?"

"I can be persuasive when I need to be." Lucy smiled through her sip of tea. She ignored the glitter of the green eyes across the room. Neither of them had forgotten the strained conversations about the kiss with the baker's son.

They went back and forth for the rest of the visit as though Aurora wasn't there. Every now and then, Peter interjected something, a question here and there about the name of a restaurant.

Aurora berated her the whole way home, but Lucy ignored her. The insults and accusations were tired and repetitive. The rest of the week was more of the same. Beth had found her tongue, and shot slights like watermelon seeds. They were endless and annoying.

"Your hem is atrocious," Beth would jeer.

"So are your manners," Lucy would reply, bored.

"You still wear that bonnet? It's nearly six years old. I would not be caught dead in such a relic." Beth sniffed.

"And yet you're wearing a dress the exact shade of cat vomit with no compunction of dying whatsoever," Lucy dead-panned.

Peter laughed, and Beth stormed away, ears red-hot.

The more Lucy stood up for herself, the more Peter warmed to her. It was a disturbing change. By mid-week, he seemed to have forgiven her their argument in the barn. He smiled at her when no one looked. She didn't trust those smiles and did not return them.

One night, she could not sleep. In bed, Lucy lay awake, staring up at the shadowy rafters of the ceiling. It was humid, but the open window allowed a breeze to keep her skin from growing damp with sweat. She lay on her covers, naked, thinking about Ben with impure thoughts. Her fingertips trailed down between her collarbones, between her breasts, along the seam of her stomach, and lower, down, down. She missed him so much she could hardly bear it. If only he knew what she thought of him. Did he think of her like this?

She closed her eyes and imagined Ben walking up her steps to her bed, watching her. His blue eyes would glow in the dark, and she'd ask him to disrobe. No. She'd *order* him to disrobe. He'd frown at her, deny her long enough to make her mad, then he'd take off his hat. Unbutton his shirt. He'd leave his trousers on and lower his face to hers, and kiss her. His beard would have grown in the weeks away; it would tickle. He'd replace her pale hand with his dark one, burying it between her legs—

Her frustration turned into ecstasy at an alarming rate, and she gasped with the force and suddenness of her climax. She'd never finished so fast, and she lay on her quilt, stunned, eyes big and pulse throbbing hard in her neck and between her legs. She'd never done this while thinking of Ben and found that she wanted to do it again. Immediately. Time passed swift and wrenching, and it happened twice more, that clenching, breath-stealing feeling.

When her quilt and bedsheets were skewed, her sweat drying, and her breathing calmed, Lucy was finally able to drift into a restful slumber.

The next day, the morning before the party, Lucy escaped to the post office and found a letter from Ben waiting for her. Her smile took up her whole face. It was short and sweet and dated from two weeks before. He'd purchased his horses and would be on his way home within the week. If that was true, then Ben was due home any day now!

Heart suffused with happiness, Lucy bounced home as though walking on air. She greeted everyone with a smile and 'good morning', her joy contagious.

Mother and Beth were out, Lord knew where, so Lucy hopped up the stairs to hide her letter, an activity she'd taken up again after her mother's arrival. She met Peter on the landing.

"Oh," she paused, surprised to see him on the family's side of the hotel. Her smile remained. She wondered if Ben was in Texas' state lines yet. "Good morning, Peter. Were you looking for Papa?"

"Good morning, Lucy. You're looking well." His hands found purchase on her shoulders, and he gave her a warm grin. "I was looking for you."

"Oh," she repeated. Her smile slipped. "Did Mother need me?"

"No, no, nothing like that." His hands slid down her arms and grabbed her hands. He grew serious. "I wanted to call a truce."

A truce? Her shoulders relaxed, and she released a relieved sigh. "I'm so happy that you want that, Peter. It was dreadful to think that we could no longer be friends."

"Of course not," Peter murmured, searching her face. "It became more than obvious to me that neither of us is at fault for the rift between us." He glanced down at the letter in her hand, but it was facedown.

Though she didn't fully agree with his statement, she smiled anyway. It would be nice to have him happy once again. She'd be able to relax around him for a change.

"Excellent. I may just be able to enjoy the party, after all."

He chuckled, thumbs stroking. She cleared her throat, uncomfortable, and slid her hands from his. "I'd best see if I can help Minnie with any preparations. Tomorrow will be busy enough without last-minute mishaps."

To her surprise, he stood tall and straightened his jacket. "I'd like to help. How can I be of service?"

Accepting the olive branch for what it was, Lucy smiled and pocketed her letter. "You're going to regret asking," she teased, then put him to work.

He turned out to be a lot of help, and good fun in the process. Minnie watched him with dark, distrusting eyes, but Lucy just smiled and shook her head. Peter would always be complicated. It was best to take the good in him when it appeared. Aurora had closed the diner temporarily during her stay. She said the people's constant chatter and the smells of the kitchen gave her a headache. Peter and Lucy moved tables from the dining area, carried in heavy crates of food for the party, and set up chairs in a circle for dancing. She tried to ignore his constant touches on her person and pretended not to see the hot looks he gave her when he thought her back was turned.

He may still have feelings for her, but as long as he kept his distance, there was still a chance that they could remain friends.

Aurora and Beth came in around dark, exhausted from calling on old friends in the town over. They ordered supper in their rooms and turned in for the night.

Lucy's shoulders and lower back throbbed from heavy lifting, and she rubbed the sore muscles with a moan before sinking into Tony's plush office chair. He was still at Mizz Trudy's, the stinking coward. She scowled and bent down to unlace the tight little boots her mother insisted that she wear. When both were off, she picked a stockinged foot up and dug her thumbs deep into the arch. She released another moan, head drooping from the incredible sensation.

"I thought I heard you in here," a soft voice said at the door.

Startled, Lucy dropped her foot and sat up.

Oh. It was just Peter.

He slowly clicked the office door shut, holding something surreptitiously behind his back.

Raising a brow, she sank back into the chair with a creak, trying to look around his back. "What do you have there?"

"Something we both dearly need."

"A good club to the head?"

His laugh was real, like those he'd given her all day. For a moment déjà vu stunned her into silence; she could practically smell the cigarillo smoke from her old back porch a lifetime ago.

It made her wary, that laugh.

"No, but I have the next best thing." He brought out one of the bottles of expensive wine her mother had ordered.

"I appreciate the gesture," she said slowly. Carefully. "But I don't think it's a good idea. I'll need my wits about me for tomorrow."

He gave an unaffected shrug. "If you insist. Do you mind if I drink?"

She shrugged as well and reached for one of her father's tumblers in the desk drawer. "Of course not. You deserve it, after today."

His laugh changed. "Yes, you worked me hard. I'll be expecting repayment."

She flushed at his words, unease feeding into her flight instinct. "I'm pretty tired, Peter," she said, handing over the tumbler and standing. She wiped sweating palms on her skirts. "I may turn in. Good night."

"Wait." Brows furrowed, he set the wine and tumbler on the desktop and raised his hands in surrender. "Did I say something? I just wanted to have a decent conversation, maybe play a game of cards like old times. If anything, I'll go to my room and let you finish up in here."

Had she overreacted?

Sighing, she rubbed her forehead. What could he do with her mother and sister down the hall? She was being a ninny. "No, no, everything is fine. Let's play a game of cards, then we can retire."

Lucy sat in her father's chair, and Peter sat in the smaller chair opposite her. By the third game, she relaxed. He'd kept his conversation safely about his law firm and new house. By the fifth game, Peter had unbuttoned his first three buttons, his hair was rumpled, and he was bent over laughing at one of her diner stories. She winced and rubbed her tired eyes.

"God, how late is it?" The window behind her was black and reflective, and not even shouts could be heard from the saloon across the street.

"Too damned late," he vowed and yawned wide enough to amuse her. He blinked at her with bloodshot eyes, more than a little drunk. "I almost forgot how beautiful you were."

Too tired to be alarmed, she nonetheless groaned at the hackneyed compliment. "Peter, enough. Don't make me throw you out." Maybe humor would keep him from becoming angry.

Leaning forward, he tried for a charming smile that didn't fool her for a second. "Lucy, you can't sit there, hair falling down, looking sleepy and so pretty I could eat you and not expect me to say something."

Laughing at the absurd statement, she quipped, "You're drunk. Listen to yourself, you're stark raving."

"Yes, well, you make me that way." His smile was gone, and his eyes lit with something fervent.

Lucy swallowed and bent down to don her pinching boots, wincing when the first foot was shoved in. "I'm sorry, I didn't intend to make you feel such things. Perhaps it's good we never married."

She heard him stand up, and paused, listening. He was moving around the desk. Damn and blast. Her hands burst into motion, tying faster but fumbling.

"We could still marry," he said, voice deeper. Nice Peter was gone. This was the Peter that put her on her guard, and she felt a flash of panic. He crouched in front of her, shoving her hands roughly to the side. Instead of tying her boots, he unlaced all her work.

"Peter, stop that—"

"We could elope, you know," he interrupted, ignoring her shallow breathing and the fact that she tried to pull her foot away. He captured her ankle in his hand and squeezed until she ceased. "I've thought about it. We could leave tonight. Or first thing in the morning. I have more than enough money to get us home to New York. Father will forgive you once I tell him about your mother's lies. It will be water beneath the bridge. Yes. Christ, I missed you. I'm afraid I went quite mad when my parents told me you'd run off."

His hand climbed up her leg and she began to struggle in earnest. Not so long ago, Ben was in this same position in front of her. She'd begged him not to stop, but his honor was no match against her. And now, it was Peter's lack of honor that she was no match for.

He moved in, eyes lowered on her lips.

"Peter, I said stop!" She pushed him hard on the shoulders, and he fell backward on his rear. Lucy made to move around the desk, fleeing for the other side, but he was quicker. A strong hand snatched her ankle and yanked. She fell with a muffled thump, knocking the chair to the side, and turned on him, ready to fight tooth and nail.

While they struggled, she couldn't see or think straight. Flashes of his throat and bared teeth, feelings of fear and rage, all of it was a blur while they both became more animal than human. Somehow, he'd worked her skirts up. Helplessness and disbelief overcame her rage, and she shook her head at him.

"I'll scream—" No sooner had she said it than his mouth was on hers, hand gripping both wrists so tightly that she keened. Why was he so strong? She bent her exposed leg up and tried to gain purchase against his ribs or chest with a bared foot, but he pressed closer. When she kicked hard at his calves with her hard little heels, his palm struck her across the face with a violence that stunned her.

Frozen, seeing spots, it took an entire minute before her senses returned and she realized what he was doing.

He'd rolled her over on her stomach. Her hands were clasped behind her back, losing feeling from the torturous pressure of his grip. Peter pressed hard against her bottom, then bent to her ear.

"If you won't marry me, you won't marry anyone. Not without having a little piece of me inside you. Scream, and I'll break your wrist." He wrenched up on her hands, and she gasped with the pain. "Do you think you're better than me? You've teased me, knowing how I feel, goddamn it."

He was fumbling at her back, unbuttoning his pants. Panting with fear, knowing that fighting him wouldn't stop the inevitable, she tried to bargain. "Peter, stop, stop, please, think about what you're doing."

"It's too goddamned late, Lucy. Look what you've brought me to," he cried softly in her ear, making her stomach revolt at the sour alcohol on his breath. "If you had just said yes, my hand would not be forced."

"You can still s-stop," she tried to soothe. "I won't say a thing, please. You're better than this."

He wasn't listening. His hand cupped her between her legs from behind, and then she didn't care if he broke both of her wrists.

She screamed.

His hand clapped over her mouth, wrenching her head back, bowing her neck. "Shut the hell up before you wake the whole house," he snarled.

The door to the office swung open, and they both froze. He released her. She crawled forward on her forearms while he re-buttoned his clasps, crouched with feral, bulging eyes.

It was Beth.

She stood, pale-faced and frail in her voluminous white nightgown. Her braid was thin, and wisps of hair curled around her ears as though mussed from her pillow. "Mr. Langford?"

Peter stood up, red-faced, swaying on his feet. Her blue eyes went wide, and she took in the scene. No one said a word. With a growl of rage, Peter strode to Beth.

"Say of a word of this to anyone, and all the doors in Atlanta will close in you and your mother's sour faces. Do you understand?"

Beth nodded without hesitation, terrified.

He didn't spare Lucy a glance and disappeared into the hall. It was so quiet in the office that Lucy wanted to shout. She wiped her face with her sleeves, shaking with quiet sobs, and stood up.

"I'm so happy you came—"

"You bitch." Beth's voice was so whisper-soft, Lucy almost thought she'd imagined it.

Cold pooled into her bones. "What?"

"Mother was right about you," Beth said, and her eyes filled with tears. "She was right about everything. You seduced him. You're seducing him now, right before us."

"How can you say that after what you just walked into!" Lucy cried. She wondered if she'd ever stop shaking.

"It's the oldest trick," said Beth, lips trembling. "Be his whore and force his hand. But I'll not stand for it, not this time. Stay away from him." She turned on her heel and left.

Lucy stood there until she was numb from cold, even though the windows behind her were fogged from the warm steam outside. Eventually, she stirred and doused the lamps, then crept down the stairs, legs weak and unsteady, jumping at every noise, terrified she'd run into Peter. She snuck into the stables, climbed the rickety ladder, and hid in the straw piled in the tiny loft. Sleep was impossible, but she lay still as a mouse, afraid to come out.

20

CHAPTER TWENTY

B en made it into Dogwood hours after dusk, dog-tired, and itching for a shave.

The journey home had been arduous, seconds ticking away like minutes. Trains crawled, and every prime piece of horse-flesh he'd bought fought the drive, trotting with the pace of livery nags. It didn't help that he was towing a wagon full of furniture and a new mattress for his bride-to-be. A bright gold ring burned in his pocket, and Ben patted it constantly in the fear that it had fallen out in the ride. He'd left the wagon in the barn, gave Junior a brief greeting, then left, his brother's unhappy frown piercing him with guilt.

Hell, he hadn't even bathed before running to the hotel, eager as a stray with the scent of home.

His lamp was lit and running low on kerosene when he turned out of a shortcut alley, and he pulled the reins in disbelief. Lucy's hotel was a beacon on the main street. People in inky black buggies and long-legged trotters left in droves, waving goodbyes and tipping hats to a couple of well-to-do strangers bidding farewells on the porch. He didn't recognize either woman but heard snippets of old-gentry Georgian accents calling out to guests.

Ben doused the lantern, flesh prickling, and circled the glow of light from the porch. Under the cover of darkness, he walked Reb through the alley bisecting the hotel and general store. The unlit barn beckoned, but he waited for a tall young man on the porch to flick a thin cigarillo into the yard and enter the back door before continuing forward.

What in the hell was going on? Regretting his shabby appearance, he cursed under his breath. He'd put Reb up and see if he could sneak into the family bathing room without anyone's notice. What a mess.

The little barn closeted him in pitch black for a moment before his eyes adjusted. Gaslight from the hotel windows behind him gave the breezeway in the stables a murky illumination, enough to see movement from the tack room. Dismounting, wary, he had just enough time secure Reb's reins before someone whispered, "Ben? Oh, God, Ben!"

A sumptuously dressed blur hurtled its way into his widespread arms, startling his horse.

"Luce?" His voice was muffled in her updo of curled, crisp, and faintly singed hair.

"I missed you so much Ben," she was still whispering, cinched close to him, on her toes and pressing tight. "Did you miss me?"

Pulse beating faster, he used his free hand to grasp her hair in a loose fist, pulling her head back so he could see her upturned face. "What kind of question is that? I wasn't at the ranch ten minutes before I was on the road again to see you." His attempt at self-deprecation went unnoticed.

Lucy gave him the barest of smiles before her great big eyes, liquid black in the gloom, lowered to his mouth. "I've felt crazy without you here. Kiss me?"

All questions about the party fled, and his breath came swiftly. "I've been on the trail for weeks, I need a bath and a shave—"

"And I need you," she said fiercely, sweet breath hot on his chin. She kissed the bristles tenderly, and he felt it straight into his gut.

"You're askin' for it." His laugh was strained.

"Maybe."

Her hands scratched up into the too-long hair of his nape, massaging the scalp before pulling with inexorable slowness. Her mouth opened wide beneath his, greedy, demanding. Something primal within him answered her passion, and he ceased thinking and crowded her, looped the reins around a post as an afterthought before moving her further into the barn. They were panting, tongues tangling, as he led her into the tack room, slamming the rough door shut behind them.

BEN'S MOUTH WAS hungry and hot, consuming her thoughts, demanding her body to submit. His dark, looming presence surrounded her and cornered her against an empty shelf beneath the dim light of the tack room's tiny window.

Broad, strong hands swept up from her rounded hips to her breasts, and she moaned into his mouth at the exquisite feeling. His fingers drifted back to her waist, tightened, then lifted.

Now the shelf was solid beneath her, and she spread her legs to accommodate Ben's lean hips, the sensation of him so close to that swollen, hurting place like a match to gunpowder. Their mouths separated while he pulled back and slowly, slowly pulled her bottom to the very edge. She could see his face between shifting shadows, the hot blue of his gaze, the shock of glossy black hair against tan skin.

Breath ragged, she felt him draw her skirts up and up, whispering past her knees, over her thighs, until the bulk of her hem and petticoats were bunched at her waist. Beneath them were fine muslin split-drawers and matching stockings. The unusual chill of the air around them pricked her thighs into goosebumps, but his palms were warm and rough, and they glided from her knees to the tender skin of her inner thighs. His callouses excited her, and her mouth parted. He was so different from her, his hard to her soft, and she couldn't prevent the small noises she made when his thumbs brushed over her most intimate of areas, halfway hidden in the fabric of her drawers.

Face burning at his steady strokes, she repeated, "I missed you so much. I think about you every night, wishing I was your wife."

Groaning low, he covered her mouth with his to stop the flow of words. "Careful. Keep talkin' like that, and I'll take you, right here, right now."

"So take me," she challenged, on fire for him, feeling drunk and reckless. Lucy arched her back, hands braced behind her. She bumped against the hardness jutting from the inside of his trousers with the heat between her legs. The action molded his hands to her, trapping them between their bodies.

Those hands moved lightning quick, gripping her thighs as the breath hissed out of him, and he ground himself against her almost angrily. She threw her head back at the indescribable feeling.

"Touch me, Ben, please, please..." she begged him, and when he hesitated, she raised one of her hands and tugged viciously on her bodice.

With a growl, he helped her, yanking with rough, shaking hands until her breasts sprang up, visible and pale in a square of light from the window behind her. His dark head lowered, and he sucked a pink nipple deep into his mouth. She clapped a hand over her mouth and muffled a scream.

Ben lifted his head, eyes hooded, leaving the nipple rigid and wet, and went for the other one. Oh, God, she never wanted it to stop.

Never.

The next time he pulled away, she grabbed him by the head and kissed him. To her shock, he bit her lip in warning. She froze, pulse whooshing in her ears and throbbing between her legs. Her breasts were cold, nipples wet, and puckered in the chill of the air. Was he angry? No, he was...he was petting her.

There.

His mouth softened its bite, kissing her slack mouth while his busy hand grazed that sensitive bundle of nerves between her legs.

It was wicked, and she tensed for a moment before moaning helplessly and opening her legs wider. It felt better than anything she'd ever done to herself, his big hand making its way into the slit of her drawers, cupping her possessively. Her head dropped backward, so he skimmed her neck and gently glided his finger inside her.

"Oh," Lucy breathed. Her eyes opened, and she began to pant when his finger left her to stroke up and pay attention to that most sensitive spot. She squeezed her eyes shut and gritted her teeth because now he was biting her neck.

She had a sudden irrational fear that she was about to climax all over him. Did men know that women did that?

Would it disgust him?

Perhaps she could hide it—no, what an imbecilic idea, there was no hiding *that*. She had to stop him...suddenly he was working two fingers inside of her and she cried out at the burning stretch.

It hurt.

It felt good.

Incrementally, his fingers moved up and in, then curved inside of her, stroking shallowly only midway in. His forehead was heavy on her shoulder as she tried to look between the dark crevice of their bodies. Their breath came hard, his mouth worshipped her breasts, and now she was in trouble because his fingers moved once again to that aching spot.

She was chasing that euphoric feeling, and it was coming fast.

"Ben," she warned in a high-pitched tone.

His mouth ate her alive, tongues at war, while below, his rhythm quickened until she drew back enough to whisper, "oh no, oh no", and everything turned blood red, then white, while she spasmed hard against him, hips bucking, legs drawn up tight while she rose and plummeted, spinning round and round. She was aware that the noises she made were breathy and ecstatic, particularly when Ben moved his fingers back into her, and she clamped around them with almost painful force. He clenched his jaw hard against her neck and groaned deep, a male desperately aroused to the point of violence.

Eventually, Lucy grabbed his hand away from her over-stimulated flesh and held his loose fist beneath her breasts, breathing hard and radiating a damp heat. He stole his hand back, and as though curious, he cupped her again. She pulsed gently against his palm; one heartbeat, two, three, then no more. His hand was wet, she noticed.

Embarrassed, she muttered something unintelligible before wiping him clean with her petticoats.

Ben smiled against her bared breast.

After cleaning him, she wrapped her arms tight around him, squeezing them as close as they could get with their clothes on.

"I love you," she breathed, heartbeat slowing to a normal pace again. "Never leave me again."

He chuckled, then choked on it when her hand cupped him against the iron hardness at the front of his trousers. "Sweetheart—"

"Tit for tat," Lucy tsked, kissing his soft lips, licking the seam in a slow curl of her tongue. He held still while her hand moved languidly up and down, measuring him, marveling at the size. When he thrust against her hand, she stroked him harder, nibbling on his lower lip.

"Lucy, stop," he hissed, grabbing her wrist, and holding it away. "Sweetheart, you gotta stop."

Ben yanked her skirts down and pulled her from the tac room counter. Her knees buckled, and she gasped. Her legs felt like lead, like she'd ridden bareback for the first time.

"You broke me," she accused.

"Not saddle broke yet?"

"You can remedy that once we're married." Lucy fell against his chest, erupting in giggles. "If it doesn't happen before then."

"You'll be the death of me," he said, quite serious.

She stretched, reaching her arms to the sky. "You'd die happy."

"You're damned right I would," he murmured, watching her bared breasts. "You're just about the most beautiful thing I've ever seen." He gave her breasts a loving stroke of his warm palms before tugging her bodice smartly up until she was shielded, shaking his head at himself.

TOGETHER, THEY SPENT several minutes putting each other back together, though Ben had arrived in such a bedraggled state that nothing but a bath and a shave could sort him out. They smiled and whispered teasing remarks, and when Lucy asked about his trip, they stepped out of the tack room together.

Glancing around the stable and finding it empty, he drew Lucy out and gave her a rundown of his trip, not mentioning the ring or the new furniture. They reached halfway up the yard before he realized that he was practically dragging her. Her feet had slowed from a walk to a trudge, then stopped moving at all.

"What is it?"

In the well-lit backyard, he could finally see her face. Whisker burns had roughed up the delicate skin around her swollen mouth. He was still semi-hard, but her lowered gaze made something else in him perk to attention.

Apprehension.

In the distance, the hotel's front screen door slapped shut. Ben pulled his hand away, and Lucy shifted her feet.

"Mother is here," she said without inflection.

The prickling on the back of his neck returned. "That why there's a party? You wanted to welcome her home?"

"Hardly." She was looking him in the eye again.

Sensing that going inside was the furthest thing on her mind, Ben put his hands in his jean pockets, prepared to wait out a better explanation. "I saw a coupla women on the front porch. That your ma and sister?"

"Probably. Blonde and putting on airs?" Her tone was acidic.

"They were telling a lot of folks I've never seen before goodbye. That why you're hidin' in the barn?"

For a moment Lucy's jaw set, a grim little angle against her usual sweetness. "It was a party to celebrate Mother and Beth's return. I couldn't stomach being in the same room as them." Her jaw worked and something ugly passed over her face. She didn't look at him. "There's something else. You're going to be angry."

There wasn't much that could make him mad, but he could think of a few reasons that made the sweat along his back turn to ice.

"Did your ma come here to bring you back to Atlanta?"

"Perhaps, but I'd have to be in a pine coffin for her to make me." Brown eyes spit fire.

"She didn't like that you were marrying me?"

"Oh, she quite forbids it, but that's nothing. Papa already gave his blessing, and that's good enough for me."

She hesitated.

"What is it you're not tellin' me?" He widened his stance, preparing for the worst. Something horrible, some age-old fear that she'd been unfaithful, that he hadn't been good enough to hold her crept its way into his logic and reason. And God, look at her, so damned beautiful—

"Beth's fiancé is here." Her voice was tight.

For a moment he drew a blank, and then, his lips pressed flat. "That Paul fellow?" he pretended to joke, trying, and failing, not to be angry. He was back at the Jackson hotel room the first night he'd spent with her alone, listening to her tragic confessions of seducing her sister's beau to get to Texas. Every word she'd said came back with stark, knife-sharp clarity.

She didn't correct him, but now she watched him, gauging his every move.

"Why is he here?"

"I don't know for sure, to chaperone Mother and Beth, keep them safe." She crossed her arms.

"Yeah, I reckon that could be it, or it might have more to do with seeing the girl he really wanted to marry." Now there was a bite of sarcasm in his voice.

"No, that's not it at all," she whispered, looking miserable and upset, but he didn't give a damn.

He lost his temper.

"I know when you're lyin' Lucy, don't stand there and tell me no when it's a damned lie."

Her head shot up, eyebrows knitting. "Ben—"

"He probably thought he'd come with your mama and talk you into comin' back."

"That's not true," she said, uncrossing her arms. "When they arrived, he was angry with me, wouldn't even talk to me."

Ben's hands came out of his pockets and he took a step towards her, enraged. "And why does some other man feel it's in his right to be mad at my woman, huh? Just what the hell did he say?"

"I—God Ben, I don't know!" she exclaimed, eyes liquid and mouth sharply downturned. "We got the letter the night before you were to leave that Mother was coming to visit. I would have told you, but you didn't give me an address to send letters to!"

"Don't pin that on me, I didn't know your old flame would be coming to stay under the same damned roof as you." For a moment another thought hit him with the strength of an iron sledgehammer. His voice lowered. "If he's touched you, I'll hurt him. He'll be limpin' off that train when he gets back home to his mama."

Lucy was taking in shivering breaths. A tear spilled over. "I would never be unfaithful to you, and have accepted no advances from him, you have my word. All three of them are here completely against my will. It wasn't as though I had a choice."

He could read between the lines. It meant there had been advances. So, had the bastard touched her or not?

He was afraid to ask. Afraid to know.

Something was wrong, more wrong than just a visit from a harpy of a mother, a simpering sister, and a sissified mama's boy. Lucy was visibly shaking. He took a step towards her, and she leaned in, letting her hands release their death grip on her elbows. But he stopped from embracing her. He was too furious. Too jealous.

For a moment, he thought about turning around and leaving. For a moment, it felt precisely like a shard of rusted metal had entered, then exited, his chest. Not in control of himself, he clenched his fists and brushed past her, back to the barn. Reb was more tired than Ben had to be. There was one thing a horse would never do to him, and that was to make him feel like chewing and spitting nails.

"Ben? Are you leaving? Please don't leave." Lucy's voice cracked, and Ben clenched his molars hard together so he wouldn't allay her fears.

Let her taste some of the turmoil he felt twisting in his guts.

He spent the next several tense minutes unsaddling his horse. The swish of skirts exposed Lucy's position beside him in the shadows. She tried to help put away tack, and he growled at her.

"I got it."

For a moment she held her hands suspended, then something snapped.

"Let me help," she growled back, and ripped the reins away from him, bit still warm and damp from Reb's mouth, and stormed back to the tack room.

He went to follow, then swore an oath. He'd be a fool to follow that woman back into that room. Her skirts would be up to her ears in minutes, and this time, she wouldn't come out as innocent as she'd entered.

When she emerged, he couldn't help but ask, "How long have they been here?"

"Two miserable weeks," Lucy gritted, pulling off the saddle blanket and draping it over a stall wall.

"They been givin' you hell?"

"You haven't an inkling." Her hands came up to cover her face. "Oh, Ben, please don't be angry with me. The only thing that has kept my sanity intact has been the thought of you coming home and taking me away from all of this. If we were already married, I could be at your ranch right now. Their presence wouldn't touch me because I'd have you. Don't you see? I don't care about those horrible people. I traveled thousands of miles to get away from that life. Can't you believe me?"

"Sh." Ben stopped the rush of babbled words with a soft kiss on her mouth. She responded with a fervency that went beyond passion. It was desperate. He believed her. Whether or not she was keeping something from him, he'd find out eventually. She had told him that she'd loved him, and he chose to believe it. "I believe you, sweetheart. I believe you."

THEY STOOD AT the threshold of the backdoor.

Ben settled his hat more snuggly to his head.

All the guests had left. Aurora's voice was a constant droning just in the foyer. Spitting consonants and hard-biting words filtered through the door, though their meaning was indecipherable.

"Ben," Lucy warned. "Don't let my mother or Pet—Mr. Langford, goad you, or cause you to do anything you'd regret."

Ben placed his hand on the doorknob. "Who said I'd regret anything?" He wasn't smiling.

Her hand stilled the turning of his over the brass knob.

"I am being serious." Her throat was tight with worry, and she hated the seizing convulsions that it made when she felt this way, as though she couldn't draw a breath, choking on her own terror. The bright image of Mr. Forde and his two little girls beside the church's live oak burned a brand of forewarning. "Mother has chased away people that I've cared about before. And the Langfords...they have connections. Old money. And they hold grudges." She paused, unsure if she wanted to say it. "And Peter...he's vindictive."

Blue eyes slanted to her, hard as iron. "I'm not stupid, Lucy. But I'm not a coward, either. You think I don't know what kinda poison these people spit out? Don't get their way, and start making threats, throwing names and dollars around until they get that shiny toy they want. Look at my Pa. They're just people, and I ain't gonna scrape for anybody. I don't give a damn who they know."

The words, more hurtful in their truth than any insult, bleached Lucy of any other counsel. He was right. They had both run in the past, he from the derision of the whole town, and she from the very people they were about to look in the eye.

Taking a deep breath, she asked, "No more running?"

The censure that had shadowed his features lifted, and all that remained was the fiery blaze of determination. "No more running."

He held a hand out.

She took it. Hard callouses and strong, thick fingers released the choking hold fear had in her throat. With him, she was stronger. Fearless.

Ben turned the knob and they opened the door, releasing the fragrant aftermath of a successful party; cigar smoke, sweat, expensive perfume, and the lingering scent of dinner. The unintelligible words from Aurora obtained meaning, and the gist of the argument was immediately clear. She derided Tony for being a worthless drunk, needing a child to get the failing hotel back on its feet.

"—and what is worse, I have had no less than three people comment on the company you've been keeping. You mean to tell me that some beggarly cowboy is courting our daughter? What a farce. It is best that she accompanies us to Atlanta, urgently. I cannot imagine that you've been entertaining the possibility of my daughter as some pioneer wife in the middle of nowhere—"

That helpless rage was back. Aurora could scorn her until the angel's wept, but it would be a cold day in Hell before the woman scorned Ben Stone. Face on fire, a promise of battle in her eyes, she stepped forward.

A hand squeezed, staying her.

"Lucy won't be going anywhere with you."

Ben led her, and she quickened her step to stay at his side. Aurora's eyes, paler and chillier than Ben's, looked him from the top of his ancient cowboy hat to the toes of his scuffed boots. She met Lucy's scorching gaze. "Truly, Lucille. *Him?* You cannot be serious."

"Don't you dare talk to him like that," Lucy uttered, ears full of cotton and vision fuzzy with a crimson mist.

The foyer shimmered with the heat of yellow gas lights turned all the way up. Lucy took in the scene. Tony weaving, eyes clouded with drink behind the concierge desk. Beth in a chair just inside the dining room doorway.

When they had first strode into the room, Peter was sitting at the foot of the staircase, his shoulders stooped. A scratch peeked from just below his collar. At the sound of Ben's deep baritone, he'd stood and circled the banister, face growing red and mottled, two stallions scenting the wind and quivering with restrained violence. His eyes were swollen, and Lucy hated him for it.

Beth looked between the two men, mouth parted, then turned accusingly to her sister.

Say something, Lucy dared her with her eyes. *You just go ahead.*

Beth looked away, nose and mouth pinched in unhappiness.

"I may speak in any way I choose." Aurora's eyes were wide and staring, nose flared, ready for battle.

"Not to my fiancé, you may not." Lucy heard every word she spoke, crisp and proper, just the way she'd been taught in Boston.

"You have no *fiancé*, you ungrateful child," Aurora hissed, a snake drawing back to strike.

Hand clenching hard around Ben's, she lifted it, drawing everyone's attention to their clasped fingers. "And yet here he stands, by my side. And would you wonder at it, he asked me himself." She shot a scathing look at Peter, whose lip curled and green eyes snapped.

"Watch how you look at her, boy," Ben said, soft as a whisper. He released Lucy's hand, stance widening.

For a moment, Peter's eyes fluttered before they turned to Ben. His smile was unkind. "Are you speaking to me?"

"I'm lookin' at you, hidin' behind skirts and staring at my woman like you got a right to." Ben had never looked more serious, his eyes hard and flinty.

"You dare speak to Mr. Langford in such a way, you carpetbagger." Though Aurora's voice trembled in the wake of Ben's obvious aggression, she didn't back down from a fight. "Fighting over a girl barely out of the schoolroom."

Finally, Ben's eyes met Aurora's. "Girl?" he scoffed. "I traveled with Lucy from Atlanta to this hotel we're standin' in.

"She survived a stagecoach wreck, rode into town on the back of my horse, so tired she looked half dead, head to tail bruises. The next day, she got to work putting this place back in business." It was his turn to look her up and down and judged her sadly lacking. "I've seen what happens to someone after you get 'hold of 'em." He motioned to Beth and Tony. "I'll be damned if you do it to Lucy. Her Pa may not stand up to you, but I'm here, and I ain't goin' nowhere." He spread his arms for a moment, waiting for Aurora to say something. When the woman just stared at him, bleached of color and chin in the air, he curled an arm around Lucy's shoulders.

Swallowing, Aurora snagged Lucy's gaze. "I forbid a marriage with this backwoods trash."

Standing taller, Lucy raised her own chin. "Ben, it would be an honor to be your wife, if you could forgive me my family."

Finding humor where there was none, Ben's lip curled up. "We can make a new one."

Aurora's sharp inhalation was drowned by an explosion of laughter from Peter. He wrung his hands into the short crop of hair at the back of his head, pacing, practically knocking Aurora down.

"Lucy, my God, you can't—" he broke off, laughing again, and made his way to stand in front of her with pleading eyes.

Ben's spine went rod-straight, and it was as though he grew larger before their eyes.

"You're a dead man walkin' if you touch her." All amusement had left Ben's face.

Peter's features wrinkled into a mocking grimace. "I have been there, *and* done that, you cuckolded fool."

"What the hell did you just say?" Ben's knuckles cracked, and he steered Lucy to the side.

Feeling panic as the men stood toe to toe, she cried, "Don't!"

Something wild flared in Peter's eyes. "Why don't we take it outside?"

The men turned sharply, slamming out the back with such force the screen door hung limply on its bottom hinge.

"Blast," Lucy breathed, then shouted, "Papa, do something!"

"Antonio!" Aurora screeched.

It was chaos.

Tony finally burst into action and followed the two ferocious men outside. They were circling in the grass of the backyard, Peter's jacket and Ben's hat discarded on the ground. Peter's white shirt and slim torso swayed and feinted from side to side while he taunted.

"You like the way our Lucy-girl kisses, eh?" he called.

Lucy froze in dreamlike horror. Ben stiffened as well, making Peter's erratic movements look ridiculous in the gaslight.

"Yes, I bet you do. I taught her that," Peter was saying, almost panting as he looked at Ben from under his brows. "I can't say she was the best at first, but she certainly was after I was through with her."

Ben's fist cracked into Peter's jaw, but it glanced rather than struck solidly. Even so, Peter tumbled into a cloud of dust in the dirt-packed grass. He scrambled up when the bull he'd angered advanced, and tried to resume his fighting stance.

Already the bloom of a bruise appeared on his jaw. He circled and avoided Ben, now, not staying in one place long enough for another solid hit. A hint of fear tightened the corner of his eyes.

Ben murmured a question of his own, too low for Lucy to hear, but Peter bellowed and charged. They grappled for five excruciating seconds before Ben's greater weight and muscular strength overpowered the slimmer man. Lucy heard the breath knock from Peter, and she ran into the yard before Tony could grab her.

Solid, meaty sounds of a fist hitting flesh didn't halt even when she screamed Ben's name.

His muscles bulged, squared, and flexed with the quick movements of his striking fist, only halting when Peter's arms and legs went limp, splayed like a stringless puppet. Behind them, Aurora was screaming for a doctor and the sheriff.

"We don't need a sheriff, woman," Tony shouted back in ill-concealed delight, his Italian accent strong. "He's just knocked out. Served the bastard right, did you hear what he was saying about our girl? Get a hold of yourself."

"What's goin' on, Ricci?" Mr. Hobb shouted from his second-story bedroom window next door.

Beth was sobbing hysterically on the porch.

Lucy and Ben ignored all of them.

"Ben, darling, are you okay? You didn't kill him, did you?" Lucy implored.

"Hell, no." Ben spat on the ground next to a bloody Peter in disgust. "I wouldn't kill a defenseless man. The boy didn't even get a hit in."

"What he said—" Her voice trembled.

"He mighta kissed you first, but I'll be your last, by God." The hard band of muscle encasing his arm drew her into the sweltering furnace that was his body. He was still vibrating with suppressed rage, his pupils blown to their fullest, glittering in the weak light. He pressed his lips full against hers, and she breathed him in, grateful, in love, and shamefully unworried about the groaning figure on the ground.

Peter was rousing.

"Let's marry tomorrow," she breathed when he pulled away.

Ben kissed her again, harder, bringing hot color into her cheeks.

"Is that a yes?"

"It's a hell yes, darlin'." He smiled, and now, it was genuine.

21

—·—

CHAPTER TWENTY-ONE

To Lucy's disappointment, it was impossible to marry the next day. However, with much cajoling and his favorite meal at the diner, the preacher was convinced, and a hasty months-early wedding was approved for the next Saturday.

The night that everything had come to the fore, tempers exploding and Peter getting the thrashing he'd deserved, Ben had escorted Lucy next door to the Hobb's until Aurora, Beth, and Peter made their way home the next day.

Aurora's parting words had been, "From this day forward, I only have one daughter. You are thus omitted from my will, and your inheritance will be dissolved into Elisabeth's. Do you understand? You won't get a cent from me once you realize what a horrible mistake you're making."

"She won't need your help," Ben had reminded her from beside a stoic Lucy. "She has me."

After one last scathing glance, Aurora turned and left for the train without another word.

It was two days until the wedding, and Lucy watched Ben from beneath her lashes on the back porch. He had a lean hip cocked against a square post, twirling his hat over and over again. She wondered if he suffered from the same frustration she did.

Ben had kept his distance since that night in the stables. He'd left and fetched his little brother as a personal chaperone. Junior was like his older brother's extra appendage. He was always there. Often, like at that moment, she'd pin an accusing glare at Ben from behind the golden-haired chatter-box's back. His expression was usually equally grim.

She tried to understand. It had to be that way, or she'd be pinned against the first wall in a dark corridor, innocence swiftly taken and disposed of. They both knew it. The banked coals that they both harbored for each other were fanned into flames the closer they came into contact. And Junior was the perfect buffer between them.

Besides being a bothersome annoyance, Junior was also an excellent source of anxiety for the engaged couple. On and on he talked about the tenuous relationship between his father, mother, and Ben, and its history. More than once, he'd mentioned his brother's ex-wife, and the apparition of Abby would wedge between them, an unwelcome presence.

In an effort not to wring the boy's skinny little neck, Lucy asked, "Will your father and stepmother be able to attend the wedding at such short notice?"

Ben gave a terse nod, watching Reb graze in the sparse grass of the hotel's backyard. "Pa said they would. Wanted to meet his *new* daughter-in-law."

Raising her brows at the enigmatic emphasis, Lucy paused her rocking. "I'll just bet he does. I assume he does not mean the sentiment kindly."

Junior snorted, loud as any backyard sow, from the chair between them. "Ever since he took that letter you sent to old sourpuss over here—" he clapped Ben's back with a powerful slap, "—and heard that ole Ben was getting hitched again, he's been chomping at the bit to see what kind of beat-up nag agreed to mar—Ow, shit!"

A scowling Ben had caught Junior's hand after the slap and bent it sharply back at the wrist. "Watch your mouth."

Unphased by the rough treatment or language, Lucy leaned forward. "Does your father truly think I'm an old maid?"

Snatching his hand back and rubbing the wrist attached, Junior cackled. "Why do you think I'm coming to the wedding?

I can't wait to see the old geezer's face when he gets a look at you."

It was the closest to giving her a compliment Junior had ever come. At her raised brows, he colored and stood with the hastiness of the embarrassed. He muttered something about getting a bite to eat from Minnie—of whom he'd managed to charm at the first introduction, to Lucy's disgust—and disappeared through the repaired screen door. Lucy leaned back in the rocking chair and covered her face with a groan.

"Lovely. Your father and stepmother already despise me."

"I recall your mother isn't too keen on me, either," Ben responded drolly, holding a hand out and hauling her up from her seat.

Waving her other hand dismissively, she denied, "Mother hates everyone, you are no exception."

"She liked that Paul fellow well enough."

"Peter." She fought not to be amused. "And she hated him as well when he first expressed an interest in me and not Beth."

They had hardly crossed the threshold through the back door when firm, strong fingers wrapped around Lucy's wrist, turning her to face him. Ben looked down his nose at her, eyes hooded. "Talking about that fellow makes me want to pay a quick visit to Atlanta."

Smiling slow and sweet, Lucy twined her free arm around his neck. "But I'd miss you awfully. I might even follow you—"

Warm lips stalled her flow of words.

THE DAY BEFORE the wedding was pandemonium.

Lucy stroked the lace edge of her cuff with a trembling finger while women scurried around behind her. Mrs. Hobb had a dozen pins tucked in the corner of her mouth while she finished last-minute adjustments to the ivory bridal gown Lucy wore. Minnie and the preacher's wife ticked things from a list near the window, speaking in low, excited voices. All the while, employees dashed up and down the stairs when they became overwhelmed and needed assistance with the enormous task of running the hotel downstairs. When the preacher's wife left and another set of louder, quicker footsteps dashed up the stairs to her attic room, Lucy didn't pay it any mind until Mrs. Hobb gasped.

"Franny!"

Francesca Hobb, the town's renowned shut-in and Lucy's dearest friend, had left the safety of her home with several bundles wrapped in crisp, brown paper. Her arms were full, and she breathed as hard as if the very devil was after her. She wore a long-sleeved, high-collared dress of hunter green, black gloves, and an old-fashioned bonnet that nearly encompassed her entire head and face. It was tied so tightly at the front that only a sliver of her features was visible. She looked a bit odd to be dressed so, but Lucy and Mrs. Hobb knew the courage it had taken the young woman to face the public.

Heart full of love for her shy friend, Lucy reached out with her hands. "Oh, Franny, I'm so glad you're here! Now everything is perfect."

"I would not have missed seeing you for the world," Franny said breathlessly from the depths of her bonnet. "I've just finished your veil, a night rail, and a nightgown—" she leaned in closer and whispered, "—for your wedding night."

Eyes glittering with excitement, Lucy whispered back, "You are too good to me." She squeezed Franny's talented, gloved fingers.

Franny ducked her head and set the packages on Lucy's writing desk. The topmost largest package was briskly opened. The most beautiful ivory veil Lucy had ever seen slithered out, and all the women held their breath at the elegant headpiece. Delicate tulle ran several feet from the silver comb to intricate lacework with a scalloped edge at the bottom that perfectly matched the cuffs of Lucy's gown.

"Oh." Lucy covered her mouth with her hands, looking from the veil to her friend's shadowed features, and back again. "It's too beautiful Franny, what if I tear it?"

Laughing, the tall bashful woman exposed a leaf of confidence, strode to her friend, and placed the long-toothed sliver comb into Lucy's hair at the crown. "Wear it like so."

While listening to instructions on how to wear the veil with her updo, Lucy became aware of an embarrassing tightness in her throat. She swallowed convulsively, sinuses stinging, and attempted to blink away burgeoning moisture. Minnie was the first to notice the struggle and stepped forward to lay a comforting hand on her veiled shoulder.

"Lucy-Lou? You all right?"

Staring at Mrs. Hobb, Minnie, and Franny in the reflection of her standing mirror, Lucy nodded and managed a taut smile. She cleared her throat.

"Yes, I'm fine," she croaked. "I'm just so...grateful. You are all my family, and I'm beyond blessed to have you. I love you all so much. Thank you. For everything."

Three pairs of hands swarmed her, rubbing her arms and patting her back.

She went on.

"I knew Mother wouldn't stay for a wedding she did not approve of, especially after all the events of the other night. I knew it, and am completely amenable to her absence: could you imagine the uproar she'd create?" she tittered nervously, unable to meet any eyes now. Her voice grew contemplative. "I felt so lonely in Georgia. No friends I ever made were acceptable. The servants were ordered to keep their distance, and absolutely no beaus allowed. But here I've always felt welcomed, and loved, and treasured. Even now that Papa—" she broke off loyally. Mrs. Hobb rushed forward.

"Oh, honey, we just love you. You've been family since you were a squirt, and nothin' makes me happier than to be here on your special day."

Franny and Minnie agreed. While the women chatted and clucked, Lucy let the warmth suffuse that empty space in her chest that claimed it didn't need a loving mother or sober father to enjoy her special day. So long as she had her friends and Benjamin Stone, she'd be happy.

THE WEDDING WAS held at the town church, the sky overcast and casting a gray light over the people that spilled out from the front doors and into the churchyard. In the privacy of the buggy, Tony pulled out his watch to check the time.

"Right on time." He cleared his throat.

Lucy's eyes were drawn to the riotous colors of the people's clothing, hats, and bonnets. They shuffled around, pointing at their buggy, children jumping up and down with excitement. For a moment, her confidence waned, and she looked at her Papa with wide dark eyes that shone with trepidation.

"There are so many people." She hated that her voice was so small.

Taking her two clenched hands in his one, Tony declared, "I am so proud of you, *mi amor*. All of those people are there because they love you, and want to wish you well on your blessed day." His eyes grew misty. "You're so beautiful, the loveliest bride I have ever known."

She released his hand and hugged him, breathing his familiar cigar smoke and pomade, and wishing she didn't feel so ill and nervous. "Thank you, Papa."

The walk down the aisle was a surreal blur of faces, double doors opening, the endless road of an ecru aisle runner. Through her veil, her mouth the driest it had ever been, she peered up and caught sight of the man she was to marry. Ben stood to the side of the preacher, alone, stiff, and looking utterly out of place. He was a far piece from his ranch and horses in dusty work clothes. A gray suit had replaced his sturdy day wear, and his crooked neck-tie stuck out like a sore thumb.

Hadn't anyone thought to straighten it for him?

A rush of tenderness suffused her, and her cheeks lifted in a smile.

From that day forward, she'd be there to make sure he was always straightened out.

Lucy didn't notice when Tony gave her away. It was as though she'd floated to Ben, her feet taking the necessary steps of their own volition. Her husband's intense scrutiny darted from her hemline to her veil and the smile behind it. She took large, rough hands that maintained a fine tremor. His hair was the shortest she'd ever seen it. The top swept to the side in waves tamed by stiff product. His beard was intact, sculpted impeccably from the sideburns to the sharp edge of his jawline, and trimmed close enough to reveal a glimpse of the dimple in his chin.

The scripture lasted an eternity. Flies droned amongst the guests who whispered, coughed, and fanned themselves. Her back prickled. Sweat beaded on Ben's forehead, and she wished the preacher spoke faster so everyone could pour from the building and catch a breeze. When Ben recited his vows, his voice echoed with strength. It made her acutely aware of how higher-pitched her own voice was, and she licked dry lips each time she paused for a breath.

Ben slid a plain, delicate gold band on her finger.

Lucy attempted to push a thicker, broad gold band around his second knuckle, but it didn't budge. He put it on his smallest finger with a wink at her apologetic grimace. After their 'I dos" rang in the air, Ben lifted her veil and gave her a chaste, dry kiss, pulling back with an awkward abruptness that made her giggle.

Hand in hand, they walked down the aisle together.

Once rice and cheers were thrown at them in the wide-open world outside, Ben finally laughed in relief.

"Let's get outta here," he shouted above the hoots and loud congratulations from friends and family. He helped her into the buggy and hopped in limberly behind. Snapping the reins, they fled the sting of rice missiles and the discordant cacophony of well-meaning townspeople.

LUCY WAS DISTRACTED during the hotel wedding luncheon.

As grateful as she was for the planning and preparations of Minnie and Mrs. Hobb, three hours of speaking to everyone but her husband was long enough. She was ready to go home.

Home.

Ben's home was now her home. They'd live there together, eat, and sleep together. She'd finally get to wake every morning nestled to him in semi-darkness, the cock's crow outside easing them from blissful dreams to the stretch of hairy legs against hers. But before that, there would be the wedding night.

Unnerved at drawing up such intimate images in a crowd of people, Lucy reached for the foreign feel of a wedding ring on her finger and gave the warm metal band several anxious twirls. Her eyes searched and found Ben. He was near the stairs surrounded by his family, the eldest and youngest Stones. Lucy had given the senior Mr. and Mrs. Stone the briefest of greetings when they had first arrived, but their faces were foggy, blurred into all the others. Now, the sight of the backs of their neat and tidy heads, facing her husband with stiff, uncomfortable demeanors narrowed her eyes. The corners of Ben's eyes looked drawn and tight and his eyebrows were straight thunderous slashes.

On high alert, Lucy strode his way.

Not at my wedding, you don't.

"There you are." She sidled between John Sr. and his plump, graying wife in her sumptuous pink gown and matching jacket. She smiled at Ben, planting herself firmly at his side, linking arms, an immovable barnacle.

The tension at Ben's temples eased. "You've met Pa and his wife?"

Brows politely raised, Lucy gave the rigid couple a regal nod. "Briefly. Mr. and Mrs. Stone, it's a pleasure to finally meet you. Junior has spoken a lot of you this past week."

John, a ruggedly handsome man in his fifties, smiled like a crocodile. It didn't reach his eyes. "We almost didn't make it at such short notice. Cattle brandin' takes time."

"How fortunate that you took time from your busy schedule to grace us with your presence." Her voice was sweet as sugar, smile wide.

"I wouldn't have missed my oldest boy's second weddin'. Figured I'd see if this one would stick."

Why, you miserable old geezer, she seethed internally. Outwardly conditioned to biting repartee, she rose to the challenge. Smile pasted to her face, Lucy rejoindered, "Considering I was the one that pursued him, I'll not be going anywhere."

"Then you must be that letter-writer. Can't say you were what I pictured."

"And of whom did you picture?"

"Someone who knows life on a ranch, for one. Don't look to me like you've done a hard day's work in your life."

The muscle that Lucy's nails were digging into bunched. Loretta Stone's hem swayed around her shifting feet. Dark stains rimmed Junior's underarms. Before Ben could get a word in, Lucy let a little of her dislike show in her souring smile.

"Don't I? It must be your advancing age. Perhaps you're past due for a pair of spectacles?"

Junior choked.

For a moment no one said a word, then John released a crack of laughter and slammed a palm into his oldest son's shoulder. Ben was quietly angry and unresponsive to the manly camaraderie, his body radiating that same heat it had when Peter had suggested a backyard brawl.

Something nasty gleamed in John's eyes. He looked slyly at Ben. "This one's a mite different than your first, eh, boy?"

Resentment at the continual mentions of that cowardly Abby Simms sharpened Lucy's words. She was finished playing. "I would imagine so. He got to choose this time around."

"Luce," Ben gritted.

"Mr. Stone," pleaded Loretta. Her face was gray, and she looked left and right as though for an exit. Junior held himself tightly, looking between his father and new sister-in-law.

John and Lucy ignored them both.

"A real man wouldn't have married a woman he didn't want, girl," John sneered. "I heard what happened last week. You had a lawyer from New York after you, and this is what you settle for?"

Lucy's brows knit with dislike. "Ben is worth ten of Mr. Langford."

A derisive snort was his response, and it was the last cup that overflowed her bucket, as Jimmy would say.

She turned her nose up at him as the society misses did at the Boston boarding school. "I only wish I could have met my late mother-in-law. It's clear to me that Ben took after her."

John's face mottled, and Loretta laid a hand on his arm. Too late, Lucy discovered his late wife was a touchy subject, and they all waited for him to blow. For a wild moment, she wanted him to. Let the good people of Dogwood see what a termagant John Stone really was.

His mouth worked to retort and he leaned closer to her, but Ben had hit his limit.

Ben took a step forward. "That's enough." His jaw was set and bulging.

Assailed by guilt that she was causing a scene at their wedding, Lucy murmured, "Ben, let us give everyone our goodbyes. Let's go home to the ranch."

For a moment, it looked as though he would ignore her and ask his father to meet him outside, but then the meaning of her words finally caught. His chest swelled with a deep breath and he turned to her. "You sure?"

"Yes, please."

He led her away by the arm without a farewell to his family. Sol's head above the crowd followed them, and Lucy nodded toward Junior.

Help him, she thought. Sol must have understood because he sauntered immediately in that direction.

Instead of making their rounds and giving farewells, her new husband led her past the foyer, out the front door, and down the steps of the front porch. Brow dark, he helped Lucy into the wagon full of her meager furnishings, clothing, and wedding gifts. Guests had followed them to the front porch, and in an effort to show she was simply eager for home, she waved, blew kisses, and called farewells. Worried faces smiled, some chuckled, elbowing each other meaningfully.

But Lucy's smile fell away when they hit the rough terrain on the road home.

Ben's silence was a hammer's peal on a coffin nail. Not even married an hour and she'd picked a fight with her new in-laws and made her new husband angry. She felt an awful heaviness in her stomach and pressed a gloved fist over the stone of fear in her diaphragm.

This is no way to start a marriage, she quailed.

Why did she always ruin things?

"BEN, I'M SORRY for the scene I made with your father."

They hadn't made it a mile out of town, and the guilt had followed like a storm system. She turned to him on the splintery wagon seat, uncaring if the fabric caught.

Ben's eyes—locked in a thousand-yard stare between the tree lines running parallel to the road—blinked. His brows, still set low over his eyes, knitted even closer together. "You've got no reason to be sorry."

"I was a perfect harridan to your family." Her lip started to tremble, but she sucked it in and bit it into compliance. "I let your father bait me, and rose to it, hook, line, and sinker. I ruined what should have been a perfect wedding."

Shaking his head before she'd even finished her speech, Ben relaxed his tense slouch and leaned against the backrest with the reins loose in one hand and his right arm wrapped around his new bride. "The day didn't have a chance on bein' perfect with my Pa and Loretta involved. Like I said, you've got no reason to be sorry. I'm the sorry one."

"Absolutely not. After what happened with my family last week? I'm surprised you married me at all."

His laughter was the sweetest thing she'd heard since he'd repeated, 'I will' to the preacher a few hours before.

"Promise me somethin'," he said, grin still notching his lips up.

"Anything."

"Let's never apologize for anything our family does from now on."

"I believe that's the best idea you've had since you resigned yourself to marrying me," Lucy vowed, then squeaked when he lightly pinched her hip.

"Oh, Ben, did you see Papa? He and Mr. Brewster were finally speaking. They looked very friendly, don't you think?" Unable to contain the happiness spilling over, she chattered about the reception, asked about the farm, and teased.

When the long drive up the hill came into view, Lucy grew quiet and still. It was far into the afternoon, and the late summer sun showed no signs of setting soon. It hovered, yellow and fat, above distant treetops where the trail to the water hole disappeared into shadowy woods. Ben set the brake in front of the house and made his way to her side to help her down. When she stood, the fine embroidered stitching of her wedding skirt snagged on a splinter, and she made a small noise of grief at the rend. Her worry over the tear disappeared when Ben pulled her into his arms. Her gasp when the world went topsy-turvy converted to full-blown laughter.

"What are you doing?" She wound her arms around Ben's neck as he shifted and carried her, child-like, in his arms.

Sliding her fingers into his unbuttoned collar, she smiled at the memory of how he'd dispatched of his neck-tie into the bed of the wagon the minute the town withdrew from sight.

"Carryin' my bride over the threshold." His crooked smile flashed down at her, and he looked so handsome and boyish that she couldn't resist drawing his head down to give him the kiss she'd wanted to plant on his lips since that dry peck after their vows. Beneath her, she felt his feet climbing the stairs to his house—their house—then lost conscious thought as the kiss became deep and wanton, his tongue grazing hers. Only when her legs began to slide down, down, and her slippered feet touched the floor did she realize they were in the house.

"Welcome home." His lips tickled hers.

"We're finally married," she said, eyes big with wonder, pressing against him, and ran her hands over the breadth of his chest, marveling that she had the right to do so. "I can do this any time I want to."

Ben laughed aloud, eyes crinkling in the corners. "And I can do *this* whenever I want." He swatted her lace-clad bottom. "Make yourself at home. I'm goin' to finish up chores before tonight."

THE CHORES WERE an excuse to hide.

Ben stood in the barn, leaning the flat of his palms against the tack room wall, taking deep breaths and cursing his cowardice. He had a new wife, a woman that was even more beautiful inside than out, and from that day on, it was in his hands to make her happy. The pressure to fulfill that promise was astounding.

And here he stood, randy as a goat and scared to death of reliving his first wedding night.

"Please God, don't let me ruin this," he whispered, eyes squeezed tight.

Eventually, noting the setting sun from the open barn doors, he went about the monotony of evening chores on a ranch. Feeding horses, chickens, and cattle alike took over an hour. Milking the two cows in the barn took another hour.

When he walked up the front porch steps with a full milk pail, lightly perspiring and mopping his forehead, it was to an empty room.

"Lucy?"

"In here!"

He found her cutting cured roast beef in brown wax paper into thin slices over white bread. A jar of pickled vegetables from his sparse pantry sat open, fragrant with vinegar and spices. The smell of coffee was pungent and welcome at the end of their full day. He strained the milk in a sterilized glass jar, covered it, and set it in the new ice box he'd bought during his out-of-town trip.

Once finished, he sat down gratefully at the work table, murmuring thanks while Lucy poured him a cup of coffee the way he liked it. Amused, he stifled a chuckle.

"What's funny?" she wrinkled her nose, pink-cheeked and smiling.

"You're still waitin' on me, even in your weddin' dress. You look like an angel serving a no-good cowboy." He took a sip with a low hum of appreciation.

Lucy set a plate in front of him and sat at the end adjacent to him, chewing her food thoughtfully. "You don't look like a cowboy today."

"Just a saddle buster in dandy's clothes."

It was her turn to laugh. "You're so blind I could strangle you."

His eyebrows rose, lips curving. "Yeah?"

"Yes," she said, matter-of-factly. "I wish you saw you the way I see you."

"How's that?"

She planted her chin on a fist and looked him up and down like she liked what she saw. It made him feel hot and sweaty like he was riding in the sun with a fever. A little shaky and weak.

"The first time I saw you was on the train," she began, picking at the single cloth napkin she'd found God-knew-where. "I couldn't see your face, but it didn't matter. I couldn't look away from you. Every time you moved, every time you breathed, I felt it straight through me the moment I sat next to you."

"I saw you before you even got on the train."

"You did?" Her eyes widened and she sat up.

"You were petting Reb."

Her smile was slow. "I remember now. You'd noticed me."

Oh, he'd noticed her alright. "A man would have to be blind and dumb not to. That's half the reason I stayed away. Figured you'd find yourself a nice young man rich on family money, settle down in town and not give me another look."

Lucy laid her hand on his and snorted. Her fingers twirled his wedding ring round and round his pinky finger.

When they finished supper, he lit kerosene lamps in the waning light, and wouldn't let her clean up.

"You'll get somethin' on that white dress."

While he scoured and scrubbed, he pretended not to see her leaning against the doorjamb, watching. Her wedding gown was pale and glittered in the lamplight. When he had nothing else to do but wipe his hands on a worn dishtowel over and over, he glanced up. She was watching his hands, chewing on a nail.

"Would you like to go through our gifts?"

What he wanted was to bed his new wife, but he kept that to himself. "Maybe tomorrow. I'm gonna go outside and wash up for bed."

She was silent for a moment, then, "I'll go upstairs and wait for you."

Mouth dry, he nodded to her, but didn't move as she glided past him, train untucked and dragging across his—their—dusty floor. She grabbed a lamp and glanced over her shoulder at him. Lucy's eyes looked black with shadows.

The whites were indiscernible in the doorway. She licked unsmiling lips before turning and advancing into the hallway and up the stairs.

In a trance at the glimpse of shiny lips, Ben hustled outside to the well-house. He grabbed an upturned pail and pumped icy water into it. His hands shook and his body was stiff, full of fiercely pumping blood. It knew what was coming tonight. Their supper and hour-long chatting had tempered his trepidation, had molded it into yearning. His guilt whispered to him all the same.

Animal.

You'll hurt her.

After tonight, you'll lose her.

"No. I won't," he whispered to himself, head bowed and dripping well water.

Ben pulled his suspenders off, unbuttoned his shirt, and briskly finished washing up. He dried his face with his white shirt, stiff in places from starch. One of the milk cows lowed in the barn, horses stomped in their stables, and he raised his head, calmer from the sounds of twilight at the ranch. He shrugged his shirt on without bothering to button it, and stomped up the side steps into the kitchen, slapping at mosquitos. Once the door shut behind him, he stood alone in his kitchen, bracing himself. Above him, he heard a creak from his bride. He took a deep breath, grabbed the last lit lamp, and made his careful way up the stairs.

22

—·—

CHAPTER TWENTY-TWO

Lucy stood in front of the heavy mirror she'd moved up-stairs by herself when Ben had done his evening chores. She forced herself not to panic.

Soft orange light pierced straight through Franny's creation.

White-capped sleeves cupped her shoulders. The sheer fabric was tight across the bosom, cupping her breasts on either side of a deep decolletage. Bows made of satin ribbon adorned the satin band beneath her breasts, and below the material flared in luxurious waves to the floor, interrupted only by a slit up the side where her slender leg peeked. Her nipples stood out like pink beacons behind the transparent material.

A nervous giggle escaped Lucy. Would Ben laugh when he saw her, too?

Her image put her in mind of a provocatively painted French postcard she'd found in Papa's office as a girl, her dark hair spilling over the pale, evocative material. Stricken by sudden nerves that Ben would disapprove, she grabbed her brush and raked it through her waves, sitting at the end of the large bed in the room. It bounced pleasantly.

Did this bed have springs?

Curious, she moved to the center to see if it bounced there. She'd have to tell Papa. Once the hotel produced a steadier income, perhaps he could buy some box spring mattresses.

349

That's how Ben found her when he walked in not two moments later, bouncing on his side of the bed, smiling like an imbecile, hair and breasts jiggling ridiculously.

The moment she noticed him in the doorway, she stood as though the bed had caught fire. Her face felt as though it had as well.

"Oh! Did you get a new bed? Sorry, it was just...shockingly springy."

Ben didn't answer. His eyes were too busy traveling up and down her figure, one hand still clasped around the brass doorknob, lamp in the other. Desperate, Lucy stepped away from him, clasping her hands together to discreetly cover the shadowy place at the juncture of her thighs. That he could probably see through the material *there*, how mortifying. He was probably fighting disgust.

Clearing her throat, she babbled, "Franny made this for me. As a wedding gift. Do you like it?"

He shut the door, and if possible, grew larger, taking up space and breathing in all the air in the room. Lucy felt light-headed and watched his shadow climb the wall behind him as he stalked her way. Squashing the irritating urge to break the silence with a giggle, she looked down, unable to meet the intensity of his gaze. His shirt was open. The skin of his torso was damp, hair matted and gleaming from his recent washing.

Ben still didn't speak but reached past her to set the lamp down on the sturdy bedside table. Pulling back, his large brown hand grazed her gown, lightly fingering the ripples of fabric below her waist.

"Your friend made this for you?" His voice was so soft.

"Yes," she whispered, voice not much louder than her heartbeat in the quiet room. "She designed it herself."

"Mm," he rumbled, deep in his throat. His eyes hooded, and she didn't know how to breathe when he looked at her like that.

"It was her wedding present to me," she repeated inanely.

"You'll have to thank her for me."

Not likely, Lucy thought to herself, but he was leaning down, and her thoughts tumbled away until all she could do was feel.

His close-cropped beard was soft against her as he kissed her deep, lips lush over her own. She opened them, eager. Kissing him was her favorite pastime, more than cooking, more than riding or chatting with friends.

This time, kissing felt different.

The urgency was there—it was always there—but so was something else. A promise. What they started tonight, they would finish. That promise forced her into movement. Lucy stepped into him and touched his hot skin with her cool hands, feeling the textures of hard muscles encased in velvety skin and ticklish body hair. His muscles rippled under her palms as she skimmed her fingers over his shoulders to push his shirt off and onto the floor. Ben's body radiated strength and hot, urgent tension. He lifted her, fingers gripping her bottom as he set her on the bed. She lay back against several pillows instead of just one, another addition from her room at the hotel. He blinked down at her.

"You're so beautiful."

She swallowed beneath his perusal, the buttery light from the lamp so close she could feel its warmth. Lucy wasn't shy by nature, but the boldness of her next move set her pulse fluttering madly at her throat. Hooking one finger beneath her sleeve, she trailed it down to her elbow until the duskiness of her left areola peeked over the neckline. She did the same with the other sleeve, watching with raptness as Ben's expression grew darker.

Lucy sat up, eyes wide, and shrugged her shoulders once. The material gaped forward and down, exposing her breasts, and his nostrils flared at the shock of seeing her bare to the waist in full light.

Ben sat at the edge of the bed, and pressed a thumb against her lower lip, rubbing the moisture across her mouth. She parted her lips and kissed his callous. He gave a hint of a smile before drawing his thumb down her chin to her chest, covering her left breast with a wide, rough hand. Callouses whispered over her skin as he cupped her, and her eyelids drooped at the sensations that traveled from her breasts to deep inside her belly.

Then, both of his hands were on her, kneading her breasts with an almost painful strength. Lucy dropped her head back, thrusting into his palms, liking the roughness. Thumbs brushed across her hardened nipples, and he watched her skin break out in gooseflesh.

A noise of surprise escaped him, and he waited until her skin smoothed back to its satiny sheen before repeating the gesture. It didn't happen again, so he trailed feather-light fingertips past her nipples and over her ribcage. Goosebumps rippled across her skin again, this time spreading across her arms, forcing a laugh from her.

Gently, he peeled the negligee down her ribs, to her waist, stopping at her hips.

"You're so little here," he murmured, spanning her waist at the dip of her navel with his hands.

"Corsets," Lucy replied, breathless. She gripped his wrists with both hands, then slid her palms up the black hair of his arms, to the bulge of his biceps, feeling their flex as they took his weight on the bed. Her eyes followed the muscles of his stomach to the ridge straining against his dark trousers. She felt him sliding the nightgown lower, and she glanced down, unbelievably shy. "Ben...will you blow out one of the lanterns? Please?"

Lips twitching at her uncharacteristic shyness, he leaned over, turned down the lamp at the bedside, and gently blew it out. That left only the light from the chest of drawers. He stood and lowered that lamp's flame, but didn't douse it, leaving the room in flickering shadows and a forgiving glow.

"Want me to turn this one off, too?"

She'd been watching the play of muscles at his back shift and flex. She shook her head when he turned his head quizzically.

"You sure?" His eyes glinted like two sapphire jewels and devoured her body in one quick sweep on the off chance she changed her mind.

"I'm sure." Was it shameful to want to see her husband?

Ben sat back on the bed, untying his dress shoes, and she sat up behind him, stroking his back. A groan crawled its way up his chest, and the sensuality of it made Lucy's breath catch. "That feels good."

She smiled in pleasure as his head lolled when she ran her fingers from his lower back to the crown of his head. She wrapped her legs around him and pressed her bare chest beneath his shoulder blades. "No one's ever rubbed your back before?"

"Naw, not since my mother did as a kid if I felt poorly."

Spreading kisses across his back, she murmured, "We shall have to remedy that. Stay still." Wriggling backward, she pressed her thumbs on either side of his spine, deep into muscles, and pushed up. He grunted something appreciative but practically melted into the floor when she began to massage the thick, tense muscles at his shoulders.

"God almighty."

Grinning, Lucy said conversationally, "Papa always asked for a backrub after a long day. He said my husband would be a lucky man when I was married. I have good, strong hands."

And she did. Fine, oxygen-rich veins wove across the tendons of her hands as she rubbed Ben's muscles in strong, slow circles. His neck was slack, head bobbing with its weight as she worked his back over. Tenderness spread from her chest to her toes, making them curl.

"You're gonna put me to sleep," he chuckled.

She paused. She didn't want that.

Rising on her knees, nightgown still trapped at her hips, she kneaded down his biceps and placed a hot, open-mouthed kiss at the apex of his neck and shoulder. She kissed him with all the pent-up need she'd harbored since that night in the tack room. Switching sides, she kissed his neck at the base, then bit him, running sharp white teeth across his pulse. And then—

She was facing him, looking up.

There was nothing adorable or sleepy about him anymore. His eyes flashed once before she was on her back, legs off the bed. The flimsy negligee was whipped down and then disappeared, and he stepped between her legs before she could clamp them shut. He pinned her arms at her sides and hovered over her, a solid weight.

"You drive me crazy, woman." His breath was hot in her ear, and she shivered, arching against him experimentally.

Their mouths met and fought, teeth and tongue, messy and wet. He released one of her arms, and then he was cupping her *there*, the same way that he had in the stables. The possessiveness of the action and the texture of his hand against her heat forced a moan from her. His hips kept her restless legs wide, and they inexorably stilled when he began to pet her. She closed her eyes, feeling. Fingers readied her while a warm mouth suckled at her breasts, sending flames of sensations rolling from her nipples to the place where his hand worked its magic.

"Move with me," he coaxed, "like last time."

"Last time it was dark," she moaned in objection, but obeyed, and turned her head into the rumpled blanket to gasp.

Ben rose, releasing her other arm, and peered down at her. He allowed her to cover the dark thatch of hair out of modesty, but Lucy feared he could still see every little thing his hand did beneath her fingers. She watched his Adam's apple bob once before he leaned down, kissing a trail down the seam of her ribs to her flat stomach.

Eyelashes fluttering wide, Lucy panicked. "What are you doing? Ben, no!"

"Sh, sh, just let me kiss you. Trust me, sweetheart."

Both of her hands covered her mons now with the strength of the very embarrassed. In all the times she'd imagined her wedding night, she'd never imagined him kissing her there. A memory, nighttime whisperings with Poppy, was conjured.

People did this, even paid for it. Women did it to men all the time, Poppy had explained. And now, Ben was trying to do it to her. Despite her humiliation, she was panting, loud, and breathy. Ben was kissing her hands directly over her clitoris, one of his fingers gliding in and out of her. She could feel his finger against her own, wet and warm as it disappeared and reappeared, over and over. His tongue licked between her fingers, and she groaned, helplessly aroused.

So what if he kissed her there, just this once? If he didn't like it, he could just stop and she'd pretend it had never happened. Her pulsebeat thrummed insistently against her hand, and she took one away to delve into Ben's hair. His eyelashes were so black, like dark fans against his cheekbones as he kissed lower. A flash of wet heat touched her through her fingers, and Lucy's head fell back at the incredible sensation. Taking the leap, she took her hand away to cover her face and heard Ben groan only once before capabilities of hearing or seeing disappeared.

Ben's tongue stroked her deeply in a long, wet lick, gliding with unbearable softness over her throbbing flesh, and coherent thought abruptly fell away. She didn't remember crying out, but she did, over and over as he kissed her between her legs in the exact way that he kissed her mouth. Lips and tongue played with her, and when he added another finger to the one inside her, she began to contract around them.

"Ben." It was a warning, high-pitched.

It was happening again, like at the stables, only faster. Lucy could hear the noises they made as though from a distance, but that feeling didn't ebb. It grew and coalesced until she was mindlessly pushing against his face for several long, desperate moments before her body seized. She climaxed, nerves exploding, almost screaming with a release that wouldn't stop. He was still at her, and she had to push his face away, toes curled and face flushed.

He didn't go far.

While she became boneless and limpid, reeling, Ben unbuttoned his trousers, shoving them down and off. His penis thrust forward from a dark thatch of hair, a flash of thick, dusky flesh that he swiftly notched against her swollen lower lips. Lucy felt something warm and blunt press into her. It was hard, yet velvet-tipped with a slight give.

"Sweetheart." His voice was unrecognizable, and she looked up to meet his gaze. He was as serious as she'd ever seen him. "Tell me if it hurts. If I'm hurting you, I'll stop, and we can wait."

Still speechless from their activities, she nodded quickly, and reached for him, wanting him close. A tide of emotion swelled, overwhelming. They were covered in sweat from the warm night, her exertions, and his forced patience.

He began to press into her with unforgiving pressure, and she tried not to tense up. Unhappy with their position, he withdrew enough to situate her further up the bed, then paused to notch himself as close as he could to her. She squeezed him tight, feeling the fine tremors along his back. It was the first time she'd felt weight of a man on her in this fashion. He was solid, heavy with muscle. He took a deep breath, and lifted himself on an elbow, guiding his sex with his hand. Again, that blunt heat pushed into hers, and she raised her head, glimpsing what she imagined should dangle from a donkey or horse, not a man. Biting her lip to hide her distress, she lay back.

Ben was looking down, still hesitating and tense, a dark lock of hair stuck to his forehead. She smoothed it over, and kissed him. If he hurt her, so be it, but she'd never let him know.

Returning the kiss somewhat distractedly, he flexed his hips, pushing against the natural resistance of her body. His entry was slow, and it hurt, even though she was embarrassingly wet. When her flesh finally gave and the crown of him entered her, Ben stalled. Both were breathing heavily, glancing at each other.

He gave her a questioning look. *Are you okay?*

She nodded rapidly.

He pushed in another inch, then another. The pressure was incredible. Lucy squirmed.

Swearing worriedly under his breath, Ben growled, "Am I hurting you?"

Lucy fought a hysterical giggle. She was dripping sweat, trembling with tension and discomfort as her inner muscles stretched with taut resistance, and yet she felt the need to calm *his* nerves. Minnie had explained to her that the more you did the act, the better it felt. Maybe by the third or fourth time, she soothed herself, it wouldn't hurt at all. With this insight, she steeled her spine, took a deep breath and rolled her hips forward. He groaned while she inhaled sharply, and his eyes glazed over before he buried his face into her hair.

"Don't worry, darlin', I don't think this is gonna take long." He gently pushed the remaining way in, wincing at her hiss, and rocked in and out of her. It was incredibly intimate, his heavy weight, the large columns of his thighs flexing against hers. She held her breath, clenching him to her breasts, braced as the tempo of their rocking increased.

He was right.

It didn't take long before he seemed to grow larger, harder, and hotter within her. Noises escaped his throat, guttural growls, as he pulsed deeply into her body. Even through the discomfort, Lucy decided that this was her favorite part. She could feel his climax almost as though it was her own, the shuddering of his muscles as they bunched in a moment of extreme strength.

He could snap her in half if he wanted.

Kissing his face, full of feeling, full of him, she whispered, "I love you, Benjamin."

"Love you," his lips murmured, skimming across her perspiring brow, sipping at her. When he disengaged, she squeaked at the strange emptiness, bringing a smile to his lips.

Ben flopped to his back, and she looked down her body at a peculiar sensation. She stiffened.

"What?"

Lucy snapped her legs closed. "Er..."

"What is it?" He sat up, brow wrinkling.

"There's—" she broke off, more self-conscious than she'd ever remembered being before in her life. Her eyes darted to the basin at the table against the wall.

His brow cleared, and if possible, he looked more embarrassed than she. "Oh." He rolled off the bed and walked, naked as the day he was born, to the ewer. After looking around for a moment, he scratched the back of his neck.

"Oh, Ben, your back!" she gasped. The muscular expanse was riddled with a dozen long, pink scratch marks.

The awkward moment was mercifully ended by his pleased chuckle. "I reckon you broke me in pretty well." While she groaned and covered her flaming cheeks, he gave up the search, sighed, and snagged his shirt from the floor. The muscles on the back of his arms bunched as he poured water into the basin and cleaned himself with his shirt. Watching with interest, she frowned when he turned around and encroached upon her with that same shirt.

"What are you doing?"

"Cleaning you up."

When her eyes widened in horror, he laughed.

"I can do it!"

"It's my fault you got that way."

"That's quite all right—" she rushed, but he was already on her. It was amazing that she'd ever thought he was shy or stoic. The planes of his face were relaxed, his eyes soft with humor as he gained on her with a balled-up wet shirt, of all things. "No, Ben, you don't have to—*Benjamin*!"

Laughter boomed out of him as he snagged a slim ankle and held her down.

"I could cheerfully kill you!" she cried while he briskly wiped her from front to back. Curiosity halted her struggles. "What is that?"

A sheepish glance at the pink-tinged mess on the shirt proved he was not as immodest as he tried to appear. "It's what happens when...when a man's done...you know."

"Oh. Like, horses and bulls? So it's...what makes babies?"

"I reckon."

"What is it called?"

"Ah, hell, I don't know—" he laughed, shrugging. "Seed?"

She giggled with him, enjoying his discomposure.

For a moment, they were both quiet and thoughtful. Then, "Do you think we made a baby, Ben?"

There was the sound of a wet plop on the floor as Ben threw the shirt. He bounced down on the bed next to her, and she rolled to him, throwing her leg across his waist. His hand found purchase on her leg, stroking up and down along her sleek calf. "Maybe. But I don't think it happens that fast. Some people don't have any at all, even after years of bein' together."

"That's true," she breathed, brushing her nails in the crisp hair on his chest. "Or sometimes they only have one or two. I hope we're blessed with at least three."

"Or we could be like Sol's parents. They had twelve."

"Twelve," she squawked, lifting her head to goggle at him. He was the most content she'd ever seen. Drowsy almost, with a lazy, sleepy smile. "I wouldn't want twelve, or even six, to be frank."

His eyes were slitted and glittered down at her, wrinkled at the corners. "There's ways not to get you in the family way."

Her lower lip pouted. "I don't know any."

As though unable to resist, he leaned forward, capturing her lips between his own. "Mm."

For several minutes they kissed, long and slow and in no hurry. It was different than the other kisses they'd shared. She could do it all night and not tire of it, that leisurely tasting. The silky stroke of their tongues, the occasional gentle bite of teeth. The only thing was, the longer they kissed, the faster her heart seemed to beat. She tried to ignore it, but her body had a mind of its own. Since her leg was already on his stomach, it didn't take much to slide the rest of the way over until she was straddling him. Strong hands gripped her hips, squeezing.

Her breasts swayed, brushing his chest until her nipples were hard, focused points. The soreness pulsing between her legs altered, feeling empty and throbbing along with her heartbeat.

Something brushed against her backside, and she raised her head in surprise.

"What was that?"

Amusement didn't hide the heat in Ben's expression. "What do you think?"

"It moves...by itself?"

He jerked against her again, and she raised herself to watch between her legs. He was hard again, huge and flushed, pointing toward his navel, and it twitched and flexed independently beneath her.

"That's shocking," she said, mouth dry. "I'm learning more than I could've imagined."

"So am I." Ben released her hips and grabbed her ribs, settling her straight upon his lap so he could see her.

She looked down at herself, to see what he saw. Round breasts, heavy with arousal. Lean, tapered waist. Her hips looked wider seated on him, and she glanced at the ridges of muscles along his abdomen. His hands cupped her breasts, pushing them together, then higher, as if playing with toys. She stroked along his stomach, lips parting. Her fingers found his nipples, and she brushed them with her thumbs.

"They look so different than mine. Smaller." She pinched one and watched it harden, and her lips curved up.

"Scoot down a little," he grunted, shifting her until she was poised over the head of his shaft. It brushed against her, and her sex gave a throb in response. Lucy bit her lip.

"I dreamed of this, once," he admitted, stroking back and forth over her soft entrance. "We were at the creek, in the sand, and you were ridin' me like a bronc."

Her breath caught when he angled her and pressed inside. "I dreamt of you, too. But nothing like this."

"You're pretty with your cheeks all pink like that." His voice was the merest rumble as he pushed in with his hips, filling her up, inch by inch. "This hurtin' you?"

"No," she breathed. "It doesn't hurt, not exactly. It's just...full. And tight."

"Yeah?"

"Yes." When he was fully seated within her, he stopped moving, their breathing ragged. "I can feel you," she placed her hand low on her belly, "right here."

For a brief instant, his face grimaced, and he pushed into her so deep that she cried out.

"Sorry, sorry."

Legs shaking at the intensity, Lucy lifted to her knees to ease the pressure. His accompanying groan froze her. That felt good for him. Excitement pushed any soreness impatiently aside, and her mind worked. What would he do if she acted out his dream? Experimentally, she lowered until she could feel the head of him deep inside.

Ben bared his teeth, hands gripping hard. "Luce—"

Leaning forward made it less intense, the angle more forgiving, and she planted her hands on either side of his broad ribcage, fisting the blankets. Taking a bracing breath, she rocked forward and backward, feeling the glide of him. Her breasts swayed, then jiggled as he met her thrusts with his own. Gritting her teeth at the incredible fullness, she watched his face, marveling at the intensity in his expression. Then, her eyes glazed over, and her lips opened in an 'o' of helplessness.

His hand had joined in, stroking her swollen, pliant flesh where their bodies met.

It's like magic, she thought.

When he touched her there, the sensation of that caress alone was in the foreground, and she buried her face into Ben's taut neck and keened. Their movements became sloppy. Frantic. Eyes squeezed shut, her skin erupted into goosebumps, and she ground into her husband's trapped fingers, feeling as though she'd caught fire and fallen from an incredible height all at once.

As though from a distance, she heard Ben curse, clench her tight to him in that remarkable moment of strength, and she wondered if she could die from loving someone too much.

After, they lay in that position until both were drifting in and out of sleep. The lantern, already low in oil, ran out and doused them in darkness. Ben maneuvered them until they were under his ragged blanket—there was no top sheet—and he tenderly stroked her drying hair from her face. She ran her nails along his chest and shoulder, tucked in tight to his side, while he made growling noises of appreciation.

That was how they fell asleep.

BEN WOKE UP with a mouthful of fragrant hair.

He was clutched to a soft body; he had an erection and amorous, roaming hands.

Stilling, he released a round breast and pulled a long tendril of hair away from his lips, rubbing the spiderweb feeling from them. The slow thrust of a bottom in his lap made him stiffen all over.

"Why did you stop?" Lucy murmured sleepily, nuzzling into the pillow that his left arm had fallen asleep under.

Her hair was everywhere, and it looked black in the pre-dawn. The sun wasn't quite up, but it was lit enough inside from the window to see a creamy shoulder and the hint of one breast before the blanket hid the rest of her body from sight. He rocked into her hips, flush against her, answering her motion with one of his own.

How long had he been touching her, clenching her to him? Now that he was awake, his arousal was unbearable. Her bare skin against his was warm and smooth, and with a groan, he reached for her beneath the blanket.

Lucy's eyes were closed, but her lips were parted and her cheeks were flushed. When he rocked into her again, his cock felt her warm wetness as she drew her legs up, arching her back in a stretch.

"You even know what you're askin' for?" His morning voice was gravel, barely intelligible.

In answer, she reached for his hand and led it down between her legs. The whoosh of blood in his head deafened him while he touched her intimately, sliding rough fingers over the softest, silkiest place he'd ever felt. Easing a finger into her, he groaned when she clenched around him. "Don't want to hurt you."

"It won't." She smiled and reached behind her to grab him at the root.

"Lord almighty," he gritted, not quite laughing. She was just as amorous as he was in the morning.

Although he tried to slow her down, to ready her with one finger, then two, she backed into him with an undeniable insistence, guiding him by the place where most women led men around. She pressed hard against him. He removed his hand and let the head push, push until it eased through the circle of tight muscle. Hot, wet heat seared him, but he didn't move and let her accommodate him. After a moment's thought, he pulled right back out of her, his wet crown drawing up the dark crevice of her bottom.

"Ben," she whined, and he smiled again through clenched teeth. *So impatient.*

Again, he entered her, the circle of muscle giving in easier than before. Four times he pulled out, then repeated the motion, playing with her, letting it go a little deeper each time until she was tentatively rocking backward in tiny increments. When he was finally fully seated to the hilt, he stayed still and reached between her legs again. He strummed that sensitive place, occasionally feeling how her flesh split wide to accommodate his girth and quashed the manic urge to pump her senseless.

But Lucy was already senseless; a squirming, panting mess. She reached around to draw his head to hers, but her nipple came into view, and he sucked it deep into his mouth. Hard. Crying out, her inner muscles flexed around him deep inside. Ben released her and cursed, drumming inside of her now. Their wet skin slapped and he bottomed out inside of her at an unrelenting pace, perhaps stroking between her legs too roughly or quickly, he couldn't use his brain enough to discern it.

An intense climax built too fast, and he tried to stop, to make it last.

Lucy made a noise, that mountain lion growl of frustration, and slammed backwards into him. Losing any sense of being careful, he crushed her to him and pistoned his hips against her, then came, leg muscles hard as a rock. He slowed down, drawing it out, but Lucy didn't stop. She was still trying to reach her climax.

Murmuring into her hair, he stroked into her, still hard, and reached between her legs. The sheets beneath them were drenched by the time she cried out several times, and for the second time in his life—after the night before—felt a woman climax around his cock. The strength of her muscles stole his breath, and he groaned with her. Their hearts pounded. Their backs were slippery with sweat. The air around them was perfumed with soap, salt, and musk.

When he refrained from pulling out, and just held her to him, all remnants of sleepiness were gone from her voice when she said, "Good morning."

He laughed until he slid out, nuzzling into her neck, feeling her giggle.

Outside, a rooster crowed.

23

— • —

CHAPTER TWENTY-THREE

Dressing together was another kind of intimacy. Ben dressed in brisk, industrious movements. Work shirt tucked into hardy jeans that buttoned at the fly. He was tying his boots when she cursed under her breath at her corset. Lucy saw him glance up and smile.

He was only too happy to help.

While she shoved stockinged feet into her boots, the tunes of Ben's whistling while he stoked the kitchen fire reached her. He was placing a blue enamel coffee pot to heat on the warming stove when she reached downstairs, still tying her favorite ruffled apron.

"I'm gonna milk the cows and let the horses I'm working on out into the round pen."

Lucy twined her arms around his neck and kissed his bristly chin. "I'll start breakfast. Who usually eats with you?"

His hands massaged her hips and he nuzzled her hair. "Sol and Junior. Tia and Frank like to keep to themselves. Both are the quietest folks you'll ever meet."

"I'll make sure to say good morning to her while I'm gathering eggs. It's nice to at least invite them."

"Well, now, that's real decent of you, wife." He gave her a hard, smacking kiss on her lips, his dark chuckle following behind him out the door while she watched after him like a bemused fence post. For a moment she was lost in the mem-

365

ories of their morning activities, then she reminded herself that she had things to do.

Right. Breakfast. Which meant eggs.

It was already getting warm in the kitchen, the hazards of cooking with a woodburning stove in mid-summer. One of the windows sported a fresh new screen, so she lifted that one and propped it up. A faint breeze and the sounds of farm life trickled in, and for a moment, she was overcome with happiness. Lucy gave a twirl, skirts spinning, and hustled to the chicken coop.

Five minutes later, gingerly carrying a dozen eggs in her apron, she turned toward the narrow trail leading to Frank's cabin and the creek. The oven would be hot and the coffee brewed by the time she got back from her visit.

The property was empty except for a man and woman planting seeds next to an already established garden in the distance behind the cozy house. The man was brown from years of sun exposure, and the bonneted woman was brown from Hispanic heritage. He turned rich soil with a wooden-handled ho and she dropped seeds and covered them confidently with a booted foot in a rhythm perfected with years of experience. Lucy would have known from one look at them that they were man and wife. They moved together fluidly, with a comfort acquired through years of familiarity. She'd met the man last month. Frank. And the woman was Ben's relative, an aunt? He called her Tia but introduced her as Tia to everyone. She'd been a quietly smiling woman with graying black hair and a handsome face.

She greeted them with a cheerful 'good morning', and the couple looked up, waving in unison. Their synchronism stirred Lucy's desire to reach that milestone of marriage with Ben. She wanted to be as in tune with him as Tia was with Frank. It was true she'd wanted his last name and the intimacy of his body. Now that she'd acquired them, a new goal blazed. She wanted the small things, the priceless idiosyncrasies that occurred from a long-standing commitment to someone. She wanted to be his world, his life, a part of his soul.

"Mornin'," Frank said. Shy, timid Tia smiled and nodded to her. Both had been to their wedding but had left before the reception.

"Would you like any eggs, or to join us for breakfast this morning?" Lucy lifted the lumpy apron in invitation.

"Oh, no'm, we ate a coupla' hours ago. Thank ya kindly."

A couple of hours? Lucy placed a hand to her face and laughed in embarrassment. "Oh, no. I'll have to learn to wake up earlier, won't I? Maybe next time?"

Both nodded, again in unison. It made her smile. She waved cheerily and carefully trekked back to the house without jostling the eggs.

Lucy made a mental note that ranch wives woke up at daybreak around here. Tia probably didn't play in bed for an hour before getting chores done. She giggled at the thought. And yet, Ben hadn't complained, had he?

Horses trotted easily into the yard, and Lucy shouted a 'good morning' to Sol and Junior before disappearing into the kitchen.

Soon, the warm, fragrant scents of bacon frying, biscuits baking to a golden brown, and piping hot coffee did quick work of calling the men inside.

"Smells good in here," Ben's baritone rumbled against her damp neck as he eased around her for the coffee pot. They shared a secretive glance, remembering, before two more male voices broke in.

"It sure does," Sol chirped, if one could call his deep voice anything close to birdsong. He snagged the kettle from Ben, leaning against the work table to pour a cup of black coffee, then looked around, baffled. "How do women do it?"

"Do what?" Lucy looked around. She'd tidied some, reorganized a little, and found some dandelion weeds to grace a narrow little vase in the center of the work table.

"Fancy up a place in two minutes flat, make it all homey-like."

Lucy beamed.

"I am godawful tired," yawned Junior from the doorway. He glanced slyly between the newlyweds. "What about you, Ben?"

Black brows lowered over blue eyes, quelling the young upstart. "Feel right as rain."

"You sure? You look a bit worn out to me—oomph!" Junior broke off and glared at Sol's pointed elbow, rubbing his ribcage.

Pretending her ears weren't on fire, Lucy carried platters of steaming food to the dining table with help from Ben and Sol. Junior kept quiet and sat down, chagrinned. He helped himself to biscuits, sausage, and eggs, studiously avoiding the grits and Lucy's gaze.

"What's on the agenda today?" Lucy asked, tucking strips of bacon in a biscuit, and wishing for some butter and jelly.

Ben glanced up from his plate full of food—three fried eggs, two biscuits, half a pound of bacon, and boiled grits—and said, "Horses need training, we've gotta get them ready for the cattle drive in the spring."

Oh yes. The cattle drive his father had coerced him to take charge of. Lucy frowned into her grits.

"How long does it usually take to complete a cattle drive?" she asked.

Sol, mouth full of food, answered, "Oh, 'bout three months, usually. I'm not real fond of them myself, but forty dollars a month ain't too bad. Better'n what I'm paid now." He laughed and dodged the balled-up napkin Ben threw at him.

"Aren't they very dangerous?" She couldn't help but look at Ben with worry swimming in her eyes. "I knew a man that drowned crossing a flooded river. I even remember what he liked to eat. Roast and potatoes with gravy, no vegetables."

Ben shook his head somberly. "Only a fool would go into flooded waters. Best to wait it out."

Unconsciously, Sol continued eating and told stories of how men had died over the years from Indian attacks, stampedes, diphtheria, and snake bites. Afterward, Lucy and Ben looked at each other with serious eyes.

"I hate cattle drives." Junior frowned into his plate. "You're never clean, and even when you come up on a water hole, you gotta share it with twenty other men and two thousand head of cattle."

Ben shrugged. "You don't have to go. You can stay with Frank and watch the ranch."

"I ain't gonna babysit," Junior sneered.

Lucy sat up straight. "I can take care of myself. I don't need anyone to *babysit* me." Especially not Junior. She gave him the stink eye and he returned it.

Hands up in supplication, Ben whistled. "Whoa, now, I didn't say that. But are you gonna tend our house, milk all the cows, wrangle up horses, check fences, feed and water 'em every day, watch for injuries, buy feed in town, load it up, bring it back, unload it, pitch hay—"

He continued on and on over the list of chores, and Lucy's straight spine grew limp, her eyes wide. All *that*, for one little ranch? How did he expect Frank to do it all by himself? She'd help, surely, but now that everything stacked on top of each other, she understood why it took three other men to help Ben run a ranch.

"I think she understands," Sol said around a mouthful of biscuit. He laughed. "Look, her mouth's open wide as a barn door."

Closing her mouth with an audible *clack*, she asked, "And Tia, Frank, and myself are going to do all of this for three months?" Her voice held a tremor of disbelief.

Ben was wiping his mouth with Lucy's cloth napkin, and she watched in fascination as he held it wide with two hands, starting at the top and drawing it down. She'd seen him do so when his beard was full and thick, wiping away any crumb or egg drip that could become tangled in the hairs. Now his beard was barely more than a dense black shadow. She imagined the back of her neck was red from the whisper of that bristly chin and upper lip.

"Naw, I'm gonna hire somebody I trust to come out a couple times a week and help with any heavy loading. Probably the

Picketts, they're the neighbors up north, and they have a couple older boys with sense." Then, he stood, picked up the napkin he'd thrown at Sol, and brought his empty plate to the dishpan. The other two men quickly followed suit, thanking her for the meal and walking back through the kitchen door.

After they had left, Ben drew her up from the table and planted a long, lingering kiss on her lips.

Eyelashes and insides fluttering from the arousing slide of his mouth on her, she whispered, "Have a good day."

Broad hand stroking her back up and down, he kissed her head, taking a deep breath in. "What do you have planned for the day, darlin'?"

"Clean, organize, make it homey." She snuggled into his chest.

"Put your stamp on everything, huh?" His lips smiled into her middle part, then he backed away.

"See you at dinner." Once he'd placed his hat on his head and walked out the door, Lucy got to work.

Cooking and cleaning were nothing new to her. For years growing up, that was all she'd do to while away the hours of boredom at the hotel. What she'd never done, however, was make a house into a home, and the task was as daunting as it was exhilarating

But, first things first. Cleaning.

She rummaged for cleaning supplies but couldn't find any, so off she went to bother Tia again.

Tia may have been quiet, but she reminded Lucy of Minnie in her single-minded efficiency. The petite woman smiled in understanding at Lucy's plight and grabbed a giant dishpan from a hook outside. She filled it with vinegar, bars of White Windsor Soap, dishrags, and a multitude of other things that made a home spic-and-span. Though Tia's spoken English wasn't fluent, her understanding of the language was excellent, and time flew by as Lucy chatted the woman's ear off. Ben's aunt didn't seem to mind, smiling and nodding through most of the flow of words Lucy didn't bother stoppering.

Once the cleaning was done, Tia surprised Lucy by asking for paper and a pencil and spent an hour hunched over the borrowed notebook while the younger woman looked on in amazement. Tia was drawing the kitchen, the pantry, and the den, and in these sketches, she would point and ask soft questions in halting English mixed with lyrical Spanish. Did she want hooks here? Did she want shelves? Would she like drying racks made for herbs? Lucy's excitement rose, and so immersed with their planning, neither woman realized that it was lunchtime until voices and loud, stomping boots from the porch roused them.

"Oh, no!" Lucy gasped. "I forgot to cook dinner!"

"No, no, you wait," Tia stood, gathering her sheets of paper, and tucking them in her apron. "I have *carne guisada* on the stove." She opened the door, said several rapid-fire sentences to Ben, and alighted down the porch to her house.

"I'm sorry, Ben, I lost track of time," Lucy said.

His eyes were busy looking around the kitchen, at the gleaming floors, folded linens on the worktable, and new curtains draped over sparkling clean windows. He let out a low whistle. "You've been busy. No wonder you lost track of time. Tia said she'll bring her stew over here. She makes it every Sunday. There will be plenty. She cooks for us all the time, stop frettin'."

Lucy stood solemnly with hands clasped. "I'm so happy to have married you."

"Because I didn't get mad you forgot to have dinner laid out?" He laughed at her, gold tooth glinting. It was her favorite laugh, the one that crinkled his eyes and transformed those dimples into deep creases in his cheeks. "I'm not mad," he reassured, and, a smile still playing about his mouth, he leaned forward over the table to plant a soft, sweet kiss on her lips.

As usual, the potency of his mouth on hers addled her brain, making it hard to breathe and her eyes fluttered shut. She could kiss him all day if he'd let her. When she tried to open her lips around his, to make the kiss lush and wet, he leaned back again, clearing his throat. His smile was gone, and his eyes were hot on hers.

"We'd better help Tia before I take you upstairs and let the men eat all our dinner." She loved how rough his voice got after they kissed, and her swift disappointment gave way to a cautious anticipation.

Junior walked in the door just as Lucy wrapped herself around his older brother like a wisteria vine. "Should I come back later?" he asked dryly.

"Yes," was Ben's muffled reply, but he set a laughing Lucy down. "Come on, let's help Tia bring dinner over."

Junior rolled his eyes and acquiesced.

That night, after making love twice, Ben and Lucy stayed up and talked until midnight. He played with her hair until she fell asleep, then blew out his lamp, closing his eyes only when he prayed for the first time in years in thanks for his miracle.

THE NEXT MONTH, Lucy had busily acclimated herself to life on the ranch.

All her belongings were put away or hung up. On the mantle of the fireplace, she'd set the wedding daguerreotype of Benjamin and her in their finery. Instead of sitting them side by side, the photographer had positioned Lucy to look soulfully into Ben's eyes while posed near the landing of the hotel's stairs. Ben pretended to moan every time he saw the photo, claiming he looked like he was the one making cow eyes at her. However, more than once had she caught him stroking the glass over her picture's profile and figured he didn't think it was too awful.

Thanks to Sol and Junior's carpentry skills and Tia's vision, new shelves and hooks lined the walls of the kitchen. Cast iron skillets and various pots hung in a tidy row along the wall near the stove, and spices sat neatly side by side on a shelf. Overhead was a pattern of drying racks and sturdy nails on the dark beams of the ceiling, soon to be filled after Lucy grew her own herbs.

Each day when Ben walked through the door for supper, she watched his eyes rove around in curiosity, trying to find something new. She would serve their meal, exhausted but pleased while they told each other about their day. Her own fatigue would melt as he'd nonchalantly go over the enormity of all he did in one day.

One afternoon, just before serving the men their dinner, Lucy scurried to the outhouse. Out of everything she loved about her new charming home, the dingy, dark, and smelly building in the back was the bane of her existence. While everything else had received a makeover when Ben bought the place out, the outhouse had been relatively ignored. The only thing new about it was the hinges on its rotting door.

For a moment, she danced in front of the leaning pile of worn wooden slats, fighting the urge to go. Oh, but she *hated* the outhouse. Taking a deep breath, she held it and rushed inside, slamming the door behind her. Inside, it was dark and full of cobwebs and hanging things. Sol told her once he'd stepped on a snake in there, in the middle of his business at that. Everyone had laughed while she'd looked at him in horror. Her own business was always done with extreme quickness, but this time, her skirt snagged on a jagged splinter. Cursing under her breath, she shook the skirt until the splinter broke off.

Searing fire stabbed through the flesh of her buttock. She'd been stabbed! Had a snake struck her? Screaming at the pain, Lucy ran out of the outhouse, shaking out her skirts and half expecting a rattler to fall out. Another burning stab like a red-hot rusty nail hit her, this time through the skin of her outer thigh. She screamed again.

"Something's biting me!" she shrieked.

Footsteps pounded her way and she looked up just as Ben tackled her to the ground.

"Oomph," she grunted, and then, her skirts were flung up over her face.

"What is it?" she heard Sol shout from several feet away.

"Turn your heads, damn it," Ben growled like an angry animal, swatting at her petticoats. "She's got a red wasp trapped."

An annoying, grating laugh to Lucy's left made tears of humiliation prick at her eyes. There was a crunching sound, then her skirts were yanked back down. Ben looked worried, and madder than the wasp he'd just killed.

"Stop braying like a jackass and get rid of that wasp's nest," shouted Ben.

Junior stopped laughing. "But they make me swell up something awful!"

"Tough shit!" Ben helped Lucy up, then heaved her into his arms like a sack of grain. Her bottom and leg were on fire, so she didn't refute the action. Sol picked up Ben's hat out of the dirt where it had fallen and handed it to his friend, wisely keeping his mouth shut.

Lucy waited until they made it into her clean kitchen with food bubbling on the stove before she started moaning, "I hate that outhouse. I thought I'd been shot!" She tried to laugh it off, but the pain kept her features in a permanent grimace.

"I'm sorry, sweetheart. I'll take care of it. Here, let me see." He sat her on the table, and she gingerly sat on her left buttock. The other one pulsed in tandem with her leg, as though the stings had a life of their own. Her skirt and petticoats were rucked up once again, and Lucy kept one eye on the door and the other on the two tiny dots on her leg and bottom. The center of each sting was a single red dot, outlined by a pale ring of skin.

"I thought it would look much worse than that," she said, face puckered in pain. "Like two giant, bloody holes. I can't believe they're so small when they feel so horrible. Can you believe I've never been stung by a wasp before? I figured it was bullets. Or a snake."

Ben paused, then left her side for a dishrag. He wet it at the reservoir, then brought it to her.

"Hold it here for a spell while I get something." He left and came back with a wad of something dark brown and wet that he unceremoniously split in two and pressed against the rapidly swelling flesh, holding it there with a dishrag.

"Is that...tobacco?" She took a careful sniff through the haze of pain.

"Yep, got it off Junior." Ben stroked her leg over her gartered stocking.

Her eyes narrowed in suspicion. "Why is it wet?"

"Well, I had to get him to spit it out so I could carry it over—"

Lucy reared up from the table, or attempted to, but Ben held her down with a strong forearm, laughing. "I stopped at the well, it's wet from the well!"

"Benjamin Stone, that was a nasty trick!" she cried, swatting his hand from inching up her leg any further, no matter how good it felt. The sly cur, he thought he could get fresh with her after his provoking, did he?

Ben, a broad grin stretched white and gold across his thickening beard, stood from his crouch. "I was just teasin' sweetheart. Here, hold this here." He replaced her hand with his over the compress and stepped between her legs, so large and broad that he encompassed Lucy's vision until she could see nothing but a damp work shirt, stretched over a deep chest. With one hand braced on the table and the other holding the compress, she was helpless to stop the descending mouth, turned soft with only a hint of a smile, from touching her own. Not that she wanted to stop him. The touch of his lips distracted her, melted away the pain and any sense of here-and-now. Her passions, always so close to the surface these days, bubbled over and spilled onto him. She opened her mouth wide over his, and he followed suit, their tongues meeting in a dance that often ended with Lucy thrown onto the bed.

The door opened behind Ben.

"Damnation, I knew I would get stung, you got any more of that—" Junior, gingerly probing his swelling hand, stopped abruptly at the scene he'd walked in on. When his eyes trailed from their flushed faces to Lucy's exposed stocking and garter, he squeezed them shut and backed out.

"Get out!" Ben roared, but his brother was already a blur running down the steps. His brow was still knitted when he turned back to a giggling Lucy. "Blamed fool didn't even bother to shut the door for us."

Her giggles escalated into real laughter.

Disturbing a wasp's nest was just the first of several events she stumbled across in her daily routine as a ranch wife. After a couple of weeks of wheedling from Lucy, Ben bartered with a neighbor for more young pullets for their chicken coop. One evening while he washed up in the hip tub in the kitchen, Lucy went outside with a lantern to grab a towel on the line. It had grown dark, and she'd forgotten all about taking in the dry clothes. Loud squawking and fluttering in the chicken coop alerted her, and, with a curse, she snatched a pronged rake from her sprouting flower and herb beds.

Not her new pullets! They hadn't even had a chance to lay eggs.

"Oh, Lucy, you pudding head," she groaned to herself as lantern light beamed on the narrow little coop. She'd forgotten to shut the coop. The door was cracked open, and she berated herself with audible viciousness, approaching the foreboding darkness within the coop. Teeth bared with fear, she opened the door further and thrust the lantern into the black cavern. A dozen young hens, still a month away from giving any eggs, roosted on the rung closest to the ground, the older alpha chickens in a neat row near the ceiling of the coop. They made deep, disturbed noises that varied between clucks and growls. Beneath them in the shadows limped a reedy brown pullet, a dead white leghorn with wings outspread, and a hunched figure that was making short work of the dead chicken's neck with sharp, yellow teeth.

"Ben," Lucy called weakly, setting the lantern down beside her. With the rake, she tried to nudge the injured chicken out the door, getting a little too close to the matted gray fur of the opossum in the process. Its eyes flashed green in the glare of the light, and it hissed at her, its mouth opening unnaturally wide to reveal blood-stained teeth. She screamed, loud and high-pitched, as piercing as the steam releasing from a train whistle. "BEN!"

Frantic that another one of her precious chickens not die, she continued to corral the stupid little hen out the door. It clucked and tried to fly on a perch, missed, and landed a little too near the arched back of the opossum. It struck at the clumsy bundle of feathers unsuccessfully. She screamed again, then screamed louder when the critter decided dinner was too risky and waddled toward the open door...that Lucy was standing directly in front of.

"Ahh, Ben!" She couldn't let the opossum get away! It could come back and kill more of her chickens. With that in mind, overriding her desperate fear of the giant rodent made of teeth, she struck the animal hard with the rake. It hissed at her again, its mouth yawning open and its beady black eyes as frozen on hers as Lucy's was on his. She continued to hit it with the rake, shouting expletives, until it backed up in a corner. When she tried to close the door, it attempted to flee again, so there she stood, screaming for Ben, for *anyone*, to bring a gun, while she kept the matted creature and its quivering rat's tail pinned in the corner.

"Lucy!" She heard Ben running, cocking a rifle. "Are you alright? What is it?"

"In here!" Her voice was reed-thin, and she screeched when she thought she saw the opossum move. It hadn't. She heard Ben open the door wider, and said, "Thank God, hurry Ben, before he gets away!"

There was a silence, then a suspicious noise. Choking.

Not taking her eyes from the chicken murderer, she asked, "Do you need me to move so you can get a clear shot?"

"Darlin', I thought an escaped prisoner had you at gunpoint." Ben sounded almost like he was amused.

"Worse, this *thing* was in here and he killed one of my pretty white chickens," she wailed.

"Alright, alright, back up and cover your ears." Yes, there was definitely laughter in his voice.

She backed away, dropping the rake to cover her ears. After a moment's hesitation, the problem was taken care of with a round of buckshot, and Lucy's eyes widened at the gory aftermath. Even in death, the great mouth was open. Shuddering, Lucy snatched the injured brown pullet before it could get into any more mischief, perching it up high with its sisters. Then she noticed Ben.

"You're naked."

"As the day I was born." He was chuckling, gun in one hand, gonads cupped protectively in the other. Bath water and suds dripped down his stomach and his hair. Chicken droppings and dirt coated his bare feet and between his toes. It was Lucy's turn to laugh.

"You need another bath." She covered her mouth and her poor dead hen was forgotten. "Oh, Ben. You shot a gun in your birthday suit." Helpless laughter took over her.

"What better way to shoot it?" he quipped, bending down for the rake so he could dispose of the carcasses. The sight of his bare buttocks sent Lucy into another fit. It only got worse when Sol, Junior, and Frank showed up with their own guns in hand.

As the weeks went by, an indescribable thing happened.

Lucy fell deeper in love with her husband.

The ranch wasn't easy to run, and there were always things to do, so idleness had no home here. That was fine with her; she never could sit still for a minute unless she was reading a book. She grew closer to Ben, Frank and Sol, and especially Tia.

Junior kept his distance, as usual, disappearing into town several nights a week and coming home haggard and unwilling to work. He'd taken to whiling the hours away at saloons with his distant cousin on his mother's side, Leonard.

Lucy did not like Leonard.

"His parents sent him away, he doesn't have any friends around here, I'm just showin' him the ropes," Junior had defended one day.

The man was oily and dishonest, and though many would have considered him good-looking, Lucy despised the way his eyes roved over her when he thought everyone's back was turned. Not only that, but Junior's attitude around him was sour as a persimmon, and his humor had adopted a cruel edge that made Leonard laugh, but no one else. Thankfully, the man stayed his nights at the big Stone Ranch.

Except when he was in town whoring with Junior.

It vexed Ben to no end, but he refused to turn into his father and shout at the boy. Lucy held her tongue but noticed that the less Junior would do, the more Ben would step up and double his workload, taking over any chores his brother failed to complete.

Fed up with the child in a man's body, but unwilling to turn into a tyrant, Lucy did the only thing she knew to soothe Ben's weary body.

She made love to him. A lot. She coddled him as well as she could when they were alone, scratching his scalp until he fell asleep, rubbing his back, his hands, his tired feet. She took over shaving him, not because she didn't like the beard, but because she loved how relaxed her husband became while he drowsed in his chair, blade rasping over his sharp jaw and dimpled chin. Perhaps the best thing was that he reciprocated. After a bout of lovemaking, he'd clean her up, draw her near him beneath the sheets, and run his fingers through her long hair, over and over. It put her to sleep so well that she never bothered to wear it in a braid anymore. Each morning they'd awaken entangled in each other, dress quietly, and have coffee together, the warm kitchen cozy as they murmured about their plans for the day.

Though there were moments of quiet companionship be-tween them, Lucy often wondered how far she could push Ben before she shocked him.

One such day after a week-long dry spell because of her menses, Lucy paced the kitchen, sexual tension, and frus-tration eating at her. Ben and Junior had ridden directly af-ter breakfast to check the westward fence. Unfortunately,

Leonard had shown up for breakfast, unannounced, then tagged along. It had taken everything in her not to complain while she cleaned up after them, so she'd stewed in silence until they'd left.

For an hour, Lucy scrubbed and washed and dusted and prepped food for lunchtime. She worked up a sweat, and a foul mood besides, fuming over how Ben had barely kissed her goodbye that morning. He was probably still unsure if she was still burdened with her "woman time", but she brushed off that plausibility and chose to pout. Now that the joys of the flesh had been awakened, Lucy found that she was tense without those intimate touches and physical reassurances.

Her mother would curl her lip at such urges. Aurora would make a note of it and give it to the preacher for the next sermon. *Lust is a sin,* he would thunder, his judgment mountainous from his pulpit as he sought Lucy out in the crowd. *Copulation is only for the begetting of children. Enjoying the bedtime act with one's husband is amoral.*

With a great, growling sigh, Lucy went outside, her tread heavy. She pulled the heavy, cumbersome tub from its hook and drug it inside. It took a good half hour to heat water to boiling and carry the rest in from the well pump. If her sweat had dried before, it came back with a vengeance to drip down her nose and gather beneath her arms, back, and between her breasts. A quick peek showed a deserted yard, so she quickly locked the kitchen and front door, undressed, and sat in the steaming hot water of her bath. She moaned low, and as she sank into the shallow depths with her closed legs draped over the side, a plan began to form. For the first time that day, she smiled.

24

—·—

Chapter Twenty-Four

B en squinted beneath the brim of his hat and asked Junior, "Is that Lucy riding up?"

It couldn't be Leonard. At the first sign of repairing fence lines and work, he'd made an excuse and went back to the big ranch. Ben could tell his brother had wanted to tag along.

Junior was hungover and in one of those black, sour moods that felt like a storm cloud over the two of them. When he turned to look, it was slow and disinterested. "Probably. Probably tired of stayin' home alone all the time and coming to tell you she's packing up." He snorted at his poor excuse for a joke and pretended not to see the cold steel that replaced the warm surprise in his older brother's eyes.

"There a reason you're being more of a horse's ass than usual, John Junior?"

"I ain't," Junior mumbled.

"Well, could've fooled the hell out of me. Come on. It looks like she's carrying a load."

Junior didn't move, just rounded his shoulders and spat in the dirt.

What in God's name was the matter with that boy? Ben wondered, wishing like hell he didn't care so much. Shooting the moody teenager a confused glare, he turned Reb toward the petite little palomino in the distance. They met halfway, and Lucy's fresh smiling face and damp hair eased an invisible weight Ben hadn't even known he'd carried.

He greeted her with an easy smile and a 'hey, darlin'. There was something in the way she looked at him, the way her body moved, fluid, in the saddle. It piqued his attention and his own body turned toward her in the saddle until Reb rode up beside Sunshine, her palomino mare, and their legs rubbed. She'd ridden astride, and he caught a glimpse of her petticoat beneath her split skirt.

"I just thought I'd bring your lunch to you today," she said, and her smile was close-lipped and secretive.

"What, a picnic?" Ben laughed. He didn't have the heart to tell her that he had been looking forward to coming home and washing up for dinner before finishing his chores. Already his back prickled with dried sweat and he didn't smell too pleas-ant, either. But she'd come all this way to see him, saddlebags packed full of what smelled like fragrant roast chicken. His stomach growled. "You came all this way to bring food, huh? Much obliged." He leaned over to give her a peck on the lips, knowing how she loved those dainty little kisses, but her lips caught his in a slow, loving caress. He pulled back, startled, fully aware that Junior was somewhere behind him, looking on.

As though she hadn't just kissed the hell out of him, Lucy gave him an innocent smile and nodded toward a big oak tree. "I'll set everything up for you gentlemen." She nudged Sunshine forward, leaving Ben sitting like a rock in the field. He'd much rather be at home, sneaking into the bedroom with his wife and playing under the covers.

Uncomfortable, wondering why his brother and wife's moods were so tumultuous, he followed her beneath the tree, helping pull out carefully wrapped dishes and canteens of some kind of homemade juice that she was so fond of. Junior tied up his horse, ignoring the two of them. He sat at the edge of a blanket Lucy had spread out with feet wide apart, arms resting on his knees. He swatted at a fly. "It's too dad gummed hot for a picnic."

Normally even-tempered with her brother-in-law's glum nature, Lucy's mouth turned down and those dark eyes cut his way. "It's hotter in the kitchen, and I felt like a ride. Besides," here she looked at Ben, and that mysterious smile returned, "I missed Benjamin."

Junior snorted and grabbed a canteen, but said nothing else.

What's gotten into her? Ben wondered. She'd been diffident that past week, tiptoeing around him in the bedroom with a perpetual blush, and her kisses had turned shy. Ben wasn't in total ignorance of a woman's menses, so he'd kept his distance to preserve her modesty, even though it half killed him not to touch her. Last night in bed she'd backed into him, little spoon to his big, but he'd rolled onto his back. He didn't want her to know that just being in the bedroom with her had his body randy. That morning, she'd stretched, low and flexible wearing only a nightgown while he'd frozen, only half-dressed. The quick peck on the mouth after breakfast was for her own good.

Now, however, he was getting a distinct feeling he'd been reading the smoke signals wrong. It had been a week since they'd made love. Well, six nights and seven days, to be exact. He could no more stop himself from keeping count than he could when Christmas came as a child.

Lucy stood up, shaking him from his reveries. "Where you going?"

Brushing her hands off on her skirt, she said, "I'm going back home. I already ate."

Eyebrow raised, he asked, "You don't want to sit with us while we eat?" Strange.

She was already unhitching her horse from the brush. "I feel like a ride. Just wrap those dishes in the blanket, I'll wash them tonight. See you at supper!" Before she mounted, she bent over to whisper in his ear. "The cake in the red dish towel is for you."

Then, she hopped on Sunshine and rode off without a backward glance, back swaying with the easy gait.

After she'd left, they ate in stilted silence, and Ben wondered at Lucy's odd behavior. She was good company, and though she'd talk your ear off, her conversation was never dull. It would've been nice to have a buffer between him and his brother. He chewed his roast chicken, grateful that at least the food was good.

A loud choking cough at his left broke his musings.

Junior was holding his stomach with one arm, and coughing into his other. In his hand was a folded slip of paper with delicate, sprawling writing. One glance showed an opened dishtowel with half an eaten cake on it. A red dishtowel. With the speed of a cottonmouth strike, Ben snatched the paper from Junior's hand.

"I think that's for you," Junior wheezed through strangled laughter and looked like the complete jackass that he was.

"Don't you ever keep your nose in your own business?" Ben snapped, unfolding *his* letter. When he realized what it said, he crumpled it up and stood, hovering over his idiot brother in a black fury. "What the hell were you doing reading this?"

His brother fell back a little, hands up in surrender. "I don't know! It was under the cake, I thought it was a love letter—"

"And if it was, then that would be none of your goddamned business either." Madder than he could remember being in a good long while, Ben pointed at the dishes strewn over the blanket. "Clean this mess up and take it to the house when you're done checking the fence."

"I don't have any saddlebags for all this shit!"

But Ben was already walking away and mounting Reb, wheeling the gelding around and thundering off.

He wanted to strike Junior, and paddle Lucy.

The words of her letter burned into his hand through the crumpled paper, branding into his mind words he'd never have imagined could come from a lady. Now, her secret smile made sense, as well as her swift departure. She was too much of a coward to watch her husband read about bedtime activities—and how much she wanted to do them with him. That alone wouldn't have angered him. Lucy's passions spilled over any time he touched her or looked at her a certain way. But that had been the knowledge that he alone knew. Private. Now, Junior had a window into that knowledge, having read her explicit, and almost poetic letter. Ben's whole body burned as though he'd been caught in the act.

It burned for another reason as well. Possessive anger was turning into arousal, making it damned uncomfortable to ride at such a brisk pace. He reached the house and swung off Reb in the yard. Sol was leaving the barn, shaking his head, and chuckling.

"She in there?" Ben asked, his strides eating up the ground between him and the barn.

Sol looked up. "Who?"

Gritting his teeth, and ripping off his kerchief to wipe his face, Ben asked, "Lucy. My wife. She in the barn?"

His friend's brows rose. "What's got you in such a foul temper? Junior being a lazy good-for-nothing again?" Sol's laughter dried up when Ben stopped, his sun-browned face menacing and serious. "Alright, don't get all het up. Yeah, she's in there, she just came in and didn't want help unsaddling Sunshine. You two havin' one of those lover's quarrels?" But his question was ignored as Ben and his horse disappeared inside the barn.

Lucy was humming at the end stall, brushing her mare's coat until it shone. He frowned at a sight that would have normally made him smile and tied Reb to a post. Her balled-up note was still in his hand, and he smoothed it out until he reached the stall door.

"You wanna tell me what this is about?" he asked over her humming.

She startled and looked up from the other side of Sunshine's mane. "Ben." Her mouth opened, but when she noticed the wrinkled paper he held up, her lips closed again. Her gaze became wary, and she remained silent.

"I'll have you know that Junior—" he choked on the words for a spell, brow knotting before continuing, "—he read this."

"What?" she gasped. Her mortification did nothing for him, and he plowed forward.

"What'd you think was gonna happen?"

"I thought you'd open the cake yourself, I told you it was for you!" Her voice had gone shrill as she crept around the backside of the horse to evade him.

"Well, Junior took it for himself, and got an eyeful of this while he was at it." He shook the paper while she fluttered around the stall to avoid him.

Her eyes shot sparks. "I didn't know he'd read it, Ben, it had your name on it. I just..." Brown eyes got big as he closed in on her, so she darted out of the stall intending to race toward the house.

But Ben was faster. He pinned her against the ladder to the loft and growled in her ear, "Up."

For a moment, she let him squash her between his hot body and the slats of the ladder, then began to climb up into the loft. He was right behind her, tripping her up. The loft was immense when it was empty, but it was more than half-full of hay bales, and it was a wall of these that Ben guided Lucy behind. The thick perfume of sweet hay and dust permeated the still air around them, and their breathing sounded loud to his ears.

"Ben, I'm sorry," Lucy whispered.

He cut off any further words with his mouth on hers, dropping the paper and forcing her backward onto a straw-carpeted floor. She met his tongue with her own, but he didn't want her compliance.

He didn't know what he wanted.

"You drive me crazy," he breathed against her mouth, pulling up and unbuttoning her dress from the front. "I should be yellin' with how mad I am, but all I can think about is getting your skirts up. Feel what you do to me?" His hand grabbed hers and pressed it hard against his erection, eyes glaring down with accusation.

"You do it to me, too," she hissed, stroking him, throat white and long under her upturned face. Her breasts were bare and heaving. "That's why I wrote it. You haven't touched me in days."

"I'm touchin' you now." He threw his hat to the side and bent his head to those pink tips, sucking them with force, biting one hard enough to make her gasp and flinch.

She ripped off his shirt, then fumbled at his belt buckle while he hitched up her skirt and petticoats. He froze to see she was completely bare beneath, no garters for her stockings, no slitted drawers. Burning eyes met hers when he grabbed her hips and jerked her closer to him until she laid supine beneath him. Their mouths met, angry and hard, and though she was ready, he still had to work himself into her. Once he was fully seated, he drummed into her with no little force. It had been a week, and he was dying. He wasn't going to last long. But a quick romp in the hay wasn't much of a punishment, so he stopped, breath grating into her neck.

Hips undulating beneath his, Lucy asked, "Why did you stop? No!" She cried out when he tried to pull out of her, latching her lean legs around his hips and preventing the disconnection.

Unable to help himself, he sank back in, and they both groaned. Her hands grabbed his cheeks and brought his mouth to hers. The kiss was no longer hard, but lush, lips sliding and slanting, tongues soft and caressing. He thrust in again, this time with a luxurious slowness that forced his eyes closed. For several minutes they kissed, as slow and lazy as their lovemaking. Eventually, Ben rose to his knees, massaging her breasts while she looked up at him. The whites of her eyes glowed beneath her hooded lids, and he swallowed and grabbed her hips, lifting her and changing the angle. Her mouth opened and her eyes closed.

"You're so beautiful. I could do this all day, every day, for the rest of my life and never get tired of it." His voice was gritty like he'd just woken up.

Breasts bouncing, she moaned. "Me, too. I thought I would die if we didn't do this. I need you to touch me, every single day." Her breathing had changed, and her legs drew up higher, her face perspiring and pinching. "Harder, Ben, please, oh, god."

He increased his pace, but her reaction set him off, and he could feel that buildup exploding. Pounding into her, he watched her climb while he shouted, pulsing hard, but he rode through the incredible sensation and sensitivity to help her reach her end. His fingers found her, slick and plump, and she keened high and loud, clenching hard around him until he cursed under his breath.

After, she pulled him down on top of her, holding him even though they were both sweaty and it was hot as hell in the loft.

"Are you still mad at me?" The question was small, worried.

Snorting, he lifted on an elbow, still deep inside her. "No. How could I be after that? Naw, I'm just," he sighed and disengaged, laying down beside her, "It's just now I have to look my brother in the eye, knowing he'll be thinking about stuff he shouldn't be thinking."

"You?" It was her turn to look at him. "I'm the one who wrote it. He probably thinks I'm a hussy straight out of a bawdy house."

"Well, he is partial to those—"

"Ben!" She swatted him, and they wrestled, half-naked and laughing like fools.

LIFE WAS BUSY as summer drew to a close.

The men were gone for long periods during the day branding and castrating young bull calves at the Stone Ranch, horse training, and selling off stock when customers came to pay. Sol brought over his little sister to help harvest the gardens one morning. Isadora was the youngest of twelve children, an "accident child", and was a wild thing with untamed honey-colored hair and hand-me-down bib overalls. She looked just like Sol with her long legs and big smile, but Lucy had never met anyone so different.

"Whatcha doin' that for?"

Lucy looked up at the lanky little girl from her flower bed. "Doing what? Clipping flowers?"

"Yeah, ain't it a little worthless to prune? Cold front's still gonna kill 'em."

"Oh." Lucy looked down at the flower clippings. "Well, I was going to put them in a vase for tonight's supper."

For a moment, Isa frowned down at her skeptically, then smiled. "I get it. You're wantin' it to look all fancy."

Laughing, Lucy admitted, "Well, sure. What's the point of growing them if I can't enjoy them?"

"I read somethin' once." Isa peeked at Lucy almost warily, but not shyly. The little girl didn't have a shy bone in her body. "'I slept and dreamt that life was beauty; I woke and found that life is duty'."

Lucy stared, mouth agape.

"I think the beauty part is you. The duty part sounds more like my ma." Isa's smile was so fast that Lucy barely saw it. Her teeth were big and gapped. Baby teeth were missing and had yet to be filled by her adult teeth, but she had a nice, broad arch like her brother.

"Where'd you read that?" Lucy's curiosity about the girl was mounting, and her flowers hung in her limp hand.

"The library. Lord Bryon or something. Sol takes me there on the weekends. I've got a friend there, the librarian. She lets me read the books all day so long's I help puttin' them back up."

"That's wonderful," Lucy said truthfully. She'd had no idea that Sol had such a close relationship with his sister.

"Miss Lucy." That wary look was back.

"Yes, Isa?"

"Can you teach me to speak fancy like you? I'd ask my teacher but she's got a twang stronger'n my Pa's, and that's sayin' something."

"I'd love to."

And so began an unexpected friendship.

Lucy could never consider Isa as "underfoot" because the child was so blasted useful. Her hands were fast and her wit was quicker.

One day Junior waltzed in during the laborious process of canning the last of Tia's summer garden. Isa had her long hair plaited into two scraggly braids, and he tweaked one as he walked by.

"Hey! Do it again and see what happens," Isa vowed. She flourished a tiny paring knife she was using to slice pickling cucumbers.

Junior's eyes glittered, and he raised his hands sarcastically. Then, he looked behind her and blanched.

"Holy cow, what's that?"

Isa whipped around.

Junior snatched a handful of carefully sliced cucumbers and danced away from her when, discovering his trick, she shouted and chased him around with the paring knife.

"Help, she's going to poke me to death!" cried Junior, knocking a chair over to get away from the child and the knife she brandished.

"Isa," Lucy laughed, "put the knife down and *then* chase him."

With a nod, Isa slammed the knife on the table, a promise in her golden hazel eyes, and dramatically rucked up her too-long sleeves. "You're gonna get it, Junior."

"I'm shakin' in my boots." He tugged her braid again, fast as a whip, and ran out the open back door.

Isa was hot on his heels

Leonard chose that moment to walk across the porch, and Isa barreled into him, knocking his hat off. Caught off guard, he didn't think before he shouted, "Watch where the hell you're going!"

Eyes big, Isa backed away. Lucy was storming out to come to the girl's defense, but Junior had beat her to it. With a strength she hadn't known he had, Junior hopped back on the porch and shoved Leonard off, reminding Lucy of Ben and Buffalo Jo in New Orleans.

"You watch how you talk to her, you sonuvabitch, she's just a kid."

Hiding his anger and embarrassment, catching his balance, he glanced at the row of accusing eyes above him on the porch and tried to appear contrite. "Hell, I'm sorry! She just surprised me, that's all. She knows I didn't mean it."

For a moment, Junior didn't look like he'd accept the non-apology. Then, he nodded once and turned his back on his friend.

"Hey, wanna get out of here and go for a swim?" he asked Isa.

Hero worship in her eyes, Isa grinned. "I'll beat you there."

They took off, and Lucy watched them, wondering at the hidden layer to Junior and wishing it came out more often.

Lucy stayed busy cooking, cleaning, helping to can vegetables from Tia's garden, and her least favorite activity of all.

Wash day.

Washing clothes, towels, curtains, and rag rugs took an entire day out of every week. With Tia, it wasn't so lonely, but it was tedious back-breaking work. Each Monday, a big pot was set to boil outside over an open fire. Two or three other tubs were brought out, along with a washboard, a stirring stick, soap, blue, starch, a Lovell Pioneer wringer, and wooden clothespins.

The men's clothes were filthy from working all week and were soaked overnight, then washed after the more delicate items. Tia shaved flakes of Sunlight Soap with a small knife into the steaming pot while Lucy scrubbed the whites in hot, sudsy water. That load went into the boiling pot that Tia stirred with a dolly stick. After half an hour, the whites went in a tub of rinse water with a bag of Reckitt's Blue. They were rinsed twice, wrung, shaken out, then hung until they were damp enough to iron. Then, the whole process was repeated until each load of clothes was completed. While Tia finished boiling the men's work clothes, Lucy would dry her red, irritated hands on her oldest apron and begin the long process of starching and ironing the linens.

One such day in December, they were rushing to bring the ironed and folded laundry inside before the bottom broke out of the angry, purplish-gray rain clouds when hoofbeats merged with the low rumble of thunder.

Lucy peered into the distance and her hopeful expression dropped. It was Ben's father. The only time he came over was to order Junior back to the house for important dinners Loretta Stone held. Junior, of course, complied...except for last night. He'd stayed out drinking, and his lazy carcass was probably dozing in the saloon with Leonard while Sol, Ben, and Frank worked. And now, she was going to pay for it with a confrontation.

She disliked John Stone.

No, she more than disliked him. When he rode over, high and mighty on his priceless thoroughbred, he didn't ask after Ben or his new daughter-in-law—he barely spoke a word to his oldest son at all. Ben assured her it didn't bother him.

Well, it bothered her.

Features set in stone, she waited for John to rein in his ostentatious stallion scant feet from her.

"Where's my boy?" he asked from the saddle, sneering at her flushed face, red hands, and old dress.

"Which one?" she countered, eyebrows raised in innocence.

His jaw worked. "John Junior, as you well know."

"Do I?" She was fed up with John Junior *and* John Senior. It was Blue Monday, the day she despised most, and just that morning she had unmistakable proof that she was not carrying Ben's child, even though they made love nearly every night. Her cool, even temper was no longer frayed. It simply didn't exist.

He chose to ignore that and spat tobacco juice in the dirt, a habit he shared with his youngest son. "I need a word with him. Where they working at today?"

Her hands turned into fists in her skirts. "Ben is training horses with the cattle to the south, but you won't find Junior there."

"He upstairs?"

"No, and if he were sleeping it off, he'd be in the bunkhouse. He moved there shortly after Ben and I were married."

He made a noise of offended disgust.

Taking a deep, calming breath, Lucy explained, "We can only advise him on what to do, but we can't force him to stay home or show up to work. The last we have seen of Junior, he went to town with Leonard."

Of this, John did not comment, but hoofbeats in the distance alerted them to the drive.

Junior had chosen that moment to ride up with Leonard. He looked like hell, Lucy thought unkindly. His mustache was even more ridiculous, trying to reach the bottom of his jaw in a handlebar, but the hairs were too pale and wispy to manage it. Lipstick stained his and Leonard's collar, and though Leonard looked refreshed and content, Junior was drooping in the saddle, blinking crusted eyes, and looking a little green around the gills.

John's face became florid, and he dismounted with rigid, abrupt movements. "Ben lets you do whatever you damned well please, don't he," he shouted, barreling to Junior's horse, and yanking his youngest son from it to the ground.

Lucy winced at the sound of the breath getting knocked out of Junior. Pity and justice warred within her, and she began, "Mr. Stone, Junior staying out all night has nothing to do with Ben, he's a grown man, fully responsible—"

"Stay out of men's business, girl!" A finger stabbed in her direction, then Junior was hauled back up by his collar, cutting into his neck. Choking him.

Stand up to him, Junior, don't let this evil man do this to you, Lucy willed him, eyes pricking and fists shaking.

But in the end, Junior complied beneath John's tirade, remounted his horse, and followed behind to the big Stone Ranch.

Leonard leered at Lucy for just a moment while it started to drizzle. One, then three drops of water skated from her forehead and nose. She glared back for an endless minute before he smirked and turned around, following the two men; one with military erectness, the other as stooped as an old man.

Junior spent Christmas at John's.

Besides Ben's occasional spells of melancholy at Junior's absence, Christmas at the ranch was magical. Lucy had found holly trees in the southern woods of their property and had made door wreaths with them, decorating their mantle with the excess. Spicy cinnamon and ginger aromas beckoned the men to visit the warm kitchen and underlying tones of hot coffee which was always at the ready to thaw cold fingers around a mug.

Isa and Tia were always present during the holiday, helping make cookies, writing out Christmas lists, and wrapping presents. Sol and Ben even came home one day with a little spruce tree, and Isa and the women circled it with strings of popped corn, homemade bows of red fabric from Tia's scrap pile, and frosted Christmas cookies.

Papa and Mizz Trudy came on Christmas Eve and stayed the whole day. Minnie had her own family to cook and celebrate with, but she and Lucy had already exchanged cards and presents the weekend before during their visit to the hotel. On Christmas morning, it was just Lucy and Ben, snuggled by the lit fireplace with presents around, sipping coffee and toasting their chilled toes. Lucy's new puppy napped on the rug in front of the fire, dreaming funny puppy dreams.

"This is the best Christmas I've ever had," Lucy sighed, tucking her head under Ben's chin.

Ben grunted in agreement, coasting his hand up and down her side, slow and contented. "Just wish Junior coulda been here."

"I know," Lucy soothed, squeezing him. "We can steal him away before the new year. Let's keep the Christmas tree up and his presents under it so he won't feel like he missed a bit."

Ben perked and agreed.

But after a couple of weeks, the tree began to die and turn brown, and they burned it in the back pasture. Junior didn't come back before the new year, so Ben rode to his father's ranch to check on him. When he came back, he didn't say a word to Lucy, and his thunderous expression halted any queries she had about how the visit had gone. Even though he didn't tell her what had been said, she had a good imagination. Ben stowed his brother's presents in the tack room and worked from sun up to sun down, a crease of worry between his low brows.

25

—·—

CHAPTER TWENTY-FIVE

"You wanna tell me again why we're holding a meeting with the trail hands here?"

Ben felt a prickle of unease and guilt at walking into a saloon in broad daylight. He followed a sauntering Leonard through the swinging doors, and when he stepped across the threshold, it was like signing his marriage to the devil. The saloon was the nicest of the three in town, Junior's favorite. That fact was probably due to the amount of young, pretty whores that made residence upstairs.

Leonard laughed at Ben's question. John had allowed the ambitious young man to arrange the meeting in his stead while he was out of town, knowing damned good and well that Ben thought the fool was worthless.

"It's good business sense," Leonard crowed. "I thought to myself, why not bring the boys to the saloon? Gettum drunk, gettum laid, that way they'll agree to any price." His hee-hawing was getting under Ben's skin, and he clenched his teeth, praying for patience.

Junior laughed along, but it had a raw edge to it that nettled Ben.

There had been something strange in Junior's face of late. A new bitterness and rancorous scorn. It revealed itself in the half-smile he gave Ben. Something was not right with the boy, even more so than usual.

396

They sat in the back of the room away from regulars already drunk or on their way to it. Fifteen men had pushed several tables together and talked over each other in the corner. Most of them were long-time waddies, bow-legged and born in the saddle. Ben had worked with at least half of them, but he knew that if you were to be a boss, you had to earn their respect. The men sized him up as he shook hands with each one of them, and though he'd done this for five years, that wariness was still there. There were always those few that questioned the boss, created mutiny amongst the men, or hightailed it at the first sign of trouble. The latter usually met them at the next town demanding their pay in loud, threatening tones.

Fortunately, none of the men seemed bothered that they'd met in a saloon, and Junior bought them all a round of drinks from his longstanding tab that their Pa had reluctantly agreed to pay for.

Ben didn't want to drink. He didn't like the taste, and he didn't trust that his mug was clean. But he nursed his warm beer like there was nothing to it, drinking it halfway, then getting down to business.

It was nightfall before the men dispersed, some out the front door, a few upstairs, and a couple at the poker table in the back room. Ben felt stretched thin. He had their number now after hours of talking money, steers, and the rigor of months of hard travel with almost two thousand head of cattle. One of them he'd tell his Pa not to hire—some man who did prison time in Huntsville for accidental homicide. Not once, but twice during their discussions did Willie admit that it was no accident. "An' after all that, the feller only had four dollars in his pocket," he'd slurred through missing teeth, weaving in his chair.

"I think we got us a pretty good crew," Junior sighed, relaxed after his third brew, leaning back with his feet propped up. "What do you think, brother?"

Leonard looked up from his audience; on each arm was a prostitute, both in their mid-to-late twenties. Not that Ben knew for sure. He'd tried to keep from looking directly at them. He imagined Lucy barging in those swinging doors while Ben was making eye contact with one of them, and he broke into a cold sweat.

"Reckon so. Besides ole Willie."

Junior tipped his head in agreement.

"Ooh, that's your brother?" giggled the brassy-haired woman. She wore a corset and a frayed chemise, nothing else. Her hand was inside Leonard's shirt, her thin lips painted bright red, smeared at the corner. Her eyes were half-closed, unfocused.

She was drunker than a skunk.

"Yes'm, he surely is," Leonard stage whispered, nearly as drunk as the whore. "He's married though. His wife wears the pants, if you know what I mean."

The women laughed shrilly. Ben's eyes narrowed. Junior said nothing, but he smirked when he nursed his tankard in silent agreement. It was high time Ben left for home. His brother wasn't fit for company anymore.

Ignoring the women's attention, he sat forward as though to stand up. "I'll make some notes and tallies and send them to Pa tomorrow."

Leonard asked something in a low voice behind the blonde's head, and Junior shrugged in response. He whispered in the blonde's ear, flashing a five-dollar gold piece so that her eyes lit with determination.

Junior listened, brows lowering, and Ben figured he wasn't too happy that his friend was inviting the girl upstairs with him. Was she Junior's favorite? Well, it happened when you grew attached to a girl who made her living on her back. Instead of taking Leonard upstairs, however, the brassy blonde stood and slunk around Ben's side of the table, blocking his escape.

With her came the cloying scent of perfume, so strong it burned his sinuses. He leaned back a fraction, praying to God none of it got on his clothes. Lucy had the nose of a bloodhound. Beneath the perfume was a wave of body odor, unwashed and ripe. Lucy had never smelled that way, not even after trekking across the Mason-Dixon with him, or doubled up on the saddle in the Texas elements.

When she stood before Ben, he looked at her in warning. Her intention became clear, and he moved to stand, perfume be damned.

Seeing this, the whore's open hand shoved his chest a little too hard to be playful, and when he didn't budge an inch, she sat down on his lap anyway, planting wet, amorous kisses all over his neck and collar. She was damp with sweat, getting it on his forearm, neck, and shirt.

He saw red.

Without thinking, he jumped from the chair, the little harlot falling on her rump on the spit, beer, and grime that caked the floor. He almost shouted at her, thought better of it, and lit into Leonard instead.

"You tell her to do that? What the hell were you thinkin'?"

The pissant was too busy laughing with the second whore to answer. Junior opened his mouth to speak, then blanched.

A stinging splash of warm beer hit Ben's eyes and saturated his clothing.

"You bastard!" shrieked the woman he'd just deposited on the floor, holding an empty mug and stumbling. "Nobody drops Delilah."

"What'd you do that for?" Junior shouted at her, jumping to Ben's defense. He glanced at Ben and the peculiar look was finally gone from his eyes. He wasn't scornful now. He was afraid. "Hey, don't do anything to her, Ben. You can get in real trouble from her boss-man."

Wiping his eyes with a kerchief that smelled like laundry soap from his back pocket, Ben growled, "I'm not gonna do anything to her. That son-of-a-bitch is the one I'm about to settle with."

His eyes burned into Leonard, who'd stopped laughing. The whore in his lap stood hastily and scuttled away, snagging a weaving Delilah to drag behind her. All around them was quiet; they'd become the new entertainment. The owner behind the bar reached beneath the counter, watching.

"You wanna square up, boss man?" Leonard slurred. He didn't get out of his chair. "Think your daddy'd like that? Naw. He wouldn't like that too much at all. Neither would Aunt Loretta. I got friends in high places."

"Why don't you and I go outside," Ben said softly, "and see if those friends will be there to carry you home when I'm finished with you." He hadn't felt this angry since Lucy's old beau had shot his mouth off at him, and he was itching, tingling to fight. Hands twitching, eyes staring, he didn't want anything right then as much as he wanted to rearrange Leonard's face.

But the coward just laughed, albeit weakly, then quieted after glancing around to see if anyone would step in to help. No one stepped forward. They waited for him to make a move. He swallowed and raised his hands in supplication. "Hey, boss, I was just funnin'!"

Soft snorts and quiet jeering from the men around them followed.

Ben sneered, "Yeah. I thought so." Jaw thrust forward, he pocketed his soiled kerchief and pointed a steady finger at Junior. "I know you let him plan that little stunt, and you didn't say a damned thing."

"Jesus, it wasn't as big as all that—"

"You know what Lucy's gonna say when I tell her!"

"Why the hell would you tell her?" Junior was truly flabbergasted. Ben's respect for him sank lower.

"Because she's my wife, Junior. She'd smell a lie a mile away."

"Well, you know what, maybe every now and then she shouldn't get her damned way. Give Miss Priss a taste of real life."

"What are you talking about?" Ben bellowed.

His brother clamped his lips shut.

"I don't know what's wrong with you, Junior, or why you've got something against Lucy, who's never done a damned thing to you. Until you figure it out and drop this sack of shit behind you, don't bother comin' around. I mean it. Figure yourself out." He turned his back and walked to the swinging doors.

"Ben, it was just a joke!" Junior called after him.

But Ben was already gone.

LUCY PACED IN the kitchen and tried not to worry. Their dog, Daisy, watched her wear a trail on the rug, brown eyes following back and forth.

Surely one little meeting shouldn't have taken seven hours? Of course, it took two hours just to get to town, but what if he hadn't even left yet? Where was he at? What could he possibly be doing for that long?

Frustrated and on edge, she decided to wait up a little longer and work on the cookbook she hoped to get published. Thirty minutes later, she was still staring at the same recipe, eyes glazed with scenarios of Ben laid up in a bed with another woman. Or, horribly, dead in a ditch somewhere.

She shook her head and dismissed the ridiculous notion immediately. It had taken months of cajoling just to get the man to even kiss her back, much less make love to her, *after* their wedding day. He wasn't the kind to go into a saloon and take up with another woman when he had a perfectly willing wife at home. With that thought in mind, Lucy smiled. There was something she could do to pass the time.

She was descending the stairs half an hour later, washed up and in the sensual creation that Franny had gifted her when she heard footsteps on the porch. Heart swelling with hope, she ran down the remaining steps, her dark, loose hair streaming behind her and robe gaping open. Ben's dark head was bowed when he shuffled in, shoulders stooped and tired. The last time she'd checked the clock it had been a quarter to twelve.

Surprise registered on his face, perhaps that she was awake.

"You're home," she sighed in relief and would have jumped into his arms, except that something made her pause. For one, he wouldn't look at her. His shoulders remained rounded as he carefully shut the door, locked it, and sat by the worktable to toe off his boots. Her stomach dropped. "What is it? Did the meeting not go well? Did something bad happen?" She thought for a moment, and her mouth turned down. "Did your father or Junior do something?" Anytime Ben ever acted this morose, it had something to do with those two. Drama gravitated and revolved around them more than anyone else she knew, even her mother and sister.

At her last question, Ben finally looked up at her. The whites of his eyes were pink and irritated. "Pa wasn't there. Why do you think Junior did something?"

Ah, so it *was* Junior, then.

"Because he always does," she replied, distracted by the complete exhaustion on his face. No wonder his eyes were bloodshot. "You look tired, darling, here. Let's get you ready for bed." It hadn't escaped her notice that he hadn't paid any mind to her attire, a sure sign he needed rest. Perhaps that's all it was. But when she stepped between his spread legs, he stiffened, and she discovered why. Her mouth quirked up. "Have you been drinking, Ben?" She reached to unbutton his collar. "You smell like cheap beer—*what is that?*"

He looked up sharply, brilliant blue eyes decidedly worried. Guilty.

"What's what?"

Lucy was having a hard time drawing breath. Her eyes were round and planted on his collar. She leaned forward and sniffed.

"You smell like perfume. Beer, smoke, and perfume. Were you at a saloon?" Her voice sounded foggy to her own ears.

"Pa let Leonard set the meeting up at a saloon, yes." His words were careful. Too careful.

"I see," she whispered.

Red smears stained his cream-colored collar.

Rouge.

He'd wanted to wear a darker shirt for the meeting, but she'd insisted he looked more professional in this shirt, as it was newer and no-nonsense. He'd rolled his eyes at the idea of being 'professional' for a bunch of trail hands, but had ceded to her judgment. If he'd worn that dark blue shirt, she never would have seen the red lipstick, would have played the perfume off as one of the odors of being in a saloon. The pain was a slug of buckshot to her chest, and she backed away from the vee of his legs, still staring at his collar.

"Someone kissed your neck. You have lipstick there." She reached and plucked at the shirt, then wiped her fingers.

His hand was shaking, halfway to his neck to touch where she'd indicated, and then his hands were a flurry of motion. He ripped his shirt off with vicious savagery, buttons popping and bouncing across the clean floor. The shirt she'd ironed only that morning landed in a sad wad near the door, and Ben's bare chest heaved while he glared at it. Then, he looked at her.

"It's not what you're thinking. One of those little strumpets just sat in my lap. I stood up. She fell on the floor, threw beer in my face, and I left. That's all."

"Not," she breathed, fury taking over the pain by increments, "before she had a chance to kiss you."

He shook his head and took a step toward her. She held up a hand and he stopped.

"Am I supposed to believe that? That she sat in your lap and you left, but you have lipstick all over your collar?" The last was a yell, and he flinched. Never had she spoken to him that way. But she was past caring, past thinking logically. Her eyes felt hot and her vision tunneled. She was unbelievably, horribly jealous. Worse, though, was the overwhelming betrayal.

"Lucy, that's what they do, they sit in men's laps and make their money—"

"I know how they make their money," she shouted, eyes flashing. "I'm not naive, I'm not stupid, Ben! I just want to know why some trollop thought she could make her money with *my* husband?"

Finally, that vulnerable look was replaced with cold fury. "That bastard cousin of Junior's paid a whore to do it just as I was leavin'."

"He *what*?" The disdain she felt for Leonard intensified. "Leonard told one of those—to sit on your lap?" She refused to feel hurt. It tried to wriggle free, that deceived feeling that led to hot, choking emotion, but she quashed it cruelly. "And Junior was there?"

Ben's brows smoothed tellingly, and he didn't answer.

Now she understood.

Junior had had a hand in it somewhere, somehow, and Ben was protecting him. As usual. Did her brother-in-law hate her so much?

"He was," she said, and her smile was poisonous. "Of course. And I will just bet that he and Leonard were both in on it."

"That ain't true."

"Oh, is it not?"

"Don't go getting all prissy on me, Lucy—"

Prissy?

Releasing the words that she had held back for months, Lucy declared, "Junior has not liked me since the moment he met me, you and I both know it. It probably made his night, knowing how angry I'd be about...this." She waved in disdain at his naked torso.

Ben's neck was washed with red, now.

"He didn't have a hand in it, Luce, he was just sitting there drinking a beer."

"I'm sure he was the picture of innocence."

"My Pa had more of a hand in this than my brother." His tone was heating.

"As though there's a distinction between the two anymore," she sneered. To her dismay, her voice sounded clogged, so she kept her chin up, high and haughty, just the way he hated it.

He threw his hands up, biceps and pectorals defining. She ripped her eyes away. It hurt to even look at him.

"Why are you acting like this? You've never had anything to say about it before. Remember what we agreed to when we got married?"

Her throat seized and she refused to answer.

Let's never apologize for anything our family does from now on, he'd told her almost a year ago, the day they'd married. This was different, couldn't he see that?

Swallowing, she said, "That's different."

"How is that different?"

"Because I feel like they are sabotaging our marriage, and that you," she swallowed again, but the lump wouldn't go down, and she blinked rapidly, "you are letting them."

He shook his head and ran his hands through his hair. "I don't believe this."

"Your father I can forgive you for, but not your brother. He stays out all night, knowing you get the heat from John once a week as though it were your fault. He doesn't pull his weight and you work yourself to death because of it. Everyone turns a blind eye when he brings Leonard around, who is disrespectful to you and me both, and you just sweep it under the rug, like nothing is wrong!"

He dropped his arms and looked at her. "That's enough."

"You let Junior get away with more than a child does, and he's a gown man—"

"I said that's enough!"

He'd shouted at her. For a moment she let the tears fall because he'd never shouted at her like that before, not in true anger, and she clenched her hands over her aching stomach.

Ben scrubbed his hands over his face and attempted to placate her. "I'm sorry. I shouldn't have shouted, but you're overreactin'. Let's just—let's just get ready for bed."

There was a long silence while Lucy wiped her eyes and mulled this over, pressure in her chest an active volcano, building, and building, its top waiting to fly off.

"Overreacting?" At her hurt, tender query, Ben took a step toward her again, but she snapped a venomous look at him. "Don't touch me. Not with the smell of some other woman on you."

She turned her back on him and stormed upstairs. He didn't follow.

She'd never felt so wretched, ill with betrayal. It was so quiet in the house that she could hear when he slammed the door and the faint, aggressive squeaking of the iron pump handle at the well. He was washing up. If he'd been smarter, more secretive, he could've washed up before coming inside and she wouldn't have known any better until washday. Even then, she would've shrugged off the lipstick as a smudge from one of Junior's shirts. Lord knew *that* one had enough lipstick, kohl, and powder stains on his clothing.

Junior.

Her thoughts grew bitter and her lip curled. He'd been cool to her since her marriage to Ben, and she'd returned the frosty reception in kind. But, as much as she wanted to place blame on the young fool, Ben was a grown man, mature and honest.

The betrayal she felt no longer concerned the woman that had sat in Ben's lap. It was fed by the blind eye her husband turned to his brother, enabling Junior to find increasingly reckless means to disrupt their marriage. Whether or not it was Junior's command that the whore had followed, she believed that you are the company that you keep, and it was Junior's closest friend that had started the whole, awful affair.

The first thing she did was change into the most virginal nightgown she owned, donning a thick robe for good measure. She'd never felt less like physical intimacy. Her stomach cramped and rolled, and she couldn't stop crying. Unbeknownst to her, these feelings had been coming to a head for a long while, now. Conspiring with Leonard to pay a whore to sit on her husband's lap, that had been the last straw.

Stiffening her resolve, she pulled a limp canvas bag from beneath the bed and began to pack her things.

Ben's shadow filled the door midway through, and she paused at the dresser. She'd tried to erase any emotion from her features, but at the sight of him, shirtless with hair dripping wet, beads of water clinging to the hairs on his chest, she grimaced and continued plucking out rolled stockings. Even now, he was so beautiful her breath caught. It made the thought of another woman touching him—maybe even rousing him—crushing to her soul. Never had she felt so worthless, so insecure.

"What are you doing?" There was a distinct, bewildered tremor in his voice.

She didn't speak, even when he crossed the threshold, and his eyes burned into her like blue coals.

"Lucy, stop."

Holding the rolls of stockings in her arms, she faced him. "I'm sleeping in the guest bedroom. Tomorrow I'm going to the hotel."

He cursed, fists clenched against his sides, spiky lashed and unhappy. "You don't have to do that, I already told Junior not to come back until he figures out what's ailing him."

"You should have just told him not to come back at all."

"He's my brother, Lucy—"

"And I'm your wife!" She was sick to death of him shoving his precious brother down her throat, especially now, when she was the one wronged. "He disrespected you, and he disrespected me, Ben. He watched his friend make a whore sit in your lap, and maybe that does not trouble you, but it does me."

"You don't understand." He shifted his weight repeatedly, restless. His color was higher. She had grown colder, and now he was the one burning. "I can't turn my back on my family the way you do. He needs me."

That *bastard*. The way *she* did?

Her face blanched of color and her eyes glittered. "He uses you. And now he's coming between us. I would never ask you to choose between him and me, but I won't have him in my house again until he apologizes to us and grows up."

"Your house?" His voice was dangerously soft. "I thought it was our house."

"It is!" she cried. "But you are choosing your brother over our marriage—"

"You said you wouldn't make me choose!" he bellowed, stabbing his fingers into his hair and pulling.

Lucy clapped her hands over her mouth and openly cried at this display, at his anguish. "It's not about choosing, Ben, I want your support!"

He didn't answer for a long time, and they both spent a long minute regaining their composure.

If only she could make him understand how she felt! Before she could think of how unwise it was to bait him, a plan formed.

Face set, she turned her back on him again, knowing it would infuriate him, and tucked the stockings neatly beside her shirtwaists in the canvas bag. The little devil on her shoulder poked her, reminding her of her pricked pride, and she gathered the flowing negligee from the foot of the bed and began to fold it.

"What the hell are you planning on doing with that?" he growled, watching her.

She shrugged coolly. "Perhaps I'll wear it. Lord knows I won't need it here."

Silence.

Lucy gently placed the lacy confection on the top, and continued, "Perhaps Beth will come to stay at the hotel. She is my sister, after all. Perhaps she'd even bring Peter." A frisson of fear rolled up her spine at the noise Ben made behind her, but she had to go on, she had to make him understand what it felt like. "Maybe she'd even watch Peter pull me into his lap, kiss my neck like that woman did with you, well I couldn't stay angry with my own sister—"

She broke off her tirade with a choked scream.

At Peter's name, Ben had flushed dark red and growled. At the first mention of her in another man's lap and receiving another man's kiss, he bent down and grabbed the washstand, then swung it with enormous force at the opposite wall where it exploded into several pieces. The earthenware ewer crashed, water spraying everywhere. A gaping hole in the wall stared at her accusingly.

Lucy sobbed uncontrollably and managed, "Now you know how I feel. What would you do if it was me instead of you, Ben?"

"I'd kill him!" Ben roared. His eyes were pink-rimmed, his voice hoarse. "I'd damned well kill him and I'd run your sister out of Texas and back to your Ma!"

Without waiting for a reply, which Lucy was incapable of managing at that point anyway, he turned and stormed from the room.

She never heard him come back inside, and eventually cried herself to sleep in the guest room.

THE NEXT MORNING while Ben did his chores, Lucy managed to sneak back into their room and dress. The washstand and ewer were still on the floor, and the hole in the wall looked like a sad, downturned mouth. Her bag, however, was back beneath the bed, her clothes neatly put away.

She could not find her negligee, and she clenched her jaw that he'd hidden it from her. As though she would ever have done those things that she'd said in anger last night!

Lucy repacked her bag, enough for an overnight stay, but froze at the sight of Ben in her periphery.

He stood in the doorway, drained of all anger and somehow insubstantial in the weak morning light in his shabby work clothes.

"You're leavin' me?" His face looked worn; eyes hollow but slowly sparking with something frantic. Worry?

"No." She took a shaky, bracing breath. "I'm going to stay a night at the hotel with Minnie and Pa. To think."

Anger replaced his hurt. "Runnin' away again."

"I am not running, I am thinking!"

"Sounds like somethin' a coward would say."

"And wouldn't it take one to know one!" She hated the shrillness of her voice and blinked her glittering eyes.

"I'll hook up the wagon," he gritted, shoving a hat from the dresser top on his head.

"I can go on my own—"

"I will hook up the goddamned wagon and take you to your pa!" he bellowed, then thundered down the stairs, a repeat of the night before.

She wiped her face with shaking fingers, furious and aching.

They rode to town in complete, awful silence.

AFTER WATCHING HIS wife disappear through the front door of the hotel, Ben drove the wagon straight to John's ranch.

He hadn't slept. His bed had been a concrete slab while he'd replayed Lucy's face when he'd thrown their washstand.

He hadn't eaten. His stomach was a tangle of twisted-up knots.

Without entering the yard, he asked a hand to fetch Junior. The ride had given him plenty of time to think about what he was going to say, but when Junior stepped out of the big house and across the front porch, he was at a loss.

Ben set the brake and stepped down, looping the reins around a fence post.

A wary Junior approached, looking almost as rough as Ben felt. He opened his mouth to say something, but Ben beat him to it.

"What do you want from me, Junior?"

"What?"

Feeling the crushing weariness like a ten-ton boulder, Ben took his hat off and looked his brother straight in the eye. "What will it take for you to forgive me for runnin' out on you six years ago?" Junior blinked, looking all of fourteen. It made Ben angry. He wasn't Junior's ma, who'd bow to anything the boy said with just a flutter of those pretty-boy lashes. It was time they spoke, man to man. "You want me to get rid of my wife? So it's just you 'n me again?"

"I-I, no—"

"Because I can't!" It burst from him, hot and terrible and true. "She's at her pa's hotel and not at our house, all 'cause of that mess you and your pal made."

Junior scratched his head, hair still tousled from sleep. "Hell, she knows?"

"Of course, she knows! She knew the minute I walked in the door last night, and if she hadn't, I'd've told her anyhow because she's my wife."

Junior said nothing, but he put his hands deep into his pockets and affected a sneer that almost, but not quite, distracted from the twin spots of color in his cheeks.

Ben slapped his thigh with his hat, brows together, more miserable than he'd remembered feeling in a long time. He tried again. "So, what is it you want?"

"I don't want anything from you." Junior's voice was tight, eyes glued to the ground.

"Damn it, Junior, I'm not our pa." Ben's voice broke. He turned away, fingers interlocked tight behind his neck, hat dropping, forgotten, at his boots. "What do I have to do to make you happy? You gotta talk to me."

"I am happy," Junior protested.

"Livin' in saloons with that peckerhead, getting drunk every night, not showin' up for work, that makes you happy?"

Junior stayed resentfully silent. Ben turned around to catch the boy wiping his nose.

"I love you almost more than anything on this good green earth, but I love Lucy, too. I can't keep killin' myself to work the farm, Pa's fence lines, and this year's cattle drive, keep the peace with you, Lucy and Pa, and now you and me are both knee-deep in shit and I don't know how the hell to get out of it."

Junior looked up. His eyes were swollen. "Did she leave you for good?" He didn't sound hopeful. Fear pitched his voice school-boy-high.

"I hope to God not." Ben's voice tried to break again and he cleared it. "I'm gonna pick her up tomorrow morning and...maybe she'll talk to me. But there's going to be some changes." His eyes were steel set in his haggard face. "I don't want even the *shadow* of that cousin of yours on my property. If I see him again, he and I'll be talking with our fists. You understand me?"

His answer was a quick nod.

"You're welcome any time...just as soon as you apologize to Lucy."

Junior didn't move.

"What you let happen was wrong and you know it. But that's not all. You haven't been nice to her since y'all met, don't think everyone doesn't see. You man up and apologize and maybe this—this mess we're in will blow over."

Ben climbed back in the wagon and rolled away. Junior didn't watch him go but stared unseeing at a line of ants in the dust.

LUCY WOKE UP to the raw wood beams of her attic bedroom.

The sight confused her until it didn't, and then misery returned with force. She rubbed her eyes; they were sore from crying herself to sleep the night before. It felt like she was coming down with a cold, and sniffed through a congested nose.

Something shifted at the foot of her bed, and she sat up straight in alarm.

Ben was sitting at the foot of her bed, attempting to read one of her old recipe journals in the dim, early-morning light.

"Ben?" she croaked. She cleared her throat, but it was no good. She reached for the glass of water at her bedside table and took long draughts. The water had a tepid, stale taste.

The journal drooped between his thighs, but he didn't look at her. "You've cooked some of these at the house before." He pointed at a page of looping script. "This one is my favorite."

It was a page that said "stuffed rock hens". The recipe was a familiar one. She could cook them in her sleep.

Oh, but why did this hurt so badly?

It was still more shadows than light in the room, and she glanced at the cracked attic window. It was overcast as well as extremely early in the morning. What time was it? How long had he been here?

"What time did you get here?"

"'Bout an hour ago."

"What time is it?"

"I don't know."

They were quiet for a moment, and thunder rumbled, long and low, across the countryside.

For wont of something to do, Lucy undid her braid, finger-combing its long, rippling length. They pretended not to watch each other, pretended not to notice the swollen and shadowed eyes in each other's faces, or the listless, down-turned mouths.

Finally, "I talked to Junior as soon as I left here yesterday."

Lucy remained silent and continued her task.

Flipping the pages, Ben continued, "We talked it out. Well, *I* talked it out. He didn't say much."

She bit her tongue to hold back a retort.

"Leonard's not welcome back on the ranch, and Junior isn't welcome until he apologizes to you. And not just for—for last night. But for everything." He was quiet for a moment, then said, stronger, "I didn't choose, Lucy. The choice was always his. We'll just have to see if he's man enough to make the right one, now."

Pick your battles, Lucy warned herself, because she was still angry. All she could manage was a nod. Her pride was still a prickly thing, stubborn and unwilling to budge. And yet, she *had* to. She'd never felt such misery since she'd entered the hotel and her husband had ridden away. Hiding her joy that he was back wasn't easy.

Honesty.

That's what they needed. Not shouting or taunting or witty jabs.

Lucy sucked in an audible, bracing breath, and admitted, "I still want to ride to that saloon and claw that woman's eyes out for touching you."

Ben was shaking his head. "I never should've gone in there. I knew you'd be madder'n hell, and you were right to be. If any-one put their hands on you like that..." He trailed off, and the journal's binding flexed under his hands. The book dropped, and his hands fisted, veins popping blue-green, knuckles as big as rocks.

Something besides residual anger and relief stirred at the sight.

Guilt. That night when Peter had put his hands on her was a wall between them, and Ben didn't even know about it. He'd told her the truth, and she'd yet to tell him.

"Ben—" She swallowed. God, but it was hard. "I have to tell you something. About the night before you came back when my mother was here."

She told Ben everything. How Peter had walked into Papa's office and offered her a drink, though she'd refused. And later, when he'd taken it too far. Rain pattered on the walls of the hotel, slow at first, then faster, like Ben's breathing.

"Why didn't you tell me when I came back?" he asked finally, knee jiggling, hands in hard fists.

"I was afraid you would kill him. I was afraid you would be hanged. And Beth—I don't know, Ben, I was ashamed. And I was a coward."

"You're right," he growled. "I would have killed him. You should have at least told your Pa. Or gone to Mrs. Hobb."

Lucy couldn't look at him. She looked at her hands in her lap instead. "I slept in the loft in the barn."

"If he ever shows his face—"

"He won't, Ben." She put her hand on his arm. It felt like warm steel.

Ben's leg stopped moving, and he looked at her face, expression unreadable. "There anything else you want to tell me?"

"No," she whispered, the shame so thick it felt like it was choking her. "No, I promise. I should have told you after he'd taken the train home, but I was so afraid you'd act rashly."

Snorting, he shook his head, jaw hard. "I still might take a train to Atlanta, or New York, or wherever the hell he's holed up at."

Taking a deep, shaking breath, Lucy nodded. "That's how I feel, too. It's still tearing me up inside. I love you so much, and I want to kill that woman and Leonard, and I want to hurt Junior, but do I even deserve to be angry? After what I kept from you, you must be so angry—"

His fingers captured her chin. "Angry isn't a strong enough word, Luce."

"I'm sorry," she said and meant it. His eyes were hard and blue. Her lip trembled and her eyes filled. "Do you still want me? Do you—"

Her words were silenced by his lips closing over hers, open and hot.

Relief and possessiveness roughened their hands as they grabbed, and yanked at each other's clothes until they were both bared, skin against skin.

It began to rain with a vengeance, pelting the window and outside the walls of the hotel with a muffled roar. Ben threw her on her childhood bed, biting her neck and shoving her legs open. Her fingernails bit into him, urging him closer, trying to take him inside her. He tested, found her ready. Their moans were loud, their breath ragged and mingling as they kissed with tongue and teeth. Strong brown hands spread her thighs wide, and she gasped each time he thrust to the root, unable to move, barely able to think. He was growling things into her ear, things he wanted to do to her.

Then, "I don't want any other woman but you. You're in my guts, in my head. The thought of anyone touchin' you makes me crazy, makes me want to pound their faces in with my fists." He pulled out of her, ignoring her moan at the loss, and turned her onto her stomach.

She was dizzy with lust, and let him push down on her shoulders, mashing her breasts into the quilt and raising her hips high. Needing him to want her with the same severity, she spread her legs and arched her back, not caring how exposed she was in the window light. A strangled sound escaped him, and he stroked her hips and bottom, at first with tenderness, and then with rough fingers. "You're so beautiful. The things I want to do to you."

"Do them," she challenged, her words hoarse from all the crying the night before. "Do anything you want to me, Ben."

He cursed, and she trembled when she felt two of his fingers delve deep inside of her, knowing he was watching. She felt him twitch, damp and heavy against her thigh. He spread her wetness around her most sensitive spot, making her jerk. Then, his fingers were replaced with the girth of his erection, and when he rocked all the way in, she screamed into her pillow, bucking against him. He cursed and flexed into her, then made a triangular window with his fingers where their flesh met. "I wish you could see what I see. How you can barely take all of me, you're so tight. Skin stretched round, all pink and shiny." He groaned and she burned at his words. She knew he was close by the way he grew impossibly bigger, then grabbed her hips against him in rough, even strokes. It made her wild, and she screamed when she came, like she was in pain, like she was dying. She never wanted him to stop and wasn't even aware that she was telling him so. He was loud too, shouting at the end, holding himself so deep that she writhed at the incredible fullness.

Afterward, they lay together, dazed and sweating.

"I'm so sorry," she was saying, sniffling against his neck. "For leaving."

His hand trailed over her naked belly. They barely fit on the bed. "No more secrets, no more runnin'."

She nodded. "No more saloons."

"I'm sorry, darlin'—"

"No, Ben, let's not fight anymore." She turned to him and ran her lips across his neck, and noticed that the skin was raw on one side. He must have scrubbed the place the loose woman had kissed him until it was red and inflamed. She licked it, tasted him, erasing all trace of any other lips but her own. When he grew hard against her belly, she sucked at the skin, leaving a love bruise, and reached down to stroke his length.

"And I'm sorry for throwing the washstand. I know better than to lose my temper that way, or scare you when all I want's to keep you safe." He kissed her lips, still swollen from their rough kisses the half hour before.

"I wanted to throw things, too," she admitted, and deepened their kiss, sucked his tongue. Thrusting against him with her hips, she pushed him onto his back and straddled him. He watched her with hooded eyes, a small, round bruise on his neck, and scratches on his shoulders and ribs. She lifted, then eased him inside of her, closing her eyes at depth and fullness.

They didn't leave the room for breakfast, and made love and talked until the blush of mid-morning broke through the storm clouds.

BEN AND LUCY watched from the porch swing as the sun set. Further west, somewhere beyond the pink and orange sunset that they faced, like-minded souls were already journeying north on the Western Texas-Kansas Trail. It was spring. Roundup. In the next week, he'd be on the four-month-long journey north. Even though Ben had taken this trail with his Pa many times in the past, his hand clenched around Lucy's.

Daisy sunned on the porch near their feet. Her eyelids twitched and she made small noises in her sleep.

"I wish you didn't have to go," Lucy murmured for the hundredth time.

"I have to. It's a stipulation of owning the property."

She already knew this; John had just reminded them not two weeks ago when he'd arrived home from business out of town.

"I'm worried," she admitted, brushing her fingers over his calloused palm.

"There's nothin' to be worried about."

"Don't lie to me." Her brows were straight and serious, her mouth unhappy. "Do you know how many men came into the hotel diner over the years with tales of the Chisholm Trail and crossing the Red River? Some of them left and didn't come back. If anything ever happened to you...."

He sighed and wrapped his arm around her hunched shoulders. Having a woman to worry about him was a fine thing most of the time. It wasn't so fine when those worries weren't unfounded. He'd driven cattle for five years as a boss, and a few years before that as a horse wrangler. The dangers of a trail drive were endless, depending on the weather, the experience of the waddies, illness, and God knew what else. The wind could blow the wrong way and five hundred head of cattle could stampede, killing half a dozen men. Ben didn't tell Lucy that. Instead, he told her the boring things.

"Well, it's dusty. A man could near about choke and die on it, true enough." She pulled his arm hair and he laughed. "Cookie could be bad at cooking. That'll make the men downright ornery. They could mutiny on account of nothing decent to eat."

"Oh, Ben," she groaned, but her lips were curling up. "I could go, and you wouldn't have to worry about hiring a cook. And I wouldn't make food unfit to eat."

The snort that exploded from him was loud and exaggerated. "Then the men *really* wouldn't work a lick. Could you imagine? Hundreds of heads of cattle, roaming miles away, while half my crew panted after my wife in the cook wagon."

Her laugh was loud and from the belly, and when she managed to contain it, she ran a hand suggestively up his thigh. "If I rode in the cook wagon, you'd get to sleep with me every night."

His eyebrows rose. "I'll think about it."

When he left at the end of the week to round up the cattle, saddlebags bulging with things Lucy had managed to stuff inside last minute, she waved at him from the porch until the house on the hill disappeared behind a stand of trees. Ben felt the loss like a mule kick to the stomach. The near misses over the years, events that could have killed him but miraculously hadn't, rose and wavered like a mirage the entire ride to his father's land. A man's face shone brightly in his mind's eye, grimacing in pain from a fatal rattlesnake bite. Taylor Jessup had been twenty-five, newly married with a baby on the way. He'd had everything to lose, and had died the very first night on the trail. It had been several years ago, but Ben broke out in a cold sweat, remembering the fear and helplessness as the man succumbed to the venom. He replaced Jessup's face with his own, turning gray as the blood leached from post-mortem skin.

He imagined Lucy crying over a grave with his name on the marker and knew true fear.

26

—·—

CHAPTER TWENTY-SIX

I f the first morning of the drive was a hint of what Ben had to look forward to, then he should have packed up and left right then.

He and the men woke up at the break of dawn, two hours after the cook wagon had already left, and led two thousand lowing, stumbling beeves due north from the Stone Ranch at a brisk pace. There, Ben led point with Sol and watched the men in action with a trained eye. They were good and kept the cattle in a nice, tight formation. He frowned.

What were those damned fools doing?

Junior and Leonard were off to the side with one of the younger hands, slouched forward and talking to the waddie with the enthusiasm of a housewife at a church social. Leonard laughed when the other man struggled to keep the agitated animals together, and instead of helping, reined in his horse, and reached in his shirt pocket. Ben's face darkened at the silver glint of a flask, and he thrust his jaw forward and tucked his lip, whistling shrilly above the commotion. He waved his hat, whistling until Junior—who'd helped himself to the flask when Leonard finished swigging—pocketed the booze with a sour grimace. At Ben's emphatic point, Junior turned his horse and kicked its flanks all the way to the back of the herd.

This was what he'd been afraid of. It wouldn't be good for morale if Junior and Leonard proved inept, and drank on the trail. Ben couldn't abide a drunkard when so many lives were at stake, and the normal exasperation he felt at his brother's thoughtlessness turned to fury. The boy had wanted to come instead of stay at home or help Frank with the ranch, indeed had insisted he not 'babysit'.

Funny, because it was beginning to look like exactly what Ben would have to be doing the whole damn cattle drive.

LUCY WOULD RATHER have been anywhere but on this particular front porch, but a promise was a promise. She blew out a rough breath and ignored the many glances from the remaining hands that stayed behind to help run the Stone Ranch. She rapped on the door and blinked when a maid opened it.

"Is Mr. Stone home?" she asked, polite as one could be when drenched with sweat.

The maid nodded and opened the door wide, ushering her in with a sweeping hand. "Yes, miss, please come in and I'll fetch him." The woman led her into a stuffy little parlor that overlooked the front yard and left.

It was telling that the servants had no idea who Lucy was or that she was married to the eldest Stone son.

When Mr. Stone came in, Lucy had taken her bonnet off and was dabbing her face with a handkerchief. His bushy brows went up. "What's the matter, girl? Ain't been a week since the boys have been gone."

Pinching her mouth at the man's usual condescension, she said, "Frank is hurt. And I wouldn't be here at all if he hadn't made me promise."

"What happened?"

"He broke his leg." Lucy had never met a man as quiet as Frank, specifically not when his thigh bone had snapped in half. She explained how he'd been putting a horse through training maneuvers, but the clumsy mare had turned too sharply and stumbled, falling on her side—directly onto Frank's leg. "The stubborn man wouldn't even let me get a doctor! Of all the imbecilic...." She trailed off, shaking her head. "Tia and I set his leg and he's unable to get around for a few weeks. He asked me, no, *ordered* me, to come here and ask if you could spare someone trustworthy to help at the house. So." Lucy stood up and dusted off her skirts. "I have upheld my promise, but I'll be finding someone in town on Saturday when I visit Papa."

John couldn't stop a grin from curling his mouth, and his eyes gleamed with some offensive thought, no doubt. "What you're tellin' me is that you need a hand to replace Frank, but now that you've come all the way over here, you'll just find someone yourself?"

Lucy paused, pretended to think, then nodded once. "That's exactly it. Thank you for your time, Mr. Stone, I'll just be going back home. The horses need to be put up."

"Now, now, just hold up." His voice became cajoling, and she bristled. "I've got someone in mind. Crew is a good worker, doesn't drink, and he's a loner-type, so being alone at the ranch for a few months shouldn't bother him none." John wrapped a heavy arm around the top of Lucy's shoulders and physically steered her to the front porch.

Gritting her teeth, she dug in her heels. "It's quite all right, I don't need to put you out. I know several hard workers in town and will pay one of them to come to the ranch." He nudged her forward again, and the manners from years of schooling finally compelled her to give in and be led.

"Ben would tear my hide if I let you hire some stranger to work around his new wife." John's placating tone grew more sincere. He stopped and faced her, taking his heavy arm from her shoulders and meeting her eye to eye. "I know you're prideful. Ben is, too. Must've been what drew you together, eh? But I have hands that have worked with me since they were wet behind the ears. I'll see if Crew wants to come out there for the next few months, or till Frank is better, and you won't even have to pay."

"Should I get this in writing?" She couldn't hide her sarcasm.

"Of course not."

When she only frowned up at him, he laughed and clapped her shoulder. "Come on, girl, what's family for? You head on home, and I'll send him over in the morning."

Neatly trapped, Lucy tamped down her frustration and nodded unhappily. They shook hands, and she turned away, donning her damp bonnet. While she tied the strings, a man leaning against the corral watched the sway of her skirts. She nodded to him, and he tipped his hat, eyes never wavering from her. Bold fellow. If Ben were here, he'd give the man a look that would curl his hair. At the thought, Lucy smiled. She'd inform him that if she were at the hotel, it was always best to let them stare; those men were always the best tippers.

Ben's response would be to shove her against the wall, lift her skirts, and pin her legs high. At the vivid image, Lucy mounted Sunshine and stared off in the distance, thinking lurid thoughts of her husband and wishing he were home.

BEN HAD NEVER been afraid of hard work, not even when he was ill or on the occasion someone in his employ spit in his eye. But he was finding it damned hard to put a hitch in his giddyup when each mile north took him further away from his cozy ranch and the smiling woman waiting on it. He didn't share such thoughts with his friend or his brother, but he did scowl into the fire as though it were to blame for his constant weariness and discomfort.

"What's the matter, pardner?" Sol plopped down beside him with a plate of stewed beans and tri-tip, hard biscuits, and a handful of dried fruit. The stars were appearing one by one, twinkling against a soft blue sky. Below it, the Brazos River shimmered, the bank across steep and inaccessible to the cattle that were easily spooked now that they were two weeks away from their bedding grounds. Even now, clumped together along the river, the great beasts were thinner from constant movement and sparse grazing. They bedded down and drank from the river as though content, but all around, the men kept eagle eyes peeled for any sudden movement from the lead steers.

A head shake was the only answer Ben gave.

"Well, I reckon I know what has you so moody. Can't be easy listening to him blow wind out his hind end, night after night." Sol nodded toward Junior, who had forgone a plate and was drinking his supper out of that ever-present flask. Leonard, the constant shadow, had passed out an hour ago and was bound to have a crick in his neck with the way his head was propped against his saddlebags.

Junior leaned over to a group of hands, telling what Ben hoped were tall tales about how he'd spent the night with three whores at once in one night at Waco. His audience mostly grunted, and only the youngest man gave a weak smile. They'd passed Waco a few days ago, and Junior and Leonard had inconveniently disappeared for two of them. Not that their absence had been much of a difference in the workload, but the hands didn't appreciate that the boss's little brother and cousin got to whore and drink while the rest of the men ran on only a few hours of sleep. It hadn't helped that it had rained the past week straight, and everyone was in bad humor.

But even before that, Junior had strained all the ready friendships that he'd solidified in town when he'd bought them all drinks. Now, he was always half-drunk, wanted to talk more than he wanted to work, and the men would grumble when he was gone and go quiet when he came around. He had gone from amusing, to obnoxious, to disliked within two weeks.

"He's a piss-poor hand, that's for certain." Sol blinked at Ben's vicious words but knew better than to nod in agreement. The bond between the two brothers was strong regardless of their feelings toward each other. "If I'd known what kind of trouble he'd be, I'd have left him home. Jeb and Ernest came by this mornin' and asked if I was gonna dock Junior's pay for those days in Waco. I told them he'd get what he earned, and not a dollar more. Must've been the right answer bein' as they haven't given me any more lip." He scrubbed a hand over his grizzled, haggard face, fed up already and it wasn't even a month in.

"Best to have a word with him 'fore it gets too bad," Sol murmured, and for once, his eyes didn't twinkle with humor. "There's always one or two in every trail ride. It's a sorry fact it's your kin this time around. Gotta treat him like a regular hire, is all."

Ben gave a noise of agreement and clapped Sol on the back. A better friend a man could never have.

"Junior. Eat up and take night watch. Now that the weather's clear, it should be quiet."

His brother looked up and belched. "Aw, I'm tired tonight. I rode all day to catch up with y'all."

A straight black brow rose. "You should be nice and rested from those nights in that dry, warm whorehouse."

The men grew quiet and watchful as Junior gave a crack of derisive laughter. "Ha! You know that a man don't rest when in a place like that. What goes on between the sheets ain't sleeping. You should know, with the way Lucy caterwauls—"

Ben was up and across the camp with Junior's shirt collar in a fist before anyone could draw a breath. Someone gave a low whistle, but it was quickly silenced. "You watch the way you talk about my wife, boy. I oughta wash your mouth out with soap. It'd be a nice reprieve from the whiskey. Now you get your skinny hide on that horse and watch these cattle tonight or you can ride straight home. *Comprende*?"

As still as stone, Junior swallowed and whispered, "Yeah. I got it."

When Ben released the boy, he mourned the look in Junior's eyes. That look had only ever been for their father; resentful, bitter, with fear of disappointment. Junior swiftly replaced it with apathy when he smoothed the wrinkled fabric of his shirt. Without grabbing a plate to eat, Junior pocketed his flask, found his horse, and avoided eye contact. After he'd ridden a fair distance halfway between the expanse of the herd, Ben saddled Reb again and followed.

It really shouldn't have surprised him that once Junior noticed he had company, he'd become angry. What did shock him, was that his brother saw his shadow ride up, and he screamed across the bank, "I don't need you babysitting me, Ben! I can handle a few dumb steers!"

A sober Junior would have known that even in inclement weather, the merest trifles could startle a herd and have them up and running. During the thunderstorms earlier in the week, several small stampedes had broken out from the cracking boom of thunder and lightning. Ben had helped the men turn the herds in a tight circle, and so far, they'd managed to prevent losing too many numbers or anyone's life from the milling. But now, that sudden, hoarse shout amid dozing cattle was the only incentive the nearest head needed to panic. In the quiet of twilight, the herd arose in a wave, as though the ground around them was lifting in an angry tide. Horns clashed as the animals heaved to their feet, and a chorus of muffled drums from their feet as thousands of tons of bovine moved as one away from the river.

Cursing, Ben kicked Reb to flank the lead steer. "Stampede!" he shouted and tried in vain to turn the herd into a circle while Junior watched, mouth agape and pale. "Don't just sit there!"

Junior shouted and tried to help, but ended up cutting off the herd at the neck where Ben was turning them. The group separated into two, and more were frightened. Before Ben knew it, half the herd scattered to the four winds.

JETHRO CREW WAS a quiet fellow in his late thirties. He didn't have a wife or kids, no family or close friends. Lucy knew this because the first morning he rode in, Tia told her after giving him a narrow look that he was an odd one to be so to himself. Considering how closed off Tia and Frank were from others, Lucy took the opinion with a grain of salt.

That shouldn't be a reason to dislike someone, Lucy thought. So, what if the man liked to be alone? It wasn't until she'd introduced herself over breakfast that she remembered him. He was the man with the roving gaze who'd watched her leave John Stone's ranch. When he shook her hand, he didn't linger, but his eyes did. Figuring he was just lonely for female company, she'd shrugged it off that first day as she went over all the chores that needed to be done before the day's end.

It was a habit now for her to milk the two cows morning and night, so she didn't add that to the list. Once Ben returned, she would continue the habit, and it would be one less thing for him to do. She felt ashamed for not doing it sooner. Lucy pressed her head against the warm side of Mathilda, her favorite cow with the longest lashes she'd ever seen. Milking was a rhythmic, cathartic duty, and she felt half asleep when a presence behind her made her pause.

"Mizz Stone, I'm done for the day." Crew's voice was raspy and plodding, as slow and steady as the man was at chores.

Lucy turned on the stool to glance at him. "Oh, thank you, Mr. Crew. Supper shouldn't take too long to cook if you want to wash up."

"Just Crew is fine. Need any help with that bucket?"

"Um, I'm almost finished, but you can strain the milk if you want while I start dinner. The cloth and jug are on the porch. Thank you." With a tight smile, she turned back around and continued squeezing milk into the half-full galvanized bucket. It wasn't until five minutes had gone by before the sensation, creeping as a spider's crawl at her nape, made her pause. Almost afraid to turn, Lucy cleared her throat and asked, "Mr. Crew?"

"Yes'm."

It made her jump, her worst fear realized. The man had been standing silent behind her for endless minutes, watching her milk, and not saying a word. Lucy pretended she'd known he'd been there all along. "I'm finished if you want to take the bucket now."

His footsteps were quiet behind her, and when he leaned in, a wave of body odor followed. He grabbed the warped handle of the bucket and took it away, brushing against her shoulder with his own. As he stood, his eyes caught hers with a discomfiting intensity before looking away. Ben looked at her that way when she'd been teasing him all day, brushing against him with her breasts or bottom, kissing his neck when she walked by him at the dinner table. His blue eyes on hers were like dry tinder on a brush fire; he made her body ache to be touched and loved.

The man that watched her now was not her husband, and her body was well aware of it. Crew's dark eyes were deep-set and one was a tad crossed. She'd felt sorry for him that morning, thinking he was a little slow on the draw and didn't know any better than to stare. Now, however, her body shrank into itself, and her instincts screamed a warning. Being slow with social cues did not make a person innocent. There was no telling what was going on in his mind. She was very aware that the only other man on the ranch was laid up with a broken leg.

With a polite, disturbed smile she stood and put the stool away, then got out of that barn as fast as she could.

As though he could sense her discomfort, Crew kept his distance while she went inside. She watched from her periphery through the screen door as he found a sterilized glass jug covered with a straining cloth on the porch, and poured the fresh milk without spilling a drop. Without glancing at her through the screen, he left the jug near the front door and disappeared to the pump to wash up. Lucy finished supper and breathed a sigh of relief when she spied Tia walking up the path from the window.

Normally in the evening, they took their suppers together, rotating houses. Now that Frank was bedridden, however, they'd decided to eat supper at Tia's so that the injured man didn't become too lonely. He was an independent, hardworking man with a craggy exterior and willing to help anyone at the drop of a hat. Therefore, he was an awful patient and needed constant supervision or he'd get up before his broken leg had healed.

By the exasperation on Tia's face, Lucy could tell that it had been a rough day.

"Need help?" Tia asked when she came in the kitchen door, holding the jug of milk. The jug was just small enough to fit in the ice box. She fiddled with the water tray beneath the sliver of ice that was left. "Needs ice."

"Tia," Lucy whispered, and by the tone of that single word, she had the older woman's complete attention.

"*Por que?*" Tia slid the full water tray back in, shut the ice box, and hurried over. "What is wrong?"

Lucy's eyes shifted to the window that overlooked the well. "The new hire makes me...nervous."

"He say something to you?" The accented voice was suddenly severe, almost scolding, as though the woman were already three seconds from taking a broom to the man.

It made Lucy laugh, and her tension released several notches. "No, no, it's probably nothing. I just, I don't want to be alone with him."

Tia nodded knowingly. "*Ojos de miedo.*"

Scary eyes.

"*Si, mucho*," Lucy agreed. "Don't say anything to Frank. I just want to be careful."

With that aired out between them, Lucy's shoulders relaxed from their rigid position, and she felt the courage to ask Crew if he didn't mind bringing the mountain of mashed potatoes to Tia's. Supper was an awkward affair in Frank's one-room cabin, where Lucy and Crew moved the small dining table near to the bed. Lucy and Frank discussed chores and cattle drives, but the other two were silent, one eating with full attention on his plate, while Tia picked at her food, attention glued to the newcomer with the scary eyes. If Frank noticed anything odd, he kept his opinions to himself. He did, however, ask if Ben still had his pistol in their bedside drawer.

Blinking in shock, but noting the steady, meaningful gaze of the old man, Lucy could only lie and confirm, "Yes, it's still there. Would you like it back?"

"Naw, you keep it. No tellin' if you might need it one day. Maybe a critter in the chicken coop that needs shootin'."

Everyone at the table held still, no forks moving to mouths or knives into steak. To break the tension, Lucy laughed, desperate, and asked Frank if he remembered how she'd cornered the possum in the chicken coop. He'd been there, of course, and had even witnessed Ben buck naked, but he raised his brows in interest and she told the story anyway.

Lucy walked the trail home alone after giving Crew a nervous goodnight at the bunkhouse, and once in the house, found a hidden pistol under a dishtowel in the washed mashed potato bowl. The gun was heavy, black, and sinister. It made its bed in the bedside table drawer that night, and every door in the house was locked up tight.

The next morning, Lucy washed and dressed in her plainest, dowdiest dress, and milked on the other side of the stanchion facing the stall door. She cooked dinner with the door locked and called Crew to the meal after she'd already eaten, washing dishes with her back to him, knife inches from her at all times. He was quiet and polite when he thanked her for the meal on his way outside, and not once had he given her a second glance. Her guard lowered, and guilt began to eat at her.

What a ninny she was.

Not every man was after her, this one included. The conversation between her and Tia now felt like empty accusations and judgment. Lucy had been unbearably unkind to him, no matter that he hadn't been in the room to hear them. Crew had to have gotten Frank's hint at dinner; the shot had hit the mark, straight and center. And now he'd probably walk on eggshells around her, terrified she'd scream rape.

"I'm such a simpleton," she hissed to herself, frowning into the dishpan of soapy water.

When the next week showed no change in the man's demeanor, and there had been no more lingering eye contact,

Lucy second-guessed any earlier misgivings and decided to be friendlier. She smiled at Crew around the yard, thanked him for jobs well done, and even teased him a time or two when a recalcitrant horse refused to be caught. And if the man didn't smile in return or even laugh, well, some men were just made different. Even so, the icy wall between them thawed and the silences at meals were easier.

Tia helped Lucy plant the seeds from Sally Kershaw a year and a lifetime before, and normalcy was finally established.

Then the rains came.

It rained throughout the weekend, and her plans to visit her father and Minnie were canceled. They had to do the wash in the house, which Lucy hated more than anything in the world. The air in the kitchen was heavy, steam rising from boiling pots on the stove in humid waves. Lucy and Tia perspired through their clothes and hung their clean laundry on the porch, in the den, and even over the dining table. Afterward, they peeled sticky calico from their chests and stepped onto the porch for a forgiving breeze.

"I need a bath." Lucy sniffed under her arm and grimaced, making the other woman laugh. Tia waved goodbye and grabbed her slicker, trotting home in little splashes.

The pantry was the perfect room to bathe in. Its long, narrow window illuminated the small space even on the grayest of days. Lucy dragged her washtub in and began the laborious chore of filling it up with hot water. She shut the door, disrobed, and sank into the water with a sigh. Wash day could drain the energy from even the most stalwart man, much less her, whose energy seemed to have depleted since Ben had left. He'd been gone three weeks, and the time apart left her on edge and crawling in her skin. Propping her feet up on the shelf nearest her, Lucy submerged herself in the bath, her buttocks and the top of her head brushing either end of the tub. She held her breath for a minute, scrubbing her scalp underwater, then came up gasping. Thoughts of Ben while she scrubbed her body with soft soap turned her movements languid, caressing. She stood and bent over to rinse her hair when she felt a draft of cool air. She stood reflexively, waist-length hair whipping back and streaming water down her body.

The door to the pantry was wide open and Crew was in the doorway, mouth lax and eyes everywhere.

A white haze of pure panic had her screaming, "Get out, get out!" while covering her body and plopping back into the water.

But it was too late. He'd seen her, *all of her*, before whirling on his booted heel and walking out the kitchen door. She groaned into her hands in mortification. Why was he in her house? He'd never just sauntered in before, had always knocked. Had he knocked before he'd entered and she just didn't hear? No, the kitchen door had been left open to help dry the lines of clothing hanging all over the house.

Anger replaced her embarrassment. What the *hell* had he been thinking? A person didn't just come into a woman's house while she was alone and help himself to her pantry. And no, he hadn't said anything or knocked. Splashing or not, she would have heard even the slightest of noises. He must have been sneaking.

She dressed in her clean clothes in a paranoid rush, but by the time she'd buttoned up her blouse, her anger morphed into apprehension. Crew hadn't quite had the predatory look of the stinky man she'd had the misfortune to meet on the stagecoach. Crew may not have leered, and he'd left after she'd screamed at him. Even so.... He'd gotten an eyeful and there wasn't a chance he'd forget anytime soon.

When dinnertime came around, Lucy was almost too anxious to go outside and milk the cows. Only the lowing of a miserable Mathilda was enough to force her hand. She should just take a deep breath, and go outside, she told herself. She owned the place. This was her ranch, and if he gave her even one sideways look, she'd run him off so fast his hat would spin. Courage mustered, Lucy took a step off the porch—and froze.

Crew stood at the barn doors, hat in hand. He shuffled forward like a kicked puppy, head bowed and not looking higher than his feet. His exaggerated posture was almost disingenuous. When he got within ten feet of her, he stopped and scratched the back of his head.

"Ma'am, I milked the cows for you. I don't have the tender touch you do, that's why they put up a ruckus. I just—" he paused and took a bracing breath, "I'm real sorry 'bout earlier. Frank's wife wanted me to tell you she made a big stew and to bring a coupla' bowls. I thought you was in the pantry gettin' stuff for dinner and just walked in, and I shouldn't'a. If you want me to leave, I will."

God, her face was on fire. She had never felt more uncomfortable in her life than she did at that moment. The sweat she'd washed off hours before reappeared, and she brushed it off of her lip.

"I—I don't know if you should stay...." She trailed off when the man's shoulders rolled, almost hunchbacked. Was she just too suspicious for her own good? He had to be telling the truth; she could ask Tia right then to confirm his story. And the front door had been opened. After how friendly she'd been with him these few days, he probably felt comfortable enough to come into the pantry. It was just the pantry. Not her bedroom, or the outhouse, for goodness' sake. Again, she might have misread everything and got confused. And if he'd looked at her while she was naked, what did she expect? A man was a man, and if a naked woman was in front of him, he was going to look. She came to a tentative decision. "Let's just put this behind us. Just, swear that you'll never come inside—"

"I swear, ma'am. It'll never happen again."

"Well. Good. It never happened."

"No ma'am." He sounded relieved, and his back finally straightened. He put his hat on but kept his eyes low.

"Alright. I'll grab those bowls, and you can meet me at Tia and Frank's." She turned on her heel and stopped. "Thank you for milking the cows." Then she walked up the steps, relieved that it was over and that they'd speak nothing of it to anyone.

As she walked by the window, she almost stopped in her tracks. In the reflection, Crew stood in the gray drizzle with his hands clenched like rocks, eyes no longer on the ground, but watching her every movement.

A cornered feeling hovered above Lucy all during supper. Unlike every night before, she wasn't talkative and picked at her food. More than once, she'd caught Crew glancing at her from her periphery, and she suffered from extreme embarrassment all over again. She waited until Crew had left the stilted silence of the room and approached Frank.

Studying the pale contents of her earthenware coffee mug, Lucy asked, "What do you know about Mr. Crew? John said he worked with you for years."

The married couple shared a look. Only the blind, deaf and dumb could have missed the sudden personality change in Lucy, and without saying a word, their eyes communicated a worrying question: What was wrong with the girl? It seemed that her query had come to the heart of it, and the feigned nonchalance made it all the more alarming.

Frank plumped the pillow under his leg and grunted, "Yep, Crew started work with Junior's grandpa before he died and John inherited the land. He was just sixteen, as I recall. Looked twelve."

"A boy? What about his family?"

"Ain't got none." After a moment's hesitation, Frank sighed and continued, "He was living in a whorehouse with his ma, so I heard. Swept the floors, cleaned the tables, took out bottles, and the like. When his mama died, he ran off, and John found him in the streets. He reckoned the boy could earn his keep muckin' out the stables at the ranch. I remember him, skinny and wearing rags. Didn't talk for years if he didn't have to. Still don't."

Lucy frowned into her mug.

Her childhood friend, Poppy, had a similar history. A child born to a whore and raised in a rough world where little girls and boys shouldn't be. The auburn-haired girl had striven to be normal before her peers, but behind closed doors, Lucy knew her friend had been fundamentally different. When it was just the two of them, the thin veneer of quiet diffidence was shed, and loads of information was not fit for polite company's ears spewed out. Poppy enjoyed shocking her. Nothing was taboo; not body parts nor their functions, and bedtime activities sounded like a game that could get you coin for candy and millinery, even new boots. Going to bed hungry was as commonplace as strangers entering a darkened room after bedtime. Violence against women didn't make her new friend bat an eye, and the girl had plenty of bruises to show and tell. At the time, Lucy had been entranced by the knowledge Poppy had of the grown-up world. Private parts had so many names and uses that the girls had giggled beneath the covers as they went over each one in hushed whispers.

Thinking back now, as she peered into her half-empty mug of tepid coffee, it made Lucy sick. The things that the poor child had seen and perhaps been coerced to do through money and treats, although an abhorrence, was a fact of life for so many children. If only she could talk to Poppy now...but of course, it would be impossible. Her friend had moved not long after she had, and hadn't been heard from since.

Had Mr. Crew experienced similar things throughout his childhood? Surely, he had. If Poppy had been socially and emotionally stunted by years of living where women worked on their backs, it would be of no surprise if Crew was as well. No wonder the man kept to himself. Tendrils of pity wriggled their way through the miasma of apprehension Lucy felt when she thought of Jethro Crew. The way he watched her when he didn't think she was looking unnerved her to the point of real fear, but her instincts continued to clash with that fear, each fighting a war inside her until she didn't know up from down, or innocent peeping from lecherous intent.

"You scared of him, Mrs. Stone?"

Lucy looked up at the rough question, eyes too big on her face. She felt clammy and nervous.

"What?" she asked, a beat too late, and from the dark look in Frank's eyes, she knew she may as well have screamed, 'Yes!'.

"He say anything to you?" The old man's leathery skin shifted into deep creases and became ugly. "My leg's broke, but my trigger finger ain't." He sat up and shifted his legs an inch toward the edge of the bed, and both women shot up from their seats in protest.

"No, Frank, please," Lucy cried, rushing to the bed, hands fluttering over his poised form. "He hasn't said anything untoward, I promise! Please, stay in bed, you'll damage your leg worse."

Beads of perspiration trickled down Frank's temples, betraying the stoic old man. His snort proved he didn't believe her for a second. "You best not keep something like that from us, you hear?" He pointed an arthritic finger at her, unsmiling, a stranger suddenly.

"Of course, I wouldn't, I'd tell you if he bothered me," she soothed.

The hell I would.

If she admitted that the borrowed hand frightened her, Frank would stand up and go after him, rebreaking his leg and ruining the healing process, probably to the point that it would never mend properly. If the issue with Mr. Crew escalated, Lucy would take a quiet ride to John's ranch, and order him to take the hand back. If he asked why then she'd come up with some asinine excuse. For now, she'd handle her fears, anything to keep Frank in bed.

She changed the subject to how much she missed Ben, and the gleam in their eyes dimmed from fervent to consoling. Neither was totally convinced, but Frank didn't try to get out of bed again.

Lucy walked home alone, shivering even in the humidity of a season approaching summer. The whisper of her shoes and skirts along the saturated grass was abrasive to her ears, and she cursed aloud and jumped when a chicken roosting in the coop flapped its wings. The rain had stopped, but the clouds in the night sky were swollen with the promise of more, their dense shelf omitting any possible light from the stars and moon. In the absolute darkness of the yard, the glow from the bunkhouse window reached its fingers to paint the path before her a butter yellow. Her feet stopped at the edge of darkness and light before changing direction, skirting visibility for the safety of the shadows beyond. There was no movement from the bright window—she knew because she watched with furtive eyes—therefore, when she bumped into the large, warm body in the pitch black, she screamed as though stabbed.

Hands steadied her, then disappeared. "Sorry, I didn't see you there."

Her heart beating at a rabbit's pace in her ears, Lucy snapped, "What are you doing out here, trying to scare me half to death?" Oh, she knew exactly what he was doing. He was sneaking around in the dark, waiting for her to come home. She'd place a wager that he'd listened to their conversation like the peeping Tom that he was.

"I was just visiting the outhouse, ma'am."

A likely story.

"Well, if you'll excuse me." She circled him and raced to the porch with the same speed one would if it were sunny. As it was tar-black outside, she promptly bumped her shinbone on the porch step. "Mother *Hubbard*," she hissed, and the sharp pain bent her double and rendered her immobile.

"You all right over there?" Crew's concern sounded genuine, but the squeak of his footsteps in the wet grass forced her into action.

"I'm fine," she wheezed and scrambled up the stairs. Stars winked in and out of her vision. There was no pain quite as acute as whacking one's shin bone. "I'm just blind as a bat at night and ran into the steps instead of up them."

There was a moment's pause, then, "Bats get around in the dark better than *that*." The emphasis at the last wasn't meant to be insulting, was it? Had he made a joke?

"Pardon?" Her hand searched for the latch of the kitchen door. It was here *somewhere*.

"You was saying you was blind as a bat. But they see real good in the dark. If you set on the roof at night, they'll fly around your head and eat skeeters."

Lucy had finally found the latch, but now interest prevented her from entering. Crew's voice came from the ground several feet away, and she could just see his murky silhouette beyond the porch. His words couldn't have surprised her more if they had been poetry. Her hand clenched involuntarily at the latch. "You spend a lot of time on roofs?"

"Sure do. It's real quiet up there. Peaceful." His answer was candid, like a child sharing a delightful secret.

"You like being alone, don't you?"

His trousers rustled as though he'd shifted feet. "I reckon I do, ma'am." He said no goodnight as his footsteps disappeared into the dark.

That night, Lucy lay awake in her locked house and pondered the life of a man with no family or friends, who never laughed and rarely talked, spent nights alone on rooftops in the company of bats, and then considered such a place peaceful.

BEN STARED WITH nostrils pinched at the swollen Red River.

They'd reached the Doans and Vernon Pass two hundred head lighter after Junior's little debacle on the Brazos. It had taken them another day to round up the steers that they could before the weather turned again, raining and storming so hard they had admitted defeat and pushed the cattle that remained north again. He'd reported the missing head to the Cattleman's Association and hoped their inspectors would find at least a percentage of them in the herds to follow.

The ferry sat empty and sad on the opposite bank, out of order when the flooding was too dangerous. Their cook wagon had made camp a mile back after the initial sighting of the churning, muddy waters. What was normally a medium-sized river with red bluff banks was now a wide span of water with swirling currents and temperamental whirlpools.

Water crawled along the vegetation and made the grass soggy, its sandy bank several feet underwater yards away from the water line.

They weren't the only cattle drive stuck waiting on the flood waters to recede. For miles down the river on either side were the shifting bodies of thousands of bovine, and dozens of men on horses milling in between to keep herds separate from each other. Ben imagined if God was looking down at them, they'd appear like a plague of flies, swarming over a choice carcass. Most alarming of all were five fresh graves, sitting sentinel on a piece of high ground that overlooked the uncaring river beyond.

Junior reined his horse in next to him, Leonard trailing like a fly on shit, and Ben tried hard to keep his face from betraying his displeasure. Again, they shirked their duties. They were supposed to be keeping an eye on the western side of the herd.

"Look at that," Junior whistled low, round eyes following a wet, rotten log spinning violently in the turbulent current, broken branches disappearing and reappearing like jagged teeth.

It gave Ben chills.

"Ain't no telling how long it'll take before it goes down low enough to cross," he muttered.

"I think we should go upriver some and just cross there. Cookie can meet us on the other side in a few days. There's supplies in Vernon that'll last us until then."

Patience thinning, Ben nodded at the graves. "You trying to end up like them? We can't risk losing any more cattle, much less people."

Bristling, Junior turned in his saddle to face him, swaying just enough to make Ben see red. "I told you I was sorry about that. I even rode rear for a week straight, what more do you want?"

The red mist blurred Ben's vision, and he saw rather than felt his hand snatch Junior's jacket, rooting until he found what he was looking for. He held up a tin flask, half empty. "What more do I want? You can start by quitting this." His brother's half-hearted swipe at it intensified Ben's rage, and before he thought about the wisdom of such an action, he reared back and threw the glinting tin halfway across the river.

It plopped and disappeared beneath the swift-moving water without ceremony. His deep sense of satisfaction that the unholy thing would be halfway to Witchita Falls by morning was ruined when Junior swung at him. The blow glanced on his shoulder, and Ben laughed cruelly.

"What're you doin' trying to fight me on a horse? You're about as dumb as a box of rocks." His laughter faded when he saw that the boy was halfway to tears, his lips curled back in a grimace of pain.

"You think I'm dumb, huh? Pa does, too. You two are just alike, you know, and you can both go straight to hell."

Leonard took this moment to speak up. "I'll get it for you Junior!" he slurred and spurred his horse at a gallop straight into the washed-out banks where the flask had disappeared.

"Wait, what the hell are you doing?" Real panic laced Ben's voice.

Junior wiped his nose with the back of his arm, watched his friend in shock for a moment, then kicked his horse without mercy behind Leonard. Cursing, shouting at Junior to stop, Ben followed, ice-cold terror in his blood as his brother's horse entered the foaming floodwaters of the Red River.

27

— · —

CHAPTER TWENTY-SEVEN

"We got company," Crew called from the corner of the house.

Down the twisting drive, a plume of dust was visible behind a fast-paced pair of buggy horses. Lucy stood from her crouch in the flower beds and squinted her eyes. One driver was a man, the other a woman in a brown dress and white kitchen apron. The driver held the reins one-handed, and the sun gleamed against the dark skin of the woman.

"Papa and Minnie?" Lucy shared a worried glance with Crew.

When she caught a view of the raw emotion on their faces as they pulled from the narrow road and teetered to a halt in front of the porch, her heart began to race.

"What's happened?" Her eyes shot from her father to Minnie, but couldn't decipher an answer. They both looked at her in dread, and she felt a tight wrench in her chest, as though a rope had caught her around the ribs and she was dangling helplessly, suspended in midair.

"Lucy—" Minnie broke off, and the way her lips trembled cinched the rope tighter.

"Minnie, what's wrong?" A hysterical note entered Lucy's voice, made it loud and demanding.

For a beat, there was nothing but the sound of the buggy horse's loud breathing, the desperate flex of those great lungs expanding and retracting. Was it her mother? Beth? Who had fallen ill, no, *died*, and left the pair in front of her so stricken with grief? For a flutter of an instant, as light as a butterfly's wings, a name drifted across her mind, but she slammed it behind a locked iron door.

Tony set the brake and helped Minnie down. They walked to Lucy, who was still frozen in the flower bed.

"Perhaps we should go inside, so we can sit down—"

"Just tell me, Papa."

Her papa reached into his front pocket, fingers shaky as a week without a drink. "A wire was sent this afternoon, poppet. I'm afraid—God help me, it's bad news. The worst news. Minnie, help me, I cannot—" He pressed his fingers hard into his closed eyes, as though he'd rather shove them into his skull than look at her.

Lucy's own eyes were round, the whites prominent. They turned to Minnie, pleading.

Someone had better tell her something, immediately.

Minnie openly cried. Her voice was a crow's when she finally managed to speak. "It's Mistah Stone. He drowned in the Red River yesterday."

She was floating, hanging by that rope until her heart pinched in discomfort. Mr. Stone? It couldn't be John; he'd stayed home for this trail drive.

"Junior?" she whispered with awful hopefulness, praying *God, God, please God no*.

A piece of paper that peeked out of an envelope with the hotel address in script across it was passed over to her.

"Not Junior, sweetheart." Tony's shoulders shook.

An annoying tremor set Lucy's chin to quivering, and she bit her lip to control it, hesitating only a moment before she took the scrap of paper. It wasn't Junior. If it wasn't Junior, it could only be Ben. This knowledge settled like a trap; it was there, she knew it, and as soon as she read the wire, she'd step right between those iron teeth. Her fingers were oddly steady as she plucked the paper out and unfolded it. The message lay on the paper, and she looked at dozens of letters without reading a word. If she read it, her life was over, this she knew. Like how her father's life would end if the hotel caught fire, and her mother's would end if she became bankrupt. When the letters came into focus, her breath wheezed out, suspended. Because she was dying. The trap had closed around her.

On June 22 1882 evening Benjamin Stone and Leonard Baffert swept away in Red River STOP Baffert deceased body and possessions found and recovered Stone assumed dead STOP Stones body has not been recovered after hours of search STOP

FOR TWO DAYS Lucy walked around the house in suspended disbelief.

She didn't eat, or sleep, only paced around the house at all hours of the day and night like a ghost. Minnie stayed when Tony left, but Lucy urged her back to town. The woman's grief only drew out her own, and Lucy wasn't prepared to give up hope just yet.

"Assumed dead" did not mean "was dead".

It didn't!

There was a good possibility Ben was alive somewhere.

A trip to the Stone ranch to find out more, Crew tailing closely behind, had proved fruitless. John Stone had left to pick up Junior from Wichita Falls, where the boy had raved and drank himself into a stupor. Not that Mrs. Stone had told Lucy that. Sol had kindly used his own wages to send an expensive wire explaining that John was to retrieve Junior and that they'd tell her everything when they came back.

Tia acted as though her cousin's son was, indeed, dead, and Lucy despised her for giving up.

She hid her feelings well by shutting herself in her house. Crew cooked their meals, dreadful though they were, and she refused to eat at his urgings and blatantly ignored the worry in his eyes. She'd turned into a woman possessed, sending letters to the towns downstream from the Doans and Vernon Pass, asking the sheriffs to keep an eye out for a man named Benjamin Stone, average of height, strong of build, with black hair and blue eyes. So far, there'd been no reply, and she tried not to think about the last letter she'd sent. It had been to a town over thirty miles away from the site of his disappearance. Let them think she was mad. Anything was possible, except his death.

Ben had been an excellent swimmer. No. Ben *was* an excellent swimmer. He could swim the circumference of the water hole in a minute; she'd timed him. He could hold his breath for over a minute. She'd timed that, too.

But, even with her certainty of his survival, she couldn't seem to stop the horrific images of his dead, bloated body floating in the swift current of the Red River, or trapped beneath the debris in dark water. When she did this, she'd shoot up from her place, be it the bed or at the kitchen table. She'd shake and grip her stomach, and it would be an hour before she'd be able to talk some sense into herself.

On the morning of the third day, the sun hadn't come over the rise before she was washed and dressed and headed to the stables.

"Mrs. Stone!" cried a voice from behind her.

Lucy glanced behind her but didn't stop her rapid pace. "Yes, Mr. Crew?"

Crew was barely dressed, still buttoning up his trousers, but she didn't notice. "Did you have a bite to eat today?"

She frowned. "I'm not hungry. I'm on my way to the big house. Then I'm going to Dogwood to see if there's any more news." She disappeared into the depths of the barn, but her voice floated out. "You're welcome to the kitchen, eat whatever you want."

The Stone Ranch was busy that time of morning, but they were becoming used to her frequent visits. She came once in the morning, and once in the evening. She'd ask if Mr. Stone was home, and the hands would give her sad shakes of their heads.

This morning was different.

A rider met her at the gate and shouted, "They rode in here at dark this morning, Mrs. Stone! I was just on my way to get you!"

"Oh, thank God!" She kicked her horse to the big house, dismounting in such a hurry she nearly landed on her rear in a pile of skirts. A man was there to help her down, but it was as though she didn't see him.

Lucy ran up the porch stairs, eyes burning, and burst into the front door without bothering to knock. The housemaid gasped, then looked warily up the stairs behind her. "They're all asleep, ma'am."

"Then I'll wake them up," Lucy gritted and shoved past the poor woman to ascend the stairs. She saw the maid fork to the right of the landing, but she was beyond caring. She opened door after door until the room at the end proved occupied. A lump with a messy mop of straw-colored hair lay still as death on the bed, and she could feel the sobs hacking at her chest.

If Junior, for all his faults, lay in bed here at his father's house, then there was no way in hell he thought Ben was alive. The awful reality pressed upon her, and all the grief she'd suppressed for days surged forward.

She needed answers, and she needed them now.

"Junior," she shouted, "Junior, wake up. Please, you have to tell me what happened. Wake up!" She shook him gently, then harder, but he didn't respond. Didn't even lift the covers off his thin, pale face. He was warm and alive but acted dead. Worry added to her hysteria, and Lucy ripped the blanket off him, ignoring his nightclothes.

Rough hands grabbed her by the shoulders and wrenched her away.

"What in blazes do you think you're doing?" The roar directed into her ear stunned her for only a moment before she struggled out of John's grip.

They faced each other, both bedraggled and sporting deep purple shadows beneath their eyes. His hair was unkempt, flattened on one side, and his mustache was uncombed. Her hat was askew and her lips were bloodless.

"I need answers, Mr. Stone." She gestured helplessly, her face a grimace of pain. "No one has contacted me since Sol sent the telegram that you were bringing Junior home. What happened three days ago?"

"You received the same wire I did. The damned fool went into the river and got carried away." He had not lowered his voice one decibel. The man's anger was so out of place that Lucy stared.

She forged on. "Junior has said nothing at all on the trip back?"

"No, he has not, and we are all tired and need some shut-eye."

"What about the search party? What did they say when you were there?"

John turned his back on her pleading and made his way to Junior's bed. Rough hands turned gentle as he covered the boy with the bedspread. Lucy watched in growing hysteria. One son was assumed dead, certainly, but so long as the Stones got their golden boy back, safe and sound, they could turn a blind eye to the grief of others. From behind them, an unkind voice spoke in the doorway.

"I must ask you to leave, Miss Ricci. My husband and son are exhausted. If we have any news, we'll send someone." Loretta Stone stood in the shadow of the hallway, fully dressed and sinister.

Fists clenched, Lucy glared at the woman from beneath lowered brows. "My name is not 'Miss Ricci', much as you wish otherwise. And you cannot keep Junior drugged on laudanum forever. I'll be back tomorrow morning."

Mrs. Stone stepped into the room, her jowls trembling. "You will not be welcomed back on this ranch, you have harassed us every day regardless that we have also lost someone we loved, my nephew—"

"Harassed!" Lucy shouted with laughter that didn't reach her eyes. "I've come every day for word of my husband."

"Who is most assuredly dead," Mrs. Stone screeched. "Junior has said so on multiple occasions on their journey here, which is why he is resting now, as it upsets him. You have no further reason to be in our house!"

Who is most assuredly dead? *Dead*. Lucy flinched as the barb struck.

The awful woman dropped the word like it didn't mean everything.

Again, an image of Ben's body, lost somewhere, alone, materialized before her. Her worst fear was becoming realized.

"God's eyes, woman," John choked behind her.

Mrs. Stone blinked, and guilt slackened her face. "John, dear."

Lucy couldn't remain in this room for another moment with these horrible, bitter people. Before she walked out the door, she paused beside Junior's mother.

"You disgust me. Neither of you deserved Ben."

There was plenty more to say, but she was sick in her heart and her soul, so she left. She rode home without seeing, handed her horse to Crew without thanking him, and walked upstairs to her bedroom in a trance. She didn't remember opening the armoire and grabbing an armful of Ben's shirts, and she did not awake hours later when Crew and Tia checked on her and found her laying in a pile of Ben's clothing, fast asleep.

HOOFBEATS FROM OUTSIDE roused Lucy.

She hadn't been asleep, not really. She'd simply lain there on the bed and clothes in a stupor that felt no hunger or ambition, only the suffocating weight of sad hopelessness interspersed with feeling nothing at all. But hoofbeats meant people were riding over at a quick pace. The urgency could only mean one thing: news of Ben.

Lucy rolled out of bed with dizzying swiftness, stumbling only twice.

Her feet met the stairs with clumsy force, and she burst onto the porch before the two horses in the yard had halted their trot. She blinked rapidly at the brightness of the outdoors. It was Junior and John. She counted back the days in her head. It had been five days since she'd received the wire about Ben, two since the altercation at the Stone Ranch. A glance at the cloudy sky showed it was midmorning.

"Is there news?" she croaked. Hope, fear, and mild dehydration turned her vocal cords to rust.

John stared at her for a beat, pausing. Then, "No. There's no news."

Junior didn't look at her at all.

They dismounted and handed the reins to Crew, who'd come out of the barn, slow and wary.

That insidious heaviness had been waiting for its moment, and sensing its chance, wrapped itself tight around Lucy. She folded her arms and squeezed her eyes and mouth shut. Unable to meet the men's eyes, she turned and wiped at her face.

"I'll put some coffee on." It had been days since she'd made a meal or a pot of coffee, but her hands were willing even if her mind was not. She walked mechanically to the kitchen, watched her pale fingers fill the pot with water from the reservoir, measure out grounds, and set the heavy kettle on the warm stove. Crew must have lit it while she'd slept. When Junior and John shut the door behind them, she was stoking the fire, composed once more. "What brings you here today?" She didn't really want to know.

She didn't care.

John hung up his hat and coat on the rack near the door and sat heavily in the chair Ben usually occupied. "We figured we'd come check on ya, that's all."

Her eyes stuck to the chair the older man sat in. He was rocking it back on two legs, and it creaked with every motion. It had creaked that same way when she and Ben had made love on it months ago. Forcing her gaze away, she stood stiff-backed.

"I'm fine."

"You don't look fine."

"Father," Junior murmured. He sounded wispy, like a ghost, but the censure was there.

Lucy looked down at herself. She wore the clothes of two days before, the brown shirtwaist wrinkled and unbuttoned to the collarbones that stood out in sharp relief. Her burgundy skirt was creased beyond belief, and her hair was matted and standing on end, falling halfway down her back. Her eyes slid to John while she re-tucked the few pins that remained.

"Should I be fine, Mr. Stone? Should I just carry on like it was any other day, without a care in the world?"

The chair legs hit the floor with a thump. "Things still need to be done around here."

Something foul was rising in her. At that moment, she hated John Stone, more than anyone she'd ever hated before. This was the hatred one didn't feel for oneself. It was the hatred you felt in defense of someone you loved. Her words were out before she could hold them in. "You want me to do what you did after Ben's mother died? Just go forward as if my husband never existed?"

"There's no need for that," John growled, his expression curdling. "I didn't come here to bandy around like roosters."

"Well, you did not come here to check on me, either. What is the true reason for your visit?"

It was quiet for several moments, and water hissed onto the stove top when the coffee started to boil. She took it off the stove with a periwinkle dishtowel and set it on a pot holder on the work table. She brought out mugs, sugar, and cream while John continued.

"My lawyer drew up some papers yesterday. I need you to sign a few things."

"What?" Junior and Lucy asked in unison. For the first time, Lucy and Junior shared a glance.

He looked terribly young. His hair was shaggy and unwashed, his eyes were all over shadows, and his cheekbones jutted over hollowed cheeks. "You didn't mention any paperwork. You said we were just coming here to check on her."

John ignored that to draw papers seemingly out of nowhere. He spread the thin stack open, smoothing the creases. "Got a pen?"

Once a pen was reluctantly acquired, she sat perched on the edge of the chair, alert. "What do those papers consist of?"

"Does Ben have a living will?" John asked, face blank as any lawyer.

Lucy's brows knitted and she shook her head. "I don't know."

She hadn't even thought to look.

"He tell you that he came to me for this land, and that I gave him some conditions?"

"Yes, he did." She was getting a bad feeling about this meeting.

"I'd sell him this house and land so long as he worked for me during round-up and cattle drives." He continued in this vein, telling the particulars that Lucy already knew about from Ben, and some she didn't, until her head was swimming. "—and upon the event of death, the land goes right back to Junior, and any property that comes with it."

Junior's voice was only a little stronger when he repeated, "Father."

His weak interjection was drowned out by the force of Lucy's, "No!"

"It's right here in writing," John said, eyebrows raised at her tone. He attempted to turn the pages around, but she was already ripping them away.

For several minutes her eyes read over every line, retracing certain sentences that were over-worded and confusing until she understood. John made himself a cup of coffee while he waited, and was halfway through his second mug before Lucy looked up. The hate in her eyes was shocking, and he set his cup down, preparing to do battle.

"This has no legal standing now that Ben's married," she gritted.

"My lawyer says different."

"Oh, does he?" She was sneering at him, almost spitting like an alley cat. "Nowhere in these documents does it mention where the property goes in the event that Ben marries *before* his death. A death which was not confirmed well enough for my standards, anyway!"

"Married or not, little lady, it says right there if Ben dies, then the land and all property goes to my boy," John shouted, pushing back his chair.

"I don't want it," Junior whispered into his empty cup, shoulders shaking. "It belongs to Lucy."

"The hell it does. No little girl that's been on this ranch for a single year gets the land that's been in my name for thirty." Mr. Stone stood up and snatched the papers from Lucy's bloodless fingers. "Either way, the terms of the conditions were never completed. He never finished the trail drive, did he?"

For a moment, Lucy and Junior stared at him with twin expressions of shock and repulsion.

"How can you talk like that about—" But Lucy couldn't continue. Her throat convulsed, and she bit her trembling lip.

Junior stood up, and his face was so red, it practically pulsed. He was crying.

"What the hell's the matter with you?" he shouted at John.

His father blinked, and for a moment, the heartless old bastard displayed enough emotion to look human. "It's just business, son."

"Well, I don't want any part of it," Junior yelled hoarsely. He scrubbed his eyes but was far from composed. "We—we came to check on Lucy, that's what Ben would've wanted, and now you're—you can't just take his home and his land away from her like this, it's wrong!"

"Christ, turn off the waterworks," derided John, scorn replacing emotion. "You act like your damned mama when you do this. You forget your brother high-tailed it like a lily-livered coward, now you wanna cry over him like he was some sort of saint. You even ran off to Dallas when you thought he was there, but he wasn't, was he? And I had to bail you outta jail because you didn't have a penny to your name to pay your hotel fee. And look at you now. Cryin' over a dead man that didn't give two shits about you."

"Get out of my house." Lucy had heard enough. Junior's tears had wrought her own, but her teeth were bared, and all she could picture was the derringer in her side drawer upstairs. She'd kill him. If this foul old man said one more thing about Ben, she'd kill him and send the body to his pathetic wife and not think twice.

Something in her eyes must have expressed her thoughts.

John turned to the door. "Come on, Junior."

"I'm not comin' with you."

John's fist clenched on the doorknob. "You're not stayin' here. Come home to your ma."

"I'll come home when I'm damned good and ready, you sorry sumbitch." Junior was trembling, his face almost puce now.

Whipping around, John was in front of Junior and backhanding him to the floor before Lucy could draw a breath.

"Stop!" she screeched. "Stop it, just leave!"

The door opened, and Crew was there, drawing his gun on John.

"The lady said get out." It was all the more terrifying because of how slow and conversational Crew suggested it. "I brought your horse around."

Hair askew and hat on the floor, John froze, plucked his hat from the floor, and pointed a gnarled finger at Lucy. "I'll be back next week with my lawyer. I suggest you get your things packed. And you," he didn't quite point at Crew, "you're fired. You love the lady so much? Let her pay you from now on." He slammed the door so hard behind him that the windows rattled.

After a glance to make sure Lucy was well, Crew opened the door and followed right behind, gun still in hand.

Lucy scrambled around the table to help Junior up, fighting tears. "He talks about Ben like he wasn't his son, then treats the one he has left like dirt, and I hate him for it."

"I do, too." Junior touched his jaw and winced. He looked like hell, worse than she did if possible.

If Ben were here right now, he'd force Junior to eat something, force him to get a grip.

Taking a shuddering breath, trying to find that steel that had disappeared from her backbone until just five minutes ago, she said, "I'll cook us some dinner. Drink your coffee. You look exhausted."

There was plenty to eat. Mr. Crew must have stocked the stores and pantry full in the hope to get her to eat. The first knife of guilt pricked her. She had worried everyone on the ranch, had ignored their grief as though hers was the only one of importance. She was mildly tempted to call Crew in to eat, but an uncontrollable need to have a private talk with Junior nagged at her. When their warm plates were set before them, Junior and Lucy ate for only a few minutes before halting, already full with half the food remaining.

"Junior," she inquired as soft and gentle as she could stand. "Will you tell me what happened? I tried coming days ago, but your mother ran me off."

"Yeah. Yeah, I heard about that." His cutlery rattled on his plate and his hands disappeared to clench beneath the table. "I'm sorry, Lucy. I'm so sorry."

He sounded so broken that she covered her eyes. Now that he was going to tell her, she didn't want to know. But she didn't stop him.

"We got in an argument. I'd...I'd been making it real hard for him the whole cattle drive. I was—" he broke off, cleared his throat, "—I was drinking a lot, not doin' my job much good a'tall. He was embarrassed by me. When we reached the Red River, I'd already lost him two hundred head, and I knew Father would blame him instead of me. So I kept drinking. B—He got mad, and threw my whiskey in the river. Leonard went in after it, like he was going to get it. I went in after Leonard. The river was flooded, I don't know what I was thinkin', maybe I could stop him, turn his horse around. He was drunker'n me."

Lucy dropped her hands from her eyes and asked, incredulous, "You what? You went into a flooded river—Ben went after you, didn't he?" Her voice shook.

"Yeah, he did." Junior was crying. "He came after me and turned my horse around and I made it to the bank. Leonard got swept off, and it looked like Ben was gonna make it back to the bank, but there was a lot of stuff in the river floatin' around, and a tree knocked him off Reb." He couldn't go on after that.

She shook her head. "And then what happened? They went under?"

"No," he sniffed. "The current took him to the middle of the river, but Reb got held against a bunch of floating branches and he didn't make it. Sol and I tried to lasso Ben out, but he couldn't fight the current."

"How can that be, he's always been so strong. He's the strongest man I know." It was almost a shout.

Now Junior shook his head, swallowing. "No, that river was fast, he was in a riptide. He went around the corner. It was already half-dark and I never saw him again. We even rode miles and miles down the river, calling for him, but it was dark by that time and we couldn't see anything and had to ride back for a lantern. There was just, nothing. He was gone." He paused for a moment, and whispered, "The last thing I heard him yell was, 'Somebody get Reb'. I couldn't even do that."

Could she be having a heart attack? It felt like she was.

"I can't believe this," she whispered and pressed the periwinkle dishtowel into her face. It smelled like hot metal and singed cotton. "God Junior, why did you go in that river in the first place? You knew Ben would go in and save you, he's always saving you."

"No, I didn't think—"

"That's just it, you never do think, and Ben's the one that always suffers for it! Now he's dead, and you come here, and, you bring your father to take everything away." She was breathing fast and hard and stood up to pace. Hysteria was taking over her train of thought. All she could think about was how if only Junior hadn't gone, Ben would be alive. "You should have just stayed! If you had stayed at the ranch like he'd asked you, he would never have gone in that river! But you had to be a 'man', and go, didn't you? You wanted to be a man, but you're only a child. A little boy that plays with the men and goes to whorehouses with daddy's money and makes his brother's life a living hell! And now, now he's *dead*, damn you." Tears nearly blinded her, but she swiped them furiously with the towel.

Junior was shaking with sobs, the blue of his eyes so achingly like Ben's she had to look away. Regret for the words she'd said wasn't enough to take back the truth of them, and she didn't stop him when he stood and sprinted outside toward the barn.

For half an hour, she leaned over the sink, head bowed and hurting.

"Oh, Ben," she choked. "I'm so sorry, darling. I know why you did it, I do. You love him more than anything. But did you have to die?" She bit her hand at the pain and suffered through the wracking sobs that tore from her chest, more animal than human.

Was Ben there with her, watching her? The prospect stunned her.

Oh, God, had he heard her screaming those horrible things at Junior?

Even the smallest possibility of her husband, standing there in spirit while she'd shouted at the person he'd loved most, brought the most crushing shame upon her. Ben would hate her if he'd been there. It didn't make her despise Junior any less, but panic ate at her that she'd done something unforgivable in Ben's eyes.

She had to fix it.

Ben's spirit would never forgive her if she didn't take what she said back.

"What have I done?" she whispered to herself. "Ben, what did I do? I'll make it right. I swear I'll make it right."

She splashed water on her face and took deep, calming breaths. While she walked outside to the barn, she imagined Ben was with her every step of the way.

The barn doors were closed; Junior must have shut them when he ran inside.

"Junior?" she called brokenly. She should shout that she was sorry, but couldn't get the words out. It was still too soon.

There was no noise. The horses and milk cows were in the fenced-in pasture grazing, and it was quiet and dusty. A piece of hay fell on her, brushing past her nose from the loft above. She glanced up at the dark eave where hay was stored, and made her way to the ladder. It had been knocked down, and she wondered briefly if Junior had pushed it away, wanting to be alone.

Spirit Ben folded his arms, frowning at her.

"You're right," she murmured inaudibly. Junior's privacy be darned. He deserved an apology from her.

Distantly, she wondered if she hadn't completely cracked and gone mad.

Heaving the sturdy ladder up would have been easier a week ago before she'd made a home in her bed and had refused to eat, but she managed to prop it up against the lip of the loft. She climbed it and called for Junior again.

Again, there was nothing but silence. Maybe he wasn't up here after all—

A noise set the hairs on her arms at attention, and Lucy held her breath, listening.

Creak. Creak. Creak. Thump.

She ran.

To the wall of hay bales.

Around them.

To a pair of kicking, struggling legs in midair.

Lucy looked up blankly for only two seconds while Junior hung by a rope from the rafter before she screamed and flew into action. She wrapped her arms around his shins and ankles, the only area on him she could reach. He stiffened his legs and scrambled at the rope above him, creating enough slack around his neck to take desperate, wheezing breaths.

"Help, somebody help!" Lucy had always had a set of lungs on her, and her screams echoed loud enough to make one's ears bleed in the rafters around them.

"Mizz Lucy?" Crew was stomping up the ladder.

"Oh, God, Crew, hurry!"

The seconds were hours. Her legs trembled and the desperate whistles of Junior's breathing echoed around them.

Crew searched for what felt like endless moments, found a crate, and slammed it on the ground next to Junior. He stood on it, tried to uncoil the noose from Junior's neck, gave up, and unsheathed a work knife and sawed at it like a madman.

Lucy squeezed Junior's buckling knees tighter, feeling him slipping. He was heavy, about thirty pounds shy of two hundred, but she was strong, and she held him long enough for the last fibers to separate from the rope. With a grunt, Crew caught him and the three of them tumbled to the straw-covered floor.

While Junior coughed and took desperate breaths, she crawled towards him, checking his throat and purple face, and babbling.

"I'm sorry Junior, God I'm sorry, I didn't mean it, I didn't mean it—" Over and over she apologized, shushing him when he whooped in breath after breath, trying to get a word in.

"Couldn't—do it," he gasped. "I couldn't."

"I know you couldn't." She was crying and holding him, rocking him back and forth on the floor of the loft like a child. "It's my fault, Junior. Please don't leave me. I lost Ben, I can't lose you too."

After that, he clung to her, face buried in her bosom like a child while she stroked his hair, whispering assurances. If she hadn't made it in time.... He had changed his mind. If she hadn't come up the ladder and seen him struggling, if she'd waited five minutes longer, he would have struggled until he'd finally died. And no one would know that he'd changed his mind, that he had decided to live, one moment too late.

She pulled back and forced Junior to look at her. His eyes looked bloody; the capillaries had burst around the irises. His color was fading back to normal, but his neck was raw from the rough rope and covered in bleeding scratches from his fingernails. Lucy's chin wobbled. "Oh, Junior, please forgive me."

"Nothin' to forgive. I just hope one day you can forgive me." His voice was the merest whisper, as though suffering from laryngitis.

She shook her head and grasped his face in her hands. "You're the only good thing of Ben I have left. I want you to stay here. I don't care if you own the land, just don't ever do that again." Her eyes flicked to the swinging rope. "We stick together, from now on. That's how Ben would've wanted it."

The despair dissipated from Junior's features as he listened to her, and when her words sunk in, he swallowed and nodded. "We stick together. For Ben."

"Mrs. Stone?" Crew's tone was questioning, and his eyes were affixed to the slight sway of the rope.

"Crew." She turned to him, still holding Junior. "I need you to get that rope from the rafter and burn it."

It was the second time in as many minutes that she hadn't put a 'mister' in front of his name, and he stared. "Yes'm."

"And Crew? Don't tell anyone about this."

He sobered immediately and nodded. "You got my word, ma'am."

The rope was cut down and burned in the yard until there was nothing but ashes floating in the wind.

28

CHAPTER TWENTY-EIGHT

Six nights earlier...

Ben followed Junior and Leonard into the floodwaters, ignoring the shouts of alarm behind him.

He'd only felt as afraid once before as he did then. When Lucy had gotten in that stage wreck, he'd tasted the acrid fear in his mouth, dry and astringent. It was happening again now, the helplessness that made a man's intelligence impotent and limbs weak.

"Junior!" he roared and kicked Reb hard in the ribs.

The only thing that saved Junior was his horse.

The mare reared up, balking at the strength of the current against her legs. Ben caught her harness and turned her sharply by the bit. Afraid and in pain, the mare shot in the direction of the bank behind them and managed to gain a sure footing while Junior clung to the saddle, cursing. Ben breathed a sigh of relief that went deeper than his bones and turned to look for Leonard. He was gone.

No, *there*.

Leonard's fancy chestnut thoroughbred was fighting against the current, the man a low figure pasted to the pommel. They were gone within seconds, submerging beneath a sucking undercurrent. When the horse reemerged seconds later, she was without a rider and was soon out of sight around a sharp bend.

Regret was sharp. The possibility that Leonard would make it out alive was nil. He'd have to lead the men downstream and see if they could find him and lasso him up.

Ben had just managed to turn Reb in the rough waters when he caught a glimpse of men rushing toward him, shouting and pointing upstream. The water was knee deep to Ben, and chest deep to Reb, and neither saw the dead tree floating half-submerged in the current until it knocked the gelding off his feet. They toppled sideways, cold, muddy water rushing over their heads. The water was freezing and alive. The current grabbed at his clothes and pushed into his nostrils.

Afraid that Reb would drown with him in the saddle, Ben managed to pull his boots out of the stirrups underwater and swam up. He broke out of the water with a gasp and searched around for his horse. He saw a pair of soaking wet ears surface, followed by a desperately bobbing head.

"Reb," he called and tried to swim toward the animal. The current pulled him further into the center of the river, and even though he knew better, he fought it. And when Reb was pushed toward an enormous pile of foaming, floating debris, Ben screamed as the horse was sucked against it.

He could only see his horse's head from the water, and then, he couldn't see Reb at all.

"Somebody get Reb!" he screamed hoping someone, anyone, could hear him. Knowing it was futile.

"Ben! Hold on Ben!" Junior and Sol were shouting at him from across the expanse of water. They struggled in vain past the hundreds of cattle that crowded along the bank, Sol throwing his lasso into the water again and again. Ben tried to swim close enough to grab it, and he knew they had failed when the grassy bank ascended and turned into a muddy cliff. He could see his friend and brother hollering, trying to circle it, but Ben soon disappeared around a sharp curve in the river.

The banks of the river had turned into steep bluffs on both sides. For a while, he floated on his back to conserve his energy, then, taking deep breaths, he began to swim with renewed strength. After several arduous minutes, he grew close enough that he reached a steep wall of mud, roots spidering out of the vertical cliff. He managed to cling to one of the larger roots, but it gave way.

The current was changing, Ben realized in alarm. This close to the edge of the bluff, the weight of the river pushed against him with twice the force. It was dark now, only the faintest light glowing deep blue from the west. Visibility was almost gone, and his lungs and muscles burned from the constant force of keeping his body afloat. He thought of Reb as the undertow sucked him under, foam filling his nostrils, his last hope that his friend could forgive him.

IT WAS DARK as pitch.

Ben could hear water lapping around him, could feel its unknown depths swirling gently around his legs. He was wrapped around something simultaneously hard and soggy. It smelled of mold and algae. Something jagged pressed into his side, and wracking pains in his chest and lungs suffused him. He couldn't see anything, and his head felt foggy and tender. Had he hit it on something? He couldn't remember being this cold before, and when he coughed, it was desperate and deep from the lungs.

The toes of his bare feet brushed against something, and he managed to raise his head. Blindly, he felt around with his feet, then loosened his hold on the slimy log he'd floated on for hours to get a better grip. The sandy bottom of the Red River veered to the right, on the Texas side, and he shoved the log away and swam with a swiftness borne from terror to a washed-out sandbar. When he reached bare earth, he whispered his thanks to God, crawled several yards away from the water onto rock and grass, and fell asleep.

HE DIDN'T WAKE until the sun was halfway across the sky.

A wet cough overtook his body at constant intervals, and his mind still felt muddled. Ben remembered what had happened, but when he stood up to walk, he felt disoriented, unsure where to go or what to do.

People, he decided. He needed to find people.

Twice he stopped walking in no particular direction to vomit river water, and on each occurrence, he moaned. His head felt like it'd split open from the force of the purging, and there must have been hot coals living in his lungs fit to set him afire every time he coughed. His boots and stockings had long made their new residence at the bottom of the river, and his bare feet paid for it. What he wouldn't give to be lying in bed with Lucy, or even sitting with her on the porch at the end of a long day.

She would be upset about Reb.

What day was it?

He wondered if the hands would wait for him to walk back.

For hours he went on like this, the aimless wandering only interrupted when the clouds fogging his brain cleared enough for him to pause and blink. A shack appeared over a rise, and the floating white linen on the line called to him like a lodestone. He expected to see Lucy behind one of the billowing sheets, humming a bawdy song rather than a gospel, but he had to stop and hunch over to hack one of his lungs out. Instead of a lung, a small bit of mucus came out, pale brown in color.

"Ho, there!" The voice sounded over-loud and grating.

Ben winced and glanced up. An old fellow in striped overalls and a weathered straw hat stood several yards from him. A shotgun was leveled in his direction. Ben raised his hands and shivered. Which was strange, considering the sun was so intense he could feel the painful tightness of a sunburn on his face.

"State your business," the man ordered, jabbing the air with his gun.

"Where's the nearest town?"

The gun lowered an inch. "Town's in the direction you came from, mister." It was said in such disbelief that it almost sounded suspicious. "You got business in town?"

Ben managed a weak nod and put one of his raised hands over his face. His head was blistering to the touch. "Yessir, I was knocked off my horse in the Red River yesterday. I need to get word to my men—" He was forced to stop for another cough. Nothing came out this time.

"Who's that, Lenny?" An old woman stood at the door of their shack, but at the sight of Ben, rushed down the steps and wound around her skinny husband.

"Now, dadblame it, Norah, don't go gettin' close to him, he could be faking it so he can rob us!"

"He ain't going to rob us, just look at the state of him. We should fetch Doc Robinson." The short, plump woman felt all over Ben's forehead and cheeks with the back of her hand while Lenny hemmed and hawed in the background.

"I call him out here, he'll be 'spectin' money that we ain't got," Lenny harrumphed.

"I have money," Ben wheezed, pressing a fist into his sternum. God Almighty, but it felt like fire was in his lungs. Breathing was getting harder and harder. "If you could just take me to town, I'll pay you both."

Norah was shaking her head. "No, you're in no fit condition for a ride to town. Lenny, help me get the poor soul inside. He needs some dry clothes and rest."

Ben didn't remember much of the next few days.

His fever ran hot and forced him into a weakened, permanently exhausted state. When the cold metal of a stethoscope pressed into his chest and back while he struggled to breathe, he wasn't aware. A few times he awoke enough to obey the orders of an old woman with a cloud of thin, white hair. He drank bitter water, held his head over a steaming basin of boiled vinegar water and herbs, and raised his arms for a mustard cast. Many times, he asked to send word to town, but the well-meaning Norah only hushed him and explained they didn't have any writing tools and to wait for the doctor to come back at the end of the week.

His coughing grew worse, and with it came foul-smelling, pale-green sputum that increased in volume on the third day, and subsided on the fourth. His lungs no longer felt full of Hellfire and were only tight if he breathed too deeply.

On the fifth day, his fever had regressed to a mild, annoying thing, and he woke up before the sun. After frowning at the unfamiliar beams of the tiny shack, he noted two things. First, he was ravenous for a hot, bloody steak. His stomach complained loud and insistent. Second, if he didn't get to town and send a wire immediately, his family would be notified of his disappearance and would think the worst.

He imagined what Junior must be feeling, and worse, Lucy, and the terrifying thought sent him into full-blown panic. He shot off the pallet on the floor, slower and weaker than a grandfather snail, and saw the old woman at the stove cooking weak beef tea and coffee.

"Mrs. Cleary, how long have I been sickly?" he croaked, and the suddenness of his voice made her shriek and fling a ladle full of simmering broth on the floor.

"Oh, have mercy, you scared me," she laughed weakly, holding her plump middle.

"Please, ma'am, how long?" He was in a pair of ill-fitting longjohns and snatched up a ragged quilt from his pallet. He smelled and needed to use the outhouse with a sweat-inducing urgency.

"Bout, hm, five days now. You had me right worried, young man. The Doc said as you might not pull through, but gave me a list of instructions and I followed them to the letter. He said you had pneumony from all that river water, that you'd need plenty of rest. And won't my Lenny be awful surprised to see you up and about." Her words were so rapid he had trouble following, but no one could mistake her smugness in the latter.

Lenny. He was the old man that had threatened to shoot Ben on the first day, and if his memory wasn't wrong, had also muttered threats to bodily harm him every day since if he proved to be some penniless drifter.

Damn, most of his money had been in his saddlebags with Reb when the horse had gone under. The pain of that made Ben close his eyes. That horse had been a wonderful, steady friend for several years of his life, gone in an instant. He'd have plenty of time to grieve him later. Now, he needed to get to town. A few greenbacks were usually kept in the inner pocket of his jacket. He couldn't remember if he'd been wearing it when he'd dragged himself out of the river. The stabbing pain in his feet made him recall losing his boots and stockings, then walking who knows how many miles barefoot.

"Where's my clothes? I should have some money in my jacket."

Her liver-spotted hand went to her mouth. "Oh. I washed it, dear. I didn't find anything in the pockets." She went to the corner of the room and dug in a basket. A stack of laundered clothes came out, the jacket on top.

He took it from her gratefully, and opened his jacket, breathing a sigh when he reached into the narrow inner pocket and felt a wad of damp paperbacks. With delicate fingers, he pulled half of them apart and set them on the mantle to finish drying. The other half, he tucked back into the pocket.

Norah was looking at the money with round eyes. "I didn't even think to look there," she admitted.

"That's for you and your husband, for all your trouble." He nodded toward the mantle and added. "I'll give you more after I visit the bank; they'll wire me money. You have any old boots of Mr. Cleary's?"

Speechless for once, Norah nodded and went outside, grabbing the oldest, saddest pair of boots Ben had ever seen. They were cracked around the soles and the tops were folded over like dog's ears. Nonetheless, he gratefully donned them after washing up and dressing. Lenny Cleary must have had long, narrow feet. The boots pinched.

After giving him instructions to town, Norah grasped his hand and smiled. "I'm so glad you made it through, Mr. Stone. God was watching over you, that's certain."

Ben squeezed back, careful of the fragile fingers. "He couldn't have done it without you, Mrs. Cleary. I've never had a better doctor in all my life."

She beamed.

He followed the road to town before Lenny made it home for dinner, and only the awful, pinching boots kept his feet from running.

JUNIOR FELT POORLY.

Lucy could tell. It must take a lot out of a man to almost die by his own hand.

Despite his melancholia, he worked like a dog from sunup to sundown. She was still angry enough to let him. It was his penance.

No matter her conviction that forgiving him was what Ben would have wanted, she struggled against the deep pull of loathing and resentment that Junior was alive and Ben was not. She recognized the feelings and ignored them to the best of her abilities. Still, she caught herself pausing before making Junior's plate, or pouring hot water in his washbasin, her lips tight and back stiff.

He never sat in Ben's chair, that was one consolation.

Forcing herself from the depths of her feelings, Lucy started living again. Not even her antipathy blinded her from how thin Junior had become, rawboned instead of strapping. He'd withdrawn from his dependency on alcohol but hadn't pulled through unscathed. She urged him to eat until he half-heartedly complied. At Lucy's insistence, he'd taken the guest room farthest from hers, and she could hear him tossing around at night during her own bouts of insomnia.

The loneliness of knowing Ben was dead was mountainous compared to the lonesomeness during the cattle drive when she'd known he'd been alive. Imagining that Ben was with her helped. His phantom presence urged her to be a better person and help his brother.

Ben's shade never spoke, but he was everywhere she turned.

Leaning in the corner by the stove.

Sitting in his chair during her morning coffee.

She had whole conversations with him in her head but his answers were smiles or knowing glimmers in his bright blue eyes.

She felt crazy.

If she was, she kept it to herself. Imagining Ben's spirit as a glowing halo on his pillow, filling the empty spot across the bare sheets, helped her sleep. Melancholia was a strange phenomenon. She was lethargic, and yet her mind raced. The scenarios and what-ifs exhausted her, nipped at her heels like hell hounds, giving her no peace. Often, she'd be in the middle of doing something—some mundane task like flipping an egg cooked the way Ben liked, or finding a man's dirty stocking under the bed—and the force of her sudden weeping would bend her over.

Junior, Lucy knew, was consumed by his guilt. She tried very hard not to feel satisfaction in his pain, she truly did. That's not what forgiveness was. When he looked, unseeing, out the window, so pale beneath his tan, Lucy knew he was seeing the Red River. Then he'd blink, catch her staring, and give her a tight smile before going outside to work the horses. He'd taken to wearing one of Ben's kerchiefs around his neck to hide the worst of his wounds. Above the faded red cloth, worn soft from age and washings, were long, ragged scratches.

They made Lucy's eyes smart, pushed some of that crushing hate from her chest, and replaced it with compassion.

They would both shoot worried glances at each other when the other wasn't looking, two young people, brought together by the death of a man who'd seemed so immortal. Beyond Lucy's bitterness and Junior's self-loathing, their previous differences disappeared beneath a more important truth: what would they do now that Ben was gone?

On the eighth day of Ben's death, she heard Junior pause at her bedroom doorway. She'd been rummaging through papers in the bedside table for the third time since John had made threats.

Lucy had torn the house apart for a living will.

"What're you doing?" His hoarse voice sounded genuinely curious, so Lucy glanced up and motioned him to the bed. She'd poured the contents of the drawer onto the quilt.

"I'm trying to find the deed or any papers that I can bring into town today to show Papa's lawyer."

Junior sat on the other side of the pile and frowned when he noticed she'd donned a fashionable black dress with a matching jacket and hat perched jauntily on her head.

"You didn't tell me you were going to town. And dressed like that."

"Dressed like what, Junior?" she sighed, and for a moment, a bit of life entered her face long enough to scrunch her nose. "I'm in mourning. This is my only suitable garment." She swallowed a lump and pretended to look through some envelopes until her voice felt steadier. "I need to look professional. Anything to do with money or property entails one to look their best."

He nodded and plucked a folded piece of paper up. It had neat writing in blue ink, and the paper was well-worn with many creases. "I'm going with you."

"That is quite alright." No. She wanted to do this alone. He was the last person she wanted riding with her at that moment.

"I want to."

"It's not necessary." Her voice was very cool.

Junior's was hot. "Necessary or not, I'm going. We're family, and I don't care if you hate my guts, I'm not going to be pushed aside. Let me help."

She stared at the wall in front of her, hot anger pushing mean words against her lips, begging to be released. A welcome mirage wavered in front of her. Shook his head. Finally, she lied, "I do not hate your guts."

His snort was explosive. "Go lie to someone else."

Lucy whipped her head at him. He was staring at the folded paper in his hands. She saw Ben's name written on it in her handwriting and her eyes widened. Lightning fast, she snagged it from his fingers and shoved it under the pile of discarded papers in her lap.

"What was that?" Junior narrowed his eyes suspiciously.

None of your business, she thought nastily.

Be nice, the mirage's eyes admonished.

"Ah, um, something I wrote to Ben." She blushed, and sucked her lips between her teeth, trying to stifle the tell-tale urge to cry.

There was an awkward silence as Junior pieced it together. He remembered now, it seemed. It had been the naughty letter he'd read at the picnic. Chagrin replaced his anger, and he stood.

"I'm getting ready for town. Don't leave without me." It was the question in his voice more than anything that made her nod.

WHILE THEY SIPPED coffee at the kitchen work table ten minutes later, they debated ways to thwart John's plans in exhaustive detail. The sad truth was that they were young and had nearly zero experience in legal proceedings.

"We'll talk to the lawyer today, the bank, and then the...the reverend. We need to make plans for a funeral service." Lucy took a deep, shaky breath and continued, "Then we can stay the night at Papa's. He and Minnie have been worried, and I feel bad for ignoring everyone for so many days. Before we come back home, we can pick up supplies. Crew said the horse feed is getting low."

We, we, we. She would rather have been discussing this with Ben, but the boy was alone except for her and his wretched parents. She needed to include her husband's brother in her life, now.

Ben's spirit nodded in his seat across from her in approval.

"Lucy, I need you to tell me the truth." Junior shifted in his seat, diagonal from hers.

Discomfited, she asked, "The truth about what?"

"Do you hate me?"

She clenched her jaw.

"I need to know."

Lucy couldn't stand to look at him. Instead, she looked at the empty chair across from her, willing Ben's presence with her bereaved mind. She imagined Ben leaning forward on his elbows, fisted hands pressed against his mouth. Waiting. Her eyes pricked. Why was this so hard? Forgiving was so hard.

Did she hate Junior?

She thought about it, then shook her head. "I-I hate your father. I shouldn't hate at all, but if he were to fall over dead in front of me, I would not blink an eyelid."

Junior was very still at that. He looked at his lap, but let her finish.

"No," she said with finality. "No, I don't hate you. But, it's hard to look at you. I'm trying to forgive you. Ben would want that. He loved you—God, he loved you more than anything. Did you know that he talked of you when we first met? You, and his mother. The two people he loved most in the world. He said he was coming back for you. He was tired of running, like a coward."

Junior closed his eyes tight, but Lucy couldn't stop.

"He told me the thing he regretted most in the world was leaving you with your father. That he should have just taken you with him. But he was scared John would come after the two of you, that he'd get the law involved, and that he'd perhaps, really never get to see you again."

"Did he tell you why he ran?" Junior's voice was thick.

"He hated himself," she whispered, and something connected, and she closed her eyes so she wouldn't see Ben smile proudly at her. *Oh, Ben.* "He hated himself for his ruined marriage, what everyone thought he was, and he was ashamed. But he said, what ate at him the most," she struggled to think back, to use Ben's terminology, "was that running didn't make him less ashamed. It made him more of a coward. So, he knew that to be any semblance of an honorable man, he had to come back home and make amends with you, and give you a life you deserved."

"And I shot that all to hell, didn't I?" Junior's voice was barely recognizable.

"Junior—" she admonished.

"No, it's true. Every chance I could, I brought it up that he left. And when he got with you, I don't know what happened, it felt like I was losing him again, and I'd never fixed it with him the first time. I'm a damned fool." His fist struck the table, and Lucy jumped with the dishes. "I wish it had been me that died. He should be here with you, Luce, not me!"

Now she was angry.

"What, so that he could be here, killing himself over your death like you are over his?" she cried, and Junior looked up blearily, so unhappy it hurt. "Because that is exactly what he would do, Junior. He wouldn't eat, or sleep, he'd hate himself all over again! What happened was a mistake, a horrible, ugly twist of fate and I hate it, I hate that he's gone so much I want to scream. But it wouldn't do any good. Because you're still here, and I'm still here, and this ranch is here. And...and if I hate you just a little for what you did, I love you even more, because he loved you, and one day, I'll forgive you, and you—you'll forgive yourself."

She was breathing hard. Her heart was racing and her eyes glittered with a passion she hadn't felt in eight days.

Then, because she couldn't help it, she blurted, "You have his eyes." She waved a hand at his face. The whites of his blue eyes were still terrifying, red flooding the sclera, but the blue was just as vivid as Ben's had been. "I have our wedding picture, his clothes, and maybe the ranch if your father doesn't kick me off it. But you have his eyes. So no, I could never hate you."

For several long minutes, they were silent. For wont of something to do, Lucy refilled their coffee mugs and sat back down. Awkwardness had replaced her passion, and she stared into her mug, watching as bits of fat from the cream dissolved in the brew.

Finally, Junior spoke. He sounded...nervous.

"I wondered if, well, who knows if we can beat Father's lawyer. Both are crooked and tight as a coupla thieves. It might just be easier if—Christ, why's this so hard?" he sighed, scrubbing the back of his neck. His beard was growing in, but was so blond and patchy that Lucy thought it would look better shaved. What he said next knocked the inane thought from her mind. "It might make more sense if we just married."

"What?" she whispered.

Ben's 'spirit' crossed his arms across from her and scowled, shooting daggers at Junior.

"No, not like that," he yelped. "I'm going about this the wrong way. I don't mean I feel for you that way, Lucy, but I respect you an awful lot. If the land and house come to me, I'd marry you—not right away, mind—but that way, you wouldn't lose everything."

I've already lost everything that matters, she thought.

His offer came from a good place, and her immediate panic eased. She breathed again. "Oh, Junior," she sighed. "You would do that for me, wouldn't you? And if you fell in love with someone afterward? I couldn't do that to you. But thank you. I know that must have been very hard for you to offer. Ben would be proud of you."

A flash of disappointment turned his mouth down, but was there and gone in an instant. He snorted. "He wouldn't be proud, he's probably up there shakin' his fist at me, saying what a jackass I am. First, I kill him, then I move in on his widow."

A heavy pall fell over him, and Lucy felt a resurgence of panic that he was going back into that dangerous, depressive state.

"Don't you say that," she snapped, and threw a tea towel at his face with enough force to wrap around his head. "He probably is cursing you, and shaking his head, but I bet you he knew where the offer came from. I'll say it again; he'd be proud."

Junior opened his mouth to retort but stopped.

There were footsteps on the porch, a rap at the door, and Crew poked his head in. "Mizz Lucy, your Pa's here. And he's comin' in fast."

Lucy and Junior shared a look full of meaning, and then they were moving, chairs knocked over in their haste to reach the porch. Her thoughts warred with 'not again' and 'he has news!'.

"He's going to kill himself," Lucy worried, rushing to the yard with the men hot on her heels.

Tony was on a horse alone, and he was moving at a reckless pace. He was also shouting at the top of his lungs. There was an awful sense of déjà vu with one glaring difference.

Her Papa's face was euphoric.

"Lucy! He's alive! He's alive!"

Her entire body erupted in cold gooseflesh and her lips went numb. A hand gripped her arm to her left, and she snagged Junior's cambric shirt to her right. Junior grabbed her hand tight, and the three of them watched Tony rein in next to them, too afraid to believe.

Tony was talking, beaming, eyes full of emotion. "I got a wire from Ben himself, he's in Wichita Falls. Said he'd have gotten hold of you sooner, poppet, but he was sick, almost drowned, then walked half the way to find a town with a telegram office—"

He continued, but Lucy was taking the wire from his hand and reading it fast, hope warring with the fear that it was all a dream.

Ben's spirit smiled and dissipated.

Junior hovered over her, and she could hear his choppy breaths in her ear. She read the wire aloud. It needed to feel real. She had to hear the words.

"Tell Lucy and Junior I'm alive. Was ill for days. Be in Wichita Falls till tomorrow. Taking a stage to Waco. Tell them not to come. Bedbugs are bad these parts. Tell family I love them."

Tears streaming, Lucy bit her fist and looked up at Junior. They shared a moment of pure hope and relief, all the worries of the world falling away. All was right once again.

"Bedbugs! It *is* him," she cried, laughing, high-pitched and intoxicated. "I'd brave all the bedbugs in the world to get to him. Thank you, Papa."

She hugged her father fast and hard. Her face was no longer pale and shadowed. Life and vivacity made her eyes glitter and her mouth was wide with a smile. Then, she turned and shook Junior by the shoulders in pure exultation.

"Junior! Go pack. We need to take fast horses if we're going to get to Waco in time."

Scrubbing his face with a sleeve, Junior thrust a fist in the air and whooped in shared elation.

If Ben thought they'd wait for him to come home, he didn't know them very well.

29

—— · ——

CHAPTER TWENTY-NINE

Ignoring Ben's orders to stay and wait for him was the easiest thing Junior and Lucy agreed to the entire trip.

The eggshells they'd walked on through their mutual grief were no longer there now that they knew Ben was alive. Now, they argued like siblings about how long to let the horses rest, where to stop and eat, and when they should look for a hotel. They wouldn't make it to Waco in one day; it would take another full day's travel. By then, Ben may have already found a place to stay. The thought of not getting there in time and missing him sped their pace.

"If only I knew before, I'd never have left. Father made me," Junior said on multiple occasions during their ride north.

"So you keep saying," Lucy would huff back. "But there was no way to know which side of the river he was on, if he'd even made it to a town at first, and you wouldn't have been home to get his wire a week later. By then, there's no telling where you'd be, or if we'd be able to wire you. No. It was better this way."

When they made it to a hotel that first night, staying in two different rooms as brother and sister, he looked up over dinner. "I didn't even think to tell Father." He looked stricken by the thought.

475

Lucy's appetite had been ravenous since the good news earlier that day. She didn't even pause in her eating to assure, "Oh, I'm sure Ben sent him a wire. If not, what does he care?"

Junior kept silent and looked down at his empty plate.

Oh, no. Lucy was turning into her mother. What a horrible, wretched thing to say. She put her fork down and grabbed his hand. Though they argued and picked at each other, there was an unbreakable layer to their friendship that Ben's wire hadn't severed. Respect for each other, and a genuine caring for the other's well-being now colored their conversations and changed the way they treated each other. "I'm so sorry, Junior. That was an awful thing for me to say. I didn't mean it. That man just makes me so furious."

His tense shoulder's relaxed minutely. "I'm not mad. I just didn't want to think about him." He gave her finger a playful pinch. "You want some dessert?"

"Oh, no." Lucy shook her head, solemn. "I won't eat dessert again until I can share it with Ben."

"Now that," Junior snorted, "is something I can't agree with." He waved the waitress over.

The next day, they did not argue.

They barely spoke at all, their focus and intensity on the miles ahead. They skipped lunch and took only two rests for the horse's benefit, then they made their serious way closer and closer to Waco.

Spirit Ben hadn't made another appearance, but Lucy still felt as though she was in the middle of some fantastical dream. She'd had a taste of what it'd been like if Ben had died, and for a week, had wished it had been her instead. This didn't happen to people, these changes of fates. The rug that was whisked out from under widows' feet was never neatly re-placed after a few days. For most, dead was dead. So, for most of the journey, Lucy prayed her gratefulness.

Once, after they'd crossed the Brazos River and were about to pass a sign that was painted WACO: 15 MILES, Junior stopped and looked at it, breathing hard enough that Lucy frowned and nudged her horse closer to him.

"What is it?" she asked.

His eyes were haunted when he turned to her. "What if you hadn't been there, Lucy?" She imagined when he looked at her, that what he really saw was a swinging rope.

A cold shadow drifted over them, but she lifted her chin, all confidence. She would tell him the truth. "As soon as I'd said those things to you that day, things I regret even now, it was as though Ben was standing next to me, looking at me. Disappointed. I could feel it as though he'd whispered it in my ear. *Do the right thing. Go after him.* I followed you for a reason, and though I know now it wasn't Ben, I do think someone pushed me to find you. It wasn't meant to be, Junior. It wasn't your time."

He nodded at her, and they went forward.

They rode into Waco with bated breath. The town was immense.

They started at the stage office. Ben hadn't come in on that morning's stage, but there were a few more due.

They checked the livery, but no man with Ben's description had stopped by with a horse.

They went to the telegraph office, but no one had picked up the wire sent from Dogwood for a Ben Stone.

"I think we got here before him," Junior breathed in relief.

"Let's check for some hotels nearby, just in case." Lucy insisted they separate and make the search faster, but that Stone stubbornness reared its head. He wouldn't let her go off alone. She put her hands on her hips. "You're just like your brother when I first met him."

"I'll take that as a compliment."

They bought a couple of rooms at the hotel across the street from the stage office, left their meager bags, then made their rounds. At each hotel they visited, they left a message for a man named 'Ben Stone' to meet them at the Smith's Inn, rooms five and six. They spent hours riding from place to place, not wanting to miss any possible building they thought he'd visit. Junior studiously kept far away from saloons.

By the time they put their horses up, it was getting close to supper time. Their travels and the constant snuffing of hope when strangers shook their heads at every question had exhausted them.

"I'm starvin'," Junior grumbled, hands deep in his pockets and head sagging with dejection.

"So am I," Lucy agreed, rubbing the grit from her eyes. "Let's go to our rooms and wash up, and we'll go find something to eat." She didn't mention asking anyone else about Ben. Neither of them could take another sad head shake.

The Smith's Inn was a welcome sight, and Lucy murmured thanks when Junior opened the door for her. Unable to help herself, she made her way to the concierge. She would check again, just one more time. A man coughed behind her, and she thought with a brief unconcern that he should see a doctor about it when several things happened at once.

The clerk nodded at the area behind Lucy, a small smile on a prune mouth.

Junior made a strangled noise from the door.

And Lucy realized, the cough.... Ben had been sick.

She turned with the slowness of someone submerged underwater, too afraid to believe, half expecting to see a phantom, or worse, an old timer with a cold. Junior was faster. He was a blur of movement across the shabby foyer, crashing into a man that could have been Ben, except this man was far too thin, and wearing a stranger's clothes.

But it was him. His head was bare and the black hair curled, reaching into the softness of an overgrown beard that was untamed and lush.

"Ben," she croaked, and then she was moving. Reaching. An arm whipped out and grabbed her, yanking her with vicious strength into the group embrace. She shoved her face into a warm, blessedly alive body, and she took deep, shuddering breaths of his scent. The faint smell of body odor and leather from traveling in a coach was ambrosia to Lucy, and she pressed hard against him, sharing the space with her brother-in-law. They were all shaking with feeling, too emotional to make out any decipherable words.

"I take it you found the man you were looking for?" came a voice from behind the concierge desk, and Ben broke away first.

"I reckon they have."

Junior stepped back, pinching his eyes with the middle finger and thumb of one hand. He was flushed and his eyes shone like glass as he took his brother in. His well and alive brother. "I'm so sorry, Ben. I'm so—"

"Hush up." Ben's voice was as rough as the hand he clasped to Junior's shoulder. "I'm fine, you see? Now. Why didn't you wait for me like I told you?"

Lucy wasn't so willing to release him. The floodgates had opened, and she clung to him. He was familiar and strange all at once. With her face against his chest, she could hear a very faint wheeze with every breath, but also, his strong, fast heartbeat. He *was* thinner. He must have been very sick indeed. She raised her head and cupped his beloved face in her hands. "You've been ill. We should see a doctor."

Ben's smile was crooked, white teeth gleaming around gold. "I'm about doctored out, darlin'."

Her lower lip trembled, but she fought it back. "Please? For me? We can do it tomorrow before we leave."

As though he'd just now noticed the differences in his wife and brother, Ben's sharp sapphire eyes took in their disheveled appearance, the hollows in their cheeks and shadows around their eyes.

"You go off eating?" he asked them, unhappy and frowning.

"You were dead," Junior managed, then turned his back to them, pinching his eyes with those fingers again.

Lucy was shaking her head at him, all attempts to stem the flow abandoned. "What happened? We thought we'd lost you, for more than a week we thought we'd lost you. It was horrible, like a nightmare. Or maybe this is the dream," she babbled, and she was crushed back into his warm chest.

"That's enough of that." It was tender but final. "I'll tell you both everything. But first, I need a bath." He pretended to sniff Lucy. "In fact, we all could use washing up. You must've rode breakneck to get here." His disapproval was marred by his obvious excitement that they were there.

The clerk ordered them baths, which had to be brought in by maids and could take up to an hour to prepare. Junior reluctantly went to his room, but for once, his shoulders weren't covered by the weight of the world. Ben followed Lucy into her room carrying a cheap carpetbag that rivaled her green one for attractiveness.

"You don't know what it means to him that you're...well," Lucy said while locking the door.

"It doesn't mean anything to *you*?" he teased.

"Oh, please don't do that, Benjamin." She turned to him, and the wretchedness on her face made him drop his bag with a thump and come rushing to her. "Don't tease me. Not about that. It means everything to me. But Junior, it almost broke him. He wasn't well. He thought he'd killed you. *I* thought he'd killed you."

Ben's eyes were questioning. "His friend made a stupid decision and I paid the price, but Junior didn't kill me. You two traveled here together. Are you two, uh, friendlier?"

"We had something in common."

"Yeah?"

"We both lost you."

He shushed her again, and she sighed into his chest, and the sigh turned into kisses, light as a butterfly's wings. "Tell me what happened?"

They held each other while he described being knocked nearly unconscious in the water, making it to the bank, and somehow finding people that would help him. "It had been five days or so when I finally thanked the woman—the *old* woman—" he added with a chuckle at her carefully blank look, "—for her help, but when I made it to town, it was so small it didn't have a telegraph office. I couldn't even send a wire for money. So I gave the last of my money to a farmer with a wagon for a ride. Halfway there, his axle broke. I know, that was about my luck at that point. He had a bad back, so I helped him fix it, and by the time I made it to Wichita Falls, the telegraph office was closed and I had to wait another day to send a wire. But I was worried about y'all. Couldn't sleep for worryin'."

"I couldn't sleep either," she admitted.

A light rap on the door interrupted before she could say anything further, and Lucy moved to help the maid bring everything in. The bath was large and heavy and took a long time to fill, so she busied herself with setting out clothes, glancing at Ben every two seconds, unwilling to let him out of her sight. When they made it home, she was going to cook him four meals a day instead of three. They'd probably ride back in the stagecoach since he didn't have a horse of his own, but she hated stagecoaches now—oh.

Oh no.

"Ben...." She locked the door behind the maid and turned to him, watching him pause toeing off the saddest pair of boots she'd ever seen.

"Hm?" he grunted, not looking up.

"I'm sorry you lost Reb," she said with a gentle softness that reached across the room.

It was as though his strength had finally waned. He propped his elbows on his knees and stared between his bare feet. "Yeah, me too." He sighed, and a world full of hurt and weariness exhaled along with his breath. Hurting with him, loving him, she went to him and started unbuttoning his shirt. "No," he protested, holding her hands. "You first."

Lucy met his eyes and shook her head, slow and with meaning. "Let me take care of you."

After a moment, he released her and allowed himself to be undressed, piece by piece.

When he sat back in the tub, he groaned. She felt something at that groan. Not just euphoria that he was alive. No, she felt a stab of lust, a ferocious need to make love to his body. Maybe then it would feel real. While he relaxed, half-asleep, she undressed and watched him watch her. When she was down to her rumpled chemise, she unpinned her hair, shaking it out until it spilled in a tangled mass around her shoulders and back. He swallowed beneath the bush of his beard, and she knelt beside him, tracing the jut of his Adam's apple with two fingers in wonder.

"I keep thinking you'll disappear. That I'll wake up and I'm back in our bed, with only your clothes to keep me company." Her fingers followed a trail between his collarbones, to the fine black hair on his chest. She tangled her fingers in it, brushing her palm across his pectorals and over a hardening nipple. His blue eyes were slits behind his lashes, and they closed completely when her hand went lower beneath the water.

"You don't have to—" he started, breath coming in ragged pants.

It was her turn to shush him. "Let me take care of you," she whispered. She needed this. Her body, her mind, her soul. When she washed him, it was with a tenderness that humbled. She drew a soapy washrag over every inch of his skin. Her nails gently raked through his hair as she rinsed it. And when he got out of the tub, she went down on her knees.

"Lucy," he choked, cupping her head in his hands as her lips brushed close.

"Let me," she repeated and kissed the tender, smooth skin of his inner thighs. He smelled of sandalwood soap and male, *her* male, and the jut of his arousal was as insistent as its owner was tentative. Lucy nuzzled against him at the root, feeling the brush of his velvet length along her cheek. She wasn't immune to his noises, and the throb between her legs matched the one against her lips when she planted a lush kiss on the head. She hadn't even kissed his mouth yet, but there'd be time for that tonight. For now, she wanted to pay homage to his body and did so by opening her mouth over him, past the crown, and as deep as she could go in a slow, sure stroke.

"Ah, Lucy," he groaned, threading his fingers through her hair.

She pulled away and looked at him, wondering at the glistening wetness that only made it halfway down his length. Determined, she grasped him in hand and kissed the head the way he kissed her between the legs, with lips soft and tongue clever. Then, she took him in deeper than the first time, shoving him into the back of her throat, swallowing hard past the urge to gag. The only warnings she had was the curse from between clenched teeth above her, and the hand fisting in her hair, then he was moving in long, fast strokes. Lucy gagged a few times, then held her breath and relaxed her throat.

He pulled out with a pop, and she looked up. His eyes were wild, and his hands were rough as he grabbed her by the arms and pulled her up. Ben picked her up and threw her on the bed, then was on her, kissing her mouth with bruising force. Not to be outdone, she met him with equal fervor and pulled her chemise up and off. It was thrown on the floor with enough aggression that the first laugh escaped her since she'd seen him. He gave her a wicked grin and then his mouth was on her breasts and he was stroking teasing circles outside of her entrance.

Yes, this, she thought in satisfaction. She thought she'd never have this again, the wild passion with the husband that she loved more than she loved herself. "Yes, Ben," she encouraged him.

"Not yet," he grunted around her nipple. He sucked the pink bud deep into his mouth and wasn't satisfied until it was shiny and red. Only then could he move to the other one. His hands were busy caressing her hips, her stomach, between her legs until they'd made their way to her ankles. Straightening her legs, he placed her ankles on either side of his head and pushed his way oh so slowly inside of her.

The pressure was intense, almost as though it was the first time. She moaned at the resistance of muscles unused for so long and tried to bend her legs so she could rock her hips upward.

"No," he rasped, watching their connection as he worked his way in.

She keened when he was seated to the hilt. "It's too much."

Sweat beaded his forehead, and his temples pulsed. He pulled back until she relaxed, and then changed the angle, giving shallower thrusts that forced gasps out of her. Gentle fingers stroked her, lighter than feathers, and she bit her lip. Any discomfort eased after several minutes of this, and it wasn't long before Lucy was begging for deeper strokes, but whispering so nobody in the rooms next to them could hear.

Finally, Ben took pity on her and spread her legs open wide. Tucking her knees back in victory, Lucy latched her arms around him, wanting his mouth, his weight, his breath. At the close contact, her orgasm climbed, and she panted into his mouth. He felt her muscles drawing tight in her legs, felt the tilt of her hips change, and when her internal muscles clamped with that inexorable suction that drove him mindless, he let himself go. Their bodies rocked together in the rare shared climax, both rigid at the intensity of falling off that nameless pinnacle, gasping breaths mingling. Lucy brushed her lips against his and said something.

"What was that?" he whispered against her swollen, beard-reddened mouth.

"I said, you're real." And she promptly burst into tears.

AFTER BEN HAD soothed Lucy with his tepid, second-hand bath, they dressed with the swiftness of the famished. A knock on Junior's door went unanswered, but she was determined.

She knocked without stopping until a bleary-eyed Junior answered the door, tucking in his shirt. "I'm comin', hold your horses."

Ben and Lucy smiled a secret smile at each other, and, arm in arm, led the way to the nearest restaurant.

The three of them ate with a large appetite, but the conversation was less than warm. Junior and Lucy went over everything that had happened since Ben had disappeared, and he listened with fingers interlocked over his firm mouth.

His eyes grew flintier with every event; Junior's unwilling journey back home, Lucy's frosty reception at the Stone Ranch, and John's visit. Lucy didn't meet his gaze and pushed her greens around on her plate as she told her husband how her father had planned on forcing her out of her home not a week after his 'death'. When a fist thumped with muted fury on the table loud enough to clang the silverware, she and Junior jumped.

"That old bastard." Ben's words had a dangerous tremor to them, and his nose was pinched, lips tight. "He'd kick my wife off the land I paid out the nose for?"

"You didn't have a living will?" Junior braved.

"I wrote something of that effect and tucked it in a bible by the bed, but I don't know what kind of legal standing it has without a witness. I'll be writing something out tonight, that's certain." There was something behind the angry words that made Lucy frown. Ben wasn't just mad. He was betrayed.

"We'll get to that later. For now," Lucy grinned mischievously, "I'd like to order dessert."

Ben remained tense for another minute, then allowed their teasing to relax him. "What else has happened since I've been gone. How's the ranch? Tia and Frank?"

Lucy explained that Frank had broken his leg within the first week, and when she went to John to relay the message, he'd sent back Crew.

"Jethro Crew?" Ben leaned back in his chair, unsmiling.

The waitress had just set small plates of pie in front of them, and Lucy was too busy poking at her meager slice to notice that her husband was unhappy at the news. "Yes, him. He's a quiet fellow, but I think we should hire him on permanently after you get home. He singlehandedly worked the farm for the past week, and is still doing so. Your father fired him the last time he came over." She took a dainty bite and made a face. "Minnie makes a wonderful mulberry pie. The cook could do with a lesson from her."

"I think it's fine," Junior argued, picking up the slice of pie with his fingers and eating it in one bite.

"You would. That's disgusting, didn't your lovely mother ever teach you any table manners?" Her lip curled when a berry fell onto his shirt and rolled, leaving a purple trail behind it. "I hope you don't expect me to wash that out."

Junior leaned back and picked at his teeth, patting his stomach. "You can get a grass stain out, I'm sure a little pie won't cause you any trouble."

They went back and forth for a while like children before Ben's continued silence halted their nettling. Lucy looked up to see him watching them with an indecipherable expression.

"What is it?"

He motioned with a hand between the two of them. "Didn't know the two of you were so friendly."

Junior sat up from his slouch. "You call that being friendly?"

Lucy snorted. "You should have heard us on the way up here. We fought like cats and dogs."

"You wanted to travel through the whole durn night, woman."

"And you thought with your stomach," she shot back.

And yet, even though they bantered, there was no heat to their words. They picked and poked with the comfort of siblings.

Ben was quiet the rest of the evening until it was time to turn in. Lucy walked arm in arm with him to the hotel, but there was a rigidity to him that hadn't been there before. Any time she'd nudge him in question, he'd ignore the small prod and continue his silent walk. They told Junior goodnight and locked themselves in their room. The bathtub had been taken out, and the bed was in shambles.

"How long's that been going on?" Ben asked from behind her.

Halfway undressed, she turned, shrugging out of her blouse. She wasn't an imbecile and was beginning to understand the change in his demeanor. Things were different between his brother and her, and Ben wanted to know whether he should feel threatened or not. Sighing, Lucy started unbuttoning her skirt at the back. "Will you help me with this? If by 'that' you mean, how long have Junior and I been talking to each other like family? Four days. The day that John came over and threatened to give the land to your brother, Junior and I came to an understanding. We weren't enemies. We were family. And whether you were gone or not, we'd remain family. So, we may as well get along."

"That was more than getting along," Ben continued, folding his arms, stubborn to the end.

"Honestly, Ben!" she cried, having wrangled her skirt off by herself. "You used to get so upset that your brother and I never got along, and now that we can tease and joke, you're angry. Come here, I'll take off your boots—where in heaven's name did you get these?"

"The old lady that helped me had an old pair," he grunted, pushing her hands away to yank the ancient boots off himself.

"They're old, all right. I bet they've been through The War and back." Though her voice was light, she was watching her husband, nervous at his mercurial mood. She crouched before him, hands on his knees. "Ben. Look at me. You have nothing to be angry about."

He refused to look at her from his seat on the bed. "I'm not the least bit angry. Just surprised that you and my brother seemed to have moved on so quick-like after you thought I was dead."

His words were rusty nails stabbing a healing wound, and she gaped. "Is that what you think? That we moved on?"

"Sure looked like it." He was watching her now.

She stood up and turned her back on him. "How can you think that?" she whispered and covered her face with her hands. "You don't understand at all, Ben."

The bed creaked when he rose and she could feel him behind her, his body warm. Her eyes closed when she felt his lips and nose touch her hair, drawing in her scent. She wanted to keep Junior's secret, but the alternative was Ben thinking they hadn't been devastated by their loss. Her heart raced. She'd have to tell Ben all the ugly things she'd said to Junior.

"You're going to hate me." It disgusted her that she sounded so close to tears already. "You'll hate me after I tell you, but I can't have you thinking I didn't care that you'd died. When I thought you were dead, I didn't want to believe it at first. I kept waiting for news that you'd survived. But the days went by with no word, and I just knew you were gone. I'd never see you again, kiss you, talk to you, have your babies. Grow old with you. When your father and brother came over that day, Junior stayed." She paused, afraid to go on. Afraid he'd know how unworthy she was.

Ben wrenched away from her, and the groan that came from him rivaled a dying beast from her nightmares. "Christ, I don't want to know. Don't tell me. I thought I could hear it—but I can't."

Realization of what he'd misconstrued from her words whirled her around. He was facing the empty corner, hands fisted in his hair with white-knuckled force. Did he honestly think she'd do anything like that with Junior? "Do you think that little of me? Ben, no! Junior stayed and told me what happened. Everything. Think, will you?" Her voice had tapered down to the merest breath of sound, but he'd released his clench on his hair. He was listening. "Your brother told me that, in a drunken temper tantrum, he and his friend had ridden into a flooded river. You came after him to save him. He lived. You died. Ben, what do you think I did?"

He faced her, and his expression was suffused with misery, lids pink and eyes bloodshot.

"I raged at him. I said awful things. All the bitter feelings I'd had for him…it was terrible. If you had seen his face…I'll never forgive myself." Strong arms embraced her and she soaked it up, sure that when she was finished, he wouldn't want to touch her ever again. "He ran to the barn. I regretted it immediately, what I had said, even if some things were true. I pictured you there, disappointed in me, so I followed him to apologize. At first, I couldn't find him, but some hay fell on me from the loft. He'd knocked the ladder down. So, I put it back and climbed up, and I heard a noise, and please, please don't tell him I told you, but Ben, he had hanged himself," she sobbed. The arms around her had become stiff as iron vices, entrapping rather than comforting. "And he was fighting it, but it was too late. He had changed his mind but it was too late—I screamed and ran to him, grabbed his legs, and picked him up enough for Crew to show up and cut the noose off. I was so sorry, Ben, please don't hate me. He—he almost died because I was cruel, and no one would have known he didn't want to die after all. After that, we had an understanding, do you see now? We didn't want to live without you, but we had to for each other. Because you were gone, and—"

"Sh, all right darlin', hush now," Ben murmured in her hair. "I understand."

"I love you so much, Ben. Don't ever leave again, I couldn't take it."

"I love you, too, and I'm not goin' anywhere." He tilted her head up, and they kissed, soft and trembling.

He didn't hate her, she realized with a moan of relief. And when he made love to her and held her through the night, whispering things, normal things, about the farm, their life, and their future, she got a full night's sleep for the first time since her waking nightmare over a week before.

LUCY FAWNED OVER Ben with a tenaciousness that a grown man should have found suffocating. Instead, he reveled in it, giving her only the smallest protestations for pride's sake. Her worried eyes and discerning hands passed over his body any time he let a cough escape, and she kept a steady stream of orders at him that would make a general proud.

"As soon as we get home, you're going straight to bed while Junior gets the doctor," she bossed, nose in the air after he'd shrugged off her concern for the third time.

"I'm fine, darlin', stop fussin'." *You should have heard my cough a few days ago*, he almost said, then decided against it. It was best she didn't know. "It's getting better every day."

Junior and Lucy wanted to take their time getting home, but Ben had had enough of being away. He'd sent a letter to Kansas for Sol, but it'd be a few weeks before his friend would make it to the end of the trail. He sent a silent prayer for the man's safety.

They were forced to stay the night in another town before making it home, and he smiled when Lucy checked the mattresses and linens.

"What're you doin'?" Junior watched, incredulous, as his sister-in-law untucked the sheets from his room's bed.

"She's checking for bedbugs," Ben smiled from the doorway, fingers tucked in his pockets, shoulders against the doorjamb. "I thought she was crazy as a cuckoo the first time I saw her at it in Mississippi."

Junior's blonde brows rose higher. "You two shared a room back then? Before marriage? My, my."

"Oh, don't act so high-and-mighty," Lucy huffed, running her fingers along the seams of the bedding, pausing and squinting now and then. Ben watched the straight line of her back that ended in the lush curve of her derriere, half-listening as she regaled how they met to his brother, who laughed and whistled throughout.

"I was such a chore to him," she was giggling, re-tucking the sheets and blankets beneath the bed, satisfied in her searching. "I felt like a chastised little girl every time he spoke to me. Such dressing-downs he gave." When she met his eyes, her smile disappeared, and she bit her lower lip. She held his hot gaze for a moment, then cleared her throat. "Well, I believe you shouldn't have any unwelcome visitors in your sleep. Goodnight, Junior."

"'Night."

Ben was hot on her trail while she walked to their room at the end of the dingy little hall, and he gave her barely enough time to lock the door behind them before he was pressing her up against it.

"Ben," she whispered, swallowing, and watching him with hooded eyes.

"I had to treat you like a child back then," he murmured against her neck, trailing his lips and soft beard along the silken skin until it erupted in goosebumps. "That way, I wouldn't picture doing this to you."

He breathed her in deep, biting the skin at the juncture of her neck, and running rough hands to the sweet roundness of her bottom, squeezing and bringing her against the rock of his hips. A low moan escaped her parted lips, and she returned the favor, gripping his hips tight against her. Ben lifted her high enough against the door that he could nuzzle the soft place between her breasts, and she released his hips to stroke the hard tendons of his arms.

"Do you know what I wanted to do to you?" Lucy nuzzled his hair, arching her back into his mouth as he opened it over her nipple through her shirt and chemise. "Let me show you."

Two hours later they lay naked, he on his stomach, she draped over him. Her fingertip played across his back, and, half-asleep, he murmured into the pillow, "L. O. V. E. U." He smiled. "I love you, too."

"My turn." She lay on her stomach, but he rose onto his elbows and turned her over onto her back.

This was how he loved seeing her. Looking up at him, eyes dewy and lips abused from their lovemaking, breasts bared and covered in the small love bruises he enjoyed branding her with. In the satiny area between her slightly flattened breasts, he wrote something.

"B," she whispered.

He made another letter, lower, over the seam between her ribs.

"A."

Lower, across her navel.

"B."

The last letter he trailed against the sensitive skin just above her pubic bone where it was flat, hollowed now from the eroticism of his game.

"Y." Her eyes, drooping a minute before, sparked with comprehension. "Baby?"

"I want to put one, right here." His broad, brown hand splayed over her womb, fingers dark against her luminous skin, pinky brushing into the hair at the apex of her legs. "Want to watch this place, right here, get big with my child. One I put there, night after night. And when we've had one, I want to put another in you. And another." He placed hot kisses there, and moved his hand lower, feeling her shivering against his lips and fingers, listening to her gasps.

Talking about it had him ready again, so hard he could feel his rapid pulse beat down low. He dipped fingers inside her and his lips followed his hand, giving her a lush kiss in that spot that made her squirm.

"Yesss," she hissed, threading her fingers in his hair.

Ben lifted his head and met her gaze, taking in her bright eyes and flushed face. "Yes, what?"

"Put a baby in me, Ben," she ordered, and he gritted his teeth at the feeling those words gave him.

He got up on his knees between her legs, feeling like an animal and the king of the world all in one, and grinned. "Yes, ma'am."

30

Chapter Thirty

When they rode into the yard the next day, the sky was a clear blue, so bright it was hard on the eyes. Lazy wisps of clouds traveled across the yellow sun, too insubstantial to even cast a shadow.

For a split second, Ben felt the stresses of travel and the hardships of the past week melt away at the beauty of his ranch with its proud house on the hill, the barn in the distance, and the familiar people rushing across when they noticed they had company.

Ben's smile was so big it felt fit to break his face when he heard Tia crying out in Spanish. He'd never seen the reserved woman so passionate, and he dismounted a split second before she came flying in his arms, praising God and the Virgin Mary that he was alive after all.

"*Tu madre te estabe cuidando, sobrino*," Tia sobbed into his chest, the highest she could reach.

"*Si*, Tia, Mama was watching over me very well."

Frank limped up, cheeks creased in a dozen folds with the strength of his smile.

The heartfelt greeting was well-meaning, but Ben felt the strain of how the excessive emotion drained his reserves. From the corner of his eyes, he saw another man, one he remembered growing up around. Jethro Crew hung back from the others, and his cross-eyed focus was on Lucy, who dabbed

493

at her own eyes on her horse. He may have been mistaken about Junior, but Ben didn't think he was wrong about the possessive feelings that urged him forward to Crew.

"I need to thank you." Ben sized up the man, who had finally stopped watching Lucy dismount in furtive glances. "My *wife*," he said with calm emphasis, "explained how much you helped out here while I was gone."

"Weren't nothin'," Crew grumbled, chin tucked down.

"No. It was." He offered his hand and squeezed hard when the other man shook it. Their eyes met, held, and they had an age-old private conversation without saying a word. Crew nodded in understanding and Ben let go. Someone nudged him from behind, and he recognized the poking finger with a deep, audible sigh. "If you want to stay on, you're welcome to. We could use a hand like you around here." Ben tried to remember that this was the man who'd been privy to that awful moment in the barn with Lucy and Junior, but the man's insistent gaze on his wife was making it damned hard to like the fellow, much less want him working for him.

"Much obliged," Crew said, and walked around to take Lucy's horse for her without another word.

So, it's like that, Ben thought in mystification. The action couldn't have made it any clearer. Jethro Crew was staying on for one reason and one reason alone; he was in love with the lady of the house. In all the time Ben had known the man, he'd noted Crew's strangeness. The solitary man worked alone, ate alone, lived alone, and seldom went to town. He'd never had a woman (that Ben knew of), never cracked a joke, or opened up to anyone in confidence. It was as though any personality he'd had before coming to work for John had been whitewashed. Seeing the difference in that man now was striking, and wholly unwelcome.

"Rider coming in." Frank plucked a strand of grass from the ground and squinted. "Looks like y'all's Pa."

Ben's jaw grew rigid. The light, soft caress of Lucy's hand stopped his teeth from gritting.

"Sweetheart, sit on the porch for a spell and I'll make some coffee. I'm sure you and Junior have a lot to say to him." She was hiding any ill feelings for the eldest Stone better than any Sunday preacher.

Having long given up on caring if his wife managed him or not, Ben nodded and accepted her peck on his cheek. He watched the sway of her hips as he followed her up the porch, and found a measure of calm. He was alive. He was home. His wife was going to make him coffee in the kitchen he'd been raised in. And if he had to face the father who'd easily given him up for dead and tried to whip the home right out from under his wife's feet without even a week to grieve, well then, he'd have Junior at his side, and they'd face Pa together.

Junior took a seat next to him on the swing and they watched in strained silence as their father rode a limping thoroughbred up to the porch.

John Stone looked pale. He looked, more than anything, old.

The hard, powerful lines of his face sagged, and he stumbled when he dismounted.

Ben and Junior were halfway to standing before hostile eyes flashed up in warning, and the brothers shared a brief look before sitting again. The old man was getting on in years, but he wasn't infirm or dead.

Yet.

Their father grasped the wooden railing as he ascended the porch steps, holding a stitch in his side for a glimmer of a second before tucking his hands in the pockets of his suit pants. When he stood before them, his gaze arrowed into the yard beyond their heads.

"Your horse throw a shoe?" Ben asked after an uncomfortably long moment had passed where the three of them said nothing.

With the slowness of molasses in winter, John's blue eyes met Ben's gaze, and held it, a fly trapped in the ooze. He didn't say a thing, but he didn't have to. If possible, the old man grew paler, face set in alabaster, as though he were already dead in a grave. His hand had a distinct tremor that worried Ben, and he placed the trembling fingers over his shirt pocket, grasping a folded, white square of paper from its depths.

"I wanted to see—" John began, but stopped, fisting his hand around the paper. The strength was gone from his voice, and his eyes moved from Ben's face to Junior's, then back again. His parted mouth became resolute, a thin slash that erased what was almost a momentary weakness. "I got your telegraph the other day. I came here, but John Junior and your wife were already gone, and Tia and Frank wouldn't tell me anything." He shot a brief glare at the pair of backs that had made it halfway home, then his eyes returned to Ben. "I drew up another paper with my lawyer. He's got a copy in town, so there's no use burnin' this one."

Ben caught the crumpled square of paper tossed to him, and his teeth ground together again. "I don't want any more paperwork from you or your greedy lawyer. You can take this and—"

"It's a deed to the house, land, and any property within the land," John spoke over him, scowling at his son's disrespectful tone. "Look it over, sign it, have Junior bring it in tomorrow when he sees his mother—" Junior snorted once, "—and be done with it. Should've done it before you even left."

"You're damned right it should have." Ben's voice was quiet, and his eyes burned hot with anger. "There should never have been a question that the house, the land, all of it was mine. I paid what it was worth and then some, and you still had the stones to come here and try to take it from my wife, when, for all you knew, I was fish food at the bottom of the Red River."

At that, John turned his face to the side, but Ben wasn't finished. No. He wasn't finished by a mile.

"You can treat me like a horse apple on the bottom of your boot, but it's a new low when you take what was mine, what was my mother's, from the woman I love. She's my family, she wears my ring, has my last name, and will have your grandchildren." He waved the paper that had slowly unfurled. "I'll sign this, and that'll be the last I have anything to do with you. Don't darken this doorstep again. Stay off my land, and stay out of my life. Lucy!" he shouted, a whip crack that made Junior flinch next to him. "I need a pen."

He stared John down, a pathetic old man that had only the merest grasp on the rigid bearing that had done so well for him for years. Ben didn't meet Lucy's gaze when she rushed out, wide-eyed, carrying a fountain pen. He smoothed the paper over his leg, quietly thankful that his hand was steady, and perused the shortest, simplest contract he'd ever read, deeding he, his wife, and any children the property in full, no holds barred.

There were no stipulations for helping with roundups.

There was no mention of cattle drives.

It was simple and to the point.

John's signature was sprawling and barely legible, and Ben signed his name below without flourish or drama.

"Here." He handed the paper over, and the second it made contact with John's fingers, Ben stood. He held his hand out, temples pulsing and eyes flaring with emotion. "Good doin' business with you."

John almost took too long to shake his hand, and stood there, blinking his eyes like a dust storm had blown grit in them. But, just as Ben had almost lost his nerve and walked inside, his father clasped the brown hand with his own, fingers swollen at the knuckles and cold to the touch. They shook once, let go.

Without stepping back, John opened his mouth, closed it. Open, close. He was a fish on a bank, out of his element.

"I," he began, failed, tried again, "I'm glad you're here, son." Then, he turned and made his way back to the steps without pause. He was folding the contract with unsteady hands, tucking it with care back into his shirt pocket.

From behind Ben, Junior stood with a muttered curse. "I'll be back for supper," was all he said, before descending the steps and clapping John on the back. "I'll ride to the Big House with you, Mother will probably be chomping at the bit to see me."

Unable to watch any further, Ben turned and opened the kitchen door. He stood in the familiar kitchen, breathing hard, and his eyes burned something fierce. A boulder had somehow made its way into his throat, and he struggled to swallow, managing only to cough. Slender arms wrapped around him with surprising force, and breasts pressed against the middle of his back.

"Hush, Ben. Sh."

He almost laughed at her shushing, but he was terrified it would come out as a sob, so he bowed his neck and squeezed her arms until they dug into his ribs. She was real and present, and he allowed it when she rocked him back and forth in small increments. They stood like that for what could have been five minutes or an hour. Eventually, that swollen lump in his throat disappeared, and his mind slowed its clamoring. His heart stopped aching and he could breathe deep again. Behind him, Lucy was humming a low, soothing melody.

Sensing that he was once again in control, she murmured against his back, "You want to play under the covers?"

This time, he allowed the laugh to fill the room.

THE MONTHS THAT followed were some of the happiest Lucy had ever had, even compared to those first golden weeks after her marriage to Ben.

Life had a new vivacity, and each day felt like a second chance.

Her relationship with Ben had deepened like a fine wine, fragrant and layered in innumerable tones. Their eyes could have whole conversations with one look, and the mention of any certain person brought the same thing to mind. Now that he was only responsible for his land and was no longer tied to checking his father's fence line, lost steers, or having anything to do whatsoever with the Stone Ranch, there was much more freedom to train horses and focus on their own ranch.

Sol arrived home in a flurry of excitement one day, leaner and browner than when he'd left. Lucy had laughed herself silly when, once spying Ben in the paddock, Sol had yipped something akin to a war cry, sprinted, and tackled his friend full-force onto the ground. It was the first time she'd heard her husband laugh a full, rounded belly laugh since the cattle drive. And when he'd grown quiet later that evening when he saw what his friend had brought back with him, it was from introspection rather than reliving nightmares of the past.

Reb's saddle and blanket hung from the rafters at the center of the barn, wrinkled, cracked, and in awful shape, but was the best memoriam they had of the finest horse Ben said he'd ever had the pleasure of riding.

After Sol's return, the ranch felt complete again.

Junior hadn't drunk a drop of spirits since that terrible day and had so far managed to stay away from the saloons. He seemed adhered to Ben's side and helped with his portion of the workload without complaint. He had bad days, days where he'd stare off at nothing and his face would fill with hatred. Lucy knew the hatred was for himself and would lay a hand on his shoulder, or she'd send Ben his way with a flick of her eyes. Somehow, they kept Junior's demons at bay, even if they were close enough to nip at the heels of his thoughts.

Lucy's workload was back at full force, particularly the laundry. There were always clothes to wash, and they were always so darned *filthy*.

One day she woke up late. The sun bathed her room in a golden light, and she could hear someone downstairs rattling pans around.

Oh, no, she'd slept in!

It must have been all the times she'd woken up to visit the outhouse in the middle of the night. That must be why she was so tired. She'd have to stop drinking tea so late. Then, she realized what day it was.

Blue Monday.

She wanted to weep. Dressing without haste, she trudged downstairs in her worst dress, grousing and wondering how big the mess in the kitchen was.

The next week, Lucy slept in again. And again, when she realized it was Monday, she really *did* weep. She dried her tears in disgust and dressed. This time, when she went downstairs, the smell of coffee hit her with the force of a sledgehammer in the gut. Gagging, she whirled and ran back upstairs. She managed not to vomit by sniffing deeply at the bag of potpourri in her drawer. Ben found her, hunched by the open commode stand, breathing into a drawstring bag, and holding her stomach.

"Darlin', you feeling poorly?" He was at her side in three strides and tried to run his hands over her face. She was clammy to the touch, and when he tried to feel her stomach, she sidestepped him.

"Oh, please, don't touch there," she moaned. She'd never felt so queasy. "Is that coffee bad? It smells awful."

Ben frowned, then his face became speculative. "The smell of coffee sent you up here like that?"

"Yes, it must be rancid. Don't tell me you drank any."

"It tasted alright to me. Come lay down." He knew she didn't feel well when she complied. Lucy was never one to lay around. "Let me fetch Tia."

Again, she didn't argue, and when Tia came in, being still had soothed her roiling stomach long enough that she'd had time to think. "Tia," she breathed, glancing behind the little woman to meet Ben's hopeful eyes. "Do you think...."

Tia was smiling a small, secret smile, and sat gingerly on the bed next to Lucy. Her tiny hand lay flat over Lucy's abdomen below the navel, and she beamed.

Now Lucy was crying. Ben crawled into bed with her while Tia ran home for some dry biscuits, and laughed into her hair, "I should have known yesterday when you turned your nose up at my fried eggs."

"Don't remind me, Benjamin," she groaned, laughing. Her eyes were shining when she looked up at him. "Oh, Ben. We did it, didn't we?"

He kissed her mouth with such tenderness, as though she'd break now that he knew. "Let's bring you to the doctor in town and make sure. How long since your...you know."

Too excited to be embarrassed, she thought back, and her eyes widened. "Not since before Sol came home. I feel like a dunce, that was over a month ago!"

"Now that I think about it, we have been having a lot of fun here lately without that monthly visitor interruptin'—"

She clamped a hand over his grinning mouth and giggled with helpless euphoria. "You hush," she warned him. "Now that I'm in the family way, why should there be any need to continue 'trying'? We can stop now—ahhh!"

Ben rolled her and pinned her on the other side, then cursed. "Aw, I forgot you were feelin' poor—oomph!" A pillow hit him in the face while his wife shrieked with laughter, so he renewed his attempts to subdue her.

Now well and truly pinned, Lucy grinned up at him. "Well," she whispered, glancing at the empty doorway. "I see no reason to stop practicing. What do you say?"

"I say that's the best idea I've ever heard." He kissed her mouth, her nose, her eyes, then, he crawled down the bed and kissed her belly. Pressing his lips to the still-flat stomach, he said, "I sure do love your mama, little one."

Lucy felt her full heart overflow.

Epilogue

Five Years Later

"**W**hy, I never had my name in no book before," Minnie exclaimed, beaming down at one of her presents from Lucy; a printed cookbook that Lucy had gotten published the month before.

Lucy fed ten-month-old Jack tiny pieces of softened roast beef from her annual Christmas Eve dinner. She'd managed to talk Papa into bringing Minnie over for a few hours before she went back to her family. The cookbook wouldn't have been possible without the hardworking woman's tutelage over the years, and Minnie was the first person Lucy had gifted it to. Minnie also received a certain percentage of the royalties, though she didn't know it. She was too proud to accept money from Lucy, so Tony had explained the extra money away as a well-deserved raise.

"Well, it's in there a dozen times." Lucy laughed at how big the woman's eyes got. "I marked the passages with your recipes. And in the front, you're one of the people I've dedicated the book to."

"Oh, Lucy-Lou," Minnie chuckled, shaking her head and unable to stop smiling as she ran her fingers over the crisp pages.

Every Christmas Eve, Lucy and Ben threw a dinner party for their family and friends, but this was the first year Minnie had managed to attend one. She had family and friends of her own, after all. With her old nanny's white smile gleaming in the cozy living area, hair more gray than black, Lucy knew true peace.

By the fireplace, Tia told a story in Spanish to Lucy's rapt four-year-old, Matthew. It never ceased to amaze her how her oldest son was the spitting image of his father, with his thick black hair and almond-shaped blue eyes. Their middle child, Samuel, had curling brown hair and eyes that were more green than blue. He was two and chased the cat with sure legs that were quickly losing that pudgy stockiness of toddlers. Jack, her youngest and last boy, blew raspberries, spraying flecks of meat all over the table.

"Jack-Jack," she gasped in dramatic shock, her eyes and mouth round. Jack laughed a deep belly laugh, his four teeth gleaming white, his dimples deep beneath the apples of his cheeks. Only Jack had those dimples, although all their boys had inherited the Stone cleft in their chin. When Lucy had given birth to her youngest, the easiest birth so far with only three hours of labor, they'd been pleasantly surprised by the baby's shocking coloring. Jack was dusky as his father but had come into the world with a shock of almost white hair, and vivid eyes that surpassed even Ben's for their true-blue hue. With an aunt and uncle with fair hair and pale eyes, the ten-month-old had acquired the recessive genes two-fold and promised to be as stunning as a grown man as he was beautiful as a child.

Feet stomped outside the door, and Samuel let out a scream of delight.

"Daddy!"

He ran as fast as his little legs could carry him, and would have barreled straight into the legs of his father if Ben's strong arms hadn't snatched him up and tossed him high, shrieks emitting from the little boy loud enough to shatter glass. Ben always teased Lucy that Samuel had gotten his lungs from her.

Not to be left out, Jack-Jack yelled, turned halfway round in his high chair, arms extended. Ben picked him up with ease, not minding the food all over his bib a whit. He gave both boys, one in each arm, a smacking kiss and asked in a deep baritone that brooked no mischief, "You boys been good for Mama?"

Samuel nodded. Jack pulled his father's beard and laughed hysterically at the wince it caused. Matthew, who had walked at a more sedate pace, finally reached his father and squeezed the big man's legs in a tight hug. Eyes warming, Ben crouched down and asked for a proper hug, and, once Matthew wrapped his arms around the muscular neck, stood while his first son squealed in delight, dangling feet from the ground with just the strength of his thin arms.

Lucy watched with all the love she felt for them in her eyes, then stood and took the baby from her husband so poor Matthew could have a turn. Jack, who loved his father just fine, still turned at once in his mother's arms, nuzzling her bosom with the possessiveness of a child uninterested in weaning.

Ben raised a brow as though asking, *Still?*

And she shrugged in reply, *How can I say no?*

They said goodbye to her father and Minnie, and a few hours later, they waved their farewells to Junior, who'd built his own house between their ranch and his father's. Frank and Tia had gone home, and Crew had disappeared into the bunkhouse alone where it suited him best. Sol was with his family for the week, and now, it was just Ben, Lucy, and their three little sons.

All the activity had worn the children out, so they were tucked in a large bed in the room next to their parents under several layers of blankets, the room warm from the coal in the grate. Lucy kissed each on the forehead, exhausted but replete. The next morning was Christmas Day, and there were presents for each child to open and enjoy. They were terribly spoiled, but how could they not be? They were the most wonderful, infuriating, imperfectly perfect children Lucy could have ever hoped to have had.

She crawled into bed with Ben after their nightly ablutions and sighed against his chest.

"What a wonderful day," she said. "Last Christmas I was too miserable and fat to enjoy it."

"You weren't fat," Ben reprimanded, eyes closed but hands busy against her thin nightgown. "You were nearly full term with Jack." He knew all the ins and outs of pregnancy by now.

"Did I tell you about the letter Papa brought with him today?"

"No, who's it from."

"Poppy! Remember? My friend I had to save from those bullies at school?"

Distracted, he nonetheless snorted. "You mean the friend you smoked your Papa's cigars with?"

"Yes," Lucy chuckled, though it was her turn to get distracted when his warm hands climbed higher. "She's coming to visit Dogwood this summer."

"Hm," was all he replied.

Lucy gave a sinuous stretch and moaned when calloused hands massaged her engorged breasts. "Oh, they're so sore. I'll be glad when the baby gives them up."

BEN PULLED HER gown off and looked down at her breasts, firm with milk, blue veins trailing beneath the taut, white skin. He didn't know what it was, but his wife had only grown more attractive as time passed. With each pregnancy, he'd only become randier. The sight of her, belly full with the child he'd put in her, made him stiff. Her breasts, full of milk from feeding his babies, made him stiff. Hell, her drooling on the pillow, tired from being up all night with sick little ones, made him stiff.

Motherhood had only enhanced her natural beauty with an earthiness that appealed to him. Her love for her children made him love her more, until he worried about it, if it was natural to feel such powerful emotions for one person.

He kissed her breasts, smiled when milk trailed down the left one, and caught the pearl of white liquid with his lips. The first time he'd done that was after Matthew's birth. He'd been waiting patiently for her to heal enough physically and emotionally from the trauma of birth. One night, she'd turned to him, still too sore to do much of anything, but needing him on a physical level and not knowing how to assert herself. The first time he'd loved on her breasts, they squirted milk, and she'd cried out in embarrassment. In response, he'd held her still and brought her hand to his rock-hardness, and asked, "Does it feel like I mind?" After that, it had been only too quick for him to find release, and Lucy's unease had dissipated.

Now, she watched him love her, eyes hooded as he kissed every vein of her breasts. She hooked a strong leg over his hip and flipped him. He was already naked, so she maneuvered down his body, and sank onto him slow, from tip to root, and back.

"I love you," he growled, watching the way her lush breasts swayed in appreciation.

"I love you, too." Lucy grabbed his hands, and put them on her hips, broader after having three children, and undulated against him. The sight of her in the lamp light made his throat dry, and he struggled to take his time.

Afterward, they lay together, breath and heartbeats slowing, sweat drying.

"When Jack is weaned, I want to try what the doctor suggested," Lucy mumbled into the pillow.

Ben raised his head, neck growing warm. "Yeah? Think it'll work?" He didn't know if he could pull out quick enough every time.

"It's worth a try. I love my babies, but I miss you." She laid her hand on the trail of hair beneath his navel. "It's difficult after a newborn. It makes it harder to...have fun."

He felt a smile growing on his face as her fingers began to wiggle, tickling closer to his hipbone. "Thought we just had fun."

Those devilish fingers made their way up his ribs, then pressed harder near his armpit until he finally released a laugh, one she always vowed was her favorite, from deep in the belly. "You're askin' for it," he warned and turned on her.

They wrestled, trying to keep their shouts and giggles quiet, but it nevertheless woke up the smallest.

A whine from down the hall had Ben bounding up from the bed, naked as the day he was born. He came back with a sleepy Jack, blonde hair sticking in odd directions and eyelids drooping over tired cerulean peepers. Lucy was already washing her breasts at the basin, dressed in her wrapper for easy access. Jack held his arms out and dove straight for her bosom. Small sounds of suckling made the parents smile at each other, and Ben dressed for bed, blew out the lantern, and they climbed into bed, tucking the baby of the family in between them.

"The other two...."

"Fast asleep," Ben reassured softly, stroking his son's downy hair, and pressing a kiss to the sweet-smelling crown.

He didn't know what he'd done to deserve this family, this life.

But he thanked God every day.

"Goodnight Benjamin." Lucy yawned and kissed his fingers, then, his mouth.

"Goodnight darlin'."

When he fell asleep, he was smiling.

ele

THE END

D ear Reader,

I sincerely hope you enjoyed reading my debut novel *Letters to Dogwood* as much as I did writing it! You can email me at **authortanyafischer@gmail.com** as I love to hear from readers and get their opinions.

Don't miss *Poppies and Silk*: Book Two in *A Texas Bloom Series* where the series continues with Sol's story when Poppy comes to town: Coming Soon!

Poppies and Silk

Coming 2023

With an unsavory childhood and secrets carefully locked away, Poppy wants to start over; old friends, new business, new life. Sol claims that a confirmed bachelor's life is a life for him, and helping raise his wild sister takes every courting notion right out of his mind. When Poppy returns to Dogwood after a ten-year absence, their instant attraction for each other shocks them both. A summer affair wasn't planned but couldn't be denied, and they fall hard. But someone is abducting girls across five counties, and it starts to get close to home. What's worse is that patterns begin to connect the disappearances with her past, and Poppy is afraid she knows exactly who could be responsible.

ALSO BY TANYA FISCHER

-A Texas Bloom Series-
Letters to Dogwood
Poppies and Silk (Coming 2023)
Book 3: Coming 2023!

About the Author

Tanya Fischer lives on a little Texas homestead with her husband, two children, and their pets (of which there are chickens). When she's not reading, she is writing. She has a passion for romance of every genre, though her heart lies in Historical Romance. She left her job in education and has pursued her dream of writing full-time.

She can be found on:

Facebook: facebook.com/authortanyafischer
Twitter: twitter.com/Tanyat_fischer/
Instagram: instagram.com/authortanyafischer/
Website: authortanyafischer.com